John Thornburn w
by its mystery and
gave him for his art

But then one day, as Celtic pipes played, John opened a portal through time to an Ireland a thousand years earlier, an age of magic, turmoil and bloodshed. There he lost his heart to Ailesh, a lovely young woman who had seen her family and village ravaged in a Viking raid.

Accompanied by Derval, a friend and sometime lover from the present, and Labres MacCullen, a roguish but gifted poet from Ailesh's time, John embarked on a quest for justice that would take him from a miraculous encounter with an ancient goddess, to the barbaric splendor of the court of the King of Dublin, to a holy place at the edge of the world where he would discover an awesome destiny.

Filled with vivid history and magical wonder, *The Book of Kells* is a stunning, resounding work, at once earthly and divine, a towering tour-de-force by one of the most acclaimed new names in fantasy.

Bantam Books by R. A. MacAvoy
Ask your bookseller for the books you have missed:

TEA WITH THE BLACK DRAGON
DAMIANO
DAMIANO'S LUTE
RAPHAEL

The Book of Kells

•

R. A. MacAvoy

BANTAM BOOKS
TORONTO • NEW YORK • LONDON • SYDNEY • AUCKLAND

THE BOOK OF KELLS
A Bantam Book / August 1985

ISBN 0-553-25260-7

Published simultaneously in the United States and Canada

Bantam Books are published by Bantam Books, Inc. Its trademark, consisting of the words "Bantam Books" and the portrayal of a rooster, is Registered in U.S. Patent and Trademark Office and in other countries. Marca Registrada. Bantam Books, Inc., 666 Fifth Avenue, New York, New York 10103.

PRINTED IN THE UNITED STATES OF AMERICA

O 0 9 8 7 6 5 4 3 2 1

This book is more Sharon's than mine.

I would like to give recognition and thanks to the following people without whom this work would have been impossible:

To Dr. James Duran of Oakland, California, for Gaelic and Gaelic usage and the loan of many good books; to Dr. Dan Melia of the University of California at Berkeley for help on Medieval Gaelic and medieval sources of all kinds; to Dr. Donal McGivillry of the University of Sydney on Cape Breton Island, Nova Scotia, for all Newfieisms and maritime history; to the gentlemen of Salamander Armory in California for tutoring in the handling of a medieval long-handled ax; to Ms. Anne McCaffrey for the geography of Wicklow; and to Miss Pat Lyne of Herefordshire for her history of the Connemara pony.

To Sharon Devlin, who was the inspiration for this book, and who worked with me and guided me every step of the way. All that is worthwhile in the book I owe to her; the errors are my own.

(All poems in the story itself are by Sharon, or were edited by her.)

Prologue

•

It was an hour for bog colors: the close of the workday in the Bog of Allen. The boy-os working the Bord na Mona mechanized turf cutters were just beginning to put their shirts back on in the sea wind of early evening. That wind was cool and saline and it drove forty miles in from the shore.

They had gotten low in this particular deposit, cut deeply today, and even the men on the machines thought that a pity.

Some parts of this bog, the greatest in the world, were now stripped to the rock. The demands of industry, the world market, and the new power plants had done more damage in a decade than the frugal spades of the Irish had done in thousands of years. With no chance for the sphagnum beds to regenerate, biologists warned, it would be gone in a generation.

Fine traditions would go with it. The seasonal work of "winning the turf" in great teams of family and neighbors. Heavy men's work with the long peat slans. And then women's and children's work: the stacking and drying. The *ceilis* afterward.

Missed above all would be that scent which is enjoyed even in the cities, in hearths or modern stoves. The scent of the peat as it made its slow, even, nearly smokeless flame: it was the age-old smell of comfort and *crachon*—conviviality. The smell of home.

Surely something beautiful would be gone out of the world. Besides the value they serve as producers of fuel, bogs are wonderful, mysterious places. Sometimes dangerous, they always hold secrets. Wild, eerie, with their outcroppings of rocks, their coffee-colored dim pools, their heather, gorse, and bog willow, thick with birds of all kinds, a bog is a fit place of concealment for a fugitive, a treasure, or a whisky still.

But the bogs shift. Old people can tell you about that, for their changes can occur within one lifetime. Sometimes things hidden in them will disappear. And reappear, far removed in time and place.

The chemistry of the turf does strange things. It colors and preserves. Occasionally a farmer, lifting his winter fuel in summer, will come upon a sealed bucket of long-forgotten workmanship, filled with what once had been butter, stored in the cool moss long ago. This dark grease is found to be wonderful for skin complaints, lubricating axles, and for healing the roughened udders of cows.

Roots of the red bog oak and sally will come up too. If set aside and slowly dried out, the dark wood is good for any construction that requires great streangth and resiliency. It can be made into a "creepy" stool, or a flour cist, or even (in the old days) the belly of a harp.

But every so often something appears in a bog that makes people cross themselves and go for the priest or policeman. Bodies appear occasionally. Generally, the corpse is found to be some poor fellow who twenty or even two hundred years ago got lost and was drowned for his trouble. But these finds are uncanny as well as disturbing; however old they are, the lost child of fifty years ago or the ancient sacrifice to Crom Duv of twenty-five centuries ago, they are recognizable—as intact as if they had died yesterday.

The National Museum has gained greatly from these finds. And since the Bog of Allen was first exploited technologically, it has yielded hundreds of artifacts to enrich the collective memory of the Irish people. Wooden things, vessels of all kinds, carvings, votive objects, jewelry. Ancient livestock and wild creatures. Textiles, dresses, cloaks, shoes, belts, often left deliberately in the peat by their original owners to get a fine, brown color from the chemistry of the bog, and then lost in the deep, slow currents.

Now and then things turn up which have clearly been "killed" there: objects thrown in to hide them forever. Sacred things of the old church and of paganism hated by Protestant iconoclasts or the Catholic Jansenist priesthood, these were often broken and drowned, to kill them doubly.

It had been an overcast, heavy day: warm and humid. But with the wind from the sea, the gray clouds were lifted along the horizon like a blanket, and the westering sun streamed under it, turning earth and cloud golden, deepest brown and rose.

Smasher Burke loved it like this. The changing mood of the place was one of the things that made this an interesting job. Riding like a king in a machine that took him three minutes to climb on or off, he saw everything.

The only disadvantage was the noise. The racket from the rows of blades that neatly cut the peat into briquettes was deafening, as was that of the belts that carried them to the receiver.

He lit up a fag and stuffed the packet of Silk Cut into his pocket. And then he heard it. A subtle change in the sound of the machine, followed by a grinding.

He instantly switched off the blades and brought her to a halt. As he climbed down from the cab, McWilliams, his partner, was already at the blades, trying to free them with a crowbar.

"Ya fucking bastard, ya!

"It's no good! Smasher, it's jammed. No good at all."

Burke's Wellies slowly squashed across the peat and around the cutter beams.

"It's a great fucking stone, Smasher." McWilliams squinted, the golden light picking out his yellow broken front teeth. "You'll have to back her up a bit."

"Right," Burke answered him, and clambered back on. "Stand away, will you," he shouted, impersonally as a bus conductor. Then he kicked her in, lifting the blades and rolling her five feet to the rear.

"Good enough, man," McWilliams bellowed. "Fucking great."

Within five minutes it had spread all through the crew that the Smasher had turned up a carving. An archaeologist from the museum had been called, but before he could get there it was fully dug out and examined by the men.

"When I heard the crunch I knew it was no ordinary lump of rubbish," McWilliams said proudly. "Look at her, will you? Look at that! It must be thousands of years old."

"It's a cross, man," Burke countered quietly. "It's not thousands. Couldn't be thousands."

It was old, though. Anyone could see that. Spirals. Spirals all over.

"Look there. Yer woman in the middle, with her little cunt stuck up, just as shameless!" McWilliams laughed nervously.

Burke had bent down to examine it more closely. Following it with his finger, he had discovered that the spirals—hundreds of them—seemed to be made from a single line.

"It doesn't look Christian," McWilliams stated.

The Smasher didn't answer.

Chapter One

•

Bound to Render the King of Laighin
Horses and Drinking Horns to Caiseal
Gold and riches brought across the Sea
Are what is due from the Leinstermen.

The Leinstermen are comrades to Munster
Against the Foreigners in any battle.
Should the Gaill come to them truly
The King of Caiseal must repulse them.

Leabher n-gCeart,
The Book of Rights

Perhaps the sound of the Uillean pipes was knocking plaster from the ceiling, or perhaps John Thornburn had neglected his household duties, for the ramps of sunlight braced against the floor were sparkling with white motes. Each oblong of light was broken by the shadow of window mintons, like a Cartesian grid, and each contained a single floating shadow-circle, thrown by the tatted pulls on the window blinds.

John let his gaze slide abstractedly from his work to the sun splashes and then back again. Circles on a grid. How appropriate. All over his house. He flattened the huge, blue-checked tracing tissue over the heavy paper and crayon rubbing below it and lifted limp flaxen hair out of his eye. His free hand (free except for the pencil between thumb and index finger) groped around blindly, seeking his blue fisherman's cap, which he usually used to keep his hair off his face. Not finding that, it crawled to the head of the drafting table and snatched up a paperclip. This he thrust into his forelock, bobby-pin style.

John Thornburn had a rather vague face and eyes of two different colors, which he had inherited from his grandfather. Grandpa had been a large, crusty old man who had prided himself on being one of the last of the purebred Micmac Indians in Newfoundland. On Cape Breton there were plenty of these, but in Newfoundland they were getting scarce. Grandpa even claimed that an ancestor of his had been a Beothuck taken in a raid, though as far as anyone knew there had been no Beothucks left by smallpox and English bullets even as long ago as two hundred years. (Because he was Grandfather, he had gotten away with it, despite the telltale blue eye.) John was immensely proud of his status as a Newfoundland Jack-a-tar, or half-breed, though he had noth ing of his grandfather in him except the eyes. (Unless he could count his inability to grow a noticeable beard.) He stood five feet five and a half inches tall.

He had come to Ireland because Derval O'Keane asked him to, and because the Book of Kells was here. He worshiped that scripture in a way that had nothing much to do with its religious content. It grieved him that after coming so far, he was only permitted to see a single page at a time, and that through glass.

Circles on a grid—spirals, really. Winding and unwindin to wind again. John overlay the nubbly soft suggestions of form with spirals exact and mathematical. He knew he had exactly one thousand spirals to copy, for he had counted them. The tissue crackled beneath his hand.

This was a high day for John: a day of fulfillment. The cross whose bog-brown fragments he had traced was in a peculiar sense his cross, for it had lain in the basement of the Museum at Trinity College, untouched, for five years. No one before him had cared to trace its designs, perhaps because the subject matter of its central panel was not considered fit for display. But for the influence of Dr. Derval O'Keane, John would not have been given his chance.

Not that this work would make any professional or financial difference for John. No school or museum was waiting eagerly to see how the rubbing turned out; no one had suggested paying John Thornburn for the work. Nor had he academic credentials to advance, not even the bachelor's degree he had pursued for three dazed years in New York. He hadn't even an opinion on the provenance or meaning of the stone he had traced. He merely liked the looks of it.

John got by from day to day by teaching a few courses in the basics of Celtic design (also a product of Derval's influence). Though he was an excellent draftsman, he was, unfortunately, a lackluster teacher. He found life in Ireland expensive and he was not particularly happy. Except, like now, when drawing.

Outside the bright windows in the bright June morning Greystones sat placidly, waiting for evening and the commuter train from Dublin. A woman hailed and another replied, banging a mop against her iron balustrade. A bicycle flew by, casting shadow and cheeping its tinny bell. If there was other activity, John couldn't hear it over the stereo.

The blasting music, also, was a product of Dr. O'Keane's influence. It was in fact Derval's record—Finbar Furey on pipes—and therefore very authentic. John had been lent it as a learning exercise, since Derval O'Keane believed that certain elements of Irish design could best be appreciated by a study of the old pipe airs. He had been listening to this same disc all morning, while he pulled together the various rubbings he had made that week. The different surges and quavers of Furey's artistry did little for John, tone-confused as he was, so in an effort to force comprehension he had increased the volume.

He was not deaf to rhythm. His right hand (deft as the rest of him was awkward) spun the inner and outer arcs of his freehand circles to the great swagging whine of the bagpipe. So many, all alike: twinned, tripleted, touching in rank. It was easy. Not like the blush-producing, upside-down Bridget in the center of the cross. That reconstruction required thought. This required not-thinking, which John did very well.

His eyes clouded and his lower lip drooped. There was only a short piece of the last upright to complete: say twenty spirals. John counted silently as he drew, betting himself (strictly a gentleman's bet) that he had estimated correctly and there were twenty left.

Nineteen... eighteen... fifteen... eight... He began to feel the surge of elation of a man who is winning a bet with himself. The pipes skirled in sympathy. Three... two... He'd won, of course. Here was the last spiral.

One. Furey produced a last, aggressive blast of his regulators and went silent as John flourished his pencil in the air.

There was the tiny metallic busyness of the automatic tone

arm lifting and drawing away from the record. John's overused ears rang.

In the next moment they were nearly shattered by the unmistakable shriek of a woman, full-throated, heart-rending, and uttered at close range. John levitated helplessly off his stool to witness the emergence from his bathroom of a very young and rosy woman clad only in a cloud of auburn hair and howling like a catamount. She flung herself down the short hall and vanished glimmering into John's bedroom.

John Thornburn made no immediate movement, but stood behind his drafting table with hands folded. The paperclip winked silver on his head and his pale, lashless eyes were perfect circles. "So . . . so very pink," he whispered reverently.

Slowly, as though breasting a strong current, John moved across the front room toward the source of the disturbance. He felt sweat prickling his scalp. He stood before the brown-paneled door. "Miss," he called, or rather attempted to call, for as he opened his mouth his shocked brain slipped into gear again.

The girl was naked, it told him. (She must have gotten in through the bathroom window.) She was naked and screaming and proabably a madwoman with (why not?) a madwoman's lies. And he—John Thornburn—was an alien in Ireland.

A Weslyan-born too.

He saw himself unjustly accused. He saw himself convicted. He saw himself in an Irish prison, carving Celtic knotwork and Eskimo figures onto the stone walls of his cell with a sharpened spoon. And so John's voice failed him halfway through his single syllable and the word "miss" came out as no more than the mewl of a kitten.

But now there was silence from behind the bedroom door. Heartened, John put his hand to the knob. The racket of breaking glass bounced him back.

He could wrap his sheepskin jacket over his arm and, using it to guard his face, throw open the door and . . . And what? Rush in and grab the girl: the pink, naked, and screaming girl? Let her break windows. Let her crawl out of a window, the way she came. Let the bored housewives on their porches see a naked girl crawl screaming out of his bedroom and then only a short hop to the Irish prison and the sharpened spoon.

The tinkle of glass recurred on a smaller scale, followed by an oddly plaintive whimper. John's terror veered toward irritation. "You've cut yourself on the glass, eh, my maid?" he called, in a voice much like that of his father. Immediately the whimper was cut short, to be replaced by the sound of wallboard tearing. John saw in his mind's eye his heavy brass candlestick reading lamp ripped from above his pillow. He grabbed a kitchen chair (the only kind of chair he had) and wedged it firmly up against the door.

John backed down the hall and into his empty front room. The sun lapped his feet, beckoning him. He let it carry him out the doorway and into the handkerchief-sized front yard.

Bright June air touched John's shoulders and told him they were knotted. It felt the line of his jaw and caused his teeth to unclench. It communicated to him the fact that his house had been stuffy and the garbage might have better been emptied a few days ago. It riffled the tiny leaves of the neglected box hedge and made John want to go away.

He could take a bus somewhere—out to McCaffrey's stable perhaps, where Derval worked her horse. He remembered the thud of hooves, felt through the earth, as she cantered her enormous beast along the fence. He remembered, with much more fondness, the thud of the waves against the wooden side of his dory, at home. The coast was only a few miles from Greystones—it was not his coast, but no matter. Anyplace would be better than sharing his empty house with a naked crazy woman. John strode over the lawn to the street.

Here, standing between his house and the next, he could see his bedroom window, new-punched with a jagged patch of black. Within there was a flash of pale skin.

John's spirits sank in a manner even the airs of June could not buoy, and at this moment he heard the small creak of a door opening across the street, and a woman's voice hailed him. "Good morning, Mrs. Hanlon," John replied, not looking up, and then all courage deserted him and he had to run. Since he was twenty-nine, rather than nineteen, he ran not away but back into his afflicted house.

Hands stuffed into the pockets of his jeans and shoulders at his ears, he approached the blockaded bedroom door. "I'd like to know what you think you're doing in there," he said to the door, tacking a shamefaced "miss" onto the end of his sentence.

The moment's silence which followed allowed John to hope that the creature had actually found her way out the window.

Mrs. Hanlon or no, that would be a blessing. But then he was answered by a rant of verbiage incomprehensible to him.

Incomprehensible, but familiar sounding.

"I'm sorry," he replied. "I don't speak Irish at all well, eh?"

Nothing. John knew he would have to call the gardai. He wandered into the kitchen, where the phone was. He nibbled his fingernail, staring down at the square black box. Finding this comfort insufficient, he bit down on the cuticle as well. It hurt.

What was the number? Where was the phone book? He found it, and his torn cuticle left bloody smears on the paper. Derval was always making fun of him for his bitten-down nails. Calling him "frog fingers." Also for his indecisiveness, which he felt was really too bad, since ambidextrous people more or less had to be indecisive.

Derval would not be paralyzed by the arrival of a crazy woman (or man) in her bathroom. She'd take such an invader firmly in hand. John found he was dialing Derval's number instead of the garda.

"Irish Department," answered the secretary in impeccable British English.

"Doctor O'Keane, please."

There was a long silence, during which John had nothing to do but lean against the kitchen sink and stare out the window of the back door, which was too warped to open easily. His nose told him he definitely should have emptied the garbage. About the time he had decided he should hang up and call again, the secretary came back on the line. John listened.

"Writing? Can't she be disturbed? Oh, *riding*? I see. No, I know the number, thank you." He spun the heavy dial again.

She must have been at the jumps, it took so long to call her. Derval was going to be very upset, being called not only from her precious riding hour but from the jumps as well. John swayed back and forth against the enameled sink, thinking how unfair it was that he should be trapped between a crazy woman, the police, and Derval's temper. He reflected and sucked his damaged cuticle. When she was fetched at last, he tried to cut off all remonstrance.

"Derval, this is John. Please don't talk Irish; I can't follow it right now. I know you don't like to be disturbed at the stable, but I'm rafted as all hell. I've got this... this crazy woman... in my bedroom, and I have no idea how to get her out."

Two seconds of silence was followed by laughter which blew static into the phone. "You should have thought of that before you bedded her, love."

"Eh? I've never seen her before. It's a pure mystery to me how she got there . . .

"Here . . . listen." In sudden inspiration John walked the phone as close to the door as he could and called out. "Are you still in there?" For emphasis, he leaned out and tapped the door panel with his toe. The reply from within was quite threatening in tone.

"You hear? That's Irish, isn't it?" Derval sputtered into the speaker again, causing John to smile more awkwardly than ever. "Derval, what I want to know is, do you think I should call the police—uh—the gardai? And if I do will you tell them I'm not a monster?"

Her laughter died away into low hoots. "Very, very good, John. I certainly can't ignore such an appeal, can I? I'll be right over."

John explained as politely as he knew how that he didn't feel the need for her presence, but only a word of advice. He found he was talking to a dead line. "Blood of a bitch!" He hung up.

It occurred to John that Derval might have thought the entire story a fabrication designed to entice her to his house. Since she had turned him down twice this week, she might be thinking he was desperate. He found himself blushing furiously.

Now here was a damn pretty kettle of fish. Was he expected to stand here waiting for Derval to visit him out of pity, while a homicidal and quite naked woman planned ways . . .

Quite naked. John's mind settled back on that as one of the few digestible facts of the incident. To the best of his memory, she had been entirely without clothes and of unusually high coloration. Of course, memory will play one false when one is in shock.

John remembered the crack that ran between the bedroom drywall and the bathroom, which allowed him to use the bathroom fixture as a night-light and which let mildew soften the edges of the bedroom wainscoting. Silently he slipped into the bathroom and put his eye to the crack.

It took five seconds before he could make out her shape, huddled at the foot of his unmade bed in the froth of covers he had kicked to the floor during the previous night. Her small, hair-shadowed face was round and her mouth was a rosebud. She stared ahead of her with glassy eyes and the whole pile of cloth shivered. Seeing that heartbroken countenance with none of the nubile body exposed, John was convinced that this was no woman but a very young girl. His own thin face sharpened in sudden compassion, immediately touched by an equal self-concern. If he found her pitiable, what would the gardai think? Derval had been right to come.

He was dwelling on this particular topic, eye to the blue-tinged crack in the bathroom wall, when Derval arrived. He heard the sound of hooves on the pavement outside, thought, "She can't have," and immediately corrected the statement to "She would have." He stepped to the front window in time to see an animal—resembling in both size and color an elephant—sail over the box hedge and plant itself in the knee-high grass of John's front lawn. Its rider slipped off and snapped a cotton lead line onto the headstall it wore under the bridle. This she looped over one of the pineapples that topped the porch's wrought-iron balustrade.

"You're going to leave him there?" John asked incredulously, leaning out the doorway.

"Don't worry, Johnnie. Tinker's never colicked in his life," Derval said, and swept in. With a last glance at Mrs. Hanlon on her own porch across the street, John closed the door. Mrs. Hanlon was, unfortunately, his landlady.

"I like the effect with the paperclip," John's visitor stated. "The off-center jauntiness of it and all. Just like your eyes."

John Thornburn's eyes weren't really off center, and if their being mismatched (one blue and one brown) made him jaunty, he wasn't aware of it. He put his hand to his head and snatched the clip away. His limp flaxen hair fell flat into his right (or brown) eye.

Derval O'Keane was a tall young woman with black hair streaked in the most ornate manner with gray. This was pulled back severely from her face and fastened with a rubber band. Her eyebrows and lashes were thick and black and her eyes, blazing blue. She wore traditional black riding boots and doeskin breeches which became her well, and instead of the orthodox hacking jacket above, a woolen smock-shirt stitched with an amazing complexity of zoomorphic knotwork figures. She saw John's glance at it and held herself out for inspection. "See, Johnnie? I wear it everywhere I go, and tell the whole world that you made it for me."

John mumbled politely, though he was not too happy to be introduced to the world as a seamstress, and the truth was he had neither woven the cloth nor stitched the embroidery, but merely drawn the figures that Derval had someone else complete. He pointed diffidently toward the bedroom. "She's still hove up there. You can see her if you peek through the bathroom crack."

Derval snorted and rejected such voyeurism. "Haven't you got that fixed yet, love? Makes it impossible to sleep nights with all that light." She strode toward the bedroom door, but turned halfway there and added, "Or shouldn't I have mentioned that? Should I be watching my words, Johnnie? For all I know you're taping this whole exchange—much good you'll get out of it. Everyone knows how scandalous I am."

"Taping? For God's sake, Derval, are you going crazy too? Or do you think it's some kind of joke I'm playing on you? Well, there's the door and she's behind it. Just don't get yourself brained!"

Derval stopped with one hand on the doorknob and the other on the wedged chair. She gave John a very mistrustful look. Then she put her ear to the door.

She knocked and spoke loudly in Irish. The response was immediate and accompanied by the thump of a heavy object (John's lamp, he guessed) being hit against the floor.

Derval stepped back. Her eyes were half-closed and her high forehead furrowed with thought. Her lips moved soundlessly and when she glanced sideways at John there was a sort of challenge in her eyes. He watched her with the expectancy one gives to a conjurer.

Derval spoke again, this time slowly, with care in every word. John, who knew only a few hundred words of Irish and who only understood those when overpronounced, made out nothing in the exchange but the word *Gaill*, or "stranger." The effect of Derval's speech was immediate.

"She's dropped the lamp," he whispered to himself, and he heard scuffing footsteps behind the door. The girl had grabbed the doorknob and was pushing on it forcefully. Derval pulled the chair away and let it fall racketing on the floorboards of the hall. She turned the knob and let the door open.

Framed in the darkness, shining and naked, stood a girl of some fifteen years. Her hair was auburn and hung to her waist, frizzed along half its length as though a bad permanent wave had been allowed to grow out. Her face was heart-shaped, and this as well as a nubbin of a nose gave her the air of being much younger than her body declared. Her chest and rounded belly were splashed with rose-red streaks and patches of rust-red. John, regarding her from over Derval's shoulder, wondered if these marks were responsible for his original perception of the girl as rosy; now she had not the eerie glow of a neon bar sign, nor yet the red light of sunset.

She stared at John, who dropped his eyes to the floor. Then the girl spoke to Derval, who listened with a close frown.

"She doesn't speak Irish at all, Johnnie. It just sounds like it, rather."

"I thought maybe she had a speech impediment," offered John. " . . . with her 'g's sounding so much like 'k's."

"Truagh, ámh! Rom-gabsa na díbergaig, suaill nach dena dím dímbríg! . . ."

The girl spoke for quite a while, this time seeming more desperate for understanding. Derval's frown slipped a little, grew puzzled. "The words are almost right, but not the order. Maybe she's a German speaker, or something like that, and studied Irish dictionaries. That's a good way to come up with nonsense. She even pronounces a lot of the silent consonants."

Then, in response to one phrase of the stranger's, Derval's scowl grew particularly fierce. " 'Violence done by foreigners'? She said it perfectly clear. In fact, a lot of what she says has almost-meaning—like schizophrenic word-salad. Where did you get this card, Johnnie? And what did you expect out of springing her on me? I don't get the punch-line."

John Thornburn had no time to reply, for the scorn in Derval's voice sparked panic in that of the naked girl, who went down on her knees and clasped Derval around the waist, crying out in her (to John) incomprehensible words.

Derval froze in distaste, but in another moment her set frown went blank from astonishment. "I get it! I get it! She's re-invented old Irish! What a feat! Of course I can't say how authentic it is, Johnnie; who could? But still, what a work!

"And now that my mind clicks on that, my dear, let us see whether I'm worthy of the challenge."

John shifted miserably from foot to foot. "Oh Derval, you're really wrong, you know. I don't know beans about . . ."

But the girl broke in on him, and, still on her knees, she pointed first at her own breast and then toward the darkened recess of the bedroom. Derval listened to her intently, much to John's discomfort. Slowly, with care, she replied, and the girl's small round face lit with hope. "Dá ttuchta mo rogha dhamh ferr lem faesam fort. Ná hobait éim."

"What's she saying, Derval? What's all this talk about foreigners, eh? Don't I have a right to be in my own house? Ask her how she got in here and where're her clothes?" John Thornburn shifted from foot to awkward foot, a movement which carried him subtly away from the two women.

Derval snorted. "I imagine you know the answer to that better than I do. I'm more interested to know what the red paint is supposed to mean. The ancient Britons used blue, if that was your point, but . . . . Oh dear God!"

Derval reached out and flicked a finger over the girl's skin, between the pubescent breasts. Then she stood quite still for five seconds, staring at that finger.

John leaned forward. "It looks like she's soused with blood, Derval. She cut herself on the window, you know." But glancing quite shyly again at the girl, John was quite shocked to see how much of the red stuff that looked like blood she was wearing. The stranger met his eyes and talked to him. She put her hand to her reddened breast as she spoke, and then to her mottled stomach. After this she put both small hands over her pudendum and spoke again. Tears started down her face. She took Derval's hand and twined her fingers through the taller woman's. "*Impím orte*."

John, in an agony of embarrassed incomprehension, put his tattered finger in his mouth and bit down on it until he tasted his own blood.

Derval was now staring at him. John felt his face color. "Do you think I did that to her? Did she say I did? All—all that? It's ramlatch nonsense if she did. Do you really...you don't really..."

Derval shook her head slowly, as though moving a tremendous weight. "She did not. I wouldn't have believed her if she had. Not you, Johnnie. Not you."

John felt his shoulders relaxing. He glanced furtively from Derval's blue eyes to the stranger's hazel ones. "I'll go get the first-aid kit," he mumbled and darted into the bathroom.

Derval took the kit from John and sent him off again for soap and water. John rummaged around helplessly, hearing the incomprehensible strings of vowels continue. (His Irish was worse than usual today, for he couldn't get any sense at all of what they were saying.)

The marks of human teeth around the aureole of Ailesh's breast were the most painful to see, but the clean shallow slash that went diagonally from her navel to her left hipbone bled most. Derval's milk-and-roses complexion was ashen as she dabbed the still oozing wounds with peroxide. Derval could so easily visualize a knife-wielding rapist whose intention had been to slash open the belly of his victim, but apparently this girl had been fighting hard and had twisted aside, escaping just as the blade descended.

She turned her head to see John Thornburn standing beside her with a clean bedsheet spread between his outthrust arms. "I thought she might like to put this . . . er . . . on herself."

"She'd bleed all over it," answered Derval shortly. "What's the matter, Johnnie? Can't you stand the sight of a naked woman?"

John bit down on his lip. She was always slagging him about something or other—his modesty most of all. Just because he buttoned his shirts up to the top and sometimes liked it dark in the bedroom. . . . Her dig was especially disturbing now, at a time when anything sexual seemed obscene.

"You know better than that. I just thought that maybe *she* would rather not be looked at."

The older woman smiled thinly. "She doesn't seem to care." Derval peered around the girl to discover matching sets of what seemed to be claw marks on the girl's buttocks. She applied the foaming antiseptic to these as Ailesh stood stone-still, hands clenched in hard fists at her sides.

She certainly was stoical. John mouthed the word "ouch" on her behalf, and saw brown eyes slide to him doubtfully. "Of course, she may not have recognized you as a man," Derval added.

"Ouch for me too," he mumbled. Cruel as the smile of an excise man. (That was an expression Derval herself had taught him.)

"What's that, eh? No need for insults." John remembered to take his finger out of his mouth.

"I only meant she's still in shock." Derval excused herself, but she was angry at him now, in a totally unfair, impersonal way. Because he was a man.

John sighed. He turned and paced through his still-sunlit front room. The rectangles of light spattered his trousers as he moved. He turned off the power to his stereo amplifier.

He felt superfluous, unnecessary. Derval seemed to have taken over. So he said something he thought might be helpful, but deferred to her for the sake of peace. "Shouldn't I call a hospital to come get her?" he asked.

Derval didn't stop to wonder that the responsibility for this decision had been laid in her lap. She answered decisively, "You should not. They would only call the gardai."

John flung himself onto his couch, which, being on wheels, slid back into the wall, banged against it, shaking everything. A cobweb and its contents were rudely dumped onto the sofa. A big spider danced toward a crack between the cushions. Save me, Mammy, save me, save me, he thought compassionately, watching it run. "And why shouldn't they call the gardai, eh?" he said aloud. "Someone did this to her—unless she's limber enough to bite her own bosom." (He almost said "tits," but caught his tongue.) "And that someone deserves to find themself between four walls."

Derval, though tempted, let his grammatical solecism pass. Holding the girl by one wrist, she turned toward John. "Fine. For him, whoever—husband, father, or worse—he may be. But what about little Ailesh here? She says that's her name, by the by. She's been raped and nearly killed, John dear." John winced. "Didn't your demure little Newfie brain pick up on that?"

John looked fixedly at the dead fireplace. What a bitch she was. And she had the nerve to think he'd have called her after being turned down twice in a week. Well, perhaps he would have, he thought, feeling lower than ever. "Yes. It did. I did. Isn't that a matter for the police?"

He saw Derval's rage building and regretted having spoken. Hurriedly he said, "All right, what do I know about it? It's not my country, after all, and I have no great desire to explain this girl's—"

"Ailesh. She has a name, you know."

"Ailesh's presence in my house, stark naked and bloody and without a word of English.

"And that reminds me, Derval. I didn't know there was a native left in Ireland that couldn't speak English."

"There isn't," she answered shortly.

"There's her," stated John, as Ailesh picked up the white sheet John had left lying, wrapped it around herself, and settled sighing down on the floor. He was impressed to see she could crouch on her pretty haunches with her feet flat on the boards. It reminded him of his grandfather, and of other native Americans he had met at the fishing stations: Inuit, Micmacs. They sat crouched on flat feet too. But this girl's broad, speading feet, while quite handsome in shape, didn't look like they would even fit into shoes.

Derval shook her head and said nothing.

Outside, the iron balustrade rang like a dull bell, and one hoof pawed the concrete walkway impatiently. Derval had for once forgotten about her horse, and the horse didn't like it. John's mood lifted a little, for he sometimes felt he was a second-rate competitor with Tinker for Derval's attention.

The dark-haired woman turned her head to the window and stood staring out at her impatient beast. "It's a really *good* reconstruction of Old Irish she's . . ." She didn't finish the sentence.

John cast a glance from Derval to the sheet-muffled girl across the room, only to find two round brown eyes meeting his, incomprehensible as the eyes of a bird. He avoided them with difficulty. "Not modern Irish, eh? Well, I'm glad to hear it. After six months of lessons I had hoped I could understand *something*."

Derval hadn't moved, nor did she seem to notice that big gray Tinker had pulled two of the rusted balustrade posts out of their concrete anchors. Her face was averted from John, but repeated in the glass of the window. "Really good," she said tonelessly. "And she's told me just now that she's escaped a *slua* of Danes."

"Danes?" John echoed helplessly. "What Danes? She doesn't mean me, does she? I'm not a Dane; I'm a Jack-a-tar from—"

"No, Johnnie-Joe, not you." Derval laughed sadly. "Not unless you've just taken up plundering, burning, and slave-taking." She turned around and smiled at him, her tongue thrust firmly into her cheek.

"Ramlatch. Pure ramlatch!" John replied.

Chapter Two

> Then that deadly hostile army arose and went to the horses and the quays where the boats were ready for them; and they set afloat their terrible, wonderful, very dreadful sea monsters, and their swift, long, firm barques and their many-coloured sombre ships.
>
> *Cath Maighe Lena,*
> Thirteenth Century A.D.

The girl who called herself Ailesh sat at the kitchen table, still wrapped in a sheet, the look of immense sadness in her eyes warring with a sour expression around her mouth. Derval rinsed sticky honey off a spoon in the sink.

"I think she still tasted it," commented John, who had watched disinterestedly from across the table.

"Of course she did," replied the dark woman, whose heavy hair was escaping the rubber band to fall over her face. She brushed it back with one thin shoulder, while dabbling her fingers through the running water. "Valium has a taste like lye and ashes. But twenty milligrams ought to do her good."

John didn't like looking into the injured girl's eyes. He did, however, like looking at the rest of her, or as much of her as he could see under the sheet, which was a bit of cleavage, a hairy little leg, and her arms. Odd, then, that he found his gaze wandering helplessly back to her face, printed with all that mad tragedy. It seemed genuine enough to him. "I didn't know you still took that stuff, Derval. You told me back at St. John that it was only because travel unsettled you, and—"

"I don't, always . . ." said Derval, fiddling with her hair and glancing away, out the window of the kitchen door. "Just happened to be carrying it." Her vague eyes focused.

"I'll believe she didn't get in the house this way, Johnnie." She pointed to the cobwebby door.

John shrugged. "It doesn't work."

Derval put her hand to the crazed china knob and worked it. Both John and Ailesh watched her tug, grunting. "I think you could fix it, handy with tools as you are."

John Thornburn's face went more lackluster than usual. "I'm no carpenter." Then, as Derval's energetic pulls caused the warped door to spring out, he added, "Could you put the trash outside, eh, since you've got it open, Derval? It's a bit griny."

She looked like she had a sharp answer on her tongue, but picked up the odorous basket with one hand and set it on the stoop. Even on the surface the basket was disgusting; John thought it better not even to contemplate its fermenting depths: a green-haired shriveling apple, half a packet of limp potato crisps, beer-soaked cigarette butts from that last evening with Kieran Hakett just a few weeks ago.

Hakett was the only steady drinking buddy John had acquired in the time he'd lived in Dublin. Derval wrinkled her nose. She despised Hakett for his constant and disrespectful reference to areas of female anatomy.

"I just thought it would make things more pleasant," said John.

Ailesh listened to and watched this interchange closely. John bit down on his thumb and thought about her.

He wasn't sure he believed she didn't understand English. He wasn't sure he believed anything about her, except that she was female. At the same time he was smitten with the feeling he was being a very bad host. These two influences came to a head together and he found himself asking her, "Do you want some milk?"

"The word for milk is *bainne*."

"Hush," John said to Derval, and he watched Ailesh's face.

It was disappointing, for the girl met his glance with nothing but animal alertness. She turned to Derval and spoke.

Derval leaned to John. "She's asking me what you said. Should I tell her?"

Politeness overcame John's detective instincts. "Yes, of course," he mumbled. "Tell her."

Ailesh looked back at John. Her face went suddenly shy. She spoke again. "Nírbo dú dom acht gebhad-sa uait madh maith let."

Derval translated her reply. "No, but she apologizes for refusing to take food with you."

Then the girl gave a sigh and the sheet rustled as her body visibly relaxed. The alteration meant more of her anatomy became visible, but at the same time her face softened, and John found his eyes straying from the pulchritude to the single tear that hung glistening on Ailesh's cheek.

She opened her small mouth and began to speak.

Derval understood every word the girl was saying. It was becoming easier and easier.

"Ni fhedarsa cía tainm ńo cía feras in fháilti. Though it is unknown to me who you are or who makes me welcome, whether you are the saints of God, men of the flesh, or sidhe or sacred beings for which I have no name, I will tell you the cause of my grief, that my tears will not be as a shame on me.

"I am no foolish slave or coward. My father is Goban MacDuilta, son of Ciaran, son of Bascine of the line of artificers to the *taiseachs* of Muhman, the Eoinachta. As for Sabia, my mother, she also was illustriously connected. Her father was Fiachra MacThuthail, an *Ollave* of great fame throughout this whole island. And her *coibche*, her bride gift, was forty prize cows with all their calves, and the calves with collars of silver bells. Though learned, she never gained renown, as she died young. I am the daughter of their union; the only living child. My mother's sister is married to the taiseach of the Ui Garrchon. Among them I was fostered in the house of his sisters." She cleared her phlegmy throat.

Derval gripped the edge of the table.

"Have no fear, *Mo stor gal*, my bright treasure," she reassured her. "We are living people, baptized like yourself."

"God be thanked for it." Ailesh made the sign of the cross as if a terrible fear had been taken away. "Then it must be through lawful power that I was brought to this beautiful house."

Derval, at this last statement, could not suppress a snort of laughter and a round-eyed glance through the filthy kitchen.

John could not help but notice her response. "What's she saying, eh? Eh?" She ignored him.

Ailesh continued. "Only a little time ago I was in the *clachan*, taking a steam bath with the other maidens of Ard na Bhfuinseoge. Light and careless was my laughter today. Often is our joy on earth cut short by some unforeseen thing. The Gaill must have docked near the harbor of Na Clocha Líatha and marched south and inland. It was at our bath we were surprised by the enemy, dragged out naked and weaponless to ruin and murder. I was thrown down and forced by one of these hell dogs, but he . . . he was ignorant of the women of the Gael.

"Though married against my will I am a widow already. I pulled his own knife and pierced him beneath the armpit so that he got his death. Then I escaped and ran to find my father."

In her eagerness to hear the end of the story, Derval almost missed the fact that the girl was confessing to homicide.

"Pursued by one of the reavers, I found Goban. Never, even if my eyes are blinded with age, will I forget the sight. In the smoke of the burning, he still worked upon the cross of Bridget, hammer and chisel in his hand. Just as I reached him he seized me and threw me against the stone. I passed through it unharmed, and that is how I came here. Whether my father is living or dead, I don't know."

Her face was now channeled with tears. "Our home was a scared place, a community of families given to the service of God. We had few weapons, and no time to take them up. We were helpless before their cruelty."

Ailesh broke down and sobbed for a while. She wiped her face and looked into Derval's eyes, then John's. "As for myself, I killed my enemy, and though some say that is a sin, I do not regret it."

Now she began to wail in earnest. Her voice rang through the kitchen. John sprang out of his chair and made his own little moan. "Ye Gods! Why's she doing that, Derval? The whole neighborhood will hear."

John backed into the refrigerator. He grabbed its handle and wrenched the door open. His rummaging hand found the carton of milk. "Here. Make her drink this. She can't scream if she's drinking."

"She's just crying. And after what I have just heard, I wonder I'm not joining her. Truth or madness, it's the most hideous story."

Ailesh, whose eyes had been screwed shut with misery, felt a blast of cold air on her face. She looked up to see John

Thornburn with his back against the shelves of the refrigerator, with a bright rectangle sloshing in his hand and the little yellow light peeping out behind him. Out of the cold and confusion she understood one thing: John's face, lit by a cold hero-light and full of alarm. Her wailing died away and she spoke to Derval.

"She says she won't wail if it displeases you."

"Nice of the girl," he muttered, stepping out of the refrigerator. A knock came at the front door.

John wilted. He sank into the chair beside Ailesh. "Oh shit."

Derval's mouth was rather wide and grew wider as a smile stretched it. "Leave it to me, Johnnie," she said and swaggered out of the kitchen. "I feel the need for an act of bravery."

With the departure of Derval, and thus of all hope of translation between them, a sort of simplicity descended between John and his visitor. The small female with brown eyes and auburn hair sat quietly, her misery smudged but not erased by the tranquilizer. John listened to the voices from the front room and recognized that of Mrs. Hanlon. He rolled his mismatched eyes at Ailesh and put his finger (well-bitten and sore of tip) to his lips warningly.

But when Ailesh shrank into herself and began to tremble, John realized he had made a mistake. He patted her hand.

"That's a good girl," he whispered. "No need to be frightened. No one's going to hurt you. Any more, that is. Not you. Just me, maybe.

"Oh Lord." He let his head sink into his hand. How could he ever convince the gardai that it hadn't been him abusing the child? Bite prints, possibly? How? Would they ask him to bite a plate of gell, as he had done in orthodontia? Surely they wouldn't want to try his mouth against the girl's . . . against the girl's . . . He gave out a small, involuntary groan.

John glanced up in surprise to find Ailesh patting his hand. His face colored. "Oh, don't pay any attention to me. I'm very self-centered," he said. "And I worry."

Ailesh glanced meaningfully over her shoulder and put her finger to her lips.

"That was your landlady," stated Derval, returning to the table after five minutes' absence. "She heard Ailesh. I told her we were practicing for a symposium on ancient customs."

"And she believed you?"

"Very nice lady," replied Derval noncommittally. "Lost a hen, she says." Instead of sitting down, she wandered over to the stove. "Dying for a cup of tea," she said. She found the lidless kettle. Fingered the grease on its sides with some distaste.

"You know what I think?" Without waiting for a reply Derval continued, "The only thing I can think, without going insane myself. I think . . . perhaps Ailesh's background is something like mine."

"You mean she's a language teacher gone potty?" John asked innocently. "Not necessarily a teacher. She could—" Derval suddenly realized what John had implied. "One for you, Johnnie boy. What I meant was, she may have been at some time a student. And a good one, if the perfection of her story is any indication.

"Though she looks so young . . . And also, I can't remember ever seeing her face in a class, and in my field one gets to know just about everyone. But there are other schools than Trinity.

"And then"—Derval stopped, uncharacteristically unsure—"I read about a case of old Freud's, where a young girl of German parents suddenly started speaking French, and seemed utterly unable to communicate in her own language. She was very convincing, in her new identity."

John frowned. "But she knew French already, didn't she?"

"I guess. A bit. And maybe Ailesh here knew a bit of Middle Irish."

John Thornburn lowered his thin brows and gazed perplexedly at the redheaded girl. "If going crazy is so good for one's language skills . . ."

Derval smiled wolfishly. "Evidently so, Johnnie. All you have to do is marry a woman who'll abuse you like this."

"Eh? Oh, I doubt it was her husband . . ."

"Do you? Little innocent. I don't doubt it a minute. Things like that happen right here near Dublin every day. I could tell you stories about what husbands and fathers do to women in this country—"

"You do tell me those stories, Derval. Constantly." John twisted his limp hair around one finger. "But I hardly believe that a father or husband did this to our Ailesh."

The girl, who had observed this interchange with unhappy incomprehension, heard her name mentioned. She shifted in her corner and made a small animal noise. John glanced at her, let the lines of irritation fade from his face, and gave Ailesh a slight, sweet smile.

Derval looked beleaguered. "Do you have a better explanation?"

John folded his hands and let his heels kick him right and left on the high drafting stool. The spitcurl he had worried into being hung over his right eye. "I just think she's crazy," he said, as though disposing of a complex intellectual puzzle once and for all.

Derval sighed, giving him up in despair. Dust-ridden sunlight filled the silence. The next person to speak was Ailesh.

"She asks us why she's here," translated Derval carefully. "She wants to know if we're going to help her revenge Ard na Bhfuinseoge: the Hill of the Ash Trees."

John flinched at ugly suggestion of violence. "Can you think of some way of explaining to her—some way that won't set her off again—that—"

"I told her we'd help her in any way we could," replied Derval simply.

"She didn't get in behind me," stated John. "I'm not blind."

Derval eyed the positions of the high chair and the door suspiciously. "No, but you're a demon for concentration when you're working, Johnnie. I'm not sure you'd notice a cliff falling on you."

"She didn't get in," he repeated stolidly. "She couldn't have, without moving the top of the tracing, which was over the board like this—see?" Effortfully, John Thornburn re-created the situation of his morning's work. "And though I admit I might not have heard an elephant trumpeting over Furey . . ."

"You were listening to the pipes, then?"

"Yes. You'll be glad to know I played the record all morning, though I still don't understand the appeal any more than . . ."

Derval strolled over to where the stereo sat on brick-supported shelves. She turned it on and lowered the needle to the record. "You should use a record cleaner," she commented, and then started backward as the floor-shaking immensity of sound broke out. Her hand groped for the volume control. "Jesus and Joseph!" she said.

John squirmed. "Well, I was alone, you know. Not trying to carry on a conversation over the noise." His eye was caught by the sight of Ailesh, in her white swaddling, scurrying around the corner and into the kitchen. "She's looking for the piper," he remarked, and then returned his attention to the work at his hand.

"I was just doing spirals," John explained to Derval, and as he spoke he suited the action to the word. "Simple spirals in a line—two cycles in, two cycles out. Nothing that required real concentration."

"Not for you, my dear," admitted Derval, with a sly grin. "So then, how'd she get in?"

"The bathroom window. I said that before." John set his dimpled jaw and stared at the paper before him. His hand, as though self-propelled, drew the pencil over the same interwoven circles as before. Such was his mastery of this obscure craft that no smudging or thickening of the line was evident.

"It's painted shut," Derval stated, not for the first time. She was left staring at the top of his flaxen head.

She had known John Thornburn for two and a half years. Her first exaggerated respect for the man's talent had pushed her toward an intimacy—an intimacy to which John had vaguely acquiesced. He had come to Ireland upon her prodding.

And now here he was, living in dirt and teaching the odd course or two. No social life to speak of, except when she took him places. Derval bullied him mercilessly. She herself knew it. She did so because he was so spineless, and because . . . because he was who he was, with the unstudied, unteachable gift of design he had, and did nothing but dawdle and doodle along. If Derval had that flaming talent, she told herself. Instead of merely a flaming temper. With her own decent intelligence and hard work she had made a name for herself, and enough money to keep herself and Tinker in comfort. John . . . he ate moldy bread, unnoticing. She blinked miserably at the head of limp pale hair. Born to be a frigging bachelor, every inch of him.

Maybe what bothered her most about John was this. What

he was doing now. Doodling and mumbling as though he were in another world, when someone (Ailesh? Herself? Derval wasn't sure) needed him here.

Gone away, gone away . . . Derval could hear the hunt horn blow the signal in her head. Fine rider though she was, she could never follow where Johnnie went, when he went away from her.

The sad air on the stereo echoed her mood. She stepped into the bathroom, to make sure her eyes had not deceived her. No. The window was sealed shut with layers of carelessly applied, dirty paint. Ailesh, like the ghost of Banquo in her white sheet, wandered in with her and then back through the front room, her small face wrinkled with puzzlement. Derval sighed and followed. She leaned against the wall. Perhaps she should take the girl to the Home for Battered Women. Not on horseback, of course, but in the Mini Minor. John was no one to help . . . .

The air ended. John put down his pencil but his eyes were fixed on his work. The bathroom door faded behind a roseate, electric cross of light. On its surface, as if picked out in neon tubing, the thousand spirals danced like living things. Ailesh lifted her hand toward it and cried out, "*Dia Linn!*" Derval gasped and put her hands to her face.

In ten seconds it had faded and gone.

"What was that?" asked John mildly, still sitting on his stool by the front door. "I saw pink again. Like with the girl."

Derval nodded, openmouthed. "So there was. A cross of red light. And space on the other side, Johnnie. With hills like those just above Greystones Harbor, and slopes like those that run between there and here."

Derval turned to him again and fixed him with a glance. And in the middle of his wonderment he had time to wish his abilities were different or differently trained, that he could paint that vibrant dark face, with one brow down and one brow flying and mouth both mocking and warm. He remembered why he had followed her like a puppy from Newfoundland. "But it was . . . I saw a hill of oak trees, love. Black with oak trees, and the slope was black as well. There was no grass to be seen." John's vague face went peaked with confusion. "A mirage?"

Derval restrained a cutting retort. "It wasn't a mirage."

At that moment they heard the sound of iron ripped from

concrete. The ornate black balustrade went clanking down the sidewalk, accompanied by dancing hoofbeats.

"Here. Put this in your head," said John, shoving the tumbler of milk over the enamel-topped table. Then he rested his chin on his fist and regarded Ailesh's efforts to use a fork on the length of cold sausage. He had a suspicion she'd do better with a knife. He was afraid to give her a knife, so he merely watched.

His resentment of Derval had grown until it was a pall that covered him and weighed him down. That was why he had to support his head in such a manner. When he had invited (invited? No. Merely not resisted strongly enough) Derval's involvement in this puzzle, he had been only undecided. Now he felt wholly stuck. He had promised—or as good as promised—the woman he'd not call the gardai, but she'd offered no other solution. Did she expect him to adopt this crazy girl?

John was afraid of crazy people. Always had been, even of old Otto who was safe enough that Dad took him out on the fishing boat. Crazy people caused John's stomach to butterfly and the hair on the back of his neck to rise. Maybe because he knew he was a bit weird himself.

Ailesh had grabbed the handle of the fork in the palm of her hand. The long sausage dangled down on either side and she was maneuvering one end of it into her mouth, spaghetti-style. She had given up trying to talk to John Thornburn.

Odd. John's stomach was free of butterflies at the moment. His hair, too, lay with its normal limp disinterest. He guessed he had simply filled up with being nervous about the girl. Or perhaps he was simply too pissed at Derval, who had flung herself out the door in pursuit of Tinker.

How like her.

In the beginning John had been terribly impressed with the Irishwoman with the Ph.D., who had never seemed to know a moment's indecision. For months her presence had served to quell the constant floating uncertainty that was John's mode of thought. It was her idea he should come to teach design at the Trinity Extension, and only through her influence had the school invited him.

She swept all before her.

The Valium should have given him some clue that she wasn't as solid as she seemed, John now reflected. But he was more than willing to have decisions made for him, and terribly flattered to be wanted so much by anyone, let alone a lovely young professor. But since he had landed in Ireland, there seemed to be less and less to be said between them. John couldn't with the best will in the world pretend to her interest in Celtic history, politics, or language. Art was his field and his fate, and it might as well be Zimbabwean as Irish for all he cared.

Among the males who clustered around Derval—a generally hairy-chested lot cut from the heroic mold—he was a poodle amid the wolfhounds. He saw Dr. O'Keane less and less, to the point where he was not sure whether she'd yet taken another lover. (It was not like John to ask.)

John had a suspicion—just a suspicion, for no one had been so cruel as to tell him—that he wasn't very good in bed.

Ailesh had finished the sausage. Her rosebud mouth was glistening with grease, as though she were wearing lipstick. The sunlight reflected from her lips and bounced through the ell of the front room to the kitchen window. It shone so in John's eyes he wondered if he were getting a migraine. That would be the crowning shame: to get a migraine and become nauseated and aphasiac just when he had to make some decision about this intruder.

He would not get a headache! He clenched his fists in his lap and hardened his jaw, letting a cleansing rage fill him. He would not let Derval return (was she going to return?) and find him helpless in a dark room.

Little Ailesh looked at his motionless stern face with some trepidation.

The rage felt rather good, really. John felt he now had the power to do something about Ailesh, even before Derval's return. He could get her on a bus to Dublin, perhaps, and let the conductor worry from thereon. Or better, he could take her on a long walk and then hop a bus home himself, abandoning her.

He could call the gardai.

He glanced fiercely over at the object of these strategies to see the small female for whom his sweatshirt was far too big (how unusual) sitting receptively across the table, her hands folded and a look of worry, almost of fear of him, in her eyes.

John winced. He would do none of these unfortunate things to Ailesh, of course. Poor crazy girl. But it was something for him to have felt in himself that he could. He patted her hand. She looked up and smiled gratefully. Her skin was soft to the touch, soft and full of feminine power. The reassurance was brotherly and mutual. Embarrassed, John removed his hand.

She was very small. "You're the scud of the lot, eh?" he said (meaning the runt of the litter). "Well, no matter. So'm I." It was easy to say such things to a girl who couldn't understand a word of it.

John felt much better. He didn't think he was getting a migraine after all.

Chapter Three

•

> There is no human situation so miserable that it cannot be made worse by the presence of a policeman.
>
> —Brendan Behan

Derval's brain had been working so fast she felt it wasn't connected to her. In the time it had taken to trot Tinker back to the stable, finagle someone into cooling him down for her, cancel her student conferences on McCaffrey's phone, and tootle the Morris Mini back to John's house, she had both understood what had happened that afternoon and realized the implications to herself, the visitor, and the entire world. "I am the instrument of God," she whispered to the rearview mirror. "Or is 'Goddess' more politically correct? Or 'Gods' in their plurality?" She liked the sound of that last phrase, " 'Gods' in their plurality." It seemed less serious, somehow, and Derval was not sure she believed in any sort of God. Since the mirror had slipped out of adjustment, she was made aware once more that excitement made her nose look longer. She grimaced at her image.

She found John seated with Ailesh at the kitchen table. He looked oddly pleased with himself. Derval took a deep breath. "Johnnie," she announced, making an all-inclusive gesture with her key ring. "This thing is more dangerous than the MX missile!"

John Thornburn blinked vapidly at her. "The Morris, eh? It *is* tiny, but then so are most of the cars around here. If you get hit by a Volvo, though—"

"You know what I mean," snapped the dark woman, and she skidded a third chair over to the table. "The dimensional warp."

John furrowed not just his brow but his entire face. "Dimensional . . . you mean the pink mirage? I'd forgotten about that."

Derval sagged. "You . . . you forgot? A woman comes screaming into your house from another world and you just . . ."

"I certainly haven't forgotten the screaming woman. I've been feeding her, you see, and teaching her to use a paper napkin. But the pink mirage-thing—"

"It was NOT a mirage. It was real!"

"Mirages are real," John continued reasonably. "They're just from somewhere else. A trick of light."

Derval rose to her full height. He had something there. It might even be relevant, but she was in no mood to give him credit for it. "That girl," she stated, pointing at mystified Ailesh, "is not a trick of light. And she came through the phenomenon out of somewhere to here."

"Don't be silly," John said with some asperity. "She came through the bathroom window."

"The bathroom window is painted shut!" shrieked Derval. "Painted, mildewed, molded, and cobwebbed shut!" In an excess of passion she dragged John's chair across the kitchen and the dining ell to the hall before the bathroom door. She tipped the outraged householder over the threshold and closed the door on him.

Ailesh watched the scene with friendly interest, for all the activities of these semidivine beings were probably deeply significant. As soon as the effort-flushed Derval returned to the table, she asked her all about it.

John came back five minutes later in a brown study. "The bathroom window can't be opened," he said, and he sat down on the edge of the table. "I tried with all my strength."

"So what are we to do?" asked Derval triumphantly. As it was she who uttered the question, it must have been rhetorical, for Derval always knew what she was to do. John gave her a wary glance, wondering what improbable, impractical, and completely unshakable resolve she had hit upon.

"I don't think that's up to us at all," he murmured, continuing, "If this thing is as big as you say it is . . ." The trite fatuity of his phrase hit him, silencing him as no scorn of Derval's might have done. "I mean, if the girl honestly came here through time—"

"If she . . . !" Derval rose from her seat and her blue eyes were the centers of a face flushed to the color of a lit match. Her hands went to her breast and then extended outward. "Johnnie boy, I am perishing—absolutely perishing—for another, alternate conclusion. If you can give me one, you will have my undying gratitude and I can go back to my tedious graduate students a sane woman." Derval caught the response murmured under John's breath but decided to ignore it.

"A hoax," he answered her aloud. "Not the hoax you first thought of, with me pulling it off, but a hoax just the same. Someone at the college, or in one of my own classes, with . . . with lasers and . . . and hypnosis, possibly."

He stared at the dusty floorboards as he spoke, so he wouldn't have to look at Derval when she answered—as he knew she would. "Someone willing to bite a young woman all over her privates in an effort to make the crack good? Not to mention somebody willing to get bit. Do you think they used a local anesthetic before ripping her up, or would that numb the mouth too much for subsequent bites?"

John didn't fight the ruination of his idea. He couldn't raise his head. His vision swam with motes of dust gone brilliant, and he blinked and swallowed with difficulty. He felt floaty. That was a very bad sign. All the suspicious symptoms of the past hour returned to visit him again. "Whatever, Derval," he whispered, and was glad to find that he still had control of his voice. "Either hoax or dimen . . . dementedal . . . time warp, our response must be the same."

"And that's?"

"Call the gardai." Now, having said what he had to, John relaxed into a miserable passivity, watching the dust motes increase, spread, and occlude the left half of his vision. It was all very predictable.

Derval gave a half-strangled wail. "For Christ's sake, man, why not call the Pentagon directly?"

John opened his mouth. No sound came out. Derval continued, "Don't you know that's the first thing our beloved taiseach will do? Give the benefit of the discovery away to the Yanks, like the faithful dog he is. Not quite for free, of course. He'll expect benefits. Bigger immigration quotas probably."

This statement was bizarre enough to rouse John from his impinging private catastrophe. "What in hell do the Yanks want with all this?" he asked, and although he was reassured to find his words still echoed his thoughts, the effort of making sense leaked tears from his eyes.

"What do the . . . ? Ah, Johnnie, you're a blessed innocent!

"And not only the secret of the dimensional warp will disappear in Washington, to be pulled, hewed, and twisted into military usefulness—are you listening, Johnnie? But you yourself, having been the one to discover it, will be whisked away without a trace."

"M'not an American," he grunted, squeezing his now useless eyes shut. He tried to rise.

"Will that matter?" barked Derval. "Will Ottawa object to her big bully neighbor squeezing one small, very poor expatriate Canadian, without living family? Will Ottawa even know?"

Derval's sincerity shook through every word as she continued, "And myself as well. I'd vanish like a woman of Chile! Do you know what I'm going to do if you insist on giving this child over?" Derval was not a cruel person, but only an emotional one, and so did not understand why John only shook his head dumbly, like a horse scattering flies. "I could kill you, I suppose, and run off with Ailesh. But I might flub the job. Probably I would, being so fond of you and all.

"What I *will* do is go underground. Today. Turn the provos to some good for once. Lose my job, and my name, what friends I have. Then maybe I'll join a band of gun patriots striking out of Portadown." She laughed at this idea, disparagingly, but half-fondly. "The last place anyone would think to find me!

"Or maybe I'll go to Brittany, or . . . London . . . or hell . . . Chicago. I'm told there are more Irish in Chicago than . . ." She paused, her breath coming hard.

John was standing by now. His left hand had struck the table, a blow he scarcely felt. He rubbed his numb left cheek with fingers like wood. He heard Ailesh's slushy, musical voice.

"She says I'm being hard on you," Derval drawled ironically. "She says you seem to be sick."

"I am," admitted John hopelessly. "Migraine." His slow, pachydermatous turn knocked his chair over. "Please, please, someone help me to the bathroom. I can't see."

He wouldn't take his medication until he knew he was finished throwing up, over an hour later. Derval sat beside him in the bathroom. "Just break a plate over my head when I act like that, Johnnie," she whispered. "It's my own blindness, you know. I get carried away."

John did not answer. Could not. But Derval looked closely at his hunched shoulder blades for signs of forgiveness. She petted his cold, sweating, rigid back and tried to explain to the girl out of time how John had these . . . attacks. She tried in her incomplete, text-learned vocabulary of Medieval Irish to emphasize that the problem didn't make John any less of a man. Ailesh squatted on her very limber ankles at the bathroom door and agreed so easily that Derval believed she must not have communicated the matter correctly.

When he said he could keep his codeine down, Derval made John a slurry out of tea, honey, the narcotic, and (secretly) her last, cherished Valium pill.

It was dark. John stared into the kind murkiness of the dining ell. His female companions were shadows. He felt as disinterested as the dead.

Derval's throat caught at the way his infantile blond hair reflected the distant streetlamp. His white undershirt made him more pitiable, and the weary way his head rested against the hard chair back was even more affecting. But his eyes had the look of a harbor after storms.

"So it was the Danes, eh? How unfortunate. I don't think that I, in her position, would be able to draw distinctions between Vikings and—er—Dublin Danes. What year would that make it, Derval?"

She whispered into darkness. "Ailesh says the year is nine eight-five. Irish rekoning has not always agreed with the one we use now, but even with slippage, that's quite a while after the Norse settlement of Dublin."

Derval yawned. "Right about then the Vikings were very bothersome. In fact, I remember that there was a second wave of raiding activity all around the Irish Sea."

She sighed and knuckled her eyes. "It's likely our Ailesh doesn't know much of what's happening outside her immediate area. People rarely do, even today. I'm not sure we can really establish her time at this remove—"

John cut her off. "Say a thousand years ago. Nice, round number. One year for every spiral on the cross, and if it's not accurate, who's to care?"

Derval's mouth tightened at this cavalier treatment of history, but she said nothing.

"Poor thing," he said, sighing. "I begin to feel she's my responsibility, Derval." His eyes, both the blue one and the brown one, rested on the mouselike figure of Ailesh, who was peering out at the street from a corner of the window blind. She had found John's cap (he wondered where) and was wearing it helmet-style, the brim low above her nose. John thought she looked charming in it.

"Just begin? From the moment she landed in your bathroom . . ."

"Maybe. But I didn't feel it." John bit down especially hard on his ragged thumb end. His face expressed some sort of resolution. "I don't claim to know politics, Derval. You do."

"Claim to, you mean," growled Derval, who could be as hard on herself as she could be on anyone.

"Probably do. Ailesh isn't going to get swallowed by the military maw. Not if I can help it." He cleared his throat and continued. "But she can't stay here. Not with Mrs. Hanlon only a hundred feet from the front door."

Derval giggled. "All right, Miss Prim."

"I don't mean that. I mean she'd never pass. Can you see her walking into Bewly's and ordering a cuppa?" He laughed at his own joke. "So what we have to do . . ."

John paused and folded his hands on his lean thighs.

". . . is send her back through the dimensional warp." Derval finished for him. "Of course, love. That's the only way."

"But safely," he added, his lower lip protruding thoughtfully. "Not into the Vikings' lap."

"Certainly not the Vikings' lap." John did not see Derval's sly, superior smile.

Ailesh was now leafing through John's portfolio with exaggerated care. Now she pulled out two line drawings and extended them. One was a complex, circular zoomorph and the other, which interested her more, was a design in traditional Eskimo style for a kayak paddle. She spoke to John in tones of great approval. John Thornburn sat beside her on the sofa, smiling and nodding at her incomprehensible noise, like a father watching over the infant of his old age.

* * *

Ailesh ran the length of the tin whistle through her fingers. Its smoothness pleased her and she couldn't find the seam: good metalwork. She held it up to the light of the window of clear glass. That was also good work, better even than the Frankish glass bottle that the Welsh traders had sold to her father.

What was this place to which Saint Bridget and Goban had brought her? Not heaven, surely. One doesn't enter heaven bloody and shrieking. (But perhaps that wasn't the truth. After all, how did martyrs enter the kingdom of God?) Nor was one reincarnated in the same body, complete with scars.

Ailesh lifted the teacup that sat beside her in both hands and drank a little of the hot brew. It burned her tongue; obviously she wasn't in heaven. The drink was clearly an herbal medicine, though tempered with milk and honey.

Ailesh blushed to think how she had shamed herself with that display of panic in front of the fair man.

The fair man. She gave a peek at John Thornburn from under her eyelashes. So odd he looked, pinch-faced and slouching, with his long trousers like the bark of a tree over his skinny legs. He looked like a man who'd never run a mile nor sat a horse.

Despite this, Ailesh knew he was no ordinary fellow. Even had she not been sent by miraculous means to this great house with walls of crystal, the skill of the man's hand would have revealed the divine spark in him. Well, the Goban was no ordinary fellow, either, and she was his daughter. And there was a comfortable feeling about this one, perhaps because he was no larger than her father. Looking at the pull of the fair man's thin shirt over his shoulders, Ailesh laid wager with herself that like the Goban, he had a strength of arm and hand. And he was the gentle one, too, though tight-strung. Ailesh made him nervous. She knew that, and she smiled.

Should she be smiling over a man with her father in danger and her home in ashes? Ailesh thought of Goban, with his round face like hers and his massive torso, and in her mind she asked the question of him. He came to her eyes, laughing the way he did when at work with the stone, red-faced, his lips pulled back from his teeth. He asked her if a young man was any less fine because an old man might be dead. Hadn't it been Goban himself who had lifted her off the ground and dashed her against—no, through—the great cross?

To the house of the fair man.

Out of the corner of her eye she saw Derval watching her watch John. Ailesh lowered her eyes to the whistle once more. There was something between these two, and there would be no honor in going between them. Probably she would make a fool of herself, if she tried.

The whistle had six holes, three more than a cuislean. It was tuned similarly to the strange box that had the *Buíon* pipes in it. She put the whistle to her lips. When the dark woman started the box going, Ailesh tried to play along.

"I'm getting tired of that record."

Derval put down the dust cover of the turntable and looked over her shoulder. "I'd think you'd be tired of making circles sooner," she remarked.

John shook his head, then winced at the effect this had on his vision. Sick headaches left all sorts of reminders. "I hardly notice I'm doing that. But I'm going to wear the paper through if we have to go through this one more time."

Derval stretched her arms above her head and cracked her fingers together. She yawned. "That we will do, Johnnie," she said, filling the silence between the bands on the Furey album. "Or do you want to shove the girl through willy-nilly and trust to fate?"

Ailesh, the person in question, was leaning over John's shoulder all this while, watching him work. She lifted her frizzed russet head and spoke to Derval.

"She says you have a gift," translated the taller woman. There was no time for John to answer, for the pipe hummed and tweeted and his hand began to trace. In two minutes the pink cross glowed in the bathroom doorway, and Derval, swallowing her heart, reached her long arm in and snatched back the broomstick (with ancient, useless bristles) she had thrust through the time before. On impulse she pulled it halfway through the shining haze and let it lie there on the floorboards. The pink glow faded and Derval O'Keane knew an instant of horror. What would happen when the past pulled away from the present? Would the wooden stick divide with it, down to the veriest submolecular particle?

What happened was the broomstick scooted across the floor as though kicked, hitting the woodwork of the hallway and scraping paint as it clattered. "Jesus H. Christ," She said. "What got into me to try that?"

"Eh? What was wrong in it?" asked John, who still sat slouched over his draftsman's stool. "What harm could the broom come to?"

"Ripped electrons," stated Derval. "Pulverized atoms. Ireland a thermonuclear accident and the world a smoking cinder twenty minutes later. That's what."

John shifted in his Valium-induced torpor. "You *are* pleasant company, Miss O'Keane, aren't you? Well, even I could have told you that wouldn't happen."

Derval raised her eyebrows very high. "And how would you be knowing that?"

"Air's made of atoms as well as wood," John told her. "And the mirage . . ."

"Stop calling it—"

". . . has been full of air every time it's happened."

Derval, who couldn't deny his logic, stared sullenly at the floor. "Still did a bit of damage to your hallway. I wouldn't want to be halfway through when the gate closed."

John rose slowly from his chair and paced toward the hall with the steps of a much heavier man. On the way he stopped to rumple Ailesh's hair. "I wonder what she thinks of all this."

Derval spared a glance at the girl, who squatted huddled Indian-chief fashion against the wall, her eyes half-closed and reddened and her mouth drooping. "She thinks it's a blessed miracle, of course," said the tall woman. "Why wouldn't she? Pulled away from some squarehead's vicious attentions. God, I wonder how her village is doing."

"Maybe she's right and it was a miracle." John slid down the wall beside Ailesh. His ankles were not nearly as flexible as hers, but his narcotized relaxation made up for much.

Derval looked down at the two. She had given away her own peace of mind, she thought dispiritedly. In pills of ten milligrams. "We're not allowed miracles," she told John. "We traded them in for technology some years ago and now we're stuck with finding out how things work. Get up, Johnnie." She sighed. "We've got to do it again."

The hen had been found on the front porch. It was a plump copper-red. Once Derval pinned its wings to its back it stopped struggling, but by the dilation of its reptilian eyes and the silently gaping beak it showed small appreciation for the music of Finbar Furey. "Mrs. Hanlon has missed her, you know," John remarked, as at Derval's command he tried a loop of twine around the bird's foot. He then took his position. "She has no business letting the creatures roam," replied Derval.

The slow air started. John traced lines. The gate opened and Derval threw the hen through the pink haze.

The fat bird landed flat on its belly, producing squawks quite audible to John at his worktable. It stood up and shivered its feathers into place. The pink phenomenon gave it a dried-apricot hue.

Derval was counting. When she got to eight she pulled her end of the twine, hissing, "Now!"

The chicken fell over, the twine slipped off its foot and piled limply at Derval's knee. The pink haze glimmered and died.

Derval stared confusedly at the string in her hand. "You—you made the loop too big. Far too big! It came right off."

John yawned and shrugged. "I didn't want to constrict her circulation."

"You didn't—" Derval took a deep breath. "Well, do you know what that's led to?"

"We've lost Mrs. Hanlon's chicken," answered John, slightly perturbed.

"We've created a paradox," Derval corrected him. "Rhode Island Reds did not exist in the pre-Cromwellian oak forests of Ireland."

John Thornburn shrugged. "Just one. It can't matter."

"Can't matter?" said Derval in ascending voice. "Such a protein source could change the diet of ancient Ireland."

"Hindersome, but after all, what if it did? It's done and you, at least, still look the sa—" John began equably, only to be interrupted by Ailesh.

"She wants to know to whom we sacrificed the chicken," announced Derval, after the necessary laborious translations. "I told her we sent it to prepare the way for her."

"How bibical. Saint Cluck the Baptist." John glanced out of the corner of his eye at the girl. Her evident weariness struck a chord in him. "Poor thing. I worry about her. Can't we sleep now and shoot her through tomorrow, in daylight?"

"In daylight, certainly," agreed Derval. She lowered her

tall form onto John's musty sofa. "And Johnnie, you needn't worry too much about our Ailesh. I'm going with her."

Morning, and once again sunlight threw spears at John Thornburn's floor. Ailesh wore enormous cuffs at the feet of her trousers—John's trousers—and his sweatshirt was a baggy tunic over her thighs. When she moved, she rustled with gauze bandages. Before her on the floorboards rested John's huge khaki frame backpack, stuffed with what supplies Derval could find at the local market: a packet of Green Label tea, a can of Bachelor's peas, Chef's salad creme, a bottle of orange barley water.

She had torn the labels off everything, in attempt to protect history.

Derval herself stood beside the girl, wearing her knotwork smock and carrying her own blue daypack, with the tin whistle poking out like a standard. "You'll give us only the length of time it takes to run the record again, Johnnie, so if the Danes are still running about—"

"It won't take them but a second to hit you on the head," he muttered, depressed but hopeless at the thought of turning Derval from her purpose. He straightened the half-completed tracing over the rubbing of the work Ailesh called Bridget's Cross.

While Derval had been shopping and preparing Ailesh for her crossing of time's border, John had been hard at work replicating the pattern which had opened the gate. He feared one more imprint upon the old tracing would pop out the spirals like so many tickets punched. The much-penciled tracing was torn to lie in the dust on the floor, and now the fresh sheet was ready for business. John had his cap on his head and all his front hair tucked into it. Derval thought he looked silly that way.

It was very quiet on the street. Not even a dog barked. Then from somewhere came a woman's voice, shrilling, "Here, chicky, chicky, chicky . . ."

John's shoulders rose to his ears.

Derval heard Mrs. Hanlon also, but she dropped the needle to the record. The driving rhythm of a hornpipe filled the air. "Okay, Johnnie. You know when to begin."

John put his pencil to the paper and was struck with a

sudden panic. It didn't seem sharp enough, though it was the same implement he had just finished so carefully rounding off, lest it tear paper. Absurd.

But this tiny surge of emotion was enough to set off the leftover throb of headache. John felt eggshellish. He was not at all certain he should let Derval do this thing. He had no other ideas. It was time to begin.

With the first stroke on the paper his nerves ceased to bother him. John traced the spirals of Bridget's cross. This was better. This he did well and neatly. Sun glinted off the walls of the room onto the perfect white paper. John Thornburn forgot what it was he hoped to accomplish, tracing the cross. He just did it.

When the spirals were complete—all one thousand of them, he raised his eyes, irritated by the gleaming pink light.

From this angle he could barely see through the glow. There were dark shadows, none of them moving. There was a bright horizon. Derval gave a wave both gallant and impudent and plunged into the bathroom, turning rosy pink as she vanished. Ailesh paused and looked over her shoulder at John. She said something in her soft and slushy Irish. She gave him a sober smile.

Derval's hand reemerged and dragged the girl through.

The gate became an afterimage and was gone. John blinked dryly in his lonely living room. He got up and put the needle back to the end of the hornpipe. His hand shook so that he scratched the record.

Dear God, what if the needle had dropped, broken, or cut a swath across the magical air that followed the hornpipe? His breath was ragged as he returned to his stool.

Mrs. Hanlon was closer now, calling her red hen on this side of the street. John's ears turned as red as the hen's comb, thinking someone might have seen him taking the bird in. His stomach had tied in a knot and his head was aching sadly by the time he began the design that would open the gate for Derval to check in.

But the slow air had suffered no damage and Mrs. Hanlon was no longer audible. John worked his spirals, feeling for the first time vaguely sorcerous and imbued with power.

The music ended and so did the drawing. The air in the bathroom glimmered and glowed.

John waited the ten seconds, but nothing more happened. No one came through the gate.

He sat very still for some seconds, holding his pencil in his hand. The pencil broke in two pieces.

Then John tried to speak, to say, "No." But panic had grabbed him by the throat and no sound came out.

What had he done wrong? It must have been something he did wrong or else Derval had . . . no. It must have been something he did wrong. Perhaps the tracing hadn't been exact, or more importantly, in time with the music. Or was this a punishment for his overconfidence? John deeply believed that overconfidence got punished.

But the cross of Bridget *had* glowed in his bathroom doorway. What could have stopped Derval from . . . no. It must have been something he did wrong.

John trotted to the stereo once again, and then rushed back to his drafting table. Furey worked his art and so did John. The cross filled the hall with light.

He stood in front of it expectantly, trying to make sense out of the pattern of shadows behind the glow. He came closer and finally stuck his head through.

Green grass parted as neatly as a head of hair, running along a path between twisted oaks whose leaves looked black. Down the path the land dipped and then rose again to the forested slopes. No stones were visible now, but there were gray roofs protruding from the declivity closeby. And there was smoke.

John Thornburn was picked up and flung backward as though by hurricane winds. His head hit the drywall of his hallway and left a bowl-shaped impression. He hit the floor hard, and his cap came sliding after.

He was neither quite conscious, nor was he too numb to feel pain. He suspected his tailbone was broken, but the ache involved in moving his head made the effort of finding out not worth it.

Concussion. Brain hitting the inside of the skull. The very idea made him dizzy. John felt a deep need for his codeine.

He rose to his feet, using the cracked wall for support. Gathering his courage together, he entered the now-harmless bathroom. He opened the medicine chest.

Where was the yellow vial with the impossible-to-open top? Not behind the Feenamint, nor concealed behind the

Egyptian key patterns on the Ramses prophylactics foil pack. It hadn't fallen on its side, nor was it left on the sink beside the toothpaste tube. Gone.

John was desolate. Tears stung his eyes. Not only was he bound for an Irish prison, but between now and then he would suffer untold agonies. He blundered out of the bathroom.

But wait. Derval had opened his pills last night. (And how strong the dose she gave him had been. Usually the things didn't make him quite so mellow.) Where had she left the bottle?

There. On the sideboard of the sink. John plunged toward it. He pulled futilely at the plastic child-proof top. To gain time for himself, he poured a glass of water.

The doorbell rang. By pure reflex, John pulled the tracing from the board, folded it and stuffed it in his pocket, as though it were evidence of criminal action. Then he turned and stepped toward the front room, still holding pill bottle and water. He was in the dining ell when he realized he did not want visitors at this moment. Through the little glass panel in the top of the door he could see Mrs. Hanlon's permed ginger hair. He paused, uncertain.

The air was bright on his sore eyes. It was bright and rosy, and the brilliance was emanating from the hallway, from whence darted Ailesh, babbling ancient Irish. She plucked him by the sleeve and he found he was standing on the cap.

"No," said John plaintively. "The door is knocking. I mean—" He was being dragged toward the bathroom. "Ailesh, no!" John cried in alarm. "If you pull me in with you, then we'll all be . . .

". . . stuck." The little Irish girl was remarkably strong for her size. John finished his sentence standing on green turf under the black leaves of the oak. Water sloshed in the tumbler in his hand.

Chapter Four

•

> "A sword's across your throat," said Laghaid. "Eating a mouse includes its tail."
>
> —Tenth-century Irish story

"Ailesh! Now look what you've done." John swiveled from the girl's stubborn face to the pink glow again.

But it was neither the shining haze nor the doorjamb of his bathroom he saw behind him, but a tall and massive cross carved in sharp relief out of white limestone. In the center of it was the figure of the saint or female deity, knees drawn up as though to give birth: the Shiela na Gig. Around her wove twisted animals holding their own tails in their mouths, and about the whole, a border of exquisite, clean-edged interlocking spirals—hundreds of them. They extended the full length of the cross and out the arms as if the Shiela literally floated on the waves of the sea.

"Ye Gods and little fishes," whispered John. He went down on his knees before the work. Ailesh tugged at his shirt.

John's knees grated over stone shards. His left leg touched something soft. Peering over the water glass in his left hand, he saw a heap of canary-colored cloth. It was heavy against his foot. There was a hammer lying in the middle of it. The hammer was held by a hand. It was stained, covered with dark clots. John's eyes refocused and perceived the dead man.

He wore a smock much like Derval's. Round face, stubby nose, balding. No—not balding. The man had shaved his scalp back to his ears; it was the old tonsure for monks and all the lower orders of clergy. Behind the ears . . .

John sloshed water over his left arm. Behind the ears the

man's skull was staved in. John Thornburn had twice in his life gone netting for men the sea had taken, once in Newfoundland on the Grand Banks and another time in the Bay of Fundy. That was an ugly death, but not like this. He made a noise in his throat. His right hand involuntarily slapped the freshly cut limestone.

"Goban!" Ailesh sank down beside the body. She picked up the square, stubby-fingered hand of the dead man in her own small, stubby-fingered hand.

John had eyes. He looked from the gray face to Ailesh's. "Your . . . father?"

She made no reply, of course, but sat with her small mouth open, her whole body frozen with loss.

Derval appeared from somewhere. John shared a glance with her, unspeaking.

With her eyes closed, her head thrown back, Ailesh began to chant. She spoke slowly at first and then with growing conviction. A song rose from her grief. Dropping the hand of her father, she raised both arms over him. Derval stood beside her, helpless to comfort. Helpless even to touch, for in the midst of their danger, Ailesh had begun keening like a heroine of the *Táin Bó Cúalnge*.

"Without the blemish of envy
Clean of the blemish of hatred
Such were your eyes, Goban my father
Sharp and insightful was your glance
Quick to see the need of the pitiful
And quick were your hands to feed the hungry
Swift to give comfort
Swift in gift-giving
Swift to see beauty your eye
Eager to give it birth your hand
Ochon o! Crows of the hill of Ard na Bhfuinseoge
Sweet will your feast be at noon and sunset!
Noble your meat! Bitter my grief
Ochon o! Goban, father, my heart's pulse is spilled out!"

John was lost in the sound of the words, even though he didn't understand them. He stood listening to the song, so sorrowful and yet still filled with a kind of proud joy, and found himself wishing he could speak Gaelic like that.

Derval, on the other hand, who did understand it, could only think of the fact they were surrounded by dead people. The smell of death—of blood in the sun—was already heavy. The air was dancing with jewellike green flies, and the crows, so poetically invoked in the keen of Ailesh, were already picking out the eyes of the unburied.

This is real, she thought to herself. We could die here. And fear sent adrenaline rushing through her veins. Suddenly she knew that Ailesh must not finish the keen. The verse would be followed by the cry, and that might carry a long way. The Danes could still be with in earshot. Perhaps the jealous squawking of the birds had shielded them so far.

She clapped her hand over Ailesh's mouth. "Quiet, my treasure, my sister. Or we will join him."

Ailesh at once saw the sense in that and nodded in agreement. "We will bury them later," Derval soothed. "We'll come back and raise a stone over them."

"At least we will live to do that." Ailesh wiped her tears away. "He will have a stone. I myself will carve it."

Derval had spoken phrases pulled from the old stories she had taught so often. They seemed to her hackneyed, stereotyped, but they had been what was needed.

Ailesh pried the heavy mason's hammer out of the clenched, stiffened fingers. She held it up to the light for a moment. "A good blow, my friend, but not timely," she whispered to the weapon. "Still, the blood of my father's enemy has cleansed you from shame."

It appeared that Goban and the ax-wielding Dane had slain one another almost simultaneously, for the dead Viking lay half-hidden in the long summer grass behind the cross. His temple had been smashed in by what seemed to be a single hammer blow. His eyeball lay (so far unnoticed by the birds) along his cheek.

Ailesh cleaned the hammer off on her father's clothes and then, for a moment, her hard-won control crumbled as she bent to touch him one last time. Her face went into a distorted grimace of pain, and then she turned away from the corpse she had no time to bury, slipping the hammer into the belt of her trousers.

"*Dean deifir, Eoin Ban,*" she whispered.

"She's telling us to hurry. We've got to get to the clanstead," Derval hissed to John. She led him by the arm down the length of the grassy path and up an embankment on which stood the village of Ard na Bhfuinseoge.

It was a huge round house of wood, conical-roofed, and like some great sow it had farrowed little copies of itself all about it. To make the porcine image even more realistic, the great house and all the outbuildings were surrounded by a penlike palisade of wattle. It looked to John Thornburn disturbingly African, but he hadn't time to waste on the architecture before him. The great house was smoldering; its roof had collapsed. All the smaller houses were reduced to charcoal.

Bodies lay everywhere.

John turned on his heel, but along the path that blind-ended at the cross of Bridget no help was forthcoming. The black oaks rustled in a summer breeze, shadowing the late-morning earth. The air was full of woodsmoke. It smelled close: a bit foul. A red hen wandered over the packed earth, busily aimless.

Something crackled in John's hand. He looked down to see he was holding the tube of codeine—holding it too tightly. Sweat broke out on his bare arms, chilling him. John became aware of Ailesh's insistent tug on his hand.

She led him through a gap in the palisade into the devastated cattle enclosure. John stumbled over the body of a spotted dog and into the branches of a freshly felled ash tree. Around the fence more trees were down. His confused mind paused to wonder why anyone ravaging a village would stop to hack down trees.

The cows, the people, and their dogs lay together, butchered with equal savagery. John was led past a man with blond hair very like his own, staring sightlessly at the sky. Beside him lay in an ungainly heap a woman whose mantle of coarse wool lay bunched under her legs. She had been strangled. Her body was covered with bites. The entrails of a black bull lay spilt around her head.

John raised his eyes to Ailesh, as his mind filled with memory of her wounds, and how Derval had bandaged them, squatting by the toilet in his bathroom. He grabbed at the girl's forearm, in a strange fear that she might lie down now with all these horrifying others and be dead. He dropped the codeine.

Ailesh picked it up. She turned her face from him and led him across the cattle enclosure to the one building the fire had not consumed: a rectangular shed made of saplings and daub.

In the light of the doorway he caught up once more with Derval, who was leaning forward in a peculiar manner against a wad of torn cloth. John could not understand the purpose of this position. He knelt before her.

She gazed through him and he saw that her eyes, too, were filled with shock. Finally she focused on the glass in John's hand, and the plastic vial held by Ailesh. "How'd you know I wanted that?" She took the vial with one stained hand and broke off the top with her teeth.

John opened his mouth. "You didn't come back," he wanted to say. He wanted to say, "We're stuck." He wanted to share with her the horror of this place they had come to—to embrace her and support her and simultaneously to hide his head against her neck. He wanted to punch her with both hands for getting him in such terrible trouble.

"I didn't know you needed it," he said at last. "I only knew I did."

Silence fell again. Ailesh asked Derval a question and the darker woman answered, but to John it was so much babbling of the birds. He looked around him.

The shed was dim and floored with packed dirt, like some of the toolsheds at home. It *was* a toolshed, in fact, for saws and chisels of iron, some of them wooden-handled, hung neatly from the walls. The beams were carved and over the doorway hung a strip of suspiciously Victorian-looking gingerbread. Two backpacks leaned heavily against the door. John heard a hiss coming from the floor beside Derval.

There was a man lying there and he wasn't dead, for the square face was taut with pain and the teeth shone in the dark. The sufferer raised one hand as John watched and wiped it over his shaggy forehead. He glanced with effort at Derval and spoke. The voice, though weak, was resonant and modulated: held in complete control. Even in his confusion John noticed that voice.

He didn't trust it at all.

Derval shook pills out of the plastic vial. Two of them went into the injured man's mouth. This action took a good time because it was accomplished single-handedly. Her right hand remained pressed against the pile of rags which John could now see rested against the man's body. She took the tumbler from John. Her fingers left dark smudges against the clear glass. "Go see if you can find a harper for this man, will you, Johnnie?"

John gawked. "A . . . harper? Is that like a priest?"

Derval grunted a negation. "He's just missing one. Won't rest until he knows. And . . ." Her shoulders relaxed for a moment. She glanced at the wad of rags, which was black with blood, and peered through the shadows at the black gaping wound she had uncovered. Reapplying the pad, she leaned into it again. ". . . and if he doesn't stop moving, he's going to die. "He might anyway."

John stood. Ailesh was going out the doorway again. Clear sunlight fell on her ruddy frizzed hair, turning it gold. John began to follow her out, but a thought turned him.

"Derval, isn't this the kind of paradox you were talking about? I mean, your coming from the future? If he doesn't die, and he was supposed to—"

"Goddamn you to black hell, squarehead," she said without raising her voice or moving from her task.

John backed out of the shed. "It was you who was worried about such things," he muttered. "Not me."

Ailesh waited for him. Her fingers stroked the squat hammer in her belt reflexively and her eyes were raised to the hill, where freshly cut stone gave off a white light against the oaks. When she noticed John Thornburn she pointed back into the shed. "Labres MacCullen. *Ollave,*" she stated. John only sighed.

He wandered over the packed earth of the enclosure as aimlessly as a cow, gazing vaguely at carnage. His gaze was vague because his eyes had had trouble focusing since the accident with the wall. His head throbbed distantly, like someone else's complaint.

So many dead people. Had it been possible to feel any sicker, he was sure he would have. What was the purpose of it, after all? What wealth had these peasant folk that a Viking would want to take away? Nothing but their cattle and their land. Their cattle were uselessly slaughtered and the Norsemen had evidently no use for the place, for they had immediately packed up and left.

They had, hadn't they? John shot a glance at Ailesh. "The Danes. Where?"

Her face registered nothing. Then John remembered the word. *"Na Gaill?"*

Ailesh pointed, not east to the nearby ocean, but northeast to the much nearer hills. John's breath caught in his throat. He peered carefully at the dusty-green rises only a quarter-mile away. He was not sure he saw figures.

"They're still here? Ye Gods!" He spun and ran back across the enclosure toward the shed. Flies were everywhere at the scene of slaughter. They buzzed in his ears. Dived at his head. John stepped on the hand of a dead person and apologized.

"Derval," he shouted into the gloom. "The Vikings are only in the hills. They might come back any minute!"

The sick man turned his head at the shouted English. He raised up on one elbow. Derval heard him say, "Who is this stupid Saxon dog who calls them back on us again?" She pressed him down again, hissing in English. "Mind your manners, Johnnie. You're not helping."

"But we've got to get out of here," he said lamely.

"Not without the Ollave here," she replied. "He's the only one left alive. Out of the whole community."

"Don't forget Ailesh. She's alive. And it was she who told me about the Danes."

Derval looked up at him. Her eyes were shadowed. There was blood on her nose. "The Danes. Yes. Well, how do you like the behavior of your sex now, Johnnie?" John stole a glance out the door at the brooding hill. "You're really the nevers, Derval. What do I have to do with all this? I'm three inches shorter than you and not half as dangerous when provoked. Besides, there're as many murdered men here as women, and no easier on them. Can't we drop this guilt business? All I want to do is go home, and that we can't do, with no one to work the spell on the other side."

Derval had a supercilious eyebrow. "Oh no? Then didn't Ailesh's penny whistle work like a gem, and without a bit of help from you?"

John started. "The penny whistle? Is that how—"

"How did you think?"

John rubbed his palms against his trouser legs. "I don't want to think. I want to go home."

Derval nodded. "This is no proper place for us. Though"—her face softened—"if it weren't so damned dangerous. To the future, I mean. I almost feel . . ."

Her blue eyes sought out John's. "This place and time is

where my heart lives, Johnnie. With the oaks and the free herds. Before it all . . . slid into shamrocks, leprechauns, and potato patches. You know."

"I don't know," he answered. "Given all, I think one place is as good as another—except when covered with dead bodies, with berserker killers not a mile away and probably coming back. To bury their dead, if for no other reason."

The injured man gave a breathy sigh. Evidently the narcotic was taking effect. John rather envied him. "You decide, love," said Derval. "Should we take him with us? Or should I stay and take care of him?"

"Stay and—" John snorted furiously. "You're completely around the bend, Derval."

"I won't abandon him."

John sat down hard on the dirt floor. "Who's asking that you abandon anybody? We'll take him back with us. And Ailesh. And anyone else you want. But let's do it now, eh?"

Derval appeared uncharacteristically undecided. "The paradox is enormous." She pressed harder against the Irishman's wonded side. He smothered a groan.

Ailesh's treble voice sounded outside. "They're coming!" cried John.

"She only said she saw movement on the hill, Johnnie," Derval retorted, but too late. John squeezed between Derval's patient and the wall and lifted the man in his arms.

One who didn't know John Thornburn would have been surprised at the ease with which he hefted a man much larger and heavier than he was. But John had spent his youth hauling nets and lobster crates, and his adult years working with stone and clay as well as paper. Derval squeaked as the pad started to slip from the Irishman's wound. "Be careful, love. There may be spinal injuries."

John's great difficulty was not the man's weight, but the fact that he couldn't see over him. He felt a panic that he would step on a dead person again. "Derval," he called. "Guide me to the stone, would you."

But instead the woman stood in front of him, and the pressure of her hands seemed like to knock him backward. "He's bleeding again, Johnnie!"

It was a miserable, stumbling journey. John slipped twice but it was Derval who fell, flat over the head of a red cow, banging her arm sadly against the mottled horn of the beast.

John couldn't see what was happening. He leaned his left shoulder against the wall of the *céilí* house.

Suddenly the man whom Ailesh had called MacCullen strained in John's grasp. One leg swung free and then he was standing, swaying. John caught him about the waist as the man cried out, and half-restrained, half-supported him as he blundered into the smoking ruins of the house.

Within was more bloodshed, around the sad small remains of a hearth. There was a woman who had been stripped of all clothing before being decapitated. There was a single bench the fire had missed, and on it lay a gray-haired and heavy-bearded man, also naked, transfixed to the wood by an oaken spear.

MacCullen wasted only a moment on this scene before sinking down on hands and knees among the ashes on the floor. "Stop him, Johnnie," came Derval's voice from the doorway. John Thornburn followed, cursing as he set his hand on a living ember.

Fallen beams made the floor an obstacle course. And it was still being formed, for even as John crawled a section of wall sagged in and collapsed a few yards from his head. Smoke filled his lungs and confused him. He coughed and retched.

When he caught up with MacCullen the man was crouched by the wall, beside a figure with scorched skin and hair burned away. It seemed no more than a boy. The wounded man moved the body aside and uncovered a thing of wood and wire.

"He's found his harper," John called out. He took the instrument from MacCullen and helped him drag the body across the breadth of the house and into the sunlight.

The air outside the building tasted impossibly sweet. John's eyes wept away the ashes and charred wool. After a moment he heard the noise.

"Is he keening now?" he asked Derval resentfully, for MacCullen stood over the shockingly burned body of the harper, holding the *clàirseach* in both hands. The instrument seemed more or less intact. His fair head was raised to the blue and white heavens and his resonant voice must have carried for miles.

Derval listened astonished, as the man who had a moment before been semiconscious orated with a self-possession united with great feeling.

"Sharp my grief!
The pain pierces me
Child of my kin
The strings of your heart are broken!
The song of your life ended!
Fitting for you all to lie here together
Under the sun three things are most pitiful,
The burial of youth,
The cutting of ancient trees,
The—"

Derval at last put an imploring hand over his mouth.

John turned to Ailesh, who was still as a statue, her hand white-knuckled on the handle of the hammer. Her eyes were fixed on the seared young face on the earth by the ceili wall. "Explain to him," John asked her. "Tell him we're not being unfeeling, but that we have to go."

She did speak, though not from John's prompting. The poet stared from Ailesh to John. Then his knees gave out and the tall Irishman sank over the body of his harper. John hoisted him again.

Once over the palisade the going was easier. Ailesh led and Derval pressed against the now fouled and filthy wound on MacCullen's side. Out of the corner of his eye John saw the white shape of the cross bobbing nearer. Assuming Derval's tin-whistle trick worked, he'd be back home in minutes.

Had anyone remembered to bring the codeine?

Ailesh clapped her hands and darted back into the ruins of the village. "Eh?" said John, and Derval made a noise of frustration. But the girl returned very soon, flourishing a little silver tube on a chain. She opened it under Derval's gaze. "My sewing needle," she announced. "It is the only thing of value left to me, except the hammer."

Derval nodded in understanding. John merely sighed. He tramped on.

If the placing of Greystones Hill meant anything, this abbey had been built where his house would be someday. Or almost. His house was (or would be) along this path a ways. Perhaps by the stone. And perhaps, just perhaps, that rosy glow in his bathroom doorway was actually produced here—in the same place, but a thousand years earlier. The coincidence was—

Suddenly John felt himself shoved violently sideways. His

feet left the path and floundered in deep grass. In brush. Ailesh hissed into his ear.

Derval grabbed his shoulder and yanked him into the trees. After hopping a frantic fifteen yards he fell among briars under the shade of the black oaks. Derval and Ailesh belly flopped beside him. The weight of MacCullen lay half over him. He raised his head to see, along the bright ribbon of the path, some twenty or more figures striding.

Men. Not wearing horned helmets. Not all blond. Not especially large, by modern standards. But they wore heavy swords and assuredly they were Vikings. They stopped by the cross of Bridget. Five of them leaned against it and the white gleaming stone went down with a crash and fell in pieces.

"Jesus and Joseph," whispered Derval to John. "Now we are stuck." He did not reply.

Ailesh hissed vituperation in John's ear. But the girl's anger did no more than match John's own. For though John Thornburn was no fighter by nature, and though human disaster left him ineffectual, this desecration of art filled him with a glowing, simple rage that overcame both fear and the lingering confusion in his head. John rose to his feet in battle heat and started after the departing ravagers. Derval and Ailesh held him back by the arms. They huddled in the dark woods till the Vikings were out of sight.

"Yeah, we're stuck," muttered John. He squatted on the dead oak leaves with his head between his two hands. Derval, who was standing between two mossy tree boles, a hand on each, gazed down at him with some compassion. "Looks that way, Johnnie. For a while, at least." She paused, looking closely at him. "Does it depress you that much? This could be a lovely place."

John grunted. "Eh? No. It's just my head. Again. I hit it. Pay no attention to me."

This command was easy to follow, for there was much else to attract Derval's eye. The forest itself, for one thing. Having grown up not too far from Phoenix Park, and having spent most of her childhood holidays at Kilronan, on Inishmore, she found the woods' shadows a heavy presence. Uncomfortably heavy. Almost awful. The oak trees stopped the wind and blackened the sky. Through them pierced the lighter spears of the *ailm* and the *coll*—or at least Derval suspected these were the elm and the hazel. She'd mastered the words, but had never had the chance to become good at identifying trees.

The high canopy sheltered a brittle undergrowth of hazel, which made too much noise when it was stepped on. And underneath, which in this season should have been grass and meadowflowers, was the acid, rotting carpet of leaves with its faint odor of tannic acid.

Derval felt the forest crowding her close. She felt judged. She remembered the backpacks, left leaning against the shed door. She reflected on what she had done.

She thought: all of time is hanging on the edge—here, on this day in these woods outside a smoking village filled with the bodies of the dead. Either I am making the future or destroying it.

But (she added in her own defense) it was never my idea.

At a crack of dry wood she started and glanced down at Ailesh, who was using branches to weave a pallet for the sick man. Derval made a shushing noise and pointed significantly toward the Viking-infested village. The girl regarded her patiently. "They won't be hearing this," she said. Derval had only to think a moment before replying, "Not at the dun, surely, but they may send"—what was the word for scout?—"riders. They may send riders to look for enemies."

Ailesh's gold-brown eyes flashed with the first touch of sharpness she had yet shown. "Riders on what? Boat riders?"

Of course. The Vikings had come on longboats, too small to carry horses. They must have marched inland very quickly, to come at the monastery without warning. Only forty men could fit in a longboat, Derval remembered. Could forty Vikings, or eighty, or even a hundred have done all that killing? She shivered.

Chapter Five

•

"McKeogh," said O'Donnells Kern, "I have worked your cure, but if you come back at me once over with your rudeness and stinginess, that same leg I healed I will break again, and the other to go with it."

The Kern of the Narrow Stripes
Irish Folk Tale: Silva Goedelica

Labres MacCullen came to himself remembering pain. After some confusion it localized in his left side. Like the wound in the side of Christ, he thought. A nice image, and he might be able to use it sometime. Not that he dared compare himself to Christ, of course. Not out loud.

He was used to misery, for he was Ollave of Leinster—the "spouse" of the realm—and the pain of Leinster and of Leinster's king was his own. But this was not the usual bitterness that ached in his side, nor yet was it a Roman spear that had pierced him, but an iron sword in the hand of a Dane. Even now, in the dark of the forest, that cold-eyed face rose above him—intent, almost seeming afraid. And he saw the stubby hands, and the spiky short hairs on the arms which were red as slabs of meat.

And him with no protection but a leather-bound book in his hands.

MacCullen felt it a marvel that he should be alive at all, for he had seen the abbot slain like a heifer of sacrifce on his own table, and the abbot's wife killed on the dirt below. Then had come the blow in his own vitals and MacCullen had fallen. He had watched the burning thatch cave in over his head. MacCullen's pain-narrowed eyes went suddenly wide, remembering something else.

Caeilte: young Caeilte, his sister's son, his harper. Only twenty and full of enthusiasm for the life he had chosen. Not yet among the renowned musicians, Caeilte had been trained since leaving the academy to accompany his uncle's verse. They were to gain their renown together, the young poet and the younger harper. No more. Caeilte, like the trees of Ard na Bhfuinseoge, was fallen and dead.

What would he say to the boy's mother? What a miserable homecoming it would be.

He had made a poem over his body, MacCullen remembered. A lament. In between grief and his wound's agony Labres MacCullen wondered whether the poem had been any good.

He lifted his head. Dizziness made him put it down again, but in that moment he saw he was out of the village and in the wood, lying on a pallet of branches. Captive? The Vikings hadn't seemed interested in taking captives. They were doubtless the dreaded worshipers of the god of slaughter. Of course if they were seeking ransom, he was the likely choice to be spared, for both his clothes and natural bearing (MacCullen told himself) marked him out as a man of worth.

Wouldn't they be surprised when they tried to find some relative of his who could pay their price?

He heard voices talking. Not Irish, nor yet Norse, both of which MacCullen knew well. They spoke something like the iron tongue of the Saxons, in which he was less fluent. He couldn't make out their speech at all. Painfully he raised himself up again and looked around for a person of sufficient quality to treat with him.

The poet recognized the tall gawky woman in the way one would recognize something once seen in a dream. He recalled that she had appeared above him and dragged him from the fallen great house. By his feet. Her nursing, too, had been clumsy and her tongue that of a baby. Or an idiot.

The blond man was even less familiar, but his outlandish dress and hangdog look marked him as a fellow of no account. With relief MacCullen recognized Ailesh Iníon Goban, gouging the earth with her knife and ramming stripped hazel suckers into the holes. She was weaving a shelter, using the earth itself as her loom.

"Are we captives, daughter of my friend?" he called to her, his voice whisper-thin and shaky.

She raised her eyes in surprise from the basketlike crescent. "Indeed we are not captives, Ollave. These heroes have rescued us from the Gentiles." MacCullen glanced from Derval to John. His mouth opened as though he would laugh, but the effort was too much. "Heroes," he echoed and then sank flat back on the ground. "All else are dead, then?"

"They are dead," said Ailesh shortly.

"Your father among them?"

"My father. Your sister's son, Ollave. The abbot and his wife and the old women and the old men and all the children. The cattle too. It must be that the harbor people ran off at the sight of the reaver's ships, and not one of them stayed the moment to warn us. Or else they are all dead, as well."

MacCullen closed his eyes and swallowed. "Between the treaties of the Gentiles and those of the *Ri* of Leinster (himself so much worse than the Gaill), we have come to destruction! And where is it we will find our murder price?"

Ailesh put her eyes back to her work. "It is certain we had no treaties with the king's brother, Ollave. Our trust was all in Dublin."

MacCullen winced as memory drifted back to him. "Goban. I lay in my blood and heard them fall—the compass trees of the abbey. Each screamed with the voice of a man."

"By Mary's face! Perhaps it was men he was hearing," whispered Ailesh to herself. She crawled over the moist earth to the place where the Ollave lay. In the dim light of evening she put her face close to his bandaged side.

He was a tall, square-built man, with fine features. His eyes were the same blue was Derval's, but against his bright complexion they looked darker. The once-careful coif of his yellow hair was plastered to his skull with sweat and mud. "You're not bleeding any more," Ailesh said. "For that you have to thank Derval. She nursed you like . . . like a champion."

"A champion I'll believe her," MacCullen countered. "At digging onions! She prodded into my side as though she would start a bed there. But what could I expect from a great girl with a shape like a tree? Had it been your hands now, Daughter of the Arts . . ."

Ailesh recoiled. "What hard speech is coming out of you? Do you think the woman sitting there has no ears, MacCullen?"

He puckered his mouth, feeling irritation that his flattery had gone wrong. "In the pain I'm in I'm not likely to care what a serving woman, a foreign slave, thinks of my language."

Derval sat motionless not two feet from MacCullen's knees. As she was not yet perfect in their dialect, MacCullen's insults struck her slowly but struck hard. As understanding dawned, her face remained set but her blue eyes glittered. She took a breath. "I am," she began, "Derval Siobhan Iníon Chadhain. My mother is a scholar and a teacher. My father, too, has an academy education."

Gaining impetus from her anger, she rose to one knee and rested forward, an arm upon it, as she continued. "I myself have traveled over all Europe and to the West where you have never been, man of Erin. I am lettered in five languages. I am master of the horse and hound. And the clàirseach.

"I am no man's servant."

MacCullen stared astonished at the woman above his head. By her language he would take her for a foreigner. A Saxon, perhaps. By face and title, though, she was certainly a Gael. Whatever, he had made a mistake. That knowledge made MacCullen feel weaker. His weakness made him angry. "Are you such a prodigy as that, woman? Well, I tell you in turn that my name is Labres, son of Cullen of the Ui Fáeláin and I took my mastery of poetry at Munster, but it is in sad Leinster I hold my rank of Ollave. What else you need to know of me you might ask of any lettered man in Ireland."

He stopped to breathe. He had exaggerated a bit. Not any lettered man in Ireland would know his reputation, for he rarely stepped too far from Dublin, and more seldom still out of Leinster, but Ailesh certainly would back him up.

But would she? She had sounded quite angry. MacCullen decided this war should be carried onto enemy soil.

"Far from insulting you, Iníon Chadhain, I intend to pay you the high compliment of surviving your nursing. But I beg to know, O great traveler and master of all the arts. Why do we languish in this cold forest if you have horses to carry us off? And if you are a harper, like my poor young Caeilte who is dead, then where is your clàirseach, and the servant to carry and tune it for you?"

"Where are your servants, then?" Derval countered, but MacCullen's eyes were firmly closed, and perhaps he slept.

"Should you yell at your patient that way?" asked John Thornburn of Derval. The dark woman sat with her jaw jutted forward, her cheeks licked with flame. She gave him a glance that pushed his head down between his shoulders.

"Do you know what he said about me?" she demanded. John shook his head. Derval glared at the unresponsive features of the sick man and snorted.

"Never mind."

"But I'd like to know."

John flinched back from her clenched hand. "Well, you brought it up," he reminded her.

Derval settled slowly, as a bird will settle its angry feathers. "Damn. Damn, damn, damn. When I think that but for that slob we'd be home by now. Warm and at home."

At this reminder, John huddled his knees to his chest. "It is rather chilly for early evening. Especially for June."

"It'll get colder," said Derval, grinding her teeth. She gave a frustrated sigh. "Already I've stood up two undergraduate classes."

John Thornburn smiled sadly. He edged closer to Derval, for, angry or not, she was warm. "No you haven't. You won't miss them for a thousand years yet. Plenty of time."

Ailesh called to them. Her little hive was finished. It was only about six feet in diameter and had no door at all. But it needed none, being built like half a basket. She gestured for John to come help her, and together they lifted the construction, shuffled it sideways, and dropped it over the wounded man. Then Ailesh began dragging brush over the entrance. "I'm beginning to understand her," said John over his shoulder. "I got 'lift' and 'right' and 'down.'"

"You're a marvel," Derval said shortly.

John shrugged away her sarcasm. "I've never had a little sister before, you know."

Derval smiled crookedly. "Not so very little, Johnnie. And why a sister, anyway?"

John gave her a look of reproach.

Ailesh pried the heaped brush aside and crawled in. She crooked her finger to them. John followed her under, giggling nervously. Derval was last in.

"We ought to keep a lookout," she murmured. "We're only an eighth of a mile or so from the bastards."

Derval's whisper was loud in the confined space. The odor of blood and sickness was evident. But Derval snuggled in between John and Ailesh, who gave way with alacrity.

The shelter Ailesh had made grew warm with body heat.

"Maybe they'll be gone tomorrow," Derval said to Ailesh. "And then we can get the cross back and try to put it together again."

Ailesh, who was pressed against the other side of MacCullen from Derval, lifted her head. "But the cross is broken off, Bhean Uasal. How can it still help us?"

Derval shrugged, jostling the wounded man just a little bit. "It's broken worse at our end. I mean at John's house."

"You . . . do not live there?" Ailesh's question was diffident.

Derval shot a quick glance into the darkness. Ailesh was staring up at the moonlight through the woven branches. "Not always.

"But the cross being broken won't matter, I think.

". . . I hope."

"You wait for the . . . the power of heaven to take you home?"

Derval couldn't miss the forlornness in Ailesh's words. She tried to remember why it was important that the redheaded girl be left back here. Paradox. The military-industrial complex.

Sounded like so much bullshit with the Vikings next door. So what if the destructive technology of this period was primitive? It was shockingly effective, and Derval would not consider leaving the girl to the sword's threat. All that was necessary to avoid temporal repercussions was for Ailesh to learn English and keep her mouth shut about her past. Easy work, in comparison to dying.

"You, too, Ailesh. You can come back with us."

Ailesh turned over. Derval saw with a bit of surprise that the girl was stark naked, except for her bandages. "To John's house? That is a strange place. It is not on this island, is it?"

Derval sighed, not for the first time. "It is . . . and it isn't. This place, now"—and she thumped the earth with her hand—"is much more Ireland than that is."

Ailesh nodded, as though she knew it all already. "But I will stay, when you go, for I have to go up the Slige Chualann to Dublin."

"Dublin?" It was John who spoke. Both women started.

"To Dublin?" repeated John. "Why to Dublin?"

Ailesh smiled. Her teeth gleamed in the broken moonlight. "You talk!" she whispered. "How nice."

"I begin," he said, after some thought. "Little bit."

"John has been studying," drawled Derval. "Studying especially hard today."

"I have to go to Dublin," Ailesh said slowly and distinctly to John. "For though we are of Leinster, we bought the protection of the Dublin Danes at a high tribute, and we did not get it. I go to get the murder price for my father and for the fallen trees of the monastery, as well as redress for the profanation of the body of Christ within our altar. It is my right and my duty."

"This I don't like!" answered John with some force.

Derval nudged the edge of the basket, which swayed. She begged pardon. John Thornburn could not see her. He lay curled in the half-hedgehog position, his knees as near his chin as his tight tendons could manage.

The wind came through, there was no doubt about that. It was marginally colder than it had been ten minutes ago. Little dead branches dug pits into his shoulder, his cheek, his ear. John listened to the ragged, effortful breathing of the poet, whose head rested near John's midsection. Evidently every breath had to be grabbed through pain.

Poor fellow. Although John could not feel for him the kind of pity that had grown in him for Ailesh—MacCullen was neither winsome nor smaller than John—still John Thornburn was aware of a sort of participation in the man's suffering. (How had he insulted Derval—so tall, confident, and athletic? He must have made fun of her temper. John decided.)

The redheaded girl was sleeping snuggled against MacCullen; her breathing was gentle and deep. She seemed comfortable.

Tomorrow morning John, too, would stand up a class. It was a small class and didn't pay him much, but it was a professional responsibility. Both his head and chest swelled with the familiar "oh, do leave me alone" feeling he got whenever he had failed in something, and people were set to fix him with hurt, reproachful glances. But of course he did not have to apologize for missing his appointments. It wasn't his fault, for once. It had been an Act of God, like the insurance forms say. In fact, he was not even present in the world where the appointment had been made any more, to receive possible hurt, reproachful glances.

Might as well be dead.

For John Thornburn that realization was not tragic but comforting. Unlike head colds, broken equipment, and smudged appointment books, death was an excuse no one could deny. He was dead to the twentieth-century world, at least for a while.

There was noise: insistent, repetitive noise that was neither his companions' breathing, nor the beating of his own heart in his ear. Chanting. Heavy, in five-beat rhythm. The Vikings were making noises in the night.

John huddled closer to the wounded poet. His sense of comfortable distance faded. Actually, he'd rather be teaching the mathematical bases of Celtic design at Trinity and be dead to *this* world's bloody appointments.

He was getting tired of that word: dead.

For years, whenever John had had trouble sleeping, he was in the habit of calling to mind a page from his masterbook—the Book of Kells. It was always the same page: the Chi Rho page, which consisted of two Greek letters so intricately, endlessly elaborated in line and color that there was no white left on the page.

One could look at the piece from many different focal lengths. At greatest remove there was the lettering itself, strong and solid against the fine grain of the background. At a closer look it was a pattern of linked circles. With nose to paper one could make out that each individual circle was a complex work in itself. At all distances, it was perfectly satisfying.

John liked to set up the page behind his closed eyes, prodding himself to remember the placement and form of each individual spiral, bird, or tiny human head that ornamented the letters. Always he was asleep before half-reaching his goal.

But tonight the figures would not behave; they twisted before his eyes in great indecision: heron's head into man's head and key pattern into scallop. It was not as though his own abilities had been blocked, nor yet that his odd, unreasoning discipline had deserted him. It was as though the template from which he worked—the Chi Rho page itself—were missing.

Could it be, he asked himself, that the illumination did not exist? That it had not yet been penned and painted by its anonymous master hand?

No, of course not. The book was late ninth or early tenth

century: already seventy-five or a hundred years old. It must be John's nerves giving him trouble. He let his efforts lapse.

But the splashes of color which would not follow direction would also not let him be, and John found himself the helpless observer in a play of light and line which spread without limit over the canvas of his mind. There was a saint's head with a halo of carmine hair and a saint's hand pointing, with each finger ending in a spiral like no natural fingerprint, and all the power and radiance of that hand expressed in golden double braid.

The eyes of the bird were golden too: the odd, fat bird with each feather a square knot and its long legs stretched out sideways and lost in the tight, three-dimensional pattern of line behind the whole. And the bees were gold, around the hive of knotted willow.

That red blazon was a mouth—or rather the stern lips were flat and heraldic. And the black brows beneath the black hair of the saint (but hadn't it been red—like Ailesh's?) were the shape of an ouzel in flight, and the crest of twin spirals like weeping eyes.

Around, bordering the saint, and the bird and the hive with its golden, sleeping bees and the argent swords in the hands of bone and the shadowed figures, unrecognized because never yet encountered . . .

. . . were looped, endless, oceanic spirals. They closed in the picture like seasons of history. Binding. Making inevitable. When the spirals multiplied in their colors of blue and silver John knew the work was finished.

I can do this, he said to himself. I can put this all down. His heart was pounding as though he'd climbed a hill.

Now he was nowhere near sleep. He wondered how he'd even thought to try, here in a strange world without language and no jacket at all. John sat up and huddled into himself.

The damn squareheads were still grunting away down there, he growled to himself. He—John Thornburn—was of course not a squarehead but a Canadian. A peaceful people; Canadians. Never hurt anyone but the Indians and he was part Canadian Indian too. He hugged his national harmlessness to his bony sides, shivering.

The rhythmical noise came closer and John knew a moment's awful panic. But this was not the chant of the Danes.

It was somebody crunch-crunching through the damp oak groves. Numb with fear, he put his eye to the wickerwork.

Out there in the moon-touched dimness, in the direction of the village, something white moved. It was large. It sought left and right over the ground. It was only twenty feet away. For a moment John Thornburn simply could not breathe.

He reached over the sleeping poet to shake Derval. His groping hand scraped the dry boughs that floored the hutch. In an agony of fearful impatience, he leaned over and pawed the empty bedding.

Derval was gone.

John's fear overcame him and his senses failed for a brief moment, and then that overambitious fear extinguished itself. "Dear, dear, dear," he whispered to himself, relishing his own control. "One damn thing after another."

It occurred to him that the two strangenesses—the white apparition and Derval's disappearance—might cancel each other out. If it was Derval creating the disturbance out there . . .

Would a yellow smock look white under moonlight? Certainly. Would Dr. O'Keane muddle about the wet earth alone at midnight with Viking raiders carousing only a few hundred yards away? Of course. Indubitably. How could he doubt it? John pried up the edge of the hutch as Derval had done and slipped out.

The prowler saw him and started violently. John saw the prowler and did the same. It was not Derval, after all, but a . . . a creature of some variety.

Domestic, apparently, for after its initial spook it came up to him readily and laid its heavy head against his hand.

It was fat, stocky-legged, and bigger than a goat. Its tail was slight and dangly and its little ears pricked. It had a round forehead covered with curly white hair, as was the rest of its body. Its nose was delicate and it had tiny hooves conical as elephant's feet. It made a sort of gasping sob as it nuzzled John's stomach.

A deformed horse, John decided with some amazement. A deformed horse living alone in the black woods. He regarded the thing with pity mixed with revulsion.

Should he tell his companions? John was subject to some indecision. There was such an air of unimportance about the creature. Surely Ailesh wouldn't welcome being hauled out of her sleep of exhaustion to be shown this. And if he did wake her, would he be able to communicate his message? Wouldn't it be more pertinent to convey to her that Derval was gone?

No. The little Irish girl, not knowing O'Keane's mettle, would assume she had been carried off. John Thornburn knew better with every fiber of his being.

Most likely she was spying on the Vikings. Horrible thought. It implied worse—such as that John should go after her. He shuddered and remembered it was very cold out here. John snuggled against the pale, downy side of the deformed horse.

Hearing a crackle and a crunch, he turned to see the thing setting its square teeth into the fabric of Ailesh's woven hutch. It pulled back and the great inverted bowl swayed perilously. John took hold of the creature's skimpy mane and hauled it back. With no sign of rancor, it set its legs against him and returned to its destructive task.

"Hush!" said John rather loudly, and he threw his slight body in between the animal and the shelter. With the large, boxy teeth against his T-shirt he wondered if he had done the wisest thing, but the horse seemed bent on vegetable pillage, and bent its lean ewe's neck around him. Shoulders larger than his crowded him back.

Now John was stretched back over the arc of the shelter. His feet hardly touched the earth and the branches sagged dangerously under his weight. Pulled among irritation, fear of discovery, and the seeping chill, he made a small mewling noise. The animal's head was above him. He grabbed it by its long jaw and little chin and, Samson-like, forced it back.

The retching, gasping sound it made turned John's bones to water. He released his grip and the animal stepped in again, gape-mawed. John felt the ribs of the hutch crack beneath him.

"Come now, hinny dear," whispered Derval, and she led the creature away with an ear between her two fingers.

"Ye Gods!" hissed the blond, sliding down to his feet again. "How did you do that? I couldn't do a thing with it!"

Derval's smirk was lost in the darkness. "And Hinny was well aware of your inability, Johnnie. Shame on her." But was she spoke she petted the creature's large rounded forehead and little nose.

John shifted from foot to foot and hugged himself from the

cold. "You . . . you know this thing?" The animal was melting beneath Derval's expert caress.

"Not this one personally: just hinnies," she replied. "Look how she gleams in the moonlight!"

"I noticed. I only hope the Vikings don't." He examined the animal dispassionately. "Birth defect, eh?"

Derval's dark head started in the darkness. "Birth . . . ? Oh, John!"

He found her snigger quite offensive.

"She's a hinny," the woman lectured. "Offspring of a donkey jennet and a stallion."

"Eh? That's a mule. I might not know much about horses, but I know that much!" John's voice was a bit loud. Derval touched his lips with a feather finger. "And this . . . this abortion doesn't look like a mule," he concluded more quietly.

Derval stroked the pointy head with a tenderness she had never showed John Thornburn. "Abortion! Did you hear that, Hinny? And you as cute as a teddy bear.

"Isn't she rather like a stuffed animal, Johnnie? All white and rounded, with her little feet and her little ears? And they're not mule ears because she gets them from her daddy. Along with her color. But her size and stuffiness are asinine, aren't they, Hinny. Honey-Hinny!" She kissed the thing on the end of its black-nostriled white nose.

John Thornburn turned away from Derval in disgust and made to crawl under the rim of the hive. "Hold it for me, John. I've got stuff."

Propping up the woven edge, John remembered about Derval. "You've been spying on the Vikings," he accused.

"I've been raiding the Vikings!" she retorted, and pushed a large, soft lump of something before her into the shelter.

The body warmth was welcome within. "Ye Gods, Derval! Why? What craziness could be worth—"

"This craziness, Johnnie," replied Derval, very close to him, and she shoved into his hands a weight of soft, clinging, very warm wool. "I couldn't get to the packs, Johnnie . . . but have a *brat*. It's the same color as your eyes—er—your right eye."

He fingered it in unwilling gratitude, feeling the instant warmth in his hands. "Give . . . put it on the sick man," he said with effort.

"The Ollave will have one," stated Derval. "And so will

Ailesh, and myself. There was no lack of cast-off clothing at Ard na Bhfuinseoge."

John shuddered, only half from the cold. "It's not bloody," said Derval. She began to strip the bundle of its layers. It revolved with an oddly solid thump.

"When I got through the palisade I wished my Norse were better. They were singing, and I'd love to know about what."

"Can't you guess?" mumbled John.

"In general. But they're behaving oddly, for raiders. They're cleaning out the wreckage."

"Eh?"

"They've piled the Irish bodies in a cow byre: I guess to burn." Derval ground her teeth together. "Don't tell Ailesh. And they've set up a sort of headquarters in the square shed where I put the Ollave."

"What about the cross?" asked John.

Derval shrugged. "I don't know. It was dark. But you know what they do have set up there, Johnnie?"

John sighed his strong disinterest in the question.

"Two dragon heads! From the bows of longboats."

John Thornburn's curiosity woke. "How styled?"

"Styled? Jeezus, John, I don't know how styled. Of painted wood with big eyes and teeth. But the important thing is—"

"Is whether it's representational or simply zoomorphic," replied John with certainty. "If it's representational, then it's probably degenerate."

Derval remained silent a moment before saying, "There is about you, my dear, a certain heroic consistency. In *my* mind these Gaill are by the nature of their calling a bit degenerate.

"But what is important to me is that there are two ships in all, which means eighty men, and that they took the figureheads off their ships and set them up in the clearing. I was always taught that when Vikings touched a foreign shore, they would take off their figureheads and set them down on their sides, lest they offend the local gods. These fellows must be very confident in themselves."

John frowned in the darkness. "Or maybe they're planning to stay for a while?" he ventured.

"Could be." Derval finished unwinding her bundle, and revealed its center, strung with shining bronze.

Chapter Six

•

God is strong and he has a good mother.
—Gaelic proverb

Ailesh was not truly asleep, but she had sunk into that depth of physical passivity that will rest the body while the mind watches. Her thoughts, too, were restrained, for every warp and weft of them led to the grief which was too great yet to be touched. She was cold and not aware yet that she was cold, for the chill seemed only the echo of her abandonment.

But she was not abandoned, of course. She was in the midst of divine assistance. She promised the saint she would feel grateful when she had the energy.

Ailesh saw Derval duck out of the hive without wondering where the woman was going, but when Eoin went out to talk to Colm's old white hinny, her eyes followed him through the gaps in the weave.

Eoin Ban was going to ruin her *bothan*, playing such games with the animal. She wondered why he didn't merely send the old beast off. Ailesh heard the crack of the hazel ribs. She moved to crawl out and tell him to be careful (and wouldn't that be a great battle, with hardly a word shared between them!) when Derval returned.

This woman who called her "my treasure, my sister" was a great warrior, to have raided the Gaill so neatly. Brats for everyone against the night's cold and Caeilte's harp as well. Most cunningly, she had sought out and found the key of the harp, which many wouldn't think to do, and the heavy, crystal-studded tuner was in her hand now, tuning the bronze strings. Ailesh had every confidence that Derval's challenge to MacCullen had been true, and she was a master of the clàirseach.

"It's scarcely out of tune," she hissed at John. "Nicely made, well-aged instrument."

"Be quiet with it," John replied. "Between you and the . . . jinny out there . . ."

"I'm making no noise at all." Plucking two strings together at the middle of the instrument, she nodded sagely. "Good. The sisters. Now we know for sure."

John refused to ask what we now knew. He tightened himself into a ball of objection and peered out at the hinny, which was lying flat on its side like a dead horse beside the hutch.

Rather than making no noise, as she had said to John, Derval was playing the clàirseach.

He knew she was considered good on the harp. She couldn't have friends over without being importuned to play. Certainly she moved her fingers fast enough. And he found the sound pleasant, of course, for it was the harp she was playing and that can hardly sound bad.

But there was a time and place for everything, and John refused to enjoy this music which might lead to their discovery. He leaned his cheek against the rough branches and kept an anxious watch, never knowing when the swirl of bell sounds put him to sleep.

Ailesh listened, nonplussed. It was a very strange music the dark woman was making: like the clàirseach and yet not like it. It was as though she were trying to play three pieces at once.

Obviously the woman worked hard at what she was doing, but it seemed to Ailesh that she was like one of those apprentices who learn to plot knots and then so fill a piece with knotwork that it becomes muddy and doesn't mean anything to the eye. Pity.

MacCullen stirred next to her. "By the wounds of Christ, is a cat sharpening his claws on the harp?"

Ailesh immediately buried her own doubts. "Labres *adhvine Uasail*, keep your tongue in. It must be fever that keeps you from knowing music when you hear it."

Derval glanced up, eyes bright as a hawk's. "Having gone to the trouble to rescue your nephew's instrument from his murderer, Ollave (of what kingdom you have not deigned to tell me), it may be I deserve better from you. But no matter: I know the streams of harping of more nations than one. If what I play isn't what your ears are used to hearing, you need only give me a sample of what you do understand. I'm sure I'll have no difficulty with it."

MacCullen narrowed one eye in premeditated scorn. "Give you a sample . . . ? Woman, I'm not about to teach you your trade."

Derval's hands lifted together on the heavy wood of the clàirseach.

But Ailesh spoke out of her own anger. "To this man the most important thing in life is getting the last blow of every discourse. Even with Goban he was like that, and my father was a man with whom one could not argue. MacCullen would sooner die than be bested."

"He is about to, my treasure," snapped Derval, with the harp still uplifted.

Ailesh made a placating gesture. "But such a slave's triumph it would be, and him a sick man! Surely you, who have raided the camp of the steel-armed enemy this night, can give him his small bitter spite?"

Derval set the instrument down.

"She's humoring me," she growled to John.

The first light was consumed by rafts of heavy clouds which an east wind had blown in overnight. White limestone went gray and shiny as the day turned to rain: a fine, throat-catching rain that spattered the undersides of the oak leaves and made the grasses go pale.

The night's wind had blown fluffy ash through the ruin of Ard na Bhfuinseoge, and in the cracks and crevices of the few buildings which had been allowed to stand: the square buildings. Now the ash crumpled in on itself, its dove-white fuzziness gone quite slick and black. One Norseman camped in what had been Goban MacDuilta's stoneroom discovered a leak in the roof and cursed the builder, while another wondered if it were raining in Orkney, his birthplace, where he could not return. The Viking chief heard the rain fall glumly. They would not be able to burn the dead today after all. He hoped it would stay cold.

Water fell unprevented into the great house, sheeting down the walls of charcoal, infiltrating the powdery wood. Loosening it. Like a tent the building sagged inward and slapped to the ground. The earth boomed. Every Norseman grabbed for his sword.

Derval grabbed John, who had just gone from the doze of a bad night's morning to painful wakefulness. "Bomb!" she cried.

"No bombs," replied John, feeling extraordinarily intelligent. "Not in this Ireland."

"By all the powers of the world, what was that?" whispered Ailesh, starting up under her damp brat. (The *bothi* was good, but not perfect.)

MacCullen opened dry, cracked lips. "Iníon Goban, that is the sound of a house falling. Nothing else can be so terrible to hear, except the sea in its full anger."

Derval scrabbled like a rat at the hole the hinny had made. She peered out one-eyed.

There was no more to see today than yesterday. The black, rain-gleaming boles of the trees prevented any glimpse, even of the embankment on which the village had been built. But she did see something, and in another moment she had darted under the rim of the hive and was tearing her belt from her garment.

"Whoa, Hinny-honey. Slow up, girl." The ancient animal, even more unlikely in appearance under daylight, had heard the noise from the village and taken off toward it at a trot. Now she suffered Derval to loop the *cris* around her straggle-maned neck and lead her back. Ailesh wiggled out like a mouse from a hole and came to help.

"Old Muiregan is afraid of nothing!" the redhead chided, hitting the hinny on the nose with one finger. "Because all the children spoil her. And then their children grow up and do the same."

The animal tried her parroty brown teeth out on the wool of the cris. Derval stared at Muiregan's mouth.

"She is over forty years old," said Ailesh, understanding that stare. "That's why her teeth are so bad." She added, "Her mother came on a ship from Spain. That's why we call her daughter of the sea.

"Our horses are somewhere," Ailesh continued, scratching the beast's round back. "In the fields to the south. Ronan and Naoise were tending the herd." Her eyes held an almost childish pride as she said, "We keep thirty mares and a Spanish stallion.

"Did keep." Ailesh turned her face away just as John also appeared in the daylight. He wore his brat wrapped unscientifically over his head and his face was screwed up against the misty rain.

"Why didn't you let the dumb animal go, Derval? We'd be better off without it."

Derval puffed, letting the cowl of her brat fall back ostentatiously from her black hair. "Better off without? A lot you know about it!"

"I know she shines like a . . . a diamond in the sun."

"How poetic, Johnnie!"

"And makes noise like a steam engine! How can we lie low with a mule bawling out to heaven—"

"How can we move the sick man without her help?"

John blinked.

"We can't lie low forever, John. Not if the Vikings have taken up residence next door."

Ailesh had been listening carefully. Now she said, "Does Eoin Ban believe Muiregan a danger to us? She is not a noisy lady, this one. If I tell her our plight, I don't think she will betray us."

Smiling, Derval turned to John. "See there, Johnnie? Ailesh's going to explain things to the daughter of the ocean, and then she'll not make noise any more."

John scowled briefly at the back of Ailesh's head. "Eh? That's very silly."

Derval kept her smile. "Oh, I don't think so. Young Ailesh is a woman with a lot of tact."

They sat once more under the woven shelter while rain fell harder without. MacCullen, in the middle, lay in moaning dreams. Ailesh prayed for him.

"Damn infection," muttered Derval. "Nothininhell I can do about it." She held in her hands the square, double-handled wooden cup she had found in her raid on the Vikings, and from it she slipped rainwater between the poet's parched lips.

John's head was on his knees. He was rehearsing a sentence. "Ailesh."

The girl lifted her head.

"Ailesh. How did Goban take stone?"

Ailesh's brow lowered in confusion. Derval turned also. "What is it you want to ask, Johnnie?"

"I'll ask," said John Thornburn stubbornly.

"Stone carved in . . . house, eh?"

"'Eh' isn't Irish," snapped Derval.

"The cross was carved mostly in my father's workshed," Ailesh replied slowly. "But when he saw it in sunlight he took the fine chisel to it again."

John nodded. "How . . . to carry stone from workshed?"

"Oh?" She understood. "Six men lowered it onto a slidecar, and a horse pulled it down the slope."

"You're thinking of stealing the cross back?" asked Derval. "I couldn't lift the smallest of the pieces they'd whacked it into."

"You tried to lift the cross?" John's eyes widened. "You were busy last night."

Ailesh watched the interchange. "If we can kill the Gaill, then we can take the cross back and set it together again . . ." She looked hopefully from face to face, before Derval's expression dampened her.

"Your abilities are so great, Bhean Uasal, I don't know when I am asking too much."

Then it was Derval's turn to stare at the ground between them. "I would get your father's blood price for you, my treasure, if I only knew how."

John sighed helplessly. He pressed his knobby knees to his chest. He smelled wet wool in his nose. He heard the crackle of paper.

Paper. His face lit up like a lantern. "Paper!" he gasped. "I still have the paper in my shirt pocket."

Derval gazed at him between hope and alarm. "What paper? The tracing paper?"

He tried to stand up, hitting his head against the dome of the hive. Old bruises throbbed. John began to tear at his brat, which now seemed unwilling to come off.

"But, but . . ." Derval stood beside him, her hands balled before her mouth. "Will it work from this end? Will it perhaps only take us to the spot where the cross used to stand, or to the rubbish heap where they've put it?"

"Don't care! Got to try." John stamped himself out of his woolen wrap.

Ailesh didn't rise, but turned her face up to the two. "You have found your way?"

"Yes! No. Maybe," shouted John, and he reached his hand under his filthy, stained shirt.

The tracing paper came out in one piece, neatly folded. It was also a uniform color of reddish-brown, and when he unfolded it, it made an unpleasant sticky sound.

"Blood," said John tonelessly. "Completely soaked in blood. The marks are gone."

"Take it out in the light," Derval suggested.

"No. All gone," John mumbled, as the rain wept over his shoulders. "And how ironic."

Derval lifted in interrogative eyebrow.

"I should have stayed with the old sheet, where the lines were almost worn through. Then I could have at least felt the pattern."

Derval stared fixedly ahead, blinking fast as the rain hit her eyelashes. "No matter, Johnnie. It was a thing we hadn't thought of five minutes ago." She retreated from him under the wet and glistening creelwork.

John Thornburn let the paper float to the ground, where raindrops beat on it with a rattling noise. Because it was his own creation, he took pity on it, picked it up once again, and gave it the shelter of his pocket.

The white hinny, still tied to a tree limb, glared at him with protuberant brown eyes. Its lower jaw jutted out with very human dissatisfaction. Its wet hair smelled. "Don't blame me," John muttered to the creature, and his own small, cleft chin mirrored its expression. "I'd love to see the last of you."

"So it's decided then," Derval was saying as he crept back into the odors of sweat and sickness. "We all head for Dublin."

John wheezed from sheer surprise. "Dublin? How decided? By whom?"

Ailesh glanced from him to Derval. "Eoin must be asked yet, Bhean Uasal," she said diffidently. Derval did not drop her gaze from John's face.

"Well, what else is possible, if you can't get us home?"

"If I can't . . ." be began weakly.

"If your paper doesn't work, and you can't reach the pieces of the cross. Have you got another idea?"

"That's not fair!" he expostulated. Derval shook her head.

"I'm not interested in fair. Just in getting home. The Gaill aren't leaving, and this neighborhood is going to get more and more dangerous. Can you think of a safer place to be than Dublin?" Her raptorial eyes softened. "I'd love to see the place."

"I'll bet you would!" replied John, stung into playing personalities. "I bet you'd glory in it, every rotting middenheap in the city and every croak of incomprehensible, dead Gaelic! I, on the other hand, would rather be back in L'Anse aux Meadows with a glass of Labatt's, watching my history on the telly. Or even better, a good game of football!

"And," he continued, stopping only momentarily for breath, "I think there's something very indicative about our . . . about you and me, that we're where you want to be, and not where I want to be."

Derval did not rise to the bait, but remained peering thoughtfully through the dim damp at him. "But you don't follow football, John."

He hissed at her.

Derval shrugged. "Well, really. It was your bath . . . Never mind. Just tell me what we're to do, then."

John glared sullenly and said nothing. He pointed at the huddled poet on the branches, shivering. "What will we do with him, if we set off for Dublin? Leave him here?"

Derval tightened her lips, and John pressed his point. "You don't care about his life or death so much maybe, since he doesn't appreciate you?"

Derval put one long arm out to either side, along the struts of the weaving. There was something vaguely crucified in her attitude and her face was expressionless as she said, "Of course not, John. We'll have to take him with us."

John snorted and flexed his arms, remembering MacCullen's weight. "I'm not a horse."

"No. Muiregan is. Or close enough. Ailesh will rig up a litter. We'll take turns with the other end of it. That's what we've been talking about in here."

John looked at the girl with a reproach she did not in the least understand. She spoke to him.

"I'm what?" he replied uncertainly. Ready to take offense.

"She suggests you're not feeling well," Derval said. "Good, sisterly concern, she shows."

John turned away from both of them.

It was all well and good to say that they would share the hauling of the sick man, but the plain truth was that John was far better fitted for the work than Derval. And none but he had been able to rip from the wet earth the straight saplings necessary for the litter. The roots of these saplings stood out in matched aureoles behind his hands as the little band marched through the trees. Derval led the hinny, which carried the heavy clàirseach as well as the front shafts of the litter, while John used the back shafts to force the sad beast's hindquarters into greater effort. When the hinny hurried, John stumbled. When she balked, which was far more frequently, his arms were wrenched. With every jolt MacCullen groaned in his fever.

Ailesh walked next to the sick man, but her head was over her shoulder, looking at John.

"It will be easier when we reach the Slige Chualann," she promised.

"Easier on him or me?" John was not sure of his grammar, but Ailesh smiled.

"Both."

Perhaps they had come a mile. A mile farther from Ard na Bhfuinseoge and the Viking camp. Derval's shoulders settled down from her ears. She looked behind at John's flushed face. "Not cold any more, are you, Johnnie?"

He opened his mouth to snarl at her, but then decided he hadn't the energy.

The tall woman led the hinny to the black moss-streaked bole of a fallen oak. "Here, let the shafts rest on this for a while."

John did so, and he sank back wearily on the tree trunk with his hands in his lap. Ailesh turned them over.

"Your hands are none the better for this work, Eoin," she noted. John, not understanding, merely stared as Ailesh lifted her brat and stepped over the near shaft of the litter. She lifted the saplings, and the hinny, by reflex, moved forward.

John found the litter moving on without him. Clearing his throat he bounded after.

"That's too heavy for you," he said. But Ailesh denied it,

and in fact the girl was moving on with a good stride. John skittered beside her.

Her sleeves were rolled up and her forearms angled with muscle. John noticed the heaviness of the tendons at Ailesh's wrist. "You are too short," he told her. "The . . . things you hold go down and the weight of the man is on you instead of the hinny."

She turned an amused hazel eye on him. "It is not bad, Eoin."

Derval kicked leaves at her feet. "You weren't so damned worried about *me* when I was trying to carry it."

"You're not short," he replied. "Besides, you gave up after thirty paces."

Derval was quiet for a few seconds. "I've no experience in that line of work. Now, if it had been a sword you wanted me to carry . . ."

John smiled, but Ailesh appeared quite impressed.

They grew less careful as the day progressed. After another hour's rough progress they reached what Ailesh called Sliege Dala, which was a forest trail twelve feet wide, studded with tree roots.

"North is Dublin," Ailesh informed them, pointing. "South are the fields where our horses graze. It is perhaps twice as far to the city." She looked to her companions for advice. Derval, in turn, looked to John.

"What say, Johnnie? You're totin'."

John pointed north with his chin. "I'd rather walk twenty miles than walk ten and ride thirty."

Much to John's amazement, his words decided the issue. They headed north.

The hinny picked up her pace on the smoother ground. John also trotted. He had tied the shafts to his wrists with strips from the tail of his shirt.

Now the injured man rode quietly—so quietly that John wondered whether he was alive—but the harp sang with the hinny's jouncing trot. After a few minutes he voiced his worry. "Is he alive—the olive, I mean? Hell! Is anyone alive in this dreary place? We haven't seen a soul."

Derval let the animal's steps patter to a stop. "Don't complain, John. A little while ago we were thanking God we'd seen no one. And as for dreary . . ." She raised her head and peered above her, where the oak and elm had given way to a net of pale birch leaves which shuddered in a wind from the west. The rain had given up, except under the trees. "You just wait till the sun comes out. This wood will look like fairyland!"

"Tra la, tra la," muttered John Thornburn, sniffing wetly. He gripped the litter shafts afresh and pushed the hinny forward.

"It is time to rest," stated Ailesh in a voice of great authority. Both her companions gaped at her, but her small mouth was set firmly and she pointed to the right. "There is good water in a hollow to the east of the road—that is, it will be good if no cattle have wallowed here today—and we can make a fire."

John looked at the sky. How far had they come? Five miles? Ten? Not ten, surely. His shoulders ached as though they had been beaten with sticks, and his stomach gave a loud and disheartening growl. "Because she mentioned fire," he said to Derval, explaining the noise. "Now it thinks it'll get something to eat."

Derval stared anxiously along the road and bit her lip. "I . . . I'd hoped to make better mileage today."

John hung his head resentfully. "Oh, I don't mean to fault your hauling, Johnnie," and she slapped his withers affectionately. "But while there's still daylight . . ." At last Derval shrugged and let Ailesh undo the hinny's trappings. Suddenly John's earlier complaint filtered through her brain.

"Your stomach, John? Well, tell your expectant stomach to fix itself for roast chicken, okay?"

John winced. "Don't do that, Derval. Makes it worse."

But Derval had waltzed to the small pile of wraps and baggage which had been lowered from the hinny to the road. She pulled out the harp and removed the back from the soundbox. It came off easily, and Derval pulled from beneath it a naked thing which looked much like a rubber chicken, complete with beak and scaly feet. "Da DA!" she bugled. "The paradox is resolved."

John's eyes refocused. "It's . . . real? It's Mrs. Hanlon's chicken?"

"Hardest part of my work last night, wringing its neck without making noise. And cleaning it in the dark, with only the harp key as a tool."

"Mrs. Hanlon's chicken!" John almost wailed. "You killed her! She was a pet! I won't touch the thing!"

His stomach made a noise of contradiction.

They built their camp next to the spring Ailesh had recognized, and the chatter of the water both quieted the company and made them realize their weariness. Derval laid the fire but then fell unexpectedly asleep. John felt it incumbent upon him, as part Indian, to start the fire, but upon opening the pack, he discovered that Derval had neglected to pack matches. He managed anyway, using a willow sally and a strip of cloth for a fire bow. But the earth beneath the bed of twigs and branches was rock-hard and his efforts to build a rotisserie were frustrating. At last he got one forked stick propped securely and another, pointed stick resting on it, with the pale and gory bird hanging over the fire. The other end he held between his knees.

If his eyes closed, he knew, he would fall asleep. Luckily John's eyes showed no inclination to close, but stared, dry and smarting, into the orange fire.

He had camped in much colder weather, such as the time his father had taken him out to try his hand at the seal trade, and the boy had thrown up all night. (His farther had called it a virus.) But never had he felt so poorly prepared to face the elements. In his mind's eye he saw the window behind the woodstove at his childhood home, with the six panes of the inner window steaming and the big sheet of the storm window frosted and the outmost sheet of plastic shivering in a winter wind. It was a warm and comforting vision to John Thornburn. He wished fervently he had stayed home and fished like his father. But no—he could not wish not to be an artist, for then he'd be someone else entirely. And that would not take him home.

And where was home, anyway? With his father dying, John had come back to L'Anse aux Meadows. A short and disappointing homecoming it was, for the old man didn't know him and was last off calling for the wife who had left him twenty years before, heading for Banff with a dashing young dentist.

And though eight years in New York had left John feeling completely alien, Newfoundland had then become just as strange. And how was he to make a living in a place like L'Anse aux Meadows? He could not go back to fishing at his age.

For a while Derval had seemed to offer . . . John glanced over at the slim ivory face, its power softened by sleep. He could hardly blame Derval for what she had "seemed to offer."

MacCullen woke up thirsty. He felt the heat of the little fire stroke his face like a curtain. He saw John at the other side of the fire, his long, rather foolish face slack, his mouth open. The smell of raw meat searing turned the Ollave's stomach. He clapped his hands at John. "Bring me water," he said.

Ailesh had been drawing together the living branches of the hazel bushes that surrounded the stream, making a pavilion to protect the wounded man from night's damp. She stooped now and rummaged in the pack for the wooden cup Derval had liberated. "He's busy, MacCullen," she whispered. "And you mistake Eoin, if you think him a servant."

MacCullen smiled with great pain. "This one, too, daughter of Goban? He is without language entirely, and, to look at him, brain. Surely some pigboy of the Dubliners . . ."

John caught only the word "language," and the fact that he had been marked as one of the Danes. He raised his head, worried.

Then Ailesh's arm was around his shoulders. The girl was wearing only a brat, and in the corner of his eye he could see her hairy armpit and her swelling breast. "Eoin is a master of the arts," she said, so slowly and clearly that even he understood. "His work is blessed by Bridget, and he is"—she hesitated—"the foster brother of my father: his equal in skill."

John had seen the cross. Indeed, he knew the quality of Goban MacDuilta's work as few others could know it, and the strength of this praise made his hand on the spit begin shaking. The skin on his arms flushed. "I am only an apprentice," he said in his best modern Irish.

"At least this one isn't full of himself," said MacCullen. Ailesh brought him a cup of water.

At Derval's first scream John dropped the chicken in the fire. He plunged his hand into the flame to rescue it before going to Derval.

She was screaming in English. "No! No! Oh God, it's coming! The bombs!" John patted her awkwardly, ineffectually. At last he took her hands in his. She opened her eyes and saw him.

"What was it, Derval my maid? Bad dream?"

Her blue eyes shone like glass in the firelight. "Bombs! Over Dublin. Wicklow. New York. London. All . . . white powder. Bright light and white powder."

John lifted her head in one hand. His eyes went triangular with concern. She needed him too, he thought. (Or someone like him.) Derval buried her face in John's sore shoulder.

"I think, Derval," he said. "With all the problems we have here, that's one worry you can put on the shelf. Besides"—he raised her chin—"it's probably all a symbol for sex, don't you think?"

Derval, despite her upset, could not miss what was for John an unusually blue joke. "More likely Vikings."

"What is frightening you, my true sister?" asked Ailesh. She crouched beside them: diffident, respectful of their intimacy.

John rehearsed his Irish answer. "She has bad dreams. She . . . dreams the end of the world."

Ailesh compressed her lips and took one of Derval's long hands in her own. "Noble woman, my sister, you must trust in the mercy of Christ and his blessed Mother." Derval's eyes slipped from the small Irishwoman to John, to whom she shot a weary, cynical glance. But John was looking intently at Ailesh.

Across the wavering firelight MacCullen cleared his throat. "Fear not, daughter of Chadhain. The world must have fifteen years more."

Derval peered over to the poet confusedly. She sighed and lifted herself from John's support. "Fifteen . . . ?"

MacCullen slicked his lime-frizzed hair back from his face. "Indeed, the millenium is not for so many years yet, and although these invasions and slaughters portend the end, still in fifteen years many deeds of high renown may be accomplished."

Ailesh snorted. "Indeed, Ollave, you sound like one of the Gentiles yourself, with your inevitable doom and your 'deeds of high renown.' Neither Christ nor His saints have made known to us the hour of our deaths nor that of this world of men, and the year one thousand and one will follow the year one thousand!"

Derval listened to the young woman confusedly, still half in her dream. MacCullen's answering smile was tolerant but unconvinced. It was John, who couldn't follow Ailesh's eloquence, who heard the rustle of cloth and turned around.

Above, behind them on the bank of the road she stood, with the evening light turning her all to black. She picked her way down amid the gorse and the eglantine, her motions stiff and jerky, and her old hands reaching out for help. It was only the yielding arms of the coll and elder that took her hands, however, and she came into the fireglow sliding awkwardly on mud.

"Listen to the maiden! By my bees and brews, just listen to her!" The voice was cracked and quavering, but not high as senility will often prove, but deep as a lowing cow. "Such authority! You'd think she'd eaten the head of the salmon. You'd think she spoke for the old dark woman herself."

She wore a nun's habit of dark and dirty crimson which dragged on the mud at her feet, and a hood wich sagged over her face like aged skin. Beneath the hood could be seen the tip of her nose, red-nostriled and swollen, and a large mouth with the lips sunken.

But the cloak which hid her face was not pinned in front, and as she stood near-straddling the fire she pulled it aside to expose two empty and withered breasts, with nipples each as large as a baby's fist, hanging down to the last of her ribs. Her belly was folded like linen cloth and the grizzled hair of her pudendum, which she arched forward to the warmth of the little fire, hung halfway to her knees in long sausage curls, like the tail of a hills' pony. Her legs were straight and her knees and feet very large. John stared at her feet, for she was so shameless and horrible he dared look no higher.

How could anyone walk around so nearly naked, in the wind and the wet of Ireland, even in summer? John knew about ascetics and anchorites, of course, but he felt quite ascetic enough in his woolen right now, and besides, nakedness might be denial of the body for a man, but on a woman he could see it as nothing less than brazenly sexual. Artist though he was, John needed to find sexuality pretty.

Yet as he stared at the old woman's feet, he had to admit they were beautiful beyond words.

The reheaded girl hopped up. "I beg your pardon, *a shiun*—Reverend Mother. I never meant to say I speak with the voice of Bridget."

The hag scratched her pubes casually. "Of course you didn't mean to speak so, little heifer. You did speak so, and that's what counts." She laughed inordinately at her own joke, if it was a joke, while Ailesh's round face blushed.

"Yet if I offended, *a shiun*—"

MacCullen cut in. "Make you welcome at our fire, *a shiun*. What we have to eat is God-given, and so given to all with need." He had raised himself to a sitting position, and his formal invitation was so mellifluous as to take all about him by surprise.

The old nun gave him a glance out of cataractal white eyes and smiled more broadly yet. "Well said! Well said! You make a fine prancing lad at the courts, don't you, my sweet? A good mother's precious son, too, I'll bet, and a loyal dog to your master! Well, no shame in any of that, though it's not the way to heaven. And your day will come to curse like a hero, before you make an end." Then she plumped herself down with force between Derval and John, who just managed to fling himself sideways in time to avoid being sat on. She put one arm companionably over each.

MacCullen gazed through the fire at her with the weary tolerance of one whom fever has given a rest. "May we know what abbey holds you for its treasure, Old Mother?"

The crone bellowed jovially. "Abbey? Why, what abbey would take me, nowadays, scholar of Munster? And what abbey could hold me, such as I am?"

The arm laid under John's eye jerked him back and forth with her merriment. Its skin was scaly but not withered, and the wrist and forearm were heavy with muscle. He could feel the heat of the old woman's body. He could certainly smell her too. He tried not to stare at the thatch of hair that ran down the underside of her arm as he wondered how a body composed of parts each interesting in itself could be so unbearably repulsive to have near him.

She had silver hairs on her face, each the length and thickness of a surgical needle.

Derval, too, he saw out of the corner of his eye, was staring at this apparition with blank terror. John felt a stab of concern. Could his wild and expansive Derval still be so in the power of a nightmare? Or did the awful old woman affect her as she did him? But it wasn't terror John felt, only an overwhelming urge to get away from the old creature. He tried to meet eyes with Derval, for question or reassurance, but hers were locked on the old nun like a sparrow on a snake.

"Yet if I offended . . ." Ailesh repeated, squatting before the hag, letting her own brat fall back. (Ailesh had the same beautiful feet, John noticed. But her pubic hair was nicer. He no longer minded looking at Ailesh's pubic hair. He stared riveted at the young girl's crotch, as a way of avoiding the other so near to him.)

The nun made a sound like a pig. "What a waste of effort, worrying whether you've offended old Bride the Brewer! Why, people offend me every day, and does the sun fail to shine for that?"

She turned to John to share the joke, and he was transfixed, looking into the catastrophe of her sagging, bleary-eyed face. His head slid down between his shoulders. "Ah! Now, I'll have you know I've bred my share of cattle, too, and I must have a look at this little bull-calf here . . ." She took his cheek between dirty-nailed fingers and gave it a very painful tweak. "Och! Eyes of sky and earth! How auspicious! I am amazed the flowers don't bloom as he passes. Now, here's one who doesn't worry about offending me. Indeed, he thinks I'm an offense against him, doesn't he? With my flapping dugs and the holes in my mouth where I once had ivory. It scares the young to see what life has in store for them."

John tried very hard to misunderstand the old woman's words, but they came clear to him as his father's back-throated Newfie English. "Please," he said to her. "I don't. I'm not. I didn't say anything at all. Please . . . just leave me alone."

Instead the old hag put both her arms around John and rocked him to and fro. "Leave you alone? What a sad request, from a fair lad lost in the wood like this! Poor little bull! You've a twisted horn, haven't you, then? Never mind. Old Bride likes you none the less for it."

Without releasing the mortified John, she turned her agate eyes on the group around the fire. "Old Bride sees very well, though you might not think so to look at her. She watched you come in, with your grand white horse and your grand wounded poet and the bright woman and the dark woman and my little bull here, hauling away with a frown on his face!"

When her smile grew sly it was like stretching cobwebs over an old helmet, for her face was all cheekbones and sharp nose bridge. "But I was at work, my darlings, and had to let you wander by yourselves. It was my time to put the old must into the new must so the ale would take.

"That is how it is done, you know, if you would have an ale with life in it. You seal the old with a bit of the new, and you baptize the new with the old."

"So it is, a shiun." Ailesh nodded politely. "So that the yeast is not lost." She reached fingers gingerly into the fire and pulled on a charred foot of the chicken. Part of the leg came off in her hand and she extended it to Bride. "Give us a prayer and bless our food by sharing it with us."

"I'll do that for you, my heifer of the sweet thighs." The old one grinned and stretched out her right hand, palm extended toward the chicken on the spit. "Power of God on this flesh!" she called in a deep and mighty voice. "And power on those who will eat it, to be worthy of the life taken here to nourish them, for the fire of all life is from God. It is finished."

Old Bride, who had been embracing the miserable John with both arms, released him long enough to take the chicken leg. Then she wrapped him around once more, so that the greasy and odorous drumstick hung just below his chin. "Eat for strength and courage, my son!" He moaned between hunger and nausea, and she chided, "The weak who shun food don't deserve to have it.

"But, Daughter of Wisdom, do you know what happens if the brewer is careless, and adds too much of the new batch into the old and then seals the keg nicely?"

"It blows up," replied Ailesh cheerfully. "And the flies crawl over everything, licking it up."

Derval flinched in the darkness where she had retreated. The old nun turned her head in her hood, and white eyes gleamed with an amusement that seemed pitiless. "What a tremble I've put you in! You're afraid I may lose my ale, warrior woman?"

Ailesh felt compelled to explain. "The Bhean Uasal O'Cuhain

has had a bad dream, old mother, and a bad dream may blacken the day after it."

"Or many days," added the hag, still gazing coolly and without particular sympathy at Derval.

Derval wiped the cold sweat of her hands onto her thighs. Unreasoning fear drove her to honesty. "What I am afraid of, Bride the Brewer, is you." She stammered as she said it.

The old crone smiled with three teeth. "I won't be heart-wounded over that, warrior. Untried woman of fierce words, you may fear whom you like."

Derval's jaw hardened. "Tell me one thing. Is this batch you brewed your last?"

MacCullen cleared his throat and grinned tightly at the fire. "Once again the shining daughter of Chadhain displays her fine courtesy. Forgive us, Old Mother, that that one there knows no better than to talk of death in the face of an ancient."

From under the hood came a flash of green. "Shut your mouth, boy-o. You'll have your own time to piss your legs; pray to the twins that you do it so bravely!" Then she turned back to Derval and brushed her hair, coarse and gray as a pony's forelock, from her eyes.

"Daughter, it is the new brewing that gives life to the old. There is always a new malt ripening as the old goes down the throat! And as for this old cow dying, I promise you she's far too busy."

Derval faced the hooded figure with a cornered, white-faced courage. "Why is everything going so deadly bad for everyone? Is it our fault?"

Bride's heavy laughter brought the chicken leg in contact with John Thornburn's nose. He rebelled. "Take it away!" he cried in bad Irish. "It's making me sick!"

"Ocho!" The old woman clapped as though John were a baby who had shown a cunning trick. "The one doesn't trust Bride, and she makes the other one sick! It's a sad life for a mother, isn't it?"

She proffered one limp dug to John. "Surely you remember the teat in your mouth, little bull?" Dropping it, she leaned forward and spread her legs. Her hands reached between them. "And surely you have some fondness for your first and kindest home, and the red tunnel that gave you to the world?" She presented herself to John Thornburn.

He fainted.

The old hag blinked at him. Carefully she set him on his back and petted his silken hair. "*Fulya, fulya!* Poor little bull-calf! What herdsman would breed from you, I wonder? Yet, look here . . ." She lifted John's pale, raw, and red-blistered hand and showed it to the others as though displaying a wonder.

"Who'd have thought it!" Her voice held a senile satisfaction.

Ailesh stepped around the fire. Carefully she detached Bride's gnarled fingers from John's wrist. "He has an illness that comes upon him," she said softly to the old woman. "And he doesn't know our ways. But Eoin's no cull, for all that."

Bride pulled down on her upper lip until the end of her nose almost touched her mouth. "Treasure of my heart, why do you apologize for everyone? Not even a mother is responsible forever."

"Don't speak!" whispered Derval in a strangled voice to Ailesh. "Don't talk to her. It's too dangerous. We don't know what she means to do to us!"

The old woman let her thighs slap together and she leaned back against the bank. As she glanced back at Derval, her eyes were sly. "You make me tired, maiden, with all that fear. What old Bride will do is what she's always done; she'll turn to her *caoruheacht* and she'll brew her beer. Maybe that's fearful and maybe it's not.

"She's not afraid; that's certain. What does it matter if all the priests turn her out, or the birds shriek from the ash trees?"

She sighed rheumily. "But once she had two sons who loved her, and that she'll swear to. One was light and the other was dark. The finest of men: wood carvers both.

"Gone to earth they are, of course. I bury them and I bury them and I bury them again. It doesn't seem to matter how many times."

She looked down at the black earth and met the opening eyes of John. She took a handful of his silky, flaxen hair. "Little Thor with the white head and the white callused hand," she murmured. He didn't move.

Old Bride rose and stalked off, away from the road, and up the hill again. "And little Iosa Dubh with his eye for wood. Such a good worker he was, and how the ladies loved him."

She barged between Derval and Ailesh, who gave back

silently. Her cataractal eyes were weeping. "They used the nails, you know. Always the nails." But as she clambered up the gentle hill she looked over her shoulder at them, panting. "What a shame on you," she said, as she caught her breath. "That you should wish me to get out from you." Then she started up again. The four of them heard her deep, loud laugh, like the lowing of a cow.

MacCullen rubbed his hands together before he spoke. "That one is growing very close to her savior this night." He pointed to his head. "Poor old *cailleach*."

Derval gave a strange little giggle.

With the departure of old Bride, the timidity—the revulsion—fell from John like bedsheets sliding to the floor. The knowledge of his own clownishness awoke.

"I'm sorry," he said truculently, in English, to Derval. "I'm sorry. God save the mark, I don't do that on purpose: falling apart like that. Some can be jack-easy about themselves, and I wish they were me. And I know you do too." He took a cold breath. "But I'm too much the nuzzle-tripe—the scud of the lot—and it's not going to change."

Derval turned her eyes to him for a moment, but they were empty, for his lapse into the dialect of his father had left her behind and she was too busy with her own fading panic to ask what it all meant. Ailesh gazed at John with worried eyes, trying to hear past the foreign language. MacCullen pursed his mouth. Only Bride ignored him, choosing her ancient, cautious way into the dark. The wind picked up amid the forest and the dry twigs of the hazel rattled. They told John to look up.

Whatever is least expected, that is the very thing that will happen.

As the old nun mounted the bank, that spine that was bent with all the sadness and work of women straightened. The silhouette against the golden moon changed.

Derval had been watching too closely to be mistaken in what she saw. Her throat contracted now. She grasped John's arm for reassurance, as her fear multiplied itself beyond all bearing. Fear became not-quite-fear.

John didn't notice Derval at all, for he was staring into Her Face.

The brat had fallen back. The golden hair—curling, glowing with light like a rayed sun: it looked alive. It reached out as if in blessing to the teeming shadowy creatures that suddenly filled the air around her.

They were long-horned cattle, golden bees, heavy-hooved horses, and dogs thin as a sickle moon: all kinds of animals of the forest, farm, and sea, their limbs intertwining harmoniously and in constant movement. A confusion of life. Exquisite form. Translucent color. And beneath it all a rumble in the earth, like the sound of a great heard of cattle.

John fell headlong into the wellspring of the illuminators—the source of inspiration. It was an infinity of order, color, line. Beyond formalism, encompassing chaos, it was his own art—the art of his midnight visions—taken far beyond what one life would permit a man.

And it was not his alone. No. More accurate to say he belonged to it—to her—along with a host of other hearts and souls that worked toward her gentle glory. And John felt a heated joy to know that he lived and breathed now among others with eyes like his, who had brought into being manuscripts that Cambrensis would say "seemed more the work of angels than men."

But from this wonder John's eyes were drawn to the center of it all: her beautiful face. Her eyes.

Heavy-lidded, huge, and patient like those of a cow, yet filled with unspeakable serpent wisdom, they shone like moons of blue. They were the color of sunlight reflected off the white sand bottom of deep bay water. Those were the eyes of Bride: old hag, perfect maiden. Milk mother of Christ.

And this sight cut open John's heart, tearing at everything in him that he felt was weak and petty. Then it was mended with beauty.

Derval stood up. She cried, "Mother! Don't go!"

Then throwing her cloak over her head, the cailleach—the hag—broken double with age, left the top of the ditch and was gone. Ailesh, whose concern for her champions had held her eyes until now, turned just too late to see.

Bending herself onto the earth until her forehead touched it, Derval wept like a child, while John's tears fell silently. He licked his lips, over and over, savoring not salt but the strong taste of honey ale—of mead—that filled his mouth. He laughed, feeling phlegm rattle in the back of his throat, and then leaped up the little bank after Bride, light as a lover.

He gasped. The spreading, black-ringed horn of a cow caught him in the ribs. John lost his wind and grabbed, as the cow swung its massive head and lifted him off the earth. He bent in the middle and jackknifed over the horn gracefully to touch down beside the running beast once more. As his hands refused to let go, John was dragged along.

A yard from his face was another cow, equally heavy and as terribly horned. Shaggy as a buffalo. And as a third pressed him close he screamed and was tossed aloft. He clutched handfuls of rough hair and found himself lying flat out on the broad back of the first animal, where he clung, bawling weakly, like the calf old Bride had named him. The beast bellowed in response.

All around him were black backs and flashing horns beneath black oaks and the stars. The hooves of the cattle poached the damp road to bog. He pulled himself onto the cow's neck, squatting, with both feet together over her shoulder blades and his hands locked in the coarse ruff, begging gods he couldn't name to let him escape impalement. He cried out wordlessly, in rhythm to her canter.

Where were the others: Derval, Ailesh, and the injured poet? Trampled, turning the mud red? Gored mindlessly and left in heaps? Surely the small embankment would not have stopped this endless, unnatural invasion.

He dared turn his head, to see behind him a glimmer of white. The hinny? No, bigger.

A horse's head. A man's leg. A saddle rug of gold and red embroidery. John swiveled on the cow's flat back, caught by the sight of that saddle rug. The rider squeezed his horse closer and shouted at John. He had a whip, and laid it right and left as he came, whistling shrilly. The cattle gave back without dispute.

The man was bearded, blondish, and round-faced. He looked somehow familiar to John, and he cried a question over the thunder of the herd.

John shrieked in reply, "My Irish is very bad! Very, very bad!"

The herder choked on dust and laughter. With a quick flick

of the wrist he wrapped his whip around the base of the cow's horns. The white horse, dwarfed in size by the cow, set its legs and lay back its tiny ears. It stared fiercely, shaking its pale pony head.

The great-horned cow dropped her head and allowed herself to be led out of the path.

John dropped his legs to the sides of the cow's neck with a sigh of relief. He pointed at the churned road behind them. "My friends! Your cows hit my friends, I think."

The rider's eyes narrowed in worry. It was of Ailesh the man reminded him, John saw. Still on the cow's broad back, he was led along, watching the marvelous saddle rug sway with the horse's pace.

The cattle were now clogged and milling. The sound of whips was heard ahead, along with the splashing tattoo of horse's feet in mud. The rider led his captive cow and John (captive, too, he wondered?) to the very edge of the road.

There were four more riders, standing in a group around something. Three of the horses gleamed white with the light of a rising moon, and one was dusky, with stripes on its legs and along its back. On the path between them was a man—no, not a man but Ailesh, standing in an attitude of authority and conversing with the men. Derval peered over the lip of the road behind.

John's leader joined the group. "Be easy, Daughter of Goban. I have your far traveler. I found him standing on the lead cow's back, and she wild, with a horn of her in either hand, looking like the world's own champion."

All stared at John with awakening respect, save for Derval, who just stared.

Chapter Seven

•

> That he might not give beyond right to anyone.
> That he might not pass a false judgement.
> That no quarrel take place in his house,
> For that is the great restriction of his restrictions.
>
> Saint Benean's instructions to a king,
> *The Psaltry of Caiseal*

"That pink pudding: there was something about it. It reminded me of home," said John Thornburn to Derval, as they lay baking side by side in the sweatlodge. "Something fishy. Salty. Was it salmon?"

Derval managed to shake her dripping head. "No, Johnnie. Not salmon. You don't want to know what was in that pudding."

Slowly John turned on his side. He prodded her. "Go on, Derval. You can't say that much and stop, eh?"

Derval gave a wet sniff. "It was blood, then. Raw blood and milk, set to congeal by itself."

John flopped back. "I didn't want to know that," he said reflectively, and added, "Just like the Masai?"

"Just like the Masai. They bleed their cattle here, more often than slaughter them."

John shifted and swallowed. He stared up at the thatch of the sweatlodge, which hung like a dark circle over the white clay walls. "What about the yogurt with honey? What was it, really?"

"Yogurt with honey."

He belched, grimacing. "And the onions? And all that oatmeal? Why so damn many onions? I'm swollen like a car tire."

Derval examined him with an ironical eye. "I guess so. I can see your little air valve sticking up from here."

John glanced at her self-consciously. Surely she knew that remarks like that destroyed his ability to . . . to approach her. (John could phrase it no other way, not even to himself.) And she was the first to complain when the strength of his desire, or more likely its endurance, let her down.

But much to his surprise, his cock only bobbed at her wit in the most defiant manner. John grinned with embarrassed pride, but Derval's attention seemed to have shifted already. She propped herself up on one elbow. "So. I've finally seen you ride. And I think you've found your destined mount too." She laughed softly in the heated air.

John settled back on the sweat-damp plank, breathing in the thick comfort of warm air. Steam stung the raw patches on his hands and the bruise on his ribs, but the relief he felt in his bones and muscles outweighed any irritation. Besides, his full stomach made him unwilling to move. His shrug was invisible in the darkness.

"Why not? She was going fast enough."

"But I'd hate to see her try a fence," Derval murmured sleepily. She laid her moist cheek against John's arm.

"But I don't mean to denigrate your achievement. You looked like thunder and lightning, sitting on that huge mother beef."

John giggled. "The thunder and lightning of Thor—nburn." He stroked Derval's rich hair.

She was certainly mellow tonight. So was he, if he came to think of it. And they were alone in the clanstead's sweathouse, now that Ailesh and the poet had gone to talk with the taiseach. Were it not for his digestion . . .

In the blackness of closed eyes came the image of Bride's old tits and yawning vulva. John's shoulders stiffened under Derval's head. Flooding behind this came the vision of the face of Bridget with her shining arms outspread: star pale, sun golden, with all creation multiplying around her like echoes of her wonder. His hand slipped in idle circles over Derval's slippery, sweet-musky skin. John sighed and stared at the ceiling, shaking his head slowly.

"It's not Thornburn they call you here, but Eoin Ban—Blond Eoin: like Ailesh does. Or Eoin the cattle leaper." Derval took one of John's raw hands and laid it in her own, half-curled upward, like a cup. She touched the palm with one fingertip. "I've also heard them say 'Bridget's Owen,' because of all Ailesh has told them." John's hand closed over her finger tightly, remembering. Derval looked over and met his eyes. "Changed everything, didn't it?" she whispered.

He put his other arm over Derval's lean shoulder. "Yes.

"Or on second thought, no. No: what should it change? Sunlight? Cows? The way hair curls?"

"The way one lives," she replied. "Only to know that man isn't the only force in the universe. That there is power. Power to shake the earth . . ."

John grinned. "It was cows, doing the shaking." He nuzzled between her neck and shoulder, feeling flesh smooth and wet, like rubber. His heavy dinner was forgotten, along with all the onions.

"Don't laugh," Derval murmured. "Not at that. It was real."

"Not laughing." John leaned over Derval. His hand slipped between her slippery thighs. She, too, reached down.

The thick, oaken door creaked. John and Derval sprang apart convulsively. John raised his knees and folded his hands so Ailesh would not see his erect member.

He need not have bothered, for her eyes were not adjusted to the dark, and she stood at the door, blind.

"My dear friends?"

Derval replied warmly for them both, while John made a rustling, so she would know where he was. Ailesh shuffled forward toward the hot stones, grateful for the heat on her nakedness.

John watched her. Smooth, rounded, and once more ruddy (as he had first seen her), she held her arms over the pile of hot stones, drawing in the dry heat. John wrapped both of his hands around his penis and squeezed it absentmindedly. He had done one good thing in his life, he reflected, if his hand had helped save Ailesh. I never had a little sister, he thought complacently, and put his hands away from his organ.

Derval put her arms behind her head and yawned.

"Are we not blessed to have come to this place, when we expected another night in the cold?" Ailesh sat down at John's other side. Their sides touched and John felt his penis slap his belly. He curled up, hot as he was, and rested his chin on his knees.

"In this dun lives my own foster mother," said Ailesh. "It

was the Christ Himself who arranged it so their drive would run so late, that they find us on the road when we most needed it. And what better welcome could there be than the shelter, ale, and food they have shared with us?"

"Do they always eat so many onions?" John asked, but he spoke quietly, or perhaps his idiom was off, for no one answered.

"And this blessing came no more than a minute after the miracle when we met the saint at the spring."

Both Derval and John came to attention at Ailesh's words. Derval spoke first, haltingly. "What . . . what exactly did you see, my sister, my treasure. In the old nun? Eoin here speaks of sunlight and moonlight and the faces of beasts. I saw a great power of mercy. You . . . ?"

Ailesh smiled humbly. "I saw *siun* Bride, who seemed to me a woman filled with love and age, worthy of reverence. I was not granted any greater vision."

"But when she turned on the side of the bank," John had to break in, "she lit the sky!"

Ailesh lowered her head. "I knew that the Bhean Uasal O'Cuhain was frightened, and you, Eoin, had a swoon on you. That concerned me so at I didn't look up the hill at all."

Derval gave a sigh of sympathy. She reached out and took Ailesh's hand and kissed the back of it. John wished he had thought to do that.

"And yet you call it a miracle, just because Eoin and I . . ."

Across Ailesh's broad face spread a grin: the first John had seen on it. She stood before them and spread out her arms. "How can I deny it? Look at me, my brother, my sister. Is there not a change in this body before you?"

John wrinkled his brow. He leaned forward until his face was no more than inches from Ailesh's navel. There was a faint odor of onions on her skin.

Her belly look ordinary: child-round and smooth of skin. Her little breasts bobbed with her giggles.

"Migod! Her wounds are gone!" Derval whispered. "All gone. She's a clean sheet of paper."

"Very fine. Very pretty," said John, as though he had been asked to judge a work of art. He sat back on his haunches and tried to trap his penis between his legs.

"The saint has healed me without scar."

"The saint . . ." Another voice echoed Ailesh. At the same

moment a disagreeable chill air slid around them. Both John and Derval twisted around to discover Labres MacCullen in the open doorway behind them, supported by two villagers.

"To the very young every bird is a great singer," he said. "And every madman or woman is a saint of God." The poet saw young Iníon Duilta turn her head from him and there was such anger in that movement that he wished he hadn't spoken.

"MacCullen, you should not be up," Ailesh said, still turned away, stepping closer to the fire.

"I can manage," he replied shortly, her words killing his momentary regret. He stood staring at the orange glow in the center of the room. Then the poet lifted his impressive head and spoke with difficulty.

"I seem to remember . . . I do remember that I have been surly to you all. I am conscious that I owe my life to the three of you, and especially"—he leaned toward Derval—"to you, lady, who nursed me through both danger and my own insults."

Derval's black hair clung wetly to her forehead. She faced MacCullen directly, for they were of equal height. He, in the starlit doorway, made a black shadow, while her naked body glimmered faintly in the dark. She opened her mouth and then closed it again. At last she said, "What did you see, Ollave? In Bride?"

He shifted from foot to foot, as the rough-skinned, broken-toothed visage came before him once more. Could a man recognize divinity in that? MacCullen glanced at Derval and felt angry—angry like a man who suspects he's the victim of a joke. He showed nothing of this feeling as he replied: "In my time I have seen many old nuns." His breath steamed in the conflux of hot and cold. "It is not that I wish to deny that divinity comes down among us. If I did, I could not remain a poet. But why suspect that there was a blessed saint among us tonight, eating our chicken and casting shame over the . . . over Eoin na Leim bó." (Owen Cattle Leaper.)

"You were not healed?" asked Ailesh in a small, stubborn voice.

Equally stubborn, MacCullen confronted her, his shoulders squared by some emotion. After an awkward silence he answered her. "I was not healed. But then my wounds are not of the sort that heal in a few days."

John growled a protest at this dismissal of Ailesh's injuries, remembering her blood dripping on the dirty oak floorboards of his bungalow. But Ailesh herself said nothing, and supposedly MacCullen had come to the sweathouse to make peace with them all, so John said nothing. Besides, John Thornburn was never sure, with Irish, that he had heard correctly.

"We have come . . . my voyaging friends . . . to tell you that the *taoiseach* has called his *brehan* and a few others now to the house of assemblies, to hear our story from our own lips."

There was a general stir, as Derval and Ailesh went to rinse themselves with water. Only after both had dressed did they notice that John was still squatting on the plank, huddled and naked. He had lit a second oil lamp from the small one that belonged in the sweatlodge.

"You don't need me," he said in explanation.

MacCullen showed teeth in a smile. "But yet I think the rumor of our cattle dancer has spread, and many will want to meet the man who rides the stampede." John only put his head between his knees.

"John Thornburn: bull dancer. Or almost bull. A regular Cretan," murmured Derval, stepping out through the door.

At last he was alone. For the first time in days. Four walls between him and the world: it was a different world, to be sure, but for John the relief was the same as it had always been, after too long in company. He felt inchoate bits of himself drift out to fill the quiet space. He gazed mindlessly at the fire.

Like all shy people, John had occasionally imagined that in another place or time he might turn around and take hold of things. Well, Ireland was another place, and ancient Ireland was certainly another time, and nothing had changed at all. This understanding did not really surprise John, for he had had little faith in his imaginings. Nor was he dissatisfied with his shyness. Not enough to stand up on his hind feet and do something about it, anyway. Let Derval handle this; she was the sort who actually enjoyed talking.

This place of heat and wood smelled just like a sauna. John had never been in a sauna until he had taken classes at Cooper Union in New York. But he had become addicted very quickly, and now he let the heat of this Irish sweathouse, oddly moist and dry at the same time, soak into his body.

It wasn't now as hot as it had been, since no stones had been hauled from the fire outside the wall for the last half hour, but it was easily warm enough to go naked, and with the two small oil lamps, he could see the pale limed walls. Only a little while ago—two hours, perhaps—he had fainted. Fainted from sheer revulsion. At what? Sex? John's bouncing penis rejected that idea. Ugliness, then? He thought of old Bride's beautiful feet. He thought (disciplining himself to the necessity) of her shrunken dugs. He made himself visualize her grizzled vulva, which was, now that he stopped to consider, very little different from that of a younger woman: arches, ovals, spirals, all intricate and richly colored.

John didn't know why he had fainted, but he did know he should not have. He'd failed someone, somehow, and now he felt very bad about it.

None of which interfered with the single-minded drive of his penis, which jerked up and down all by itself and tickled against his thighs. He let it distract him.

Well, good. He could sit here by himself and jack off. Why not? It was a thing John liked to do, sometimes looking at dirty pictures and sometimes at Byzantine art. Tonight he would look at the walls.

He took his penis in a practiced left hand (always the left, for the right had to turn pages) and let his eyes unfocus until the shadows of the wall became shapes in black and cream. Became legs and arms. Breasts and buttocks. Fat bodies and withered. One gray stone was a perfect head with face.

Lamplight trembled on the pale wall. John found his right hand at his breast, seeking a nonexistent pencil in the pocket he wasn't wearing.

A need more intense and consummatory than his solitary desire took him. He bounded to his feet and ran out naked, to where the fire of wood and turf burned to heat the sweatlodge. There he scrabbled among the dead coals. Besmirched and chilly he popped back into the hot room, over to the blank white wall. His eyes measured and his mouth moved. With great sweeping gestures he began to draw.

His penis—stiff-standing, ignored—made a series of tiny smudges in the charcoal. Eventually these blended into a stripe like a chair rail around the room.

* * *

The alcove bed of the taoiseach and his family was at the second row in the dun, which meant that Derval, sitting against the wattlework lattice which separated it from the two on either side, could stare down ten feet to the middle of the hall, with its benches by the hearth and the great turf fire. Like from boxes in an opera hall, families looked out of their two storys of bedrooms, draperies and screens drawn back, to see the event of the council. Some of them were still eating as they reclined, with wooden bowls and spoons of horn, sopping the gruel with hunks of oat bread. Others were grooming themselves before sleep. Just across the empty space from them, in a room with scarlet wool curtains, a woman combed her long black hair before a polished metal mirror illuminated by a small lamp in a bowl. She was naked except for a shawl. Most of the people looking out from their rooms were nearly or totally naked, clean from the bath.

The black-haired woman noticed Derval watching her, and she nodded and smiled. With perfect friendliness Derval nodded back in reply. She felt slightly drunk with the warmth of the place. Her eyes wandered.

Derval was startled to discover an elderly couple making love in an alcove with open curtains. No one else was paying the slightest attention to them, except for a baby (grandchild, perhaps) who was playing delightedly with the ribbons in the woman's elaborately braided hair. This infant squealed with joy as the man removed his face from his wife's neck long enough to tickle its stomach with the end of a braid. He kissed the baby on the top of the head and called out. A young woman came, speaking in soft teasing fashion, and took the infant away. The couple resumed their pleasure.

"Shameless," Cambrensis had called these, the Gaels. Derval's face tightened in glad vindication of her own native stock, even as she blushed like a rose to see it. She remembered a phrase from *The Wooing of Etain:* "Come with me where there is no sin between man and woman." There was no sin here; Derval knew that.

And Johnnie was holed up in the sweathouse, alone. He could have used a little of this training. Hell, he could have used a crash course. What a man to have beside one in the freedom of the tenth century. Derval's lip curled.

But then her brain delivered to her the image of John that evening in the trees, just before Bride had . . . Johnnie crying out in great misery his shame and his need. And she had offered him nothing, not even a word of friendship. She had an excuse, certainly, for a miracle had been impending, or perhaps a string of miracles. And she was not a therapist, after all, Derval told herself. All in all she had been quite patient with Johnnie's sexual problems, which hurt no one as much as himself. She had nothing with which to reproach herself, Derval decided, but still her gloating over her Gaelic heritage seemed suddenly silly and her proud mouth softened. She looked downward, toward the hearth.

Children and dogs ran across the floor like mice in a granary while adults of both sexes chased them. Evidently it was bedtime.

The private quarters of the taiseach were dim, and consisted of a line of heather mattresses laid against the outside wall of the dun, each mattress covered with a feather bed, a double woolen cloak, and cowskins or sheepskins. There was a highly ornate ax and a shield on the taiseach's wall, and below it a carved stand displaying a prayer on parchment. Three tallow lamps hung from chains of bronze. There were no facilities for cooking in the alcove: only the huge caldron and the iron spit on the hall fire in the very center of the round wooden building.

Why did the taoiseach—the battle chieftain—live on the second story of the dun, where he (not to mention his wife, his old mother, and crippled father) had to go up and down stairs every day? Perhaps the second story was warmer, or perhaps the family had lived there before he was elected taiseach and didn't want to move. Derval cast a glance at the burly man, clad only in a blue-green cloak which was deeply embroidered about the hem and seams and closed at the top by a handsome enamel brooch, and decided that he was in no mood to be bothered with questions of that sort. A silver-bound horn of ale was passed round, and she sipped of it before passing it on. It was warm, that ale, and sweetened with honey.

The fire heated her back and the incense smell of turf filled her nose. The sweathouse had drained her nerves away. Derval gave herself another five minutes before she'd close her eyes and start snoring.

She sneaked a glance at Ailesh, to her right. The little redhead sat on her heels with her palms cupping her opposite elbows: a rather formal balance. She appeared neither weary nor intimidated as she waited for the taiseach's mother to be helped onto pillows and wrapped in a cloak with a heavy woven pile, like that of a rug.

MacCullen lounged on a mattress on the other side of the girl. He was attended by a young man who arranged his feather bed with exaggerated, awkward care. MacCullen seemed not to notice. His attitude was exaggeratedly calm, but his half-open eyes glittered. He was sizing up his audience, thought Derval, amused. He obviously expects to make an effect of some sort.

Yet twenty-four hours ago she had expected this man to die. True, she was no hospital nurse, but he'd lost so much blood . . . Derval shook her head in wonder and almost fell over from the effort.

"*Éistig ré sceál*—hear this news!" The taoiseach had spoken. He was a sandy-haired man with a ruddy face and he sat in the middle of the room, disdainful of pillow or prop. His wife, Ailesh's foster mother, sat beside him and stroked the bereaved girl's hair.

There was a murmur of assent. The taoiseach went to the lattice and bellowed.

The scuff of the children's play faded. There was silence from below. The slow turf fire and the woven lattice speckled with gold all the faces of the people facing Derval.

It was the ancient woman who spoke. "Come, Buan. Sit down and let us hear our guests' story."

The poet took this as his cue. He sat up, shifting free of his helper's arm. He took a measured breath, while his gaze shifted from face to face, commanding attention. "I swear by the Gods my people swear by. I am Labres MacCullen, Chief Poet of the kingdom of Leinster," he said. "I think there is none here whose late fire I have not shared. By the wounds of Christ and by my own wounds, I will speak the truth to you tonight." He swayed, perhaps involuntarily.

He's such a good-looking man, thought Derval. I forgot that, while he was playing the ugly for us. He's good-looking and knows how to use it.

"I come this day from the Abbey of Ard na Bhfuinseoge," MacCullen was saying, "where the compass trees lie broken, their leaves shrouding the bodies of the dead. The abbot's blood is spilled on the earth, and that of young Caeilte, my sister's son and *clàirsoir*. Goban MacDuilta is lost to us as well, let all the island lament!

"I have seen the great house of Ard na Bhfuinseoge burned; it was set aflame above me, as I lay bleeding, the only one alive after the assault of the Gaill."

Ailesh blinked at him. "Remember that I, too, am alive," she began, seeming reluctant to correct the Ollave in company.

MacCullen glanced down at the girl and blushed hotly. "Christ forgive me, you are right, Iníon Goban, and I spoke like a fevered man to forget it. There were two who survived."

"Ah! Never let truth get in the way of a good line," murmured Derval in English, quietly.

He raised his face and voice. "It was the savage pagan Gentiles who came upon us: the servants of the false devil, to whom I will not give strength by naming. Their message was death itself, for they left little even for plunder. Ard na Bhfuinseoge is no more. That is my history.

"Ailesh, the daughter of Goban the carver, has a story as bitter but yet stranger." He flung out his arm toward the girl and sagged backward.

Ailesh lifted her arms out from her sides. "People of proud Ui Garrchon, foster mother, friends of my childhood . . . Pray for me, for my father is dead, and in my own peril I have not been able to lament him."

There was a stir of sympathy, soft as a light wind. Derval saw the sign of the cross being made, as well as other gestures she did not recognize. She was aware of MacCullen's restlessness. He leaned against his helper once more. Envious, she decided. Envious of Ailesh's good theater.

"The Gaill came yesterday at midmorning. The people of Na Clocha Líatha must have fled with no thought of us, and that is little wonder, for it is a matter of dissension that their tribute is to Leinster's Rí ruirech while ours is sent away to Awley Cuaran in Dublin. The reavers sent their filid before them, to inform us they would attack, but it was an empty service, for he spoke his own tongue to us, and we did not understand. He was a small and dirty man, whom we thought to be a laborer from Dublin. Besides, my kinsmen—what would we have done had we understood his threat of doom: we who had no weapon more deadly than a stone chisel among us?"

The old woman in the front of the company put her hand to

her head and the white hair fell over her face. Her bony fingers pulled at the lank locks in an oddly restrained and formal gesture of anguish. "That was always a mistake. I told the abbot Colm from the beginning, it was a mistake not to keep at least some sling spears! Now he lies martyred for the glory of Mary's Son!"

MacCullen said, "Let you, who have not seen the war frenzy of the Gaill, not speak against Abbot Colm! Had we had axes and spears, each of us, the outcome may have been the same—for these who attacked us were madmen, biting their own shields until the blood ran from their tooth-flesh, and foaming at the mouth like dogs."

There was a moment of stillness, and it seemed to Derval she could taste a change in the air of the small assembly. So quiet might songbirds sit, while the hawk soars between them and the sun.

Berserkers. Her hands grew cold as she mouthed the word.

"I was in the sweathouse with Medb, Ardes, whom you also know, and Gignait, Mell's daughter, when the Gaill burst among us," Ailesh said. "Medb died quickly, before it occurred to the butchers they might have another use for us. I was dragged out by my hair and the motherless demon flung himself onto me. There I was raped and my body torn and my first joy of man stolen from me.

"And there I killed the brute." Some cries of joy at her revenge interrupted her. She waited, then continued. "May his punishment be hell. His blood and my own soaked me red." Ailesh spoke evenly, but Derval could see her tearing her thumbnail viciously all the while. Like Johnnie, she thought, with a new stab of pity.

"I leaped the cattle fence and ran along the road to the Ard na Scamall where Goban finished the cross he had promised to Bridget long ago, after mother died. In doing so . . ." Her voice faltered. "In doing so I led the enemy to him."

MacCullen's arched eyebrows lifted and he took Ailesh by the hand. "Do not believe he would have been spared, child. Nor would he have willingly hidden while his heart's treasure was being destroyed."

Ailesh shook her tears violently from her eyes. "Then, by my father's cross, the saint granted me the first of three miracles.

"I found my father waiting for me, with his hammer in his hand. He picked me up in his arms as the pursuers reached me, and there I thought we would die together. Instead he flung me at the cross itself and the stone gave way before me. I found myself far from trouble in the home of Eoin Ban, my father's foster brother."

In the general buzz and stir, one voice spoke up: that of the white-haired woman. "I didn't know Goban had a foster brother."

"Nor did I," said Ailesh, "until later, when I saw the work of Eoin's hand. But I was in his glass-walled house, far from violence, and there he and this warrior woman, Derval Cuhain, gave me aid and friendship. By the skill of his hand and the cross of Bridget, Eoin brought me back again, so that I may go to Dublin and demand the murder price for my father!"

"This is true? This is not a dream tale?" came a voice from the wall. An old man sat up. He was missing an arm. "Are you sure you're not all from the Ui DunLainge, out to trade joke for joke?"

The taiseach smothered a grin. "Peace, father! I don't think Ui DunLainge yet regards our raid as quite the joke you do. Nor would our kinswoman play their game upon us.

"You spoke of three miracles, Iníon Goban."

"I did. The second occurred this very evening, when an old nun came into our camp to share our food, and spoke wisdom to us. It was Bridget herself, and as she left she showed her radiance to both Derval and blond Eoin. Although I was not privileged to see her for who she was, by her presence she healed every hurt on my body. Look at me and judge!" She opened her brat and displayed her sweet, plump, naked body.

"She was injured," said Derval, stepping forward. "The blood of this brave woman's slashed belly stained the floor red! It was as though a human wolf had torn her breast open. Such injuries do not heal in a day!"

The eyes that shifted from Derval to Ailesh were uneasy. "MacCullen," said the chieftain. "You are a man who guards his reputation. What do you say to this? Did you see the face of Bridget?"

Goddamn! thought Derval. Cynical, supercilious bastard: they had to ask him. Now he will destroy her in front of her own people. Everyone will think Ailesh is crazy, and John and I . . .

MacCullen met her eyes. "I admit I am disappointed that I myself was not worthy of the aisling vision," he said carefully, looking straight at Derval. "I did not know this visitor for the saint, but the daughter of Goban the carver does not lie. And as for miracles, anyone who had seen me last night, bloodless and lost in fever from the stroke of the heathen's sword, must call my life a miracle." He turned to the company.

"I stand by what the daughter of Goban said."

Staring slantwise into Labres MacCullen's blue eyes, Derval silently apologized for her distrust. She pulled a smile from him.

"I am neither saint nor bean sidhe," Derval replied to a question from the chieftain's mother. "Nor yet am I a hero, though the young Ailesh calls me one. I am instead a student of languages; though I was born on this island of Gaels, still you can hear that Irish is not my native tongue."

"An Irishwoman without Irish? That is a riddle I haven't heard before," said the chieftain doubtfully, and then that large man lay back with his head in his old mother's lap. She patted his hair as though he were a dog.

"My parents were travelers, and much of my early life was spent among Saxons and other speakers of the hard tongue.

"And I cannot explain the miracle of Ailesh's rescue; I only know she came to us: to Eoin, who is called the Cattle Leaper, and me . . ."

"Yes. Tell of this cattle leaping. Another riddle?" asked the chieftain with narrowed eyes. "This one could easily be of the blood of the Gaill himself; is he not a Leinster Dane or an Orkneyman?"

"Not so. I speak not of a riddle but a deed. John is a craftsman and a Christian," Derval said, hoping the last was not a complete prevarication. "His home is in Eire."

"A house of glass?" The taiseach's questions brought a new sweat to Derval's face and armpits. At any moment he would evoke from her some statement either unbelievable or incriminatory. She could see herself announcing to this sober assembly that she was a woman from one thousand years in the future. She herself hadn't believed Ailesh's story of Vikings in suburban Greystones.

"Only a house with glass windows," Derval corrected the man gently.

"Flat as mica and clear as air," testified Ailesh, much to Derval's irritation. "Huge windows the size of doors."

"That is Eoin's house," Derval admitted, if only to shut the girl up.

"A magical house?"

Derval smiled. "No. Eoin has no magic about him, except in his art. Any man can have glass in his windows, if he can pay enough. And the house belongs not to Eoin but to his landlady . . . er, patroness."

"I did not meet the patroness," Ailesh said, "unless it was the woman who was looking for her chicken." She looked rather shamefaced as she added, "We raided her hen away from her and would have eaten it tonight but for your cattle."

The chieftain smiled slowly. "That's all right. We raided the cattle also. From the Ui DunLainge. Lucky for you you met us instead of them, for they are as angry as bees."

Derval's eyes opened wide. "Cattle raiding! Does the Church let you do that in this time?" she blurted. The man returned her glance with some hauteur. "I mean . . . rather . . ."

The old woman gently dropped her son's head on the ground beside her. She leaned forward. "That is enough about our guests, son. Further personal questions would be unmannerly."

The taiseach let his mother speak.

"What we must know, Scholar O'Cuhain, is where the Vikings landed and when they are going to leave. For we have only thirty among us who wield the ax at all, and none of us are champions. We will not willingly encounter Odin's mad hounds."

Derval noted the title the old woman had granted her. Well, why not? She had claimed as much to MacCullen, and she was a scholar, wasn't she? She had worked hard for her doctorate. Let the poet take note. But her face was sober as she answered. "Alas, mother, the Gaill do not leave. I crawled close to Ard na Bhfuinseoge last night and I saw the prows of their dragon boats set up in the ruins of the cattle enclosure, among the stumps of the sacred trees. They plan to stay."

The old woman said nothing. Her mouth, ragged-toothed, hung open. The chieftain rocked forward onto his haunches, staring at her. In the sudden quiet Derval heard a child crying and wondered if the sound had just begun.

"It is for that reason especially we must receive the support promised us from Awley Cuarán of Dublin," Ailesh said. "Otherwise, even here you are not safe."

"Indeed we are not!" whispered the old woman. The taiseach frowned like thunder and met his father's worried eyes.

"If he is still in here, there'll be nothing left of him," Ailesh called over her shoulder to Derval. She pried open the door of the sweathouse, expecting heat and dark.

The lamplight and gentle warmth surprised her and drew her in. Derval, the chieftain, and the chieftain's mother followed.

There stood blond Eoin, but blond no more, for his hair and his face were smudged with charcoal. He was drawing on the wall, and when he heard them and turned, he blinked like one newly awakened from sleep. His rampant manhood hung out before him, as dark as the yard of a black bull. His hands, too, were black. "Hello," he said in English, adding, "Is it late? I lost track of the time."

"It is a man of wonders who can go from a bathhouse dirtier than he went in," said the taiseach. It was he who first noticed the walls, and then his mother did. At last Derval turned and stared at what John had done. She whistled through her teeth.

Ailesh was last to look away.

On the back wall, first seen upon entering the sweathouse, was Bridget, with her calm cow eyes and her hair coiling outward, enclosing all creation. There about her were the wren and the heron, the ouzel and the osprey. There among them stood a penguin in full dress, not drawn realistically but quite recognizable. Around the saint ran deer and camels and bison, and a thing Derval alone recognized as a Morris Mini Minor, its tiny wheels filled with tinier patterns of spirals.

The right-hand wall sported both a triskelion and a large yin-yang. The Oriental symbol was worked out in fish eyes, fish scales, and fish netting, while the three-lobed circle was composed of seals and polar bears.

The third wall's decoration, interrupted by the entry of

Ailesh, was a knotwork composed of connected rectangles of curious form. "A . . . locomotive, Johnnie?" she asked, staring. "Oh yes. Had I seen the caboose first, I would have understood."

"I . . . I'm not done," said John, shifting from foot to bare foot. He became aware of his erection and turned his back on everyone.

The chieftain's mother paced around the room, holding her own oil lamp near the walls. Her son followed. At last the old woman stepped up to John and held the lamp to his face.

"You are worth a house of glass," she said, mystifying John completely. Then she added, "But young man, it is past time you were married!"

Derval sat up. "Somebody just threw the bolt! The bolt on the door!"

John tried his best to surround her without moving his body. "You're nervous, Derval. Shouldn't still be nervous."

She released herself efficiently by prying John's fingers back, and ignored his complaint. "We're locked in, Johnnie!" Derval cried, floundering through darkness toward the door. A quick pull at the wooden latch proved her point. She hissed her anger.

John Thornburn opened his eyes. It was very difficult to do and didn't help affairs much, as the only light that entered the sweatlodge was diffused starlight around the airhole near the ceiling. "What's the matter? Do you have to piss that bad? Maybe they're only protecting us from bears or something."

"No bears," said Derval sullenly. "Not in Ireland."

"Or something."

She felt her way back to the fine heather mattress and the heap of feather tickings with which the taiseach had provided them. "Don't talk like an idiot, John."

"An idiot!" John sniffed. "A little while ago I was your grand, lean-thewed, cuddly, silk-haired—"

"Stuff it." Derval crawled back under the ticking to think. Her bare skin was chilled; John chafed it vigorously. He rubbed his own body against her back. His hand wandered over her thigh.

"I said 'Stuff it'! And I didn't mean . . . John B. Thornburn, what's gotten into you tonight, anyway?"

"I'm sorry," said John, contrite. "But I can't seem to help it." He eased away from her reluctantly.

Derval flipped over, staring into the darkness where his face was. "Now, if you could just distribute that ardor over a period of, say, a fortnight, that would mark a general improvement in your performance. But not now. For one thing we're in trouble, and for another...

"... my mucous membranes are wearing thin," she concluded in a mutter.

John sighed. It seemed incumbent upon him to allay Derval's suspicions, so he brought his arms under his chest and ejected himself from the snug nest of feathers. On his way to the door he scraped the wall once with his shoulder and cursed, wondering what he had smudged. He reached the door jamb and found the latch.

"It's only locked." John spoke decisively.

"Yes. So I said."

He leaned against the door, feeling the oak boards warp ever so slightly at his pressure. It was a heavy wooden stick that was holding it, he decided. Like a two-by-four. An oak two-by-four. John sighed again.

"So we're locked in? What do you think the villagers plan to do—burn us in a wicker basket?"

"Off by five centuries," stated Derval, her contempt muffled by layers of covers.

"Not off," replied John. "Merely being sarcastic. After all, Derval, Ailesh is out there. And the olive."

"Spare me. Spare me the 'olive,' Johnnie," said Derval, with a show of bluster. "But you're right about Ailesh. I can't believe these people mean ill to one of their own, and I know Ailesh won't abandon us. Nor let us come to harm. Perhaps it was only a pranking kid who thrust the bolt."

John agreed readily, and navigated back to the bed by Derval's voice. By the time he buried himself in covers once more, he was so cold his body balled up like a sow bug. Derval gave him the warmth of her chest and belly. He lay that way for sixty seconds, shivering, and then said, "You know, I'm beginning to think we should worry, eh?"

"Stuff it, Johnnie," murmured Derval, licking his ear with her tongue.

It was only a short while later that Labres MacCullen quietly shot back the bolt on the sweatlodge and edged in.

He heard the grunts, the panting and heaving, and stepped toward the mattress in his soft leather shoes. With trained courtliness he waited till they were done with that particular bout, but when it appeared that there would be no real respite, he cleared his throat.

Derval gave such a gasp she came close to inhaling her tongue. Her reflexive huddle bounced John six inches into the air.

"Forgive me," said MacCullen considerately. "I didn't mean to startle you, nor to interfere with your pleasures. But I am sadly disappointed in the honor of this taiseach, and I thought it best no one notice my visit."

Derval sat up, denuding John of covers. "Why? What has the man done, Ollave? Why were we imprisoned here?"

Slowly the poet sat down beside her and sighed. "They mean no great harm to you, Scholarinion Cuhain. But it grieves my heart that fear should bring Irishmen to treat visitors of welcome in this manner. And it is inconvenient, isn't it? But for the respect these villagers owe to my profession I would have had my liberty constrained also." Then he leaned over until she could feel the warmth of his face over her breast and said gallantly, "What a fine woman's smell you have."

Derval felt an embarrassed heat over her face. "What did he just say to you, Derval?" inquired John, at her other side. "Did he just say what I think, eh? He didn't say that you smell, did he? He's got a right to talk, if he did!"

As John spoke in English, it was all noise to the poet. "The problem is this, my friends. The taiseach, after consulting with his mother's brother, has decided the clanstead cannot bear the force of a Viking attack, God give him a blessing for his sense! But he also fears to meet the wrath of Ui DunLainge while on the move, with all the cattle milling and babies to care for. Surely if they are caught on the road they would lose half their herd, in reparation for a raid of twenty-two cows! So they leave tomorrow and go south and inland, over the hills toward the lowlands of Wicklow."

"What has that to do with us?"

MacCullen fingered the fringe of his brat. "Her kinswoman wants Ailesh to go with them. She is clanless, but for these people, you see, and they feel . . ."

He ground his teeth. "They feel she will get no great hearing in Dublin for her trouble. This clanstead resisted the pressures of Dublin and submit only to Leinster. They feel the Dublin king, being one of the Gaill himself, takes his tribute without honor to give justice."

Derval had listened closely. "And are they right, Ollave? You ought to be objective."

MacCullen snorted. "May the saints stand between me and the men of ignorance! Perhaps the taiseach judges by his own standards of what is due a guest. Hardly half of these cowboys have been in the city at all, and they don't speak the language. I know Olaf Cuarán. I have composed before him in his own tongue many times, and he will not have forgotten me. Besides, the king in Dublin may not be a great ruler, like Aud the deep-minded, when she was queen in Ireland, but he is, after all, a king! And how could a king survive without maintaining his sword pledge?"

Derval, listen as she might, could hear no sarcasm in the poet's words. She answered with a noncommittal grunt.

"And more, inion'Cuhain. The taoiseach fears that any traveler on the road north at this time is sure to run into a band of Ui DunLainge's champions."

Derval chewed her lip. "And what of that? Would they cut strangers to the ground on sight? We are not the people who raided their cows."

"Certainly they would not cut us down on the road. But the road is rutted with fresh tracks, and they could scarcely avoid asking us what we had seen."

MacCullen fell silent, as though he had proved an important point. Derval felt she must have missed something. "Does the taiseach believe we would give him away? After all his hospitality? Or what would have been hospitality but for this."

"He knows we would not lie," answered MacCullen slowly. Derval's face heated again with blushes.

"Never would I let Ui DunLaingacht know that their enemy was in flight and to what refuge. But how could I deny having seen the raiders when my eyes did see them?"

"Did he really say that?" interjected John Thornburn, who had been listening carefully. "Did he just ask you how he could say he hadn't seen what he had seen? Tell him just how easy it would be."

MacCullen spoke over John as he might have spoken over the hooting of an owl. "I think that I suffer no peril at the hands of any Gael of this island. Ragged I may be, and without my harper, but my estate is known. Still—others may suffer the anger hidden from me."

"Like Ailesh?" asked Derval. "She may be known, you think, for a kinswoman of the raiders?" She felt the poet turn in the dark beside her. "Like the young daughter of Goban, and like others! Have you no fear in you for yourself at all, inion'Cuhain? For I warn you that strangers will not grant honor to a scholar who yet speaks with the accent of the iron tongue."

Derval had spoken at her first thought, before considering that she and John might also be considered to be involved in the matter of the Ui Garrchon and the Ui DunLainge. But although the prospect of meeting a squad of horsemen with axes and spears bent on punishment left her feeling unsettled, she found herself unable to disillusion MacCullen on the subject of her personal courage.

"If a man doesn't know me for what I am, that is his own business and none of mine. I am not afraid to meet the *sluagh* of Ui DunLainge."

"I am," said John in English. "If you're talking about what I think you are, I'm scared shitless."

Derval smiled invisibly in the dark. "Eoin Ban was never taught that it is mannerless to speak in a language one of the party does not understand. He is, however, a great one for enduring foe and hardship."

John let out a canine yelp at this, and MacCullen burst out laughing. "I think I understand Eoin the cattle leaper quite well!" he said. "Except when he tries the speech of the Irish.

"So then it is settled, Scholar Iníon Cuhain? Despite the will of Buan MacConghal, we will continue toward Dublin?"

Derval was about to reply when a thought struck her. "What about you?"

He frowned. "Me? I do this for young Ailesh. After all, I am Ollave of Leinster, and"—his scowl broke pleasantly—"a man of no small influence."

Derval had to smile. "Quite. But perhaps you're not the healthiest chief poet in Ireland. It's only a night passed since you were sick indeed."

A moment of silent tension passed, magnified by the gloom. Derval wondered why he found it so difficult to admit his weakness. Surely he could not hope she had forgotten, who had staunched the horrible flow of blood.

"I've been better in my health," MacCullen said at last. "But sick or well, I must return to Dublin immediately. I have been too long away."

"Why, Ollave? What business has a poet of Leinster in the city of the Gentiles?" Derval asked baldly. "And why were you in Ard na Bhfuinseoge anyway, with only your sister's son for company?"

If she expected gain by this directness, Derval was to be disappointed, for MacCullen's response was a long, hard stare. "My business, woman, is Leinster's business. And I see no reason why Leinster's business should be yours."

She felt her face grow hot, even to her lips. "I would agree entirely, poet, had fate not matched our paths so. Against my choosing, to the risk of my life and without hope of gain for me, I must add."

MacCullen's hauteur crumbled. "True enough, lady. But as I am not the king of this province how can I reveal his affairs? I must return to Dublin, believe me, and I feel I can now walk a distance."

Derval answered his faint, wintery smile. "Or better—ride?" She wrinkled her brow a moment. "The harp would be worth a pony, wouldn't it?"

"It would be the price of a very good horse!" replied the poet. "But as it is Caeilte's harp, it is not mine to trade.

"And I would not trade it if it were," he added, with a theatrical groan. "Not while his mother waits for his music in happy innocence, and that strain will only be heard now in the isles of the West. Not while I, MacCullen, reduced as I am, have yet a bright flame of life in me."

In the darkness Derval's grin passed unnoticed. It was not that she doubted the sincerity of the man's feelings, but . . . She rehearsed her words before answering, "Of course you wouldn't trade it, but the very honor with which you are bound to this possession of the blessed dead boy marks how well it would serve as hostage against your return."

"Hostage?" MacCullen considered the idea. "There is sense in that, scholar. I would, however, have to leave a letter of explanation. Could you pen it?"

"Of course. I'll rise to the work gladly."

John spoke in his slow Irish. "We are not going to leave Ailesh behind, are we?"

MacCullen slapped him on the back, or rather meant to. But the light was so poor, and John so huddled against the cold, that the poet's large hand caught him across the back of the head. "Eoin Cattle Leaper, you cheer my heart! No, we will not leave without Ailesh Ni Goban."

"Ow," replied John.

"Certainly not," said Derval. "Well just have to . . . to steal her away. Like a cow."

"Eh? She's not," muttered John sullenly. "Nothing like."

Chapter Eight

•

> Rats, though sharp their snouts,
> Are not powerful in battle.
> The Vermin Killing Satire "Glam-Dichenn"
> of Senchan Torpest, Ollamh of all Ireland

The late-rising moon was partly obscured by the trees, but still it made John and Derval stop to adjust their eyes. Ahead rose the thorn-hedge palisade which enclosed the dun, with only a woven archway breaking its forbidding black length, high enough and wide enough for one man at a time to ride through on a pony. The village ponies themselves milled around the perimeter of a smaller paddock outside the walls. Half the beasts were grays, which glimmered like moons, occasionally eclipsed by their invisible dun or black brethren.

Another day coming, thought Derval. The gardai must have been notified by now. My secretary must be wild. George Hormsby will be calling about the excavations in Dublin. In Dublin! I'm on my way to Dublin now. Has someone called my parents yet?

So they are leaving, thought John, peering through the gloom at the tall stone dun. Will they come back before the place falls apart? What a waste of work if they don't. Who will ever see my sketches?

MacCullen led John and Derval toward the arched gate, and there was nothing secretive or skulking in the poet's gait. Derval paused by the horse corral and looked in. "Pack ponies," she said in English to John, with no great enthusiasm in her tone. "Probably quite fit to pull a small plow as well. Christ knows where among these we'll find something to carry MacCullen."

John stumbled on the tussocks of grass while following after her. "Olive!" he whispered very loudly. "Maybe there's guards?" The man in question stopped and allowed John to catch up. "Certainly there are guards, Eoin. I passed them at their games when I went out. What have they to do with us? Do you think a taiseach mean enough to lock his guests away like cattle would admit as much to his young men?"

"Why not?" replied John. "Doesn't being boss mean you can do whatever you want?"

MacCullen looked down at John, muttered in his throat, and strode away once more. At the archway he came to a halt and leaned over the light wickerwork cattle gate, as though he had nothing to do and too much time to do it in. As John came up behind him he heard the poet address someone.

"In truth, Enan, it is difficult for an injured man to sleep the night through. A healing wound throbs all the harder."

John started as the fellow MacCullen spoke to uncoiled himself from the earth behind the gate.

In the pale moonlight John could see that the three young men by the gate were not dressed like the others he had seen. They had neither shirt nor *leinne*, but rather skintight trousers that ended at midcalf. Tight leather jackets covered their upper bodies, giving a sort of Hell's Angels feeling to the group. These jackets were embroidered or painted; in the poor light John could not tell which.

The man addressed by the poet wore also a short, shaggy cloak, and his long black hair was braided with ribbons and set off by brass ornaments which gleamed silver in the moonlight.

"The Ollave must forgive my blocking the way. We are only watchful tonight, what with Ui DunLainge and the presence of the Gaill." He reached sideways and pulled from the wall a long spear. Putting his weight on this, he raised his left leg and rested his bare foot against the side of his other knee. John Thornburn noted the picture he made thus, standing like a heron, and had an impulse to draw him with a heron's head, braids, brass, and all.

MacCullen continued to lean on the wicker gate, which creaked beneath his considerable weight. "You're watching your chess game closely enough, at any rate," he said.

The young man looked from MacCullen's bland face to the pegboard at his feet, where another youth squatted. This one was groomed in as peacocky a fashion as the first, and was also barefoot. A couple more lounged standing farther away against the wall of the cattle enclosure and did not approach. Enan dropped his spear against the wall again, shrugged his brat over his shoulders, and rubbed one finger under his nose. Perhaps he also blushed; the moonlight did not reveal it. The other player spoke for him.

"That is why at least three must watch every night, Ollave. So that not all can be playing chess at once."

MacCullen smiled like a cat. "True enough, Ainmine. But many can throw the dice. And the odd man can lose himself quite completely in his companions' game. Have I not an example here? Young . . . young—say, are you not the son of Aidhne, whom I last saw dragging at the hem of his mother's skirt?" The third guard, who had been standing against the palisade, unseen by John or Derval, stepped out.

"I am, Ollave," he replied, blinking over the poet's shoulder. He was a very tall young man, who seemed not yet to have grown into his own bony framework. His leather jacket pulled too tightly over his shoulders and exposed an inch of pale skin above the trousers. He met Derval's eyes for a moment, then dropped his gaze to the wickerwork. His acknowledgment of John was even more awkward. "My name is Delbeth."

Casually MacCullen swung the gate open. Insouciantly, he strolled in. Derval and John crowded after him.

The poet stooped down beside the wooden board with its tiny pieces of bone and affected a strong interest in the game. "Look here, Scholarinion Cuhain, and tell me if you don't think there will be a queen imperiled in three moves."

Derval bent beside him. She was flattered that he should ask her for her opinion, and at the same time angry with herself that the words of this arrogant man could flatter her. Although she played chess, and liked to believe she played it well, she had no idea which pieces the pegs represented. Nor was she certain that chess in the tenth century was the game she was to learn from her uncle nine hundred and eighty years hence. She thought it best to nod sagely after MacCullen, chewing on her thumbknuckle.

John found himself close to the youngest, largest watchman, though not meeting his eyes. Indeed, John's eyes were approximately level with the youth's nipples, which were barely visible beneath his drooping brat. He felt a stab of disappointment, for he had been told all his life that people in the past had been smaller, and had ofttimes fantasized a world in which he might be considered a sizable man. He tried to imagine himself battling through this boy to rescue Ailesh.

If I slouched a little, John said to himself, I could hit him in the solar plexus with my nose. He snorted softly in self-disgust, and gangling Delbeth took one step backward.

MacCullen rose once more, groaning. The first guard put his hand beneath the poet's elbow to assist him. Derval took his other arm, but he shook her off. There was an exchange of sparks between them, witnessed only by John. "I'm not so injured I need lean upon a woman."

"Then don't," said Derval, stepping back ostentatiously. She brushed invisible dirt from her hands. MacCullen turned on his heel and walked toward the dun. Derval followed, striding stiff-legged.

"They fight a lot," mumbled John to the guards, and without looking around he scuttled after his companions.

"Wait!" The call came loudly, before he had gone ten steps. John froze, with his shoulders around his ears. Derval also stopped dead, though with less visible anxiety.

MacCullen looked over his shoulder. The expression on his face might have withered stone. "What?"

The chess-playing guards were staring in some surprise at their gawky friend, who had uttered the command. He stepped forward, tripping on the handle of his ax, which lay on the dirt. A cow blundered into him, or he into it, as he came toward John. John decided he would have to punch the fellow in the groin.

"The cow," he blurted. "Can you teach me to do it?"

John's mouth hung open as he tried to parse the odd request.

"Can you teach me to stand on the shoulders of the lead cow?" With this out, the young man cupped his large hands on his large elbows and stared fixedly at the sky above and to one side of John Thornburn's head. His toes made nervous circles on the ground.

MacCullen was standing on one side of John. Derval put a hand on his shoulder. All three of them took a slow breath in concert.

John tried out stories and explanations in his head. All failed when he began to speak. "I never did it before," he said. "It was the fear of the horns that drove me up there. It made me . . ." Here John's vocabulary ran out. He didn't know the Irish words for "faint," "nauseated," or "hysterical." "It made me want to shit."

The tall young man looked straight down at John. He opened his mouth to reveal a row of large white teeth, one of them chipped. His smile grew until it shrank the face around it. The first guard clapped him about the shoulder. "You see, Delbeth? There's hope for you yet!"

John himself suffered under a similar embrace from MacCullen. "Eoin Cattle Leaper, I call you an honest man and a boon companion!" he said, leading John willy-nilly toward the dun.

The great door of wood and iron hung open, and by the accumulation of manure around its base it seemed to have been a while since it had been closed. The dun—that huge thatched hut—was closed to entry by nothing more than a gate of open wickerwork, identical to that which kept cattle in the outer enclosure.

The thatch was raised from the walls by its framework of salley, and this in effect made a sort of clerestory window around the building. The starlight which crept round its odd angles, along with that let in by the door, as well as a certain red glow from the banked fire, provided only enough illumination for John to see the balustrades of the apartments across the hall from him. Beyond, where the sleepers lay, was impenetrable darkness, and he could not see the second story of apartments at all. Yet MacCullen paced forward confidently, found the stone steps, and ascended them. John followed, working his fingers into the loose weave of the poet's brat for security.

Derval was beside him. John wondered how she dared walk two abreast on the open stairway. She whispered, "How will we wake her up?" into the poet's ear.

"She will wake when she feels my eye upon her," replied MacCullen.

Stone stairs gave way to straw. The air, heavy with breathing, smelled of sour babies and fresh heather. The poet stopped between one step and the next, and John's face came into sudden contact with MacCullen's broad back. He smothered an injured sniff.

Vision came as John Thornburn stood still and watched for it. They were in the center of the second story of apartments, looking in at the sleeping taiseach and his family. Most of the pallets were topped by lumps of blankets no more distinctive than the cocoon of an especially drab sort of caterpillar, but two were identifiable.

The taiseach's uncle lay on his stomach, and his white, blunt-ended arm was flung over the dark ticking beside his head. It shone with a light of its own, that injured arm.

The arm of the taiseach's wife was equally visible as it lay in a protective, restraining half-circle about a small heap based on a feather bed and topped by blankets: a heap that might have been—that was—Ailesh Ni Goban. The girl's face was turned away from her kinswoman's (as is the custom when two people eat onions and sleep together) and toward MacCullen's, and indeed as the poet stared, her eyes did open and perceived her visitors, one by one. She looked surprised.

John smiled for her. He was certain she hadn't enough light to see his smile but knew no better way to offer his moral support. Moral support was the only kind he imagined being of any use, for it didn't seem to him Ailesh had a chance in a hundred of getting out from under her protector's arm without rousing the household. He shifted his glance from MacCullen to Derval, waiting for them both to come to that conclusion.

Derval was in shadow, and MacCullen continued to stare.

As though this regard chilled Ailesh, she pulled her blanket higher, bringing a solid layer of cloth between her kinswoman and herself. That was all that happened for five minutes.

John Thornburn, who had missed the counsel in the taiseach's apartment, now got a chance to examine it thoroughly from his vantage outside the waist-high wall. First the ax on the wall became visible, and then the spear, and finally the lectern with its white parchment. Fixed, glassy staring at that rectangle gave John no hint of its contents, however, but only produced glowing circles within John's eyes and gave him an alarm that he might actually be getting a headache. He turned his eyes away.

Derval, though glad the girl had been wakened, felt irritation that the poet's self-consequence should be stoked by such success. Mere chance. She glanced at the tall man distrustfully.

Ailesh was moving again. She was turning slowly around, onto her back, and bringing up the feather bed with her like an ungainly pillow. It took a long time for this revolution to be completed, during which John knew Derval to be anxious, for she kept holding her breath to her limit and then expelling it audibly in his ear. At last the girl was face upward, though hidden from them completely by the bulky bed ticking, around which her mother's foster sister still had her arm wrapped.

Then another long wait, while John shifted from foot to foot and felt a cramp incipient in his left large toe. Perhaps the girl had fainted beneath the weight of anxiety and bed ticking, or perhaps she had merely fallen back asleep. Just when he was about to suggest as much quietly to MacCullen, Ailesh appeared at the half-wall, having slid on her back all the way off the mattress, leaving her shape in feathers behind. Clasped awkwardly before her was the harp. "We are going?" she mouthed silently.

The moon had cleared the trees and struck them all in the face as they left the dun. MacCullen explained the situation to Ailesh in an undertone. When she discovered that John and Derval had been locked into the sweatlodge, her anger found vent in a catlike cry, and she fingered the hammer in her belt and turned to go back into the darkened house.

MacCullen's square form stood in her way. "Patience, Daughter of the Arts. Will you brain all your kinsfolk in their sleep?"

"But they lied to me! MacCullen, my own foster mother has gone back against me, and done injury to those who saved my life!"

He put a burly arm around her and led her out from the doorway. Under moonlight shone the shapes of sleeping cows, lumpy as river rocks. The poet led her to one beast that lay lamb-fashion, with its sticklike legs curled around it, and sat Ailesh down beside it. Both of them leaned against the warm and smelly back as though it were a cushion. "Tonight," the man began, "you told a strange story to these people, Iníon Goban. You spoke of three miracles. Most people, you know, live their lives without seeing one miracle. Can you wonder they may have known doubt of you?"

Ailesh's mouth opened roundly. "Doubt? MacCullen, these are my foster kin!" Then, frowning, she added, "Do they think I am a child, not to know truth from my imaginations?"

The poet stared at nothing and folded his hands over one raised knee. "When last they knew you, you were a child, were you not? A father does not notice his son growing tall, I am told, until he becomes too big to cuff safely!" MacCullen chuckled at his own joke and put his arm around Ailesh's waist. "Besides, my dear heart, how many feuds can one woman maintain at a time? Forgive these uneducated cowherds and let us be gone!"

She looked troubled, but willing to be convinced. "But yet, Ollave"—and as she spoke she scratched her back against that of the cow—"They were willing to believe in the attack of the Gaill!"

MacCullen's smile was pained. "Far easier to believe in things horrible than things wonderful, woman. And the longer one lives, the more true that becomes."

Because John had no hope of following the conversation, his senses were more animal-acute, and it was he who noticed the approach of the gate guard over the dust and dried manure of the enclosure. "Heads up!" he cried.

Derval squatted beside MacCullen and Ailesh, resting her hand against the cow's horn. That long-suffering animal rose, lowing, and deposited them all in the dust. "Ollave, what are we to tell the cowboys?"

MacCullen turned his square head and watched the tall, gawky boy approach. "We will tell them the truth, certainly, Iníon Cuhain. It is up to each of them to decide whether their honor requires them to follow the plots of so mean-spirited a war chief. If it does, then we must overcome them. They are only boys, after all."

His face was calm and adamant, and Derval, meeting his eyes, had the sensation of having run full tilt into a wall. It was an experience to which she was not accustomed. Sweat spangled the woman's forehead, and she saw in her mind's eye the wicked iron axes piled in the dust by the palisade.

She thought with the rapidity of thought that just precedes panic. "But MacCullen, because they are only boys, isn't that a cruel position in which to put them—to give them the choice of dishonor or alienation from kin and clan? I think I can chart a course for us which would spare them this grief."

MacCullen half-smiled at Derval. His strong face was much improved by this expression. "I would be the last to deny you a chance to be merciful, lady warrior."

There was no chance for retort, for the gawky youth was beside them. "I—uh—we thought perhaps you might like to share our alebag," he said, proffering the sloshing leather sack, which seemed to be made from the leg of a cow. Even under moonlight, the lad's color could be seen to rise, especially when he shot a glance at John Thornburn.

Derval cleared her throat. "Delbeth, champion of Ui Garrchon, I thank you, but I think such a gift would be inappropriate. I am forced to admit that our visit here was unwelcome to the taiseach, and so we depart."

Delbeth let the alebag slowly fall to his side. His face sagged like the leather. "You . . . de—depart? In the long hour of night?"

"Even so," replied Derval. "At no other hour is it possible."

The shy boy stared at the ground and scratched his face where the beard was coming. "I am very sorry," he said. "I don't know what was in Buan's mind! A kinswoman, too . . ."

MacCullen spoke. "Do not apologize for the taoiseach. When one has the governance of an entire *finé*, Delbeth, matters of policy become complex. Be glad that yours is the simple, honorable warrior's role!"

Delbeth looked up at this, gratefully.

"We will take one horse only," said Derval. "And were it not for the Ollave's injuries, we would take nothing. Can you find us a good, solid pony to carry a wounded man to Dublin?"

The boy's eyes flashed. "Give me but a minute."

After a muted colloquy with the other guards, he passed out of the wicker gate. The four companions followed him.

The pony he led up to MacCullen was pale and wide and very strange of eye. Derval grinned and looked to John. "A blue-eyed cream. Often put to death at birth."

John started and then sighed. "I keep forgetting how barbaric it was—is—back here."

"No, Johnnie. I meant put down in the twentieth century. Can't you look at the coarse creature and see why?"

He looked closely at the beast's face. "Not at all. I think she looks very nice."

So did the poet. "This is a fine animal, Delbeth. I expected none such."

"She's mine," mumbled Delbeth. "I learned to ride on her."

MacCullen made to give the mare back, but the tall youth shook his head. "I don't ride her much any more. I have two, you see, and she doesn't get the work she needs."

"I will bring her back, should heaven spare me," said MacCullen. For a minute they both watched Derval, who was struggling through the pen of horses, trying to get a rope over the neck of an uncooperative Muiregan. Delbeth giggled at the sight, his voice breaking up and down.

"In the morning when your watch is done, Delbeth, please tell the taiseach that we have departed and that he must trouble himself no further about us. And tell him that should we meet the riders of DunLainge"—and MacCullen could not suppress a smile—"that they may derive some amusement from my strange companions and I, but useful information will be slow in coming."

"DunLainge!" Delbeth's long face was stricken. He dashed back through the wicker gate, leaving MacCullen holding the pony's bridle. When he returned he was holding his ax. "Take this, Ollave. You must not be weaponless."

MacCullen gave it back. "A poet is never weaponless, true heart. And we will take no weapons from a *dirb fine* I leave in peril. But instead I leave this with you in hostage for the return of your sage mare." And hefting the heavy harp, he gave it into the astonished Delbeth's arms.

"Ollave! I am not worthy to keep such treasure!"

"I can think of none better," answered MacCullen, and he climbed effortfully upon the cream pony's back.

They retraced the road they had taken only that evening, with Derval encouraging the unhappy hinny along with a willow wand. Within a hundred feet young Delbeth had chased after them and caught them once more. He put his hand on John's shoulder. "Eoin Cattle Leaper, I crave of you the stranger's blessing."

John looked dazedly at Derval, who explained. John tried

to put his hand on the fellow's head, but could not reach, and was covered with confusion as Delbeth knelt before him. "Tell him, Derval. Tell him that I ask Bridget and Christ and all whoever to bless him, eh? And—and tell him to look in the sweathouse when it's light. I want someone to see my sketch."

"I will, John," she said. "And I'll tell him the work is for him."

"Why not? Let it be for him."

Derval translated very earnestly for the boy, who rose, kissed John on the face, and then ran home as fast as his overlong legs could carry him.

"Eh? Is the guy gay, do you think, Derval? Not that I'm narrow-minded or anything, but he seemed to have quite a mash on me."

"Young men will develop their mad passions. Around fame and glory, of course. He doesn't want to sleep with you, Johnnie: just to be as good as you."

John scowled, shoving his hands deep into his pockets.

Derval caught MacCullen looking at her with a sort of concentrated, uncertain expression on his face. She looked away. "I didn't lie to the boy, Ollave."

"No, you did not. Not for a moment," he answered. "But Daughter of Chadhain, I admit I had doubts, when you spoke to me of your far travels. I have difficulty, you must know, associating the hard tongue with education. Yet I know now you must have cut your milk teeth at the courts of Europe. Not a lie, and yet hardly a word of truth."

John, who understood most, if not all, of the above, sniffed deeply. "Yet young Delbeth is alive and whole, and maybe wasn't to be so without Derval's wit." John was marching along with a great stride for his size and with his shoulders back.

MacCullen lifted his eyebrows high. "Indeed! Let us be thankful for poor Delbeth's sake."

The moon was no help. Instead it splashed randomly through the heavy oak forest in confusing fashion, and when the party issued gratefully into small meadows, they were glare-blind until reaching the next patch of cold damp. At least it wasn't raining, thought Derval, clutching her brat to her with her free hand while holding onto Muiregan's tail with the other.

The old hinny led them along the road, for despite her age her eyes were the best among them. Or perhaps the mare of Delbeth might have contested this superiority, but MacCullen rode on her back and if she led, he might have brained himself against the limb of a tree. As it was, Derval's height condemned her to a series of attacks about her face on the part of twigs (which she could not help visualizing as bat claws). Each time she suffered she flinched and pulled the hinny's tail, the animal snorted, and MacCullen, Ailesh, and John tucked their heads. For the last two the gesture was entirely symbolic.

It was now perhaps twelve hours since old Bride had shown Derval her power. Twelve hours. It was only thirty-six hours (or so) since they had plummeted through time. In her mind Derval clung to this short history: especially to the visit of... of... Jheez! And they called her a saint. Derval smelled the fresh cow shit on the road. Her body remembered the trembling of the earth. (Not under hooves. Not that alone.)

No last brewing. No last brewing. She clung to that cackled phrase like scripture.

Of course that didn't mean Derval O'Keane wouldn't die herself, and lose all the tastes and urgings and the picture-book memories and whisperings in the dark and touchings and readings and ambitions, fulfilled and fulfilling. And long-standing, deeply satisfying academic feuds. Like with... what was his name again? Sullivan? Who insisted (idiotically and in the face of all evidence) that the early medieval Irish either did or didn't use stirrups: she couldn't remember which. Come now, Dr. O'Keane, she told herself. You remember which side you defended in the June *Irish Sword* only last year, don't you?

But she didn't. She still felt the delightful and worthy contempt of the man (was it Sullivan? Or was it Sully?), but she couldn't remember which side of the argument was the right side. Her side. Well, there were other memories of more significance. The taste of tea, for instance. No tea in the tenth century in Ireland. Derval called on her private cellar of experience to relive a breakfast cup of black tea with thin milk and one-half teaspoon of sugar. This effort came to nothing also, being superseded by a belch of this evening's warm ale and blood pudding.

Derval knew a moment's drowning panic, for if her memories were failing her, wasn't she as good as dead already? What was she, after all, except the memory of all she had done, telling her the sort of person she was and guiding her next act consistently? Without that, what was left but blind chance and leaves blown meaninglessly through the trees? I must know who I am, thought Derval. I must know that.

Derval didn't remember herself and didn't feel very good, either, being tired and cold. And riding boots were never made to walk in all night. Nothing was made to walk all night, especially Derval, and with a tiny moan of "Mother" she collapsed forward over Muiregan's tentlike croup. The hinny stopped and looked over her shoulder.

"What is it?" whispered Ailesh to MacCullen, trying to look around his pony's rear. "Have you seen something?"

"Not I," replied the poet. "But Chadhain's daughter in front of me. I think she is listening at the ground."

Derval indeed had her ear to the earth. Her whole body lay against the packed earth of the trail and her hand still gripped Muiregan's sparse and yellowed tail. MacCullen listened intently. He grunted his discovery of sound.

"Cows once more," said John, nodding wisely.

"Not cattle but riders. Ui DunLainge," said Ailesh.

MacCullen scratched his mouth with one hand. "I think, my friends, that it is better not to meet them." He turned his horse to the right off the trail. In dark and confusion, John and Ailesh followed.

Derval opened her eyes and saw feet: both rag-wrapped and bare feet, glowing silver under moonlight. Behind these were the knob-jointed legs of horses. The fear that she might be trampled drove her to her own feet. Her brat dragged on the ground.

A redheaded man took her by both shoulders in a grip half-supportive and half-imprisoning. "Who are you, woman? What mischance has left you here on the road to die of the night cold?"

She yawned in his face, albeit apologetically, and stared

around her. A dozen ponies, mounted by men dressed in padded linen. Their spears were as limber as elongated arrows, and bobbed as the small steeds pawed the earth.

Another twenty or so men on foot, carrying axes.

Ui DunLainge, Derval's brain told her. This was a *taraigeacht* of Ui DunLainge, of whom she had boastfully said she was not afraid.

And as a matter of fact Derval was not afraid. She was too swimmily exhausted to be afraid. She made to conceal her gaping yawn with her hands and discovered she was still holding onto the hinny's tail. Looking around, she discovered her friends were gone. Confusing.

"I am," she began, straightening in the war chieftain's arms, "Derval Iníon Chadhain, and I come fleeing the destruction of the Abbey of Ard na Bhfuinseoge."

"The . . . destruction of the abbey?" The redhead let slip his hands.

"By the Gaill! The madmen called berserkers took it two days since, and hardly a soul in the place still lives." Again Derval was consumed by yawns that doubled her over like a coughing fit.

But in her extremity she did not miss the cries and groans which escaped the warriors around her, nor when the taiseach invoked the face of Mary to stand between himself and trouble did she fail to read the man's mood. Derval had always needed tea to start her intellect functioning in the morning, but sheer slyness she could call to use in a sound sleep.

"And it is my holy purpose to gather Gaels to the revenge of their innocent blood. The reavers are many, certainly, and well drenched in blood, but so much more is the reward in heaven of Christians who fall in such an undertaking. I myself expect to live no longer than my next meeting with the berserkers, sending at least one Gentile to hell to balance my own ascent!"

The silence would have been deafening but for the restlessness of the horses, who of course didn't know of the quick road to bliss Derval was promising.

She let the burly redhead stare for a few seconds before adding, "But I wake to my senses, brothers, and I see my news has gone before. For to what other purpose do Irishmen ride under moonlight, in coton and with ax and spear?"

The chieftain muttered a word to a thin gray man beside him. That one brought forth a wide-backed, platter-jawed black horse that the chieftain swung himself onto.

Stirrups, thought Derval. Of course stirrups, by the late tenth century. What an ass Sully is, after all, to say they didn't exist here.

"Our business, unfortunate woman, is our own," said the chieftain from this added height. "And it is our misfortune that we may not add our cause to yours this night. But remember—we are not coast dwellers, and Gaillic reavers are first the business of the clans who suffer them. Ui Garrchon, for instance."

"Ui Garrchon," Derval echoed without inflection.

"You will find them to the south along this very road," the taoiseach added helpfully. "And they are a band that might have been created especially for this heavenly endeavor of yours, for they have many sins to account for."

"Ui Garrchon," repeated Derval once more. "Now, I wonder if that could have been the empty clanstead I passed in the early hour of night, where the spiders had made their webs in the firepit and all the manure was dusty dry? Nay, it could not be Ui Garrchon."

"What is that?" The gray man spoke. "Cobwebs in the firepit?" He turned his suspicious glance to his taiseach. "Wouldn't it be like them? To raid before we could discover the move, and send us pelting over the night road to an abandoned dun?"

The chieftain looked undecided. The gray man bit his nails (like Johnny, thought Derval). The foot soldiers, one and all, stared white-eyed along the road Derval had come.

"Come," she urged. "I will show you the abandoned house and you yourselves may judge. But I must in truth warn you that we are like to meet the Gaill before we come there, for they cannot be now far behind."

"You are pursued?" The redhead started so that his horse shied.

Derval brushed her black hair from her face with both hands. "Noble sir, I do not stumble along the north road behind an ass's child in fulfillment of a penance!"

The taoiseach made an ursine noise in his throat and once more called upon physiognomy of Mary. "We have homes," he said. "And families left undefended against the scourge."

He swung his pony around on its hind feet. Then, remembering Derval's condition, he added, "Stranger, you are welcome to take your shelter with us, but pray God you do not bring the berserkers after you!"

The entire troop returned then the way it had come, the ponies pacing and the foot soldiers trotting with a will. Derval was left alone under moonlight.

MacCullen pressed his head against his mare's neck and allowed her to bull a path through the brush along which Ailesh and John followed, hopping and floundering. In the next whitewashed meadow the pony stopped, and feeling no hand upon the rein, put down her head to graze.

MacCullen rose and pulled twigs out of his hair. "Good old . . . Hah! I never asked your name. Well done, whoever you are, my pearl of price." He looked around him, saying, "Iníon Chadhain, you have good ears."

Ailesh was leaning against a tree, puffing hot, ragged breaths. John was pulling something out of the laces of his shoe. Balancing on one foot, he said, "She was ahead of you, eh, Olive? I never saw her anywhere else."

MacCullen shook his head blankly. "I turned first into the trees, because I had the only animal to force a path."

John looked back at the black hole they had ripped through the forest. "Oh shit!" he said in English, and he threw himself back along it. His arms up and out, warding off the branches, he looked like a running baboon. But in another second he was bowled over by the white mare, who was kicked whinnying into the forest, and MacCullen shouted, "God forgive me for an unfaithful fool!"

"He does very well for a fellow so sick," John said.

Ailesh peered into the gloom as the white rump bobbed and faded, while a cry of "MacCullen to Chadhain" echoed in the heavy air. "True," she said. "And although I do not belive the Bean Uasal Iníon Cuhain has come this cold distance to be bested by the small taraigeacht of Ui DunLainge, I am heartened to see Labres MacCullen for once acting the part of a poet."

John took the girl's hand as he picked his way by feeling into the brush of the woods. "He doesn't always?"

Ailesh made a noncommittal sound. "He is a learned man. His history is faultless and he is friends with all the people of importance, both among the Gaels and the Dublin Danes."

"But his poeting isn't very good, eh?"

She stepped up beside him. "MacCullen is a . . . considered man. His poems have never driven men mad."

John spit out a guffaw. "Thank God!" he said in English, and then added, to Ailesh, "I don't know what art is, but I know what I like."

"That is the beginning of all knowledge," Ailesh replied, and to the young woman's immense surprise, John doubled up laughing, and charged full tilt toward the road still doubled up, dragging her behind him. At last she broke free, bending his wrist around the trunk of a sapling. Their bodies continued in the arc imposed by the tree and met, chest to chest, with some force.

"You, on the other hand," she said, panting, "are a madman already." And Ailesh gave John a sweet, blundering kiss which caught only the corner of his mouth.

"Eh?" He stood absolutely still, with one hand around her waist, where the violence of their contact had carried it. "Eh?" His face was cut into scowling lines by shadow.

Ailesh turned away and floundered along the horse's trail, her short legs stepping very high. John, slightly dazed, had to follow.

Derval rubbed her eyes with three fingers of each hand. She seemed to have lost the hinny while talking to those silly Ui DunLainge men. What if it had followed the riders and was now a half-mile away? Shit.

But she heard a rustle and rummage in the trees to the left of the road. She pulled Muiregan out of a clump of briars and was only grateful she couldn't see her hands bleeding under the moonlight.

Now she had to stop and think about her companions. It wasn't pleasant thinking, for all evidence pointed to her being abandoned on the road. She imagined the lot of them, Johnny, MacCullen, and little Ailesh, tiptoeing away into the woods as she marched on, attached to the hinny's tail. But she couldn't believe that, and strange in her own mind, it was prickly MacCullen whom she could least see committing such a treason to friendship. Her mind instead filled with an image of giant black spiders depending from slimy cords in the trees to lift each of her compatriots to a terrible, shriveled death. It was *The Hobbit* she was thinking of, she told herself. Such giant spiders would not yet be invented for another thousand years. She dared to look up and saw the moon high, broken like china by the twigs of a dead oak.

She heard labored hooves again and leaned on the hinny's flank wearily, awaiting the night's next entertainment.

MacCullen burst out of the bushes eighty feet behind her. His pony came to an awkward, star-gazing stop. With his brat and long hair flying, the poet looked awfully large on that pony. Spotting her on the road, he swiveled the beast and it lunged toward Derval.

Another yawn came out of nowhere, but she smothered it. With a touch of surprise (strange—that anything still had the power to surprise her) she saw MacCullen fling himself upon the dirt beside her feet. "Woman, forgive me! It was not ingratitude but only confusion that caused me to fail you here, and I swear by the blood of Christ crucified and by his voice upon the storm of the water—I swear further by the bright edge of the sword of light—that never shall such shame fall upon me again!"

"Bright edge of wha . . . ?" began Derval, stifling a series of yawns as endless as waves of the sea. But she looked cannily at the white pony and amended her sentence. "You don't have stirrups."

Perhaps he hadn't heard her, for he still lay flat out upon the ground, with his face tilted upward, ever so oddly. Derval lowered herself down next to him. The ground was cold on her bottom. She heard her knees crackle.

"Don't . . . uh . . . fesh yourself about it," she said, shaking him by the shoulder. "Just explain to me where everybody went. And why you don't wear stirrups."

MacCullen crawled up on his elbows. He sat back, dusted the leaf mulch from his brat. "Why should I wear stirrups, woman? Am I feeble, fat, or aged, to need such a crutch? Or am I carrying weapons that require such support?"

"Only those feeble, fat, aged, or carrying weapons wear stirrups?" she asked keenly.

MacCullen blinked at her confusedly. "I simply tell you I do not."

She sighed. "Then it becomes hard to say who's the fool,

me or Sully," she muttered, not caring particularly whether the man heard or not. "Well, at least you can tell me where you all went." She glanced around. "And where Eoin and Ailesh are."

"They will come," answered MacCullen. By his beetled brow and thrusting lower lip, Derval judged the poet to be working up a case of the sullens. But hands rubbed his face into composure. "How did you escape the anger of the taraigeacht, Scholar? Or did you merely slay the lot of them?"

"Me?" Derval stood, noticing the hinny had begun to eat MacCullen's pony's tail. She separated the beasts. "I killed no one, Ollave. I merely sent them home. They had no bottom."

"No . . . bottom?"

Derval shrugged and tapped herself over the gut. "Nothing here to push with. Gave out before the race was half run." She stood by the pony's head and met its round, dark eye. She giggled. "I wish I had my horse, Ollave. I'd like to see your face when you see *him*! Now, he has bottom."

This time, MacCullen made no retort at all.

Coming off the *boreen* from Dun Dergne they heard the whistling, bells, and lowing of a small cattle drive. Ailesh called out in the darkness to the other, unknown group of travelers, and was told to hurry in front so they would not have to walk in the dust kicked up by the animals. She thanked the *buchalana*—the drivers—that they could not see in the shadow of the trees, and the three walkers and the Ollave on the horse stumbled forward. Once on the main road, MacCullen roused himself from the stupor he had fallen into long enough to call out a blessing to the courteous strangers.

"Thank you! I need your good words, noble person," the reply came back. "Today is my wedding, and this is the coibche of my beloved that we are hurrying on, here." MacCullen brightened up at that. "Then may it aid you to know that it's the blessing of a chief poet that falls on you today. May no weakness stain your bridebed or its children, strength to your piston."

A chorus of hearty cries answered him. "Honor me by eating with us at daybreak," the bridegroom called out as he rode from under the shadow of the trees into the pale starlight ahead of his company. "You and all your servants are most welcome to take food with us."

Derval smiled tightly. Of course the herders would make that mistake. MacCullen was mounted while they were walking. Derval waited to see if he would correct the man or revel in the aura of power and wealth of a man with three servants.

But MacCullen was not what his vanity made him seem, at times. Or he knew Derval would not let him get away with it. "We would be grateful for your hospitality. But we're in mortal haste. A lawsuit is taking us to Dublin today. These people are not my servants but companions in trouble. I am wounded and have been given the only horse left to us: my friends walk out of necessity."

The rider was so close now that they could see him in profile against the star-speckled sky. John thought his head seemed strangely shaped. Then he realized that the stranger was wearing a headdress. As he dismounted and walked a little way beside them, talking to the poet, John suddenly knew from the scent that he was crowned with a thick wreath of flowers. Light touched them and John saw the baby-pink ruffle of wild roses. The wreath looked incongruous to John over the fellow's brawny physique, but John shrugged his shoulders. Here was a people who went around all the time armed with mucking great axes, swords, and knives, and life seemed in constant peril. Yet men kissed, nudity was socially acceptable, and sexual intercourse might occur in public without interrupting the conversation.

The bridegroom got back on his horse. "I'm sorry for your trouble and I wish you were able to join us, for strangers can be good luck at a wedding. Good luck to us all anyway," he said in parting.

John, suspicious of his own understanding, turned to Derval and asked, "Nice and polite, but they don't want to know the name of the great poet who's blessed them. Maybe they don't believe a word of it, eh?"

Derval rubbed sand out of her eyes as she replied, "I think they believe him, Johnnie. It's hard to fake arrogance like our poet's. And I'm sure these folks would love to know his name. But they can't ask outright. Not till after they'd fed us, bathed us, and entertained us all the day would it be polite for them to ask. MacCullen could have told them, though, if he had wanted them to know."

John eyed the mounted man narrowly. "Could be he doesn't want to be known by the company he's keeping."

Derval's smile went tighter than ever.

The bridegroom had stopped and turned on his horse to have one last word. "If you expect compensation from Awley Sandal or his queen, you could wait a long time for it."

The poet fingered his reins in silence for a moment. "That may be," he answered the man firmly, "but if that's the case, I must compose such a black-boil-raising satire that he will be a laughingstock in Eire until the custom of speech dies out among humankind."

This speech seemed to daunt the bridegroom, for he backed his pony into the shadows again. "*Dia dhuibh,*" he said in farewell. "God be with you."

"*Agus aris oruv,*" replied MacCullen. "And with you."

Ailesh touched MacCullen's hand. "If you can stand it, we should quicken our pace. These cows give us an opportunity to cover our tracks."

MacCullen laughed smugly. "Your foster kin know quite well where we are headed. They won't have time to follow us, anyway. They're scuttling out of the way of the Ui DunLainge." He glanced down, then, to check whether his words had offended the girl, and added, "You're right in principle, Iníon Goban; we should not advertise ourselves, helpless as we are. But all roads in this part of the world lead to Dublin."

Their path led over the mountains for a while. The lowing, the bells, the whistling: sounds of the laboriously driven cattle continued behind them. Then the bridal party turned off toward the ocean, to the right and down, leaving them alone on the high path. Ailesh sang softly, "making the road short," as is said in Ireland now as then. Often Derval sang with her. When they were tired and became silent, MacCullen began speaking of the history of the land beyond them and where they were heading. He spoke of Bricru, the poison-tongued, blaspheming poet who demanded, in return for a verse, both thousands of cattle and to have the noblewomen of a whole province grind corn for him: a very insulting task. He told of how Bricru was stopped by the natural world itself at the ford of hurdles at the Liffey. "The waters of the river rose up and confounded him as a false poet. And the men of the South took back the cattle and their wives, leaving him with nothing to sop his pride. He was so ashamed that his face blushed as if it had been burned.

"And it stayed that way, night and morning, gray skies or blue. Even when he came back empty-handed to the kingdom of Ulster, he was red as a fresh firebrand. 'What happened to your face in Munster, Bricru? Did you suffer in the sun? Are you fevered?' Connocabhair the king would ask him, and never get an answer."

John listened to the half-understood words that rolled musically from the mouth of MacCullen. A few sentences, a phrase, a name, made sense to him, now and then. But the words, just as sound, were beautiful, soft and thick as the growl of the sea's wave receding over pebbles.

For the last quarter-mile or so it was a hard climb straight up. The first lightening of the sky made the mountain on their left visible to them. "This is Kilmasogue," Derval whispered to John. "We are six miles south of Dublin, as the crow flies."

They couldn't see anything new from the shoulder of the mountain; it was still too dark. The wind hit them, making the travelers wrap their cloaks tightly around their bodies. (Wherever one goes, winter or summer, the wind before dawn is cold.)

They began to go downhill. After a while MacCullen pointed to their left, to a dim heap of huge stones. "This is one of the beds of Diarmuid and Grainne," he said with authority. "It has a long passage inside it, and if you would like to get out of the wind, it would be a good stop to shelter ourselves. That pair was being pursued by their enemies and yet were not taken, so it's a place of good fortune."

Derval didn't like the look of it at all. She knew, of course, as MacCullen didn't, that it had been used for burials. She had read that in the archeological survey report. Ordinarily that would have made it more interesting to Derval, but since such strange things had happened to her of late, anything seemed possible. She might wake up among a people of stone axes, where she had neither language nor understanding. And besides that it looked spooky.

Among the many lessons Bridget had taught her the night before was the meaning of the word 'awe.'

"Let's go on," she said quickly.

"There would be no good in approaching Dublin in the

middle of the night. And I am fatigued," MacCullen said with infuriating finality. "A sick man can go only so far."

Derval struggled with herself. She didn't want to cross MacCullen again so soon, and for a moment she couldn't think of anything to say. Yet moment by moment she grew more obscurely terrified of the cairn. She—who had promoted herself as fearless. Derval sighed deeply, ashamed.

"Well, if you want to sleep on top of a dead man, that's up to you. I'll curl up under the trees."

"There are no dead men there," MacCullen said, gesturing broadly to the stones. "I would know it if there were, for I have by heart the Dinn Seanachus of this whole province!" His black eyebrows lifted under his fringe of light hair. "Can you say as much, Scholar?"

"No," Derval replied thoughtfully. "Not by heart. But I know nonetheless that dead men lie here, for it has been told me by teachers whom I trust, and it is *gaes* to me to sleep on a grave. Besides"—she fluttered her hands in a most uncharacteristic, feminine gesture—"you have women with you, who don't want to become barren. And you know that sleeping with the dead will do that."

MacCullen's tired face stretched in a grin, appreciating this act of helplessness for what it was. "If you fear spirits, woman, simply turn your cloak," he said.

"Turning your cloak is mere superstition," she replied, dropping into her usual brusqueness.

But MacCullen refused the side issue. "Where are these burials, Scholar? Show them to me and then I will believe."

Then Ailesh, standing beside them, shivered and crossed herself. "Do not ask that, Ollave! Derval is a woman of unusual knowledge. I beg you to give in to her."

"Give in? It is ridiculous!" MacCullen shook with frustration. "Graves unknown to learning and barren women . . . The truth is that women who have no children sleep here. They come up here with their husbands to get babies! That's how dangerous this place is to fertility."

Derval perked up. She stared at the poet for a few seconds while her brain made connections from her own childhood. Could a folk legend remain recognizable for a thousand years? She believed it could. "You're wrong!" Derval cried triumphantly, pointing due west. "I know of that place myself! Half a Roman mile is it from here, I'll place a bet, and it is a dulmen under the moon with no tunnel at all!" She saw doubt creep over his features and pressed her point. "I think your wound has changed your memory, Poet, for the spot you're mistaking this for is all the way on the far side of Kilmasnogue."

MacCullen sank back in the saddle as though he were a ball being ventilated with a pin. "The woman is right! By the naked saints, she speaks the truth and it is I who have misremembered!" he said at last. He slapped the pony's croup with his hand and it began to move slowly on again. They all walked on in silence for a while, then MacCullen looked down at Derval, who was holding onto the saddle blanket. "How many are buried there?" he asked quietly.

Derval opened her mouth to say there were a good score of people buried there, for Celtic oral history ran to round numbers—but instead she searched her memory for the right answer. After some work, she could visualize the page of the book which contained it. She answered, "There are seventeen men and women buried there. I don't remember how many of which."

"Christians?"

"No. From the ancient times." She considered how best to translate for him the idea of radiocarbon dates, and gave it up. "When Moses was in his cradle in Egypt. Before the Milesians came, these dead were old in their graves."

"I will remember that," MacCullen said with renewed satisfaction in himself. "What else do you know about them, there?"

"Nothing more. Wait—I forgot. Some are buried with their weapons, and these are made of stone."

He brightened further. "That is something. Stone. Indeed, I believe they must be old, for lore has it that the first people on the isle met the Milesians with nothing but stones for weapons. My ears hear truth, and I thank you for that. Who taught you these things?"

Derval hesitated only a moment. Her dedication to the idea of preventing time paradox had been all but extinguished by now, by all the needs of the moment. Let time take care of itself.

"A man named O'Roirdan taught me: a great scholar. And I heard it also from a Welshman named Eston Evans."

"O'Roirdan. Eston Evans. Where do these teach? In what sacred place?" Derval struggled for a response. Where were they, indeed, she wondered. Where are any of us before birth? "Neither of them are now living men."

MacCullen seemed unsurprised. "God to them." He nodded his head, murmuring softly. Derval watched his work of a practiced memory and knew that if ever he had occasion to recite what she had told him, he would finish with something like "And I heard this from Derval, the learned Iníon Cuhain, who heard it from the scholar O'Roirdan, and from Eston Evans, the Welshman."

She got goosebumps on her arms and her throat tightened. The mercurial flashes of this man's arrogance and humility caught her off guard. She did not yet feel she understood him, but more and more she wanted to.

She realized another thing about both MacCullen and herself. As she began to accept that he would not, under any circumstance of peril or personal gain, tell a falsehood, it was becoming difficult—no, impossible—for her to lie to him.

In the slowly growing light they walked on. The pony's head was drooped with effort. They were climbing again. This time no one sang. MacCullen was quiet, too, but Derval was not happy that she had silenced him. He had spoken for nearly two hours, reciting the memory of the countryside by heart. Did he really know the Dinn Seanachus—the old histories of the whole province?

She had no doubt of it. Yes, she too was a scholar, but her knowledge was in books. She knew where all the books were, and remembered little snatches like reference tags about each of them. MacCullen had the library in his head. Whole volumes leaped to his tongue when needed. This last incident, in which an accident of recall had saved her and put him to shame, had made her understand that difference, as she searched her mind in befuddled agony for the things she thought she had mastered. The way he had thanked her for what she knew—for her, till now, such things had just been data. To him, receiving the tradition from her was much more. To him, the transmission of fact and skill was a sacred thing. No wonder his person was sacrosanct, not for his own sake but for the treasure of human knowledge he carried. Killing him would be like burning the Alexandrian library. She shook her head at her own thoughts. How fragile. How fragile. How important that the knowledge not die with the man.

At true dawn, when the sun was touching the northern mountains, they came to the ridge overlooking the long valley of the river Liffey. The northern face of the Wicklow Mountains, grazed and logged bare of timber, looked over a sea of green oak forest, and wide, flat marshes with cleared farms here and there on either side of the river. Mist rose in transparent blankets from these lowlands, and the unbanked stream reached out in wide silver fingers for the sea. The low plains were still in blue shadow as the golden yellow light caught the smoke rising from the breakfast fires of little Dublin, a half-moon of what appeared to be hundreds of small brown and yellow-thatched boxes. A semicircular fortification encircled it all; the congested houses and streets packed tight around the black pool, the *dubh-linn* that gave the town its name; a natural tidal harbor, where the river Pottle joined the Liffey. From up there on the hill, the town looked like a big bitch on her side, with ships suckling her like pups.

Over to the left Derval saw smoke from other fires, from the houses of a separate village. It stood farther up the river. The great road running through it before it crossed the river. The tide being out, she could just see a shadow like a road bed on the surface of the flood plain. It was not a bridge but a wattle-bottomed causeway. Baile Átha Cliath: Town of the Hurdle Ford, the Gaelic town immeasurably older than Dun Dublin of the Strangers. Built at the meeting of the great roads there, it seemed to stretch toward but not to touch her newer sister. There must, Derval reasoned, be a church there (probably St. Mo Lua's), because the sweet, very faint ring of a bell reached her where she stood. The two communities, Gaelic and Gaill, seemed very separate, with the round houses and huts contrasting sharply with the rectangular roofs.

Around Baile Átha Cliath stood no wall, because she needed none.

Just outside the fortification, on the height of Dublin, on what Derval knew to be Christ Church Hill, where St. Auod's and the Tailors' Hall would be, was a complex of large buildings that looked as if ships had been turned keel up and used for the roofs. Barely discernible wisps of smoke rose from the louvers. "The hearth in the law hall of Awley Cuarán is never allowed to go out," Ailesh told them, proud of her own small learning.

Chapter Nine

•

Rise now in your force
With warlike, cruel wounding shield
And strong-shafted, curved spear
And straight sword dyed red
In dark gatherings of blood.
Tāin Bó Cúalinge,
Thomas Kinsella, trans.

It's a grand life, if you don't tire.
—Gaelic proverb

It was too bad about the women. Holvar splashed hot water over his face, then dipped his hands into the soft soap, first sparingly, then, thinking better of it, taking a generous handful for himself. Why not be luxurious, he thought. It had come cheaply enough. He soaped his face, arms, and neck and rinsed himself again. By Frigga, it was good to be clean again.

Yes, it was too bad they had killed the women, he decided. They would have brought a good price almost anywhere on the continent. In the Levant, or in Sicily or Gibraltar. They would have been worth a fortune. Had he known it wasn't the usual celibate monastery, he wouldn't have dedicated every living thing in it to Odin before the attack. Then that way . . .

He rubbed his arms and face dry on an odd, nubbly but soft cotton square that had been found in one of the two canvas boxes framed in metal, which had been otherwise full of cylindrical tin weights, like the anchors of small boats. Holvar wondered idly about the construction of both the boxes and the weights as he let the air finish drying him. This raid had been profitable, but he had to admit the killing of the women and children disgusted him. You are getting old, Holvar, he told himself. Still, he'd really wanted a fair fight; it was more satisfying that way. The frenzy that he worked himself into—the most sacred experience of his life—was not sustained without real risk to himself. Real danger. Unless he ended up bleeding a little himself, it wasn't worth it. "Blood bathed the bright-steel biter," he murmured inaudibly. "Hell has her horde increased."

He'd given his sword a good drink the day before yesterday, but he'd come out of the trance not at the end of the battle but just at the gate, before he could strike a single enemy. There was no barricade of armed warriors to hack through, just an old man raising his hand up as if to get the right to speak once more before being slain. The man's face had shown neither fear, nor anger, nor expectation of mercy, unlike the terrified eyes of the little boy, not more than four, that clung to his skirts. Then he had stopped, his sword frozen in the air, till another came beside him and the two Irish no longer existed. "Odin, this blood to you." He screamed the dedication. But for the first time, the ecstasy of destructive joy failed to cover the reality of what was done. Indeed, he still recalled the face of the tall Irishman upon whom he first wet his spear. Before he'd fallen the fellow had stared at Holvar as though he were so much dung.

For the next thirty minutes Holvar had murdered in utter sobriety. Even the woman he'd taken in the midst of the slaughter failed to move him. He killed and killed, more in fear of what his men would do if he failed, than because he wanted to. Fear of his men, and fear of his god.

I am being tested, he told himself, as he began to sweat, remembering the sun and the blood and the flies. Oh, the shit flies wallowing in the blood! His whole body trembled a little. He suddenly felt cold—cold in the morning sun. He thrust his hands into the heated wash water. That was better.

He is testing my faithfulness to him, the father of poetry. I've never before felt fear or revulsion like this. I must face it boldly. This is a part of a second initiation. A new stage has been reached in my priesthood.

He rubbed his chin. His tongue felt around his front teeth. I might be—once I overcome this—a greater man in his sight than before . . . a greater skald perhaps.

For a moment he felt better, bathing in the hope his

rationalization had given him. And then the terror was back: that somehow, the next time he put the wolf belt around his waist and chanted the seor verses, nothing would happen. Maybe he would never find the frenzy again.

"*Godi*? What do you think Einar is telling his old comrades now?" Holvar looked up to see Skully Crow squatting on his heels on the other side of the basin. "He must be talking fast and hard to explain how he got killed by a woman." The boy said it loudly enough to be a public joke. It occasioned lewd laughter and whistles.

Holvar smiled quickly. "He'll be asked if it was worth it, that's all." The godi must be first in wit, as well.

Every man of them was laughing now, even the dead Einar's closest friends. Part of Holvar's difficult task as leader was to keep internal strife to a manageable level. Sometimes he had to fight someone or just cuff them up a little, but if he could do it by turning aside an insult into comradely repartee, so much the better.

"I would bet she was worth it," Ospack the Old agreed. "She was a wild little mare."

"Was? She's alive, I'd guess," Skully chuckled softly. "I saw the whole of it, and I don't remember burning her! But a girl like that deserves life," he said with an air of genuine admiration. "If I had a woman, I would want her to be as good with a knife as Einar's Irish bitch."

Holvar stopped picking his teeth and looked over into Skully's face. The boy was grinning with pleasure at his reminiscence, totally unconscious of the underlying meaning of what he had just said. "No one was to escape!" Holvar shouted out, and leaped to his feet before the fire. "Why was she permitted to escape?"

Skully fell backward in his attempt to get out of the chieftain's way. "It was not my fault! It was the will of the gods! She must have been intended to survive."

"They were dedicated!" Holvar cried out. "Ulf! You were supposed to search for survivors afterward. You have failed me."

"Holvar!" Ulf spoke hurriedly. "I did search. There was nothing! What does it matter if she is gone? It's the same as if she were dead, and she would have only made a difficult slave. Their women are nothing but trouble."

"Are you so drunk you don't realize the truth? We've made an error that may cost us much. We must get out of here and keep moving now. I had hoped to rest in this place, isolated as it is. For weeks we might have sat here unknown, if we were sure no monkish visitor survived his visit. Instead, she or any others that made it out alive will raise the countryside against us." He threw his hands up in the air.

"How often do I have to explain that this is not just another raid. With Haakon's jealousy we can't go back to Norway!"

Holvar looked down around the fire again. Skully had recovered himself and was smiling, squatting on his heels like before. "Only a stupid man is happy to be rebuked!" Holvar muttered. Nothing was going well, he thought, as he sank back down in his place. He was beginning to be dissatisfied with the quality of men he was leading. This would never have happened—mistakes like this—among the others he had fought with. Maybe because it was too easy the other day, Holvar thought. It put us all off guard, and my discipline is falling apart.

Across the washbasin Skully Crow, known as Tooth Skully because of his broken front teeth, stared sullenly at the godi. Now the boy was angry. He was young and easily set off. At the same time pitifully eager to impress the older men. He hadn't liked being called stupid just now.

Of course, Skully hadn't liked it. He was an extra son—one too many for the size of the homestead. His plight was shared by many of the men there. Grudgingly given a place at his brothers' table, after his father's death, he stayed on until his idleness and drunkenness caused his mother and sisters-in-law to nag him and finally to beat him to do his share. One day the whole family turned on him and he threatened to go off reaving, never to return, only to find general agreement with this idea. "Now I can see what you are fit for, worthless, stupid thrall of a son," Mother had said. (There. That word "stupid," again.) "Good for nothing else!" his mother had shouted, as their slaves had grinned in mockery. "Be a thief! You are more afraid of work, even, than dying!"

Skully looked into Holvar Hjoer's eyes as if he would see out the back of the man's head. Then he pulled his sword out of its sheath slowly and shoved it back with a snap. Before anyone near them could see what had happened, Holvar moved in a blur and was back in his place. Skully was holding the very tip of his nose, which had just fallen into his hand. His mouth opened in amazement as the blood ran in streams down his face. Ospack the Old was bent over, head to knees, laughing. "Today, boy, you get a new nickname." He slapped the calves of his legs. "Our godi is named Holvar Sword. Don't forget that."

Not daring to show weakness, Skully managed somehow to smile, as he turned around and, taking a brand from the fire, seared the little wound closed. He only flinched a little as the fire touched him, looking at Holvar the whole time.

I'll have to kill him eventually, the older man reflected. This is what I get for taking an itinerant market duelist into my company.

Holvar stood up and turned his back on them as he walked into the woods. For a while—nearly an hour—he searched the land all around the monastery. By midafternoon he had found the creel, the bloodstains, and a bandage that had come loose and been overlooked in the escape, and the tracks of a small donkey or mule.

Holvar sat down in the booth of wattlework and watched the sun stream in broken patterns across his knees. Then, as he got up to go, he noticed a long strand of woman's hair, frizzy from braiding, caught on a snag on the bark. It was a rich, dark red-gold. "The girl in the sauna," he said aloud.

She and at least two others had escaped together. Somehow a part of him was glad, and then the other part of him, the part that was unbelievably tired, knew it would have to track them down.

Holvar grunted and ran his fingers through his limp, fine, nearly white blond hair. He had squarish hands, strangely delicate for all their strength.

We will bury the dragon beams in the woods, he thought. Hide the ships and go inland. What a shame, when he had been planning on a good month of rest.

Holvar had decided everything by the time he got back to the fire.

The sight rolling out before them, mixed with the warmth of the first sun on their hands and faces, kept the company rooted for a while. The only noise was made by Muiregan, who broke her long silence with a very asinine welcome of the day. The blue-eyed pony shook her head, as though she found the sound no more pleasing than did the human audience. Then, as the hinny prepared to continue her performance, Derval yanked the lead on her headstall and led the beast forward and down the hill.

Trees took them under again, robbing them of the feeling they had reached their goal. The speckles that were Dublin vanished, along with the dark Liffey and sparkling sea. John let out a grunt that was half a groan. Ailesh leaned on the pony's fat rump as they descended.

By nightfall, thought MacCullen, pulling his legs under the mare's sides to avoid the close-growing gorse, I will be dressed properly again in a clean, bleached *leinne* and a brat with a cotton lining. I will have my hair cut, I think. And a close shave with water almost blistering hot. Tonight my bed will be indoors and my tale will be Olaf Cuarán's worry.

He felt Ailesh's head against his side as the mare turned to the left along the descending path. My tale, but her tragedy, MacCullen corrected himself. I have lost a servitor, partner, and kinsman. The daughter of MacDuilta has lost all. The first pang of pity he felt for the girl echoed in his system long enough to spark from the poet the phrases "orphan child, crimsoned in her own bright blood" and "this daughter of art and beauty, naked upon the road." The poet had not seen Ailesh crimsoned in her own bright blood, nor naked upon the road, but he felt these images true to her condition and his mind hung over them, testing their effect, until by the great uprush of compassion for Ailesh that welled through him, he decided the lines were good.

He looked over his shoulder at Ailesh's frizzy head quite coolly, for the sight of his traveling companion could not move MacCullen half as much as the crafted words describing her. Her success with Cuarán would depend entirely upon his ability to move the king. Abbeys were torched every year, along this coast. Girls were raped and orphaned daily.

But they didn't usually have a Munster Academy poet to compose their stories.

MacCullen shifted forward on the mare's back and she paced the slightest bit faster. His challenge to the Dane king's justice had to be a great work. If it went well, it would increase his name a hundredfold. They would no more call him a speaker of learning and wit (mild praise), but instead a poet of divine passion. What else, when he stood there in his heavy wounds (and here MacCullen quailed within himself, because he felt very unsettled in this matter of his wounds.

Oddly enough, he felt guilty about them). In his wounds, bereft of kindred, new come from slaughter, with a poem on his lip—and for Cuarán it would have to be in the Norse language and form, striking its five beats like blows of Thor's hammer—a poem that would set Dublin in a month's amazement at least.

But how could a poet work under the leaves of trees in dappled sunlight, while swaying to the motion of a pacing horse and listening to birdsong? Impossible. He would have to find a room with a mattress for a few hours and pull the shutters on himself. Whose? Dublin was full of his patrons and associates, but the number of people before whom Labres MacCullen wanted to present himself in his present ragged condition, bearing with him two people whom Dublin would only see as a sort of rabble—that was small.

There was Alf Bjoergolfsson, Clorfíonn, the old *brehan* who had been his foster mother, and possibly Frodi the shipbuilder, who would not think the less of him for his condition. But the shipwright would hardly be home at the broad end of June, and Bjoergolfsson, if his memory worked correctly and the bride price had finally been settled, must have been remarried this last fortnight. That left Clorfíonn Iníon Thuathal. She was not rich, but she had enough, and the saints knew she was discreet. And she knew everything that blew in the wind around Dublin, especially concerning the court.

But as MacCullen decided his course, a high cloud obscured the sun and the dappled wood went chilly. It occurred to him that perhaps Iníon Thuathal would be away. Or would not welcome his plans. And he could not be sure a few hours would be long enough to compose. Perhaps he was not ready to create a poem to amaze Dublin. Perhaps Dublin itself (smart and cynical town that it was) had not the heart to be amazed.

And King Olafr, MacCullen remembered the last poem he had made for him, in which, by great wit and language, he had managed to describe the history of the king's line—the sons of Ivar losing and rewinning Dublin and York to the surrounding tribes, and intriguing, fighting for, and occasionally buying their way back with peace bribes—and conveying it all in a light that made them appear heroes. What a work that had been, and how much sweat it had cost him. (And all for Domnall's poor sake.)

Yet what had the Dane said? He had called MacCullen to

him, and his great wide face had smiled as he had said he had understood every word of MacCullen's Norse this time and complimented him on his more moderate use of skald's kennings.

Despite a weariness that covered him like a deep bed of briars, MacCullen stirred with remembered anger. And his confidence failed him as he remembered the blemish-raising satire he had promised to deliver—promised only bare hours before and in public—should Olafr fail his promises.

Yet why should he be expected to fail? A king need not be a scholar or a man of art in order to keep his promises. It was the job of the Ollave to show him his duty. Perhaps his greatest job. MacCullen pulled his brat tighter over his shoulders and road down through the morning chill.

Derval looked down at Dublin at the foot of the hill with a predatory exaltation. There, she told herself, in what looks (if I squint my eyes) like that town in Sweden, when I was eighteen and that bollox threw me out of his car when I wouldn't . . . and there was the village, only fifty little square houses and a petrol pump around a puddle-bay.

And there it is: Dublin. The crib sheet. The teacher's answer book. The smug refutation/confirmation of a hundred academic wrangles. There it is, and it might as well be Welsh, or Danish, or even Canadian, like the swamp hole where I found Johnnie and where Johnnie's father used to steam out in the evening smelling of engine oil and dead fish.

And there is the old, fat slatternly Liffey, brown even before she became man's char and his sewer, bulging out over her banks and making a dirty mess at the sea's edge. And that hill's the Tailors' Hall hill, the long Market Street visible as an open space even from where they stood.

And there was where the first bridge would be, in about forty years. Sitric, whose testicles haven't descended yet, will build it. And behind it—far behind it—the river wasn't peaty but light hazel, like Johnnie's right eye, and that round hill must be the Thingmount where the Norse have their assemblies.

She lifted her eyes to the north, across the river, and saw the slash and bare earth that would be Glasnevin, where she had been born, or would someday be born, or which was at least twin to the place of her birth. Ugly even then. All the stumps of cleared land alike, like row houses, and among them wandered cows dressed in dull, uniform black. In the middle of the waste was what appeared to be a monastery.

Derval swayed against the hinny. Dear God! What a fate for an historian. That she should see, hear, and touch all this, and none of it any use to her. Like receiving the answer to a math problem she hadn't the method to work out. It would do her no good with her peers to say she had seen tenth-century Dublin in a dream, visitation, or out-of-body experience. In fact, it wasn't fair to show her this, for it was Derval's job to dig for truth, either in old books or old mud, and the knowledge given freely ruined the work.

But when the hinny brayed and she pinched it on, her exhaustion made her feet stumble and the shade of trees brought miserable gooseflesh over her body. Free? Shit, she was buying this experience with her life, and it was only worthless because she could not get home, and would never be able to use what she was learning.

When the cloud covered the sun, Derval bowed her head, her eyes watering hopelessly.

Ailesh had been to Dublin before, on expeditions to buy iron tools or Italian alabaster, but it was no ordinary thing to visit the strangers' town. And she had never been there without her father. She watched the sun play on the bay water until her eyes smarted. Goban spoke the speech of the Danes, and it was always he who shepherded his daughter through the town, making jokes about how Dublin was a collection of outhouses.

Even when she'd been four years old she'd known that Goban's Norse was awful. She could see the way the Gaill—no, give them their name: the Dublin-men—smiled when he asked directions, and usually he would have to repeat his questions in a half-dozen ways before getting a response. But the smiles had been tolerant, for Goban MacDuilta dressed well, when not covered with stone dust, and the important people knew him and honored him as a carver of genius. And besides, Father's arms had been as thick as some men's thighs. No one ever made fun of him to his face.

During that first four-year-old's trip, young Ailesh had been presented to Awley and to Awley's queen, a pretty woman with yellow hair, who had smiled and called her (as Ailesh learned later) "the poor motherless chick with a little hammer in her belt."

Ailesh had never mourned the loss of the mother who had died in her birth, but now her heart quickened, and in her own mind she told the story of her father's death to the yellow-haired woman, and imagined her small eyes fill with tears. And Ailesh would tell the queen she still carried a hammer, and what use she planned for it. The girl's own sight swam, thinking of this. King Awley himself she did not include in her vision, although she knew it was to Olaf she must present her case. Little Ailesh had not remembered the king of Dublin at all.

It came to her with force that he, probably, didn't remember her either. And she did not speak the tongue of the Gai . . . the tongue of the Dublin-men. Did Derval Iníon Cuhain? Did Eoin Ban? She must not make the mistake of thinking that because they were foreigners, they would be able to understand all other foreigners. Though they were sent to her by heaven. Ailesh lifted her eyes toward heaven and found instead MacCullen, who rode before her.

The Ollave had been her father's friend. He spoke Norse like a native, it was said.

She wished she had not spoken so sharply to Labres MacCullen in these last days, for she felt entirely within his power. And she would have much rather been in Eoin's power, if she had to be in the power of a man. Eoin was her size. Like Goban.

A cloud covered the sun.

John looked at the little fishing village below them with the loose rafts of logs floating, and wondered what it was, and what that big, ballooning estuary that floated the logs was doing on the east coast of Ireland. Could such a bay have silted in entirely by modern times?

Could have, but probably didn't. With the distance they had come, it must be the realm of King Olaf Cuarán—king not of a country, but of a single city. Dublin. John stared at the river below, as at the face of a stranger who suddenly took on a familiar look. Was that—could it be—the same Liffey he had spat in for luck on the first day he arrived in Ireland?

(Goddamn waste of spit it had been.) Was that cluster of wood huts the biggest town on the island? The Micmac settlement where Grampa had retired seemed bigger than that.

Oddly enough, the realization of Dublin's insignificance put a broad smile on John's face. He let his gaze slide east, from the buildings to the harbor, where his vague eyes suddenly went sharp.

Those needle shapes weren't logs at all, but longboats. Dragon ships. Fifteen feet wide, he estimated, with no draft to them at all. Even from this distance he could see the bright splashes of color on them, the brilliant sails furled in lumps on the decks. There must have been twenty ships bobbing at the wooden docks, and half again that many pulled up on slick mud beside the water.

And the longboats weren't all. Here and there among the bigger craft were other vessels, some round as water bugs, that huddled together as though from fear of being pierced by the fierce needles of the Norse. Big coracles, he saw with blooming interest. The coracles were rolling and bouncy and so flat-bottomed they could navigate a bathtub, if they didn't spin one or throw one or turn belly up, as they would at a moment's notice.

These . . . Ye Gods—so many wild horses! John Thornburn felt a moment's hot desire to own one of the small round water bugs himself. He quickened his pace and went among the trees. When the sun went behind a cloud he didn't notice at all.

Holvar marched through the woods with an unusual grace, considering his short legs and wide frame. He felt his men at his back: a complex presence that tickled his neck. For a moment he was certain the the man behind him was Skully Crow and that he was getting closer. Too close. But he dared not look around lest he show weakness. He was uncomfortably aware how near he had been to losing his command that morning, when he told the men they must leave the ships behind. Perhaps it was only the bright weather that had saved him from insurrection. That and the support of five or six of the most respected fighters: Thorir and Ospack the Old particularly. These men were hounds of Odin, and the god must feel his own glory in them.

The man behind him was certainly drawing closer, and

Holvar put his hand in the most casual manner on his belt beside the hilt of his sword. But in another moment he let the fingers slide free, for in the footsteps he noticed a slight hitch, a fault in rhythm, and he knew it to be Ospack.

Holvar turned to catch his eye, and between them they shared their knowledge of how near a thing it had been. But Ospack smiled through his faded chestnut beard, and wrinkled the scar that ran along his scalp like an exaggerated part in the hair. "Cheer, Godi! Maybe these dark woods will open to a sweet and succulent city, filled with things to eat and drink."

Holvar snorted. "The Irish do not have such cities. They live wholly like beasts in the wood, in houses like that big corncrib we just burned."

As though the chief hadn't spoken, Ospack continued. "And maybe when we find this city, the godi will not feel it necessary to dedicate every good thing in it to the god, but will allow his poor ship-brothers some share—"

Holvar winced. "Ospack, Ospack! Is this necessary? Do you think me a fanatic of some kind? Remember the loot of Northumbria!"

Ospack's smile grew gentler. "Indeed. The harvesting of Northumbria. I wonder how it slipped through my fingers?"

"You traded it for the greatest paunch worn by any—" Holvar stopped in midsentence. He came to a dead halt and his eighty men pulled up in confusion behind him. "Horses," he whispered.

In another moment all heard the drumming on the earth. "Little horses," added Holvar pleasantly. His smile drew as wide as Ospack's. He waved his men back.

Three gray ponies appeared on the road before them, shining white in the light of midday. One of them wore a rug of blue and crimson, and on it sat an Irishman in a yellow *linnia*, his yellow hair tightly curled. This one called out, and the words no one could understand were filled with alarm. Holvar's smile was beatific as he strolled forward. "Pretty bird," he whispered to the rider, "I killed my fear and buried it at the roots of a tree when I was thirteen years old. It is unfortunate that it is too late for you to do the same."

From a loop on his saddle rug the Irishman pulled a dull iron ax. One of his companions did the same, while the other hefted a slim, pale spear, bright-headed. Ospack moved behind Holvar, but only to keep the rest of the Vikings back.

For a moment the three riders loomed above Holvar Hjor, while the leader of them stared in horror at the mass of armed Norsemen blocking the Sliege Dala. Then he spoke a word and all three ponies spun in place.

Holvar drew his sword and made two strikes. The leader's white pony crumpled, both hocks cut cleanly. In an instant the rider with a spear had reacted. Holvar saw the delicate dart, shining like a ray of light, and he stepped to the right just as much as was necessary. For good measure he cut the shaft in two pieces as it went by. He heard his men cheering.

The remaining rider was having trouble controlling his mount, which reared in terror at the cries of the downed pony beside it. Holvar slipped in under its feet and stabbed it in the belly. He cut off the foot of the rider as he darted out.

By now the first man had slipped off his disabled horse. He raised his long-handled ax against Ospack, but the old warrior merely blocked and led him back toward his godi.

Holvar was overjoyed to come to grips this way, on foot and weapon to weapon. With the gladness filling his face he thanked the Irishman and feinted with his sword. The axman took the blow on his weapon's oak handle and let the force of it carry the iron head in a circle, aimed at Holvar's head.

A helmet of boiled leather and iron strips might turn a sword stroke, but never that of an ax. Holvar was careful to step out from under the ax as it fell. Almost without conscious thought, he struck his blade across the Irishman's unprotected stomach as he did so. Then, out of consideration for his foe, he took off the man's head before he could see his own guts spilling out in front of him.

Perhaps the spearman had no other weapon and didn't know Holvar would have been happy to lend him one, for he turned his back on the carnage, kicking his pony into a gallop. Holvar looked over his shoulder with a face set with disgust and boredom and at least ten spears, propelled by leather throwers, leaped after the fleeing Irishman. Three of them found their mark, and another two entered the broad back and croup of the pony, which screamed.

Holvar glanced around him to see the second of the riders, the man who had already lost a foot, dragging himself upright by the trunk of a sapling. Bled white already, he was, and soon to die, Holvar noted, but still gripping his horse-soldier's long-handled ax. Holvar stepped toward him, to cut his sufferings short, when the man raised the ax against him. "Do you plan to throw that at me?" Holvar murmured softly. "Well, good luck to you."

The man aimed, and Holvar stood rock-square before him, giving him his chance. It wasn't much of a chance, because the weapon was not at all designed to be thrown, but Holvar approved of the fellow's spirit. But the throw that came was not what he had expected, for at the last minute the Irishman shifted and sent the clumsy missile not at Holvar but into the middle of the crowd of watching Norsemen. The Vikings scattered, their yelps of dismay turning into rowdy laughter. The ax hit flat against Thorir's shoulder point, and Thorir swore good-naturedly. The dying man bared his teeth at Holvar, who took careful aim and stabbed him in the heart.

Then Holvar was surrounded by his men like a warm cloud of love and approval. Respectful hands clapped him on both shoulders. He said little, but rubbed Thorir's bruise in comradely fashion. Thorir was still laughing about his own slowness.

"They will follow their godi anywhere," whispered Ospack to Holvar, a hint of slyness in his voice. Hovar's own glance was dry. "Odin has been very good to me this morning," he replied.

In another quarter of an hour the path was empty. In the bushes on one side lay the severed heads and the cooling bodies of men, while hidden in a declivity on the other lay three ponies, tangle-legged, their pretty white heads encircled by rings of red. The flies came.

They passed unchallenged through the stockade wall down where the river Pottle emptied into the pool that formed the harbor beside the Liffey. MacCullen was waved through. At the gate, the dirt road ended abruptly. John stumbled against the wooden sill and fell face flat onto the paving with a cry, almost breaking his nose on the rough surface of the logs. "Oh! Oh Jeezus," he moaned.

"Honest to Christ, John," Derval snapped angrily. "Watch your bloody feet!"

John struggled right up again. Ailesh looked hard at Derval. "He's your husband. You should not speak to him like that."

"He's not my husband," said Derval nervously. "We're . . . pals."

"But he has the friendship of your thighs, my sister?"

"Well, yes."

"It's not my place to tell you," Ailesh apologized, "but even if no cattle have been given, there should be honor between a man and woman who sleep together."

Derval opened and shut her mouth several times but couldn't say anything. For a moment she struggled with embarrassment, then forgot all about it, as Dublin drew her attention and held it.

They were below Christ Church Hill now, approaching a stretch of water that would be gone in later times, and all the busy activity of commerce was going on around them. They passed through a sort of open area. Derval guessed it to be the lower part of High Street. Then they descended to the harbor.

The houses and ships were all of wood. Wood greased and pitched sometimes, but mostly the natural color of wearing, silver-gray to brown. Here and there a brilliantly painted gable ornament displayed the townhouse of a rich person. But those were few: paint was costly. Walking carefully over the bumpy pavement of close-set logs, they had to maneuver around a work line of stevedores who were unloading a great longship. No, Derval realized, it wasn't a longship. It was a *knorr*—a cargo vessel—the real work vessel of the Norseman. Broad and deep-bellied, with a bow that suggested the bosom of a well-endowed matron, it could carry the contents of a good-sized farm: food, household goods, and people, and even some livestock. There were far more of these resting against the Dublin mud than the elegant, slender dragon ships, with their gilded wind fans, suitable only for travel and war.

The men in the cargo line passed the bundles to each other, the last man ordering it on top of a wagon and a sleigh that stood next to it. As he did so he called out a phrase to a well-dressed fellow with a waxed tablet and a stylus who was keeping account. He stood between the two vehicles, and Derval noticed with some surprise that his hair style and clothing looked Byzantine. Of course, how stupid of me, she thought quickly, he had been in the service of the emperor in Constantinople. He was probably part of the Varangian guard:

they were all Norse by the time of Harald Hardraade. "But that's a long time to come. This is nine eighty-five," she whispered to herself. "Ethelred the Uncounseled is king of England. Maelsechnaill is Ard-Ri. Domnall Cloen is king of Leinster." Her head swam, as they passed the clerk with the tablet and stylus. Probably a king's man, she thought. Olaf Cuarán, I understand, is/was a man of business before anything else.

"A shrewd man of commerce," MacCullen said in her ear. "That's what Olafr Sigtryggsson is. And the way we deal with him must take that into account."

Derval grinned and shook her head to hear him echo her own thought.

Looking down the street in the direction of the sea, Derval was struck by the way Dublin—or Dyflinn, as she knew the Gaill called it—resembled a traditional village in White Russia or the Ukraine. The houses were squarish or rectangular, all with peaked roofs: some flat, others bowed. Bands of fancy carving decorated the edges of the roofs. Carvings of animals and birds adorned the peaks. The dacha—the Russian farmhouse—she understood now, was descended from these. And hadn't some of the fathers of the Vikings called themselves the Russ? Didn't "Russia" originally mean the "land of the Swedes"?

It was busy here next to the black pool. It was a market, of course: the *margad*, as the Irish called it. Who would want to haul merchandise a long way from the ships, to sell it? Cloth, animals, food, craft items, were offered everywhere, right from the vessels that had brought them, from wagons, from the backs of animals, and from baskets on heads.

Dahomey by the Liffey, thought Derval.

It was slow going through the press of people. A woman in Norse dress—in pleated shift, embroidered double apron, fastened with heavy round buckles that made her look like she had an extra pair of breasts—walked by with a basket full of smoked salmon dipped in honey and salt. Derval could see the pink flesh, brown on the edge from the fire. Her mouth began to water; the smell was luscious. She didn't think she'd ever been so hungry. The woman, noticing her interest, walked up and began haggling, offering different-sized pieces and stating what she wanted for them. But before Derval could say anything, MacCullen told the woman that they weren't really interested, and she turned away quickly, giving Derval an angry look because she had wasted her time. Derval almost burst into tears. She was going to scream at MacCullen, but was stopped in midutterance by the sight of a beggar, right arm and left leg missing. The other, remaining limbs were powerfully built, and he had clearly been a man of the sword and the oar. The cripple called out to the crowd in guttural Norse.

So this was the end of unsuccessful Vikings—to drag out one's days near the ships one would never sail again. Was he a drunkard, cadging jars in the local alestalls? So it seemed to Derval.

But a small group of people gathered around him as the four travelers moved off. He collected coins and then began chanting a long poem. A town skald: a public storyteller, he was no beggar after all. Yet how different, Derval thought, this man's fate, from the famous heroes of the saga literature. No vellum book would carry the deeds of this poor fellow. His "victory luck" had failed him. He would never enjoy the dignity of a big farmer chieftain back home in the North.

She had another insight. In the year nine eighty-five, the indomitable, almost satanic Egil Skallagrimsson was growing old in Iceland. In a few more years his sight would fail him and he would be bullied and tormented by his own servants and relatives. No. Perhaps their fates were not so dissimilar after all.

In the Norse world, it was a bad thing to grow old and helpless. Among the Gaels Derval had seen in the dun of Ailesh's foster kin, it was somewhat different. The old were treasures, adorning with their years the bright energy of the young people whom they counseled, supported, and restrained. But then, the Gaels never seemed to be alone in the same way the Norse were. A Norseman was a man apart, putting his personal loyalty where conscience or profit told him. When he was ruined, he could easily find himself without support. The kinbond of the Gael was stronger. The *dirbfine* would never let him sink to a gutter seat like that one. They would have come for him long ago, brought him back to the hearth, still a man among brothers, whatever fortune had done to him.

* * *

John scanned the boats. He hardly noticed the people or houses. His eyes widened at the perfection of a magnificent merchant vessel, the planks sweeping in rhythmic curves to form the hull, the line rushing, it seemed, upward to join at the omega points of the keel ends with their carved beasts. Above it a huge brightly painted sail was unfurled across the deck. A pair of riggers, one on each side of the sail, with their needles and leather palms (tools changed almost not at all in a thousand years), searched for flaws against the morning sun and mended them.

John turned and saw the cripple too. It made him remember a popular song from Nova Scotia about pirates. "God damn them all, I was to sail/ The seas for American gold./ Fire no guns and shed no tears,/ Now I'm a broken man on a Halifax pier,/ The last of Barett's privateers." John was not shocked. This was the way of the world; he knew that well enough.

His eyes went back to the ships again. They followed the line of a mast upward. He had seen a man break his back upon a deck—a man who'd been trying to free up the seine lines from the net struts and who fell. That man still sat near the boats in his battery-driven wheelchair every day. On the dole forever. "Dead from the waist down," John's father had said.

"I'm on easy street," the injured man told his old friends in the local bar. "I live like a fucking king. I pity you poor bastards." He laughed, smoked his cigarettes, and rolled down to the wharf to watch the ships come in, looking out to sea, always.

Among the bigger vessels were many smaller, more archaic boats and skiffs. One reminded him of a sampan; it was low, shallow, and flat-bottomed, built of moss-caulked planks, with a tongue of wood at the bow that went straight up onto the mud. There were skin boats of all kinds, besides the small, round coracles. There were larger, bull-hide curraghs: one he saw was thirty five feet long, with a cross at one end and a cow's skull on the other. Several cattle lay bound up in it, feet together, ready to be sold for meat and hides.

It was leather, tanned and untanned, that had given the king his Gaelic nickame: Olaf Cuarán—Olaf "Sandal." He had a state monopoly in shoes over the whole area, and though the ones in the king's cobbler shops were for export, and of good enough quality, intricately colored, stamped, and slashed, as often as not, the *cuarán* was the footwear of slaves and ditchdiggers. It was the uncured hide knotted or bunched with hairy thongs. This was the thing they called him, because they hated him.

John saw a vessel that made him stop in his tracks in awe. It was not docked, but out in midstream. The craft was only twelve feet long or so, and a young man and his companion pulled it against the current with long paddles. The sun was behind them and the transparent skin of the little boat shone as if it were filled with light. The dark ribs of the supporting structure made blue shadows. A strange, Y-shaped projection was the only decoration of the bow.

"It's like an Inuit boat—a *ummiac* from Greenland," said John aloud. "I don't believe it." He watched in fascination as the young men paddled strongly past and disappeared. When he turned around to share his excitement with the others, he found he was alone.

In dismay he looked down at the line of medieval garbage, lapping against the bank. Scraps of fish guts, a bread crust, a rag, a drowned kitten . . . Sea gulls were eating of this noisily. A floating turd bobbed past. Reality smelled bad.

It was the smell that verified to John he was in Dublin. A thousand years had produced no change in the silty, dead-minnow smell of Dublin harbor. He stood with his hands in his jeans pockets, his brat hiked up to his hips. The glitter of the water held him, with no thought in his head.

It was so easy for John not to think, when thought might be unpleasant. He'd been practicing all his life: doing boat chores, cleaning fish, reading schoolbooks with unfocused eyes. Sometimes he got by in that manner; John (said his father) was the only boatman who could pilot reliably in and out of the Grand Banks while staring straight at the sky. (Looking like a stunned ox, the elder Thornburn usually added.) Sometimes, as in the tests at school that followed the blind study, he did not get by. But this misty trance state was the flip side of his ability to draw—or at least he liked to believe it was—and he usually let it have its way with him.

Therefore it was nothing unusual for John to turn around and discover that he'd lost all three of his companions on the way down to the town. Nor was he upset to discover this. John's usual vagueness, abetted by trauma, overwork, and undersleep, led him to proceed quite casually down to the waterfront in the Viking town, leaving to his friends the job of finding him.

And there was nothing about this little wooden town to break the trance. Here there were no riven bodies, no men in helmets of flowers, no herds of archaic great-horned cattle. Here was a straight though rutted single-lane street. Here was a blond boy with a stick, hitting the corner of a building with great concentration, making the usual private vocal accompaniment that boys make when engaged in such activity. There was another man, half-bald and half-dressed, rolling a barrel that John's nose told him contained beer.

John Thornburn stood in the street and whimpered to himself. Had he been suddenly possessed of the sea-going coracle he had lusted after so recently, he would have traded it for a single tall glass of that beer. Joyfully traded it, along with his pants and jumper.

He followed the man with the barrel, not so much in an effort to find where it was going, but because his thirst gave him no choice. The great heavy thing rumbled down the dirty road until it became lodged in one of the ruts. John found himself helping the bald man work it free. This was not a trivial task, and the effort cost John dearly; he could feel his heart pounding and his lungs laboring as he docilely applied himself to rolling the barrel down to the docks. Neither he nor the bald man spoke a word.

This barrel had become the center of John's existence, and when it rolled away into a house of bare wood, he simply had to go with it.

Even John had to duck down a little to go through the door. The dim light, which came through the raised roof louvers, showed him a long rectangular room, half-filled with drinking men. Along the center ran an open raised hearth whose smoldering peat fire sent smoke up into the eaves where it hovered among the dark wooden beams for a while before being driven out by the breeze. Sheets of flat bread hung in garlands from the ceiling, with strings of sausages and net bags of onions and garlic. A girl was chopping kale with a big knife. She looked up briefly and grinned at him, tossed her greasy brown braid over her shoulder and went back to work. There was a huge cask, identical to the one

John had helped to roll, but this one was settled and open, and the bald man set to filling horns and jugs from it. John could smell it all the way across the room, and knew it had to be something alcoholic. By sympathy with his nose, his eyes watered. The floor around the cask was so impregnated with the barley malt that the white oak had turned ale-brown.

The publican was taking coins and bits of coins and weighing them on a small scale. John reached into his pocket and took out an Irish shilling piece. He looked at the bullock, and turned it over to show the harp. It looked like silver; he would chance it. Bravely he walked up to the beer drawer, pointed to the barrel and a pint jug, and held up his index finger for "one." He fixed the bald man with his odd eyes (which held no hint of vagueness in them at all) and said quite clearly, "Eh?"

The fellow extended his palm. John put the shilling in it. At first he smiled, and then his brow wrinkled. Quizzically he examined the shilling, and bounced it against an iron plate. The sound was not satisfactory. He handed it back to John and shook his head. But with a smile of some apology he scooped curds into a bowl and said, "Take this for the help you gave me."

Curds were welcome, but not the desire of John's heart. He pointed once more to the ale cask. "I'm sorry, my friend," the publican said in Irish almost as heavily accented as John's. "You've been cheated."

John replied, "*Ni Tigim.*" I don't understand. In truth he did not understand a word of the man's base Irish.

"Your coin is worthless, you poor fellow. Don't try to pass it in here again. Don't you have something else?"

John gesticulated frantically. "*Ni Tigim.*"

The publican was not a hard man, nor was he one to be duped, either. Still, he had learned the importance, in an age when most people carried weapons, of not giving direct offense. Gently, with an air of fraternal sadness, he pressed the coin back into John's hand. John looked at it in shock, realizing his poverty for the first time, and then he dug back into his pocket and took out the rest of his coins. He spread them out on the table and gestured toward them. The barkeep sighed heavily, but when he leaned over he brightened up as if he had suddenly understood something. To John's amazement, he chose two of the huge, solid copper pennin, and smilingly handed over to John a big *mether* of ale. John took the ale and the curds with his mouth hanging open. "The buttons are truly lovely," the man said. "And well worth ale here. Pick yourself a couple of plump sausages to go with the curds." He split his beard-bottomed face in a grin and punched John in friendly fashion on the chest.

John hadn't understood much of what the man had said. The Gaelic was too mixed with Norse slang for him to get the drift of it. Holding the jug and the bowl he picked his way across the room to a corner. There weren't really any empty areas, and he wasn't sure about pub etiquette in these parts.

He took a long drink of the ale. It was not cold, but cool enough for enjoyment. He held it up and let a sunbeam from the louver fall into the vessel. It was clear, deep amber brown. No floaters and a good head too. It was a bit more "green" than he was used to, but Goddamn, eh? At this moment he didn't care.

The floor of the outer room was good packed earth, smooth as marble. The walls were raw split oak, devoid of decoration. John stared disapprovingly at them, thinking how they could be improved. Such thoughts led to a reminisence of the time he, a thirteen-year-old Thornburn junior, had added great improvements to the wall of the town bus station: improvements consisting of three nude mermaids and a complete flotilla of PT boats (he had come oversupplied with gray acrylic). But this pleasant memory led to one nearly connected, which involved a police station uglier than the bus station by far, and the rope-hardened hands of Mr. Thornburn senior. It was better to control artistic fervor than talk through loose teeth. John yawned, feeling the ale, and forced his eyes upward.

Around the discolored hole in the floor were assembled five low benches. So close to the earth were these, that the sitters upon them carried their knees by their chins, as did those who merely squatted on the floor. As many, however, were lying along the benches as sitting upon them, and almost as many sprawled on the floor by the smoldering wood fire, elbows propping their heads.

John, numb-cold as he was, was kept away from the circle of heat by that sense of disbelonging which hits a man who comes into any neighborhood pub, and which lasts until the first local decides to make a grunt or stare in his direction. He slid down against the grainy wall, using it to counterfeit the Indian squat he had lost through years of sitting at a drafting stool. He glanced covertly at customers of the ale house, avoiding eye contact that might be mistaken for a challenge.

He was the only human being in the room who was not visibly armed. Even the cook's girl, who was quite possibly a slave, had a knife. For the first time since he left Newfoundland, he took his little clasp knife case out of his pocket and fastened it on the outside of his belt. He felt very self-conscious doing this, and even more nervous about opening it, as he had to do to eat the curds. He accomplished his deed under the table, only to meet the eyes of a large, russety man sitting at his left, who grinned slyly at him, as though understanding all. He began to nibble at the curds, lifting them up with his knife blade, and following them with swigs of ale. At last he dared look around at the other customers of the alehouse.

Ye Gods, what an assorted lot. The only thing they had in common was being, as far as John could tell, all male.

The Irish he'd met so far in this time had seemed like so many pedigreed animals, so much did they resemble one another: biggish, square-set, more chubby than otherwise, with fair to brownish hair. Ailesh was small, certainly, and MacCullen not so broad of face as the usual, but as a rule they were comfortably the same.

That fellow over by the carefully locked back door of the room had olive skin, that one could see even by the poor light of roof louvers. And his high-bridged nose turned under in a lovely curl into his nostrils. He had no more shoulders than Derval. His drinking companion (each kept a jealous hand on one handle of the four-sided cup) had features equally Mediterranean, as well as kinky black hair kept back by a great deal of grease. Idly John wondered whether such toiletry might not attract flies. After careful observation, he decided that indeed it did.

Whether the very dark man who hugged the fire between his gaped knees also had the usual kinky hair that accompanies that complexion John could not tell, for everything about the man was hidden in blue gauze except for his face, and the upper part of that was concealed by an awning of the same material. But his nose and mouth managed to express an entire physiognomy's worth, for the nose was pinched and the lower lip protruded aggressively. He wore a heavy Irish brat over his gauze (also blue) and over the whole, a heavy, curved sword.

That scimitar itself did not bother John Thornburn. He had seen many horrific instruments in the last few days, as well as discovered the possible violence of his own favorite tool, the stonemason's hammer. But the combination of that oversized fish skinner with the man's jutting lower lip he found disturbing. John made of himself a very small package against the wall of the alehouse and determined to do nothing obtrusive. His determination was strengthened at the sight of another scimitared fellow sitting across the firepit from the first. This man was not so black as the Moor, but his face was equally forbidding. He wore a turban, pegged trousers, and so many gold rings they coated his fingers like a suit of armor. His disagreeableness seemed centered on the blue man, and as John observed in mouselike silence, this Turk gave utterance to words that ignorance of language could not diguise were meant as an insult.

The Moor's reply was equally incomprehensible to John, but delivered in tones of threat. John turned to his left-hand neighbor for enlightenment, but the ruddy fellow merely widened his blue eyes and hefted up his shoulders to display his own ignorance of the dispute. John looked back at the disputants just in time to see the blade of the Turk's scimitar catch in a stream of sunlight as it slipped past the dodging Moor and toward the unsuspecting face of John's neighbor.

John leaped up as though he were playing lacrosse, a game at which he had once had some expertise, stopping the bright damascene steel with the edge of his wooden trencher. The blade caught, and the swordsman lost his balance, rolling over onto the floor, the bowl burst into two pieces, spraying everyone, including the two Arab-speakers, with curds.

"Pimp and son of a pimp!" screamed the Turk, as he flung himself again upon the Moor. "Your head be a sacrifice for all true merchants!"

"Out! Out of here. No duels in my house!" bellowed the landlord. "Get out—you're breaking the market peace!"

But the Saracens were deaf to him. The struggle moved toward the hearth, with the combatants chasing one another around the four king-posts of the house which stood at the four corners of the hearth. The two of them were a swirl of cotton robes and razor-sharp blades. Everyone who could not get out immediately plastered themselves against the wall to prevent being sliced. The servant girl hid behind the open cask.

Suddenly a point of stalemate was reached. For a moment one combatant was on each side of the fire. They circled each other, teeth gritted, eyes bugged with fear and anger, blades raised. Then the Moor swung over his head, cutting the bread rope, which came crashing down on his enemy, and while the Turk tangled with that, he escaped into the street. Two heartbeats later the Turk followed him, shrieking his battle cry. It was over.

The publican, standing in the middle of his disordered room, said quite calmly, "That Moor thinks fast." The greasy-braided servant girl began to pick up the bread. John felt a heavy hand on his shoulder, and turned to see the big man who had been sitting next to him. He had a fiery red beard, brown hair, and perfectly round blue eyes.

He smiled fiercely, but his embrace was warm around John as he said in Norse, "Thank you, my friend. You saved my life." The fellow clapped enormous horny hands on John's shoulders. He had cheeks as red as his beard and slightly protuberant lips that were even more red. "My name is Snorri Finnbogison. I'm from Eyjafjord in Iceland."

John, though taken aback and speaking no Norse, knew at least that he was expected to introduce himself. He pointed to his breastbone. "John Thornburn of Newfoundland."

"Oh. Jan Thorbeorn." The big stranger grinned. John tried to correct him several times, then gave it over as hopeless. Snorri took over the conversation. "I knew a Thorbeorn at Hafurbjarnarstadir. Is he akin to you?"

John shook his head blankly.

"No? Well, that's all right. Sit down and I'll make up for the loss of your meal by buying you something far better." He pressed John back down onto the bench, and, brushing curds out of his beard, called for the alewife. He spoke to her for a moment, and then turned to John and began a long rambling speech. He seemed unperturbed by John's minimal, uncomprehending response.

John began to gather here and there, from individual words (and by the fact that Snorri talked with his hands), that the man had been shipwrecked. He heard *Grenlandinga* and over and over again *wormener*.

"Wait!" John cried out in English. "Worms. Toredo worms. You lost your ship to toredo worms, eh?"

Snorri laughed aloud. "You do not speak my language, yet you seem to understand me a little. Are you from the Anglander Dane-law?"

"No. *Nei.*" John had heard the word "Anglander." "You Graenlendingur, eh?" And he pointed north and west. Snorri looked astonished, and then smiled and grinned. "So you have heard of it?"

"Yes. Uh, *ja*." John was now feeling a frenzy to communicate. He gesticulated for Snorri to sit where he was, jumped up and searched the hearth until he found a slip of charcoal from among the kindling wood. On the table he began to draw a longship. He drew worms eating it. He looked at Snorri, pointing to the drawing. "Wormener, eh?"

The Norseman nodded and grinned.

John drew a pine tree, drew the process of pitch extraction, showed with round still and fire how turpentine could be made from it, drew the extraction of lye from ashes of the fire, showed the distillation of alcohol from barley, and then indicated that his mixture should be painted on the hull to repel parasites. Such was his gift, that without language of tongue or body language, he explained the process to Snorri. "No more wormener," John said to him, and dusting the charcoal from his fingers, began enjoying the cheese, apples, butter, loaves, and meat that his new friend had provided for him.

Snorri sat in silence for a moment, knuckle in his mouth, then embraced John again, who nearly gagged on his food in surprise. "You are an openhearted and good man," said Snorri earnestly. "Not only have you saved my life today, but you have given me, a total stranger, a precious secret of your trade. I am ready to swear lifelong brotherhood with you!"

Chapter Ten

•

May the Gods get rid
Of this ruling reaver!
Let the heavens hang him
For highway robbery.
Egil's Satire Against
the King of Denmark
Translators: A. Palsson and P. Edwards

"A corduroy road, Johnnie. What do you think of that?" Derval tapped the first log with one sore toe and turned to find Ailesh and MacCullen staring without comprehension. She stepped around to see whether the small Canadian was concealed behind MacCullen's pony. The hinny bawled protest, for Derval had not released her hold on the animal's tail. "Where'd he go?" she asked in Irish.

Both Ailesh and the poet looked over their shoulders. MacCullen rolled his eyes in his head ludicrously. "Abducted by a cow again, no doubt," he said.

Derval put her knuckles in her mouth and turned away from the ships and water, back into the crowd through which they had just passed. There was no blond figure in trousers and heavy brat to be seen. No friendly face save that of a smiling pigherd beating his charges along with a thorn stick just behind them. Nothing but cows far away on the long grassy decline to the Liffey. Nothing at all on the straight sweep to the eastern sea. Her perfect fear for him turned into perfect anger. "Shithead," she announced. "Absolute shithead action. Just like Johnnie."

MacCullen smiled at her heat. "But Scholar, what do you expect? Our Eoin is no ordinary man, I have it on authority. And I myself would be willing to wager that he returns to us, and in better state than when he left."

The authority's cheeks grew as red as her kinky hair, and she shot a glare at MacCullen. "I don't think anger is the proper feeling to show, Bhean Uasail. After all—not eight hours ago it was you who were lost."

Derval blinked, remembering. "That's right." But then the memory came in full and she added, "But about my getting lost: I think I could perhaps phrase that another way."

MacCullen nudged his pony between the women. "Perhaps you could, Iníon Cuhain, and have the right of it. But we have not yet heard Eoin's side of the story, either, and we may be at fault once more. Tell me, when last did you see him?"

Derval screwed up her black brows. "I . . . heard him. Mouth breathing, as we came out of the trees and sighted Christ Church—I mean, sighted Olaf Cuarán's Hall."

"We were all breathing heavily," Ailesh had to say. "It had been no easy descent. I saw Eoin after that, under sunlight. He stopped to pick a flower."

Derval groaned. "You go on to the brehan's house. I'll have to go looking for him."

The girl's resentment of Derval turned immediately into concern. "Bhean Uasail, I don't think that's necessary. As the Ollave says, Eoin can take care of himself very well, and surely he will remember the name of the woman whom we go to visit now."

"Will he?" Derval pushed her hair back from her face. Both the face and the hair were greasy, and her fingers were cold against them. "If you think he can take care of himself, oh treasure of my heart, then you have an unrealistically high opinion of John Thornburn."

"She does that," interjected MacCullen. "And the truth is, Iníon Cuhain, she said the same of you when you were lost."

Derval flashed hot and cold with anger, but as she glanced up at the poet, a bitter retort brewing, she saw that his eyes were more than half-closed, and so puffy that he might have been beaten about the face. This recognition awoke similar weariness in herself. Ailesh put a strong hand on her arm as she swayed. "By Mary's babe! You're in no state to go seeking through Dublin after anyone. When we are settled, then I will find Eoin Ban for you."

It was with a sense of wonder that Derval noted Ailesh's

hazel eyes were bright and clear. "You will, my sister? What is your secret, then? Are you too young to feel tired?"

The girl turned away, shyly, fingering her hammer in her belt. "No. I am tired also. But there is something..."

But in between exhaustion and her irritation at John's disappearance, Derval found herself interrupting to ask, "Or is it that you would rather find 'Blond Eoin' alone?"

Ailesh flinched. "Derval! I meant... I have a task in front of me. A great task. Heavier than I have the strength to perform, perhaps. When that is done I can rest, but until then... Though I have the love of a kinswoman for Eoin, I would dare make no move to step where I—"

"Shaa!" MacCullen made a mouth like he would spit and turned his pony's head sharply around. "I will stand and listen to this no longer."

Ailesh trotted up beside the pony, her face fixed despondently on the oak logs of the road. Derval followed them from the low valley and away from the heart of Viking Dublin, feeling absolutely wicked.

Away from the black pool, they passed along the river and out toward the west gate. There the imposing character of the houses they passed changed. They got smaller and lower. Thatch, bright gold to dull gray, began to replace the wooden-shingled roofs. The walls became wattle and daub. Often there were little gardens surrounding the houses. Often the walls were whitewashed. Here and there a banner or symbol proclaimed the shop of a craftsman or merchant, but these became sparse and then disappeared altogether. Razor-back pigs scavenged the wooden gutter, along with chickens and dogs. The street began to level out. The stench of a tanner's yard made them gag, and then they passed it by. On some of the houses the clay was falling off the wicker panels. This part of town looked as though it had once been as prosperous as the rest, but had fallen on hard times. Some of the houses and yards were abandoned and burnt out. It was a sad sight.

They left the stockade behind them and walked across the common fields for a little way. The cattle, sheep, goats, and horses of the city dwellers were scattered all over it. A number of children and a couple of ragged slaves watched the animals not-very-intently. Gathering together around the warmth of a small fire, they didn't look up as the travelers passed. A little while over the muddy cattle track, and they were back in streets again.

They were now in the Gaelic town: the old village of the hurdle ford. The road was still muddy, but the mud had a foundation. Slabs of rock paved it more or less. Some houses were of limed stone here, most of them round, with round gardens and cattle enclosures.

A round thatched house just before them had a look of faded magnificence to it. Thick stone flags formed a porch before the door, which was beautifully carved with patterns of many-feathered birds. Traces of paint and even some gilding could be seen on it. The yard in front was fenced with sally and soft with new fuzzy kale, leeks, turnips, green onions, and many herbs. Two figures bent side by side to work in the garden: a very large man with an iron-shod hoe and a very small woman with a straw hat and one leather gardening-glove on her hand. She stood up and squinted at them from under the hat brim. Her nose was snub and her mouth wide. Her heavy-lidded eyes shone like blue glass, and when they met Derval's (who stood behind MacCullen and Ailesh at the remove of one who is not quite on the best terms), Derval had the dizzying impression that her trip through time was either over or had been an illusion from the start, for there was such a comfortable, familiar stability about the aged face, and the hat seemed so familiar (it had feathers in it), and that single, clumsy weeding glove . . .

But the eyes of the brehan passed by and returned to MacCullen. "Is it Labres MacCullen I see, my fine poet, my fosterling, looking like he's been rolling in his own cattle's dirt?" Her voice was scarcely audible across the five meters that separated them.

MacCullen glanced down at his stained leínne and the ill-fitting brat Derval had filched for him. "It is, myself, that it is. And to Clorfíonn, Daughter of Thuathal, seed of Niall of the Nine Hostages, he has come, like a bird storm-soaked, out of murder and great loss, bringing with him the companions of his ill fortune." Her hooded eyes widened, and MacCullen added in a voice that took ten years off his age, "It really has been terrible for us, foster mother. It has that." Slouched upon the mare's back, he told the brehan an abbreviated version of their story.

Very slowly and deliberately Clorfíonn pulled off the dirty glove, and gestured for the large man beside her to take the pony's reins. Derval found the hinny also being led away behind the house. Without the beast's support, she almost fell.

"That's not the best flattery in the world, my boy. I try not to remind others of that, around here: that I am Niall's seed." She stepped between the wandering rows of green onions with delicate steps and turned-out toes, and opened the wicker gate. "A hundred, hundred welcomes to my house, Labres, my child, my friend, and the son of my friends. A hundred welcomes, his companions. Please God that you find help here for all your need."

Derval came through the gate last, stiffly, almost reluctantly, feeling she accepted hospitality under false premises. Without actually regretting a word she had said—for in her physical misery all lashing out seemed legitimate—she loathed herself cordially. Consequently, when MacCullen presented her to the brehan first, before Ailesh, as the scholar Derval Iníon Cuhain, her response was a shamefaced mumble. It seemed to her that the brehan regarded her warily.

Derval had to notice the knocker, which was a strangely calm-faced bronze man whose knees held an oar. His arms swiveled up and, when brought down, made a loud metallic thud. "A brass knocker. Dublin never changes," she mumbled to herself.

Entering the house, she stood with her back against the wall, while both Clorfíonn and a woman in a brownish-red linnia moved in practiced fashion to put hospitality into effect.

After the serving woman gestured and grinned for a few moments, Derval realized she was expected to remove her boots and socks. The bucket was waiting, and the "foot-water." Sitting on a little bench provided for that purpose, Derval submitted to this ritual of welcome. She winced as the slimy cold soft-soap was rubbed over her feet and ankles. The rinse, again cold, was over swiftly. Clorfíonn stepped over with a towel she had warmed over the fire. As a sign of special welcome, she dried the guests' feet herself. "I will prepare a bath for you all."

"Thanks for that," Derval said, and got the first real smile from the brehan. She smiled back. Her hostess dried the feet of the others and was gone again, leaving Derval to look about her.

A yurt, Derval decided. The house was like a great yurt, with limed walls. John would love it, if the silly fuck-pig ever showed up, for these walls were so closely and intricately painted in the colors of red, green, and gold that it took a good hard stare to make out what they meant.

At least there was plenty of food, she saw, for from the rafters opposite the door hung at least a dozen cured hams. But looking more closely, Derval realized that what she had taken for legs of pork were really leather bags, each painted, riveted, and embroidered carefully, and containing hard, flat, lumpy . . .

Books. The brehan had her library hanging from the ceiling. Derval smiled. How better to keep them from rats and damp? Being Derval O'Keane, she could not help herself from approaching the bags, almost colliding with the rufous-clothed woman, who scuttled by with a pot of hot water. Derval apologized, feeling another emotional jolt as the woman replied in an Irish as badly accented as John's. Without touching the precious leather bags, Derval followed this woman back to the door.

The brehan was already out in the yard beside Ailesh, who stood in a wooden tub, and standing on a box she doused the girl with warm water out of a sprinkler-headed leather bag. Ailesh let out a gasp. The two spoke, but Derval could not make out the words. She turned at a sound to find MacCullen standing beside her. He put a cup of warm milk into her hand. On his face was no reminder of their last exchange. "That woman," she began. "Not the brehan, but . . ."

"Hulda?" His face already had regained some color.

"She speaks oddly."

The poet's smile was only slightly malicious. "She speaks with an accent. So do you."

He mistook her silence for offense taken. "Not so badly as she, of course, Scholar. And yours is not quite the same accent. But in Dublin you will have to get used to hearing Dublin Gaelic, for most of the people are Danes or of mixed kindred."

"Are those people her servants?" Derval tried not to seem wounded by his last remark.

"They are not." MacCullen smiled. "They are her fosterlings also, though legally I suppose they could be called bondmen. Clorfíonn fished them out of the Liffey when they were infants." Seeing her expression, he added, "That's the way the Norse dispose of their unwanted children, especially" —he hesitated, making sure no one but Derval heard him— "the children of slaves. Clorfíonn knew the mother. She was a Saxon, taken on a raid in Wessex. She tried to buy the woman and free her. It is a most shameful thing for a Christian woman to be enslaved, and still worse to bear children to the one you hate most."

Derval shuddered. She was going to ask more, but the conversation was cut off as Ailesh came bustling in, wrapped in a leinne that glistened. "Next one," she said. MacCullen pushed Derval out the door. "You first, Iníon Cuhain." She peered back at him, distrustful, and he added, "I wish to stand here and delight my eyes with your many charms." Derval found herself blushing.

The water was not very warm, but it was welcome nonetheless. Clorfíonn held the bag for her with her own hands. Afterward they put over her head a clean leinne belonging to Hulda, for the brehan's would scarcely have reached her knees. When this was done Derval really did feel better, and went to find the poet for his turn at the bath.

He already wore clean linen and his hair was slicked back. Ailesh stood beside him, looking fresh but combative. "I washed from a pot by the fire," he explained.

"He won't let me look at his injury," Ailesh told Derval, and then added, with an adolescent eagerness, "Help me hold him, Bhean Uasail, and between us he won't be able to do a thing about it."

MacCullen's eyes issued a warning.

"No, heart's treasure," Derval said calmly to Ailesh. "I won't touch him. A man's body is his own business."

"Good woman!" said the poet, with a grudging smile.

It was a heavy porridge, flavored with butter, leeks, and onions. Derval watched Hulda cutting the onions, noting that she did it in a bowl of water. It had been only three years previously that Derval had learned this trick for avoiding tears.

Ailesh was no more than a face peeking out of a pile of heather beds at the other side of the house. MacCullen sat on a pillow with a great shawl over his head, facing the wall. He was either deep thinking or asleep. The manservant sang in the yard as he fed and groomed the animals. His voice was good and his style complex. None of the airs were familiar to Derval. A fly buzzed through the air before her face and exited out a large flap window in the thatch. The house smelled of melting butter and raw onions, mixed with the scent of heating cider.

Something cracked and opened within Derval: a kind of guardedness or shock, and she looked around her as though seeing this new/old world for the first time. She found the brehan Clorfíonn looking up at her.

Those heavy, deep-set eyes were not really blue. In this light, there was an amethyst cast to them. "Tell me, my heart," the older woman said. "How many bowls?"

Derval wrinkled her forehead. "Did you ask how many beds?"

"No, of course not. I have enough heather beds to spread across most of the floor, and cloaks and cowhides to cover them. Bowls. I ask," continued the brehan very quietly, "because who is eating together is such a sensitive subject, and through my years I have found it impossible to understand the ties among my guests within the first few hours, and if I guess wrongly, I'm sure to offend someone. I need to know how many bowls to set out for the three of you."

Derval smothered a laugh by turning it into a sigh. "Bhean Uasail, Brehan and daughter of the kings, I am in many respects a foreigner to this island's customs. But I can tell you that four days ago I had not met either the poet or Iníon Goban." And as though it were torn out of her mouth, she added in a whisper, "And since then I have scarcely been an hour with Labres MacCullen without some sort of sharp word between us."

The old woman's smile broadened into an immense grin, and in the same whisper she replied. "An hour is not so bad! Be comforted, Scholar, for Labres is a very young man, who has had to work hard, and often feels the great world his enemy."

Hearing the Ollave described as a young man who had had to work hard so astonished Derval that she stared slack-jawed at Clorfionn, who walked to the fire still grinning, swaying her hips from side to side as she went. The brehan's eyes, just before she turned away, had been green.

In the musty shadow of his woolen shawl, Labres MacCullen tried to block out his appeal to King Olaf, but he was distracted to torment by the light, the buzz of flies, and the buzz of women's voices. Not to mention the smell of butter-fried leeks.

His mind wandered back to Derval's temper at Ailesh, which had been shameful. Shameful and impossible to understand, unless the little man was her husband. Yet MacCullen doubted this. If it were true, then Eoin was most terribly henpecked. MacCullen grinned at the thought, for he found everything about John Thornburn very humorous. Except for the man's skill of hand, of course. But a fellow who was a buffoon as well as a craftsmaster was a delightful paradox.

But that did not mean he made a suitable mate for a fine big woman like Derval Iníon Cuhain, here. She was far too much woman for him, just as the great cow had been far too much mount. By Mary's face, though, that woman might be overmount for anyone. At the thought of Derval, MacCullen's grin faded, grew tentative. He reminded himself he was a poet and not a trainer of horses. He heaved his thoughts back to Olaf Cuarán.

Derval wished she had half the flexibility of the old brehan, who sat cross-legged beside a little traylike table, spooning porridge out of a riveted iron pot. At either side of her squatted her servants, and they ate out of the same bowl as their mistress. MacCullen's wooden bowl was dyed red, Ailesh's green, and Derval's bleached white. The center of the table was occupied by a roasted joint of venison, which Hulda had run out to buy, ready-cooked and hot, from someplace along the waterfront. There was hot hazelnut cider to go with it. Derval caught the old woman staring from one of her guests to another and was suddenly convinced that the brehan had chosen the bowl colors deliberately to match her various guests, and wondered what the choice meant.

White.

She felt herself blushing.

With the first edge of everyone's hunger blunted, Ui Neal began to speak. Her voice was so soft that all three leaned forward across the table to hear. "Labres, son of my heart, I have thought now for a good hour on your question, and I believe you are in the right. If you must approach Awley Na Ri do so under the mantle of your art, rather than at law."

"If I must approach Cuarán . . ." MacCullen's voice rose. "How can there be any question I must approach the king? His lands of cattle tribute are ravaged and left full of dead men! Wild Gaill are seated on the trunks of an abbey's sacred trees—"

"Do not forget that Awley Sandal, too, is a Gentile born," said the brehan in the same quiet tones.

MacCullen's head was up and his nostrils twitched like those of a mettlesome horse. "You, I know, will never forget that." He turned to his companions and said, "Forty years ago this woman before you instigated an uprising of the Gaels that whipped every Dane in Dublin back to the sea. Such is her power in this kingdom!"

"Instigated?" The brehan stopped to chew and swallow. She smiled ruefully. "Did I cozen those Ui Neals and Ui Fáeláin, Labres? If you think that, then I think that you weren't there. Besides, Awley then had York to worry about. That may have made him clear off as well as what we did." Looking straight at Derval she said, "I was then newly ordained at my calling, and I spoke the law as I learned it."

"And now you don't, Daughter of the Ui Neal?" he rapped back.

"Now . . ." and the brehan spoke even more softly and left a premeditated pause between her words. Derval listened so intently she nearly lost her balance and fell into the porridge. "Now half of those heroes of our island are dead and the other half are old. Their sons, now, are as rotten as Cerball MacLorcan or as luckless at Domnall Cloen. And any man—or woman—with the spirit to lead has been bought off by the gold that won Olaf back his law hall. What a merchant's victory that was, and a king's daughter for his bed to seal the bargain. Gold and what is greater than gold, support for a claim and the swords to back it. Awley and his fathers have always had that.

"First Congalach sold himself to Awley. He learned too late! Maelsechnaill is no better an Ard-Ri—he of my own blood. His mother bought Awley's loyalty to her claim by her own flesh. She even bore him a son." Clorfíonn shook her head. "After her, another king's child was served up. Another daughter of my clan. I am safe here, Scholar Iníon Cuhain, because of the fornication of my own blood: the southern Ui Neal with my sworn enemies. But I can watch them here!" She raised her hand for emphasis.

"There has been much to watch too. Kings and subject kings of this island have killed each other for the profit of these foreigners, or have stood by while the Dubliners killed them. I don't know which is worse: when they hold the weapon themselves or when they drink with the murderer after.

"Lorcan MacFealin," the brehan almost chanted, "you were the choice man. Your blood was the cleansing of this place for a while. For you Congalach and Cellach of Leinster and Bran MacMealmorda rose and struck a good blow. I spoke the judgment! I knew there would be no murder price to be got out of Sigtryggsson."

Tears welled up in Clorfíonn's eyes. "My brothers were with them that day. I remember the smoke rising from the burning—how it hung heavy and thick along the river. We won, avenging Leinster at a stiff price. And it's all gone to smash, what we did then. Nothing was really changed, except that after it my father had no sons. I bore children to comfort my parents. Never took a husband: only concubines. Ochono! It's over and long over!"

She lifted a spoonlike strainer of perforated bronze, placed a small piece of linen in it, and poured the hazelnut cider fresh for everyone. She took a little sip and passed the meather. She looked dreamily down at the fire.

MacCullen put down his spoon and pushed the bowl away. "That's not quite the truth, Iníon Thuathail." He caught first Ailesh's eye, then Derval's.

"Look at this woman and see the power of the Word on her. A daughter of the Ui Neals, she is, and all of Northern Leinster would follow where she led."

Both Hulda and the manservant sat up straighter at these words, but the brehan seemed unaffected. "Easy to say, when you know I am not in the business of leading, Labres." She winked at Derval and added, "I told his father he had to be a poet, for he had such unbendably noble ideas he would fail at anything else."

"Clorfíonn!" cried MacCullen, outraged. "Will you never let me grow up?" The old woman broke up laughing and he dissolved in blushes.

"Labres, my heart, was your singer killed as well as Caeilte?" Clorfíonn asked earnestly.

"He was not, God be thanked," MacCullen answered earnestly, shaking his head. "Beoan is ill. He went home to his parents for care. He has a trouble of the lungs which makes him bleed from the throat. The physician in his grandfather's house is the only one who can turn the illness from him. So I sent him back with a rich payment. It was his great luck that I did that; I would to God that Caeilte and I had gone with him for the journey."

Clorfíonn looked anxiously at her foster son. "Let me hire a harper and a singer. You can rehearse here with them. It's shameful for you to appear before Awley speaking your poems like a common bard."

Labres laughed softly. "Mother of my soul, their poets of greatest renown speak before them without such niceties."

Clorfíonn flushed with sudden anger held in tight reserve. "My fosterling, do not degrade yourself!"

"I am degraded! Before high heaven and the blessed earth!" MacCullen choked on the words. Derval turned sharply from her eating to see a tear well up glistening in the eye of the chief poet. It did not run down his cheek but hung there while he spoke. "I am a slave and less than a slave. Slave Ollave to a slave king. Just now you spoke of luckless Domnall Cloen, my lord to whom I am the conscience and the honor, whom Olaf holds imprisoned."

Clorfíonn covered the side of her face with her hand. She had let her tongue run away with her, and was now aware she so had pierced MacCullen with a knife of grief.

"Do you thing I've spent all those weeks," MacCullen went on, regaining control of his voice with every word, "licking the feet of Olaf Sigtryggsson because I wanted gold and horses?"

Clorfíonn reached up to touch his face. "No, my sweet boy. I knew you better than that."

"You did, my mother of affection, as many did not."

He turned in bitterness and found the eyes of Derval. "And that, Scholar Iníon Cuhain, is why the Ollave of Leinster is found kenneled at the court of the Gaill."

"I didn't know," answered Derval.

Ailesh, taking the blame on herself as always, spoke up.

"That is my fault, my sister. I ought to have known to tell you, far traveler that you are."

MacCullen grinned thinly at the both of them. "No matter what you thought, dark woman. My name is shit from here to the border of the Shannon!"

"Forgive me, dear foster son," the old brehan insisted with maternal tenacity, "but I still think you should have two artists of skill to put the poem to him, while you stand by in dignity."

"You never give over, do you?" MacCullen laughed suddenly. He scratched his head. "I need to rest, Clorfíonn."

"You will have your own way of it. I would never dream of trying to influence you." This time MacCullen's answering laugh held real amusement.

Derval found herself staring at MacCullen's profile. Was it Clorfíonn's influence that made the man seem five years younger? She felt an irritating urge to comfort him, and yet she was afraid to speak. That was even more irritating.

In the confusion Derval found Ailesh looking at her across the table. Derval mouthed the words "I'm sorry I used my tongue on you before." Ailesh gave back a broad smile which broke in the middle, as happiness made the girl remember her own grief once more.

"Listen to me, my new friends and old," said the brehan, and such was the power (gift of sovereignty or long training) of her voice that everyone turned to her face, including the stolid manservant. "I said I could not recommend the case to Cuarán, not because I distrust the man, but because the time is very bad to bring such business into Dublin. Know that ever since April he has been expecting the wedding visit of his son-in-law, Olaf Tryggvason, prince of Norway. It is three days since the arrival of a Moorish ship that had passed the king's longboat along the coast, coming from York. Until Tryggvason arrives safely, with Olaf's daughter, I don't think he will have ears to hear of a raid off the coast; do you?"

Ailesh's round head drooped forward. She ran her spoon along the smooth wood of the edge of her bowl. But her eyes were more belligerent than daunted. And MacCullen squeezed her small hand in his. "A king's pledge does not await his convenience," he said, bringing his other hand, palm down, onto the table.

The brehan nodded. "Quite. And perhaps he will accept

that lesson if offered to him in verse. But if I present it as a matter of law—"

"He must accept it however offered, unless he wishes the Powers of the World to take his kingship from him."

He is protective of Goban's daughter, thought Clorfíonn. While she is beside him, he will consider it a defeat to listen to reason. He would probably consider it so, anyway. Poor Labres. Clorfíonn's deep, mutable eyes gazed at him dispassionately, remembering how few cows MacCullen's father had left, after paying for his long schooling, and how nervously both father and mother had watched his progress in the world, until sickness took them. It was no fun to be the most renowned in the family.

Poor young Labres. He would have to go up to Navan to explain about Caeilte too.

She glanced at Ailesh and away again. Nothing wrong there. She was certainly to be pitied, losing a father like Goban MacDuilta, but it is better to have lost such a man than to have never known him at all. Though Clorfíonn had never met the stonecarver, she knew his work, and the stories of his immense good humor had spread beyond the Boyne. She was glad to see that the girl hadn't stuck that hammer of hers, pasted with dried blood, into the belt of the silk linnia Ui Neal had brought all the way from the Holy Land.

Then she shifted her hooded, almost invisible regard to Derval. What was the foreign woman doing with them? Dare she ask? Did she really want to know? The brehan decided she really did want to know, for the severe beauty of the young woman, as well as her air of proud isolation, attracted her. She was glad she had chosen her a white bowl, to go along with her ivory face and silver-rooted black hair. Clorfíonn remembered a snatch of poetry from the *Voyage of Mealdun*: "Her skin was snow-white under her white shift. Her cheeks and mouth were as red as the foxglove, and her hair as black and shiny as the raven's wing. Here is a fit woman to sleep with our chieftain tonight, said the men to each other. Let us woo her for him." Clorfíonn smiled and her soft eyes turned bright green.

Holvar glared at the ocean below from under scowling brows. His men shuffled tentatively around him at the cliff's edge.

"Perhaps they flew off from here," suggested someone from behind, giggling nervously.

Holvar did not take the bait. Instead he cursed the stony ground, adding a malediction upon himself for letting himself be led wrong. "We should have continued north."

"North? To Dublin?" asked Ospack. "Why would these Christians flee to a pagan city?"

"Because it's the only city they've got," Holvar replied. "And but for the Danes, they'd have none at all. But I had thought their refuge would be nearer to hand."

Thorir spoke, diffidently. "Godi, the earth was not that hard. Didn't it rain only yesterday? If we lost the tracks of the little ass, perhaps it is Odin's work, and he is taking this deed away from us."

Though the man had meant his words as a comfort, Holvar gave a shudder. The god taking the deed away. Taking Holvar's frenzy away. His priesthood away. He turned on his heel, ploughing through his men without meeting their eyes.

The east path had looked so right. Holvar had believed himself led to it—led to the edge of a cliff above deep water. He gave a ragged breath, filled with an unlawful resentment. He stalked back along the rocky, broken trail, anger obvious in the set of his head and shoulders, and in the way his hands gripped his swordbelt.

Wind off the ocean had shrunk and shaped the few trees that grew there. Holvar, coming down from the last hill, felt dreadfully exposed at all sides. No matter that a force of eighty battle-hard Vikings was in no danger from anything that might be brought up to oppose them along the wild countryside of Ireland: a battle against some Gaelic cowboys now would be an endeavor without gain at the end of it, and it might interfere with the search. Holvar breathed easier once the heavy oak forest took him under its shadow.

Here once more was the intersection where he had gone wrong. Holvar stared at the road north, where the outcrops of stone had been scored and whitened by the wheels of carts, and the litter of oak leaf and mast blew lightly in the brisk air. No sign whatsoever of an ass's hooves, nor of the intricate and distinctive patterning of the boot soles one of the fugitives was wearing. Instead, much to Holvar's dismay, the ground was liberally scuffed by the soft boots of his men. He groaned aloud.

But when exactly had he last seen the light track of his quarry? Holvar was now not sure the footprints had been seen in the previous few miles before the turnoff. It was possible—quite possible—that they had struck off into the woods far behind. Holvar bit his beard in frustration.

Joyous cries from his men roused him. Holvar glanced around to see four or five Norsemen with something between them, which they hung from like dogs on a deer. As he waited a woman was dragged before him.

Great gladness turned sour in his heart, for it was not the girl he had been chasing, but a dark woman of middle age, who stared at Holvar with absolute blankness. Two men held her arms, while a third, his hands locked in her hair, tilted her face toward the godi's. Her struggles were silent.

Ospack didn't need to be told this was not the fugitive of the abbey. Smiling dryly, he held out to Holvar a large wicker basket, mounded with cloth.

Without hurry, Holvar stooped to the basket. His knees cracked. Something was wrapped in the cloth, he discovered, and carefully he picked up a section of it. Eggs. He sighed and stood again. He gazed at the woman speculatively, and she, seeing no malice in his face, spoke a few words.

Holvar turned to Ospack. "Though this is not the one we follow, yet she may lead us to them."

"But there is not a man of us who can tell her what we want of her," the old warrior objected. "I doubt she speaks any proper language at all."

Holvar smiled. "That isn't what I meant." He turned to the prisoner, rested his hand gently on her shoulder, and said, "I am going to send you with a message. When you come before Odin, you must say that we are his men and will accomplish our sworn pledge to him, but that he must show us the way."

The woman stopped struggling as she listened to Holvar. Very carefully she said, "I have no Norse. I have no Norse."

"It doesn't matter," replied Holvar, and his hand on her hair was a caress.

The holy rope was unwound and hung from the lowest limb of the oak beside the intersection of the two roads. As they pulled the brat and linnia from the woman she began to fight again. She had a strong body with dangling breasts and brown nipples. Her arms, legs, and crotch were thickly hairy. When she saw the noose she arched her back like a hooked fish and began to scream. Ospack ripped off a section of linen and stuffed it into her mouth. "Do we tie her hands, Godi?"

Holvar shook his head. "Not necessary for a woman." The oldest men of the troop carried her to the hanging noose and placed it over her head, carefully pulling her long hair out of the rope's way. Three men took the end of the rope which dangled from the limb and pulled, lifting the sacrifice into the air.

Evidently they should have tied her arms, for the woman's hands clawed upward and clutched the rope. Wild-eyed, she pulled herself up toward the limb of the tree. It was so large a branch she could not get around it, so she dangled just below, yanking at the tight noose with one hand. Holvar could hear the breath whistling through her nose. He frowned at this imperfection in the ritual and walked over to where the woman's feet flailed and kicked. He leaped upward and grabbed her about the knees, raising his own feet off the ground. Her hands slid down the rope and the noose tightened again. Holvar whispered a short prayer and then let himself down.

Now the legs kicked without coordination and the hands did no more than twitch at her sides. Holvar looked up into the blue, swelling face and raised his sword before him. "Tell Odin we await instruction." At the moment her legs sagged straight he took his blade and sliced cleanly down from her throat to her belly, letting both blood and offal spill at his feet.

Her long hair was cut off and braided into a black noose, which Holvar put around his own neck. He went off into the bushes. Seventy-nine men awaited him, flush-faced and reverent, staring at the corpse with the large brown nipples which spun lazily in a circle in the air. Bowels and bladder were voided down its legs.

Holvar was gone only ten minutes. "We are to continue north," he said.

Derval awoke at the table with her hand lying greasy in her porridge bowl. She glanced confusedly around to see if any had noticed her nodding. It seemed everyone had.

"I think that is a very good signal that the meal is over," said the brehan in her almost-whisper. "Is everyone replete?"

MacCullen did not demur, but he swallowed a last bite of venison and raised the three-handled metham once more to his lips. After drinking deeply he passed it on to Derval, who imitated his action, passing the cup to Ailesh.

There was something in the way the young woman took it—a kind of prodding awkwardness—that caught Derval's sleepy attention. She looked carefully at the three brass handles on the wooden cup to discover that two of them were jellied with grease, and Ailesh was searching for the third. A close, covert inspection on Derval's part revealed that the second, third, and little finger of Ailesh's hand were soiled with food, but the index finger and thumb were not. Derval glanced under her lashes at MacCullen to discover the same. When she looked over at the brehan, that woman was giving the cloth into MacCullen's hands, to be passed in turn to Derval and Ailesh. Derval blushed furiously to notice that only she left dark stains on the fabric. In trying to avoid all eyes she was caught by those of Clorfíonn, which were once more green. The old woman smiled at her blandly.

"I will spread out my mattresses now and we will all take a nap. At my age I need one in the middle of the day." To forestall MacCullen's budding protest, she added, "It will be only self-punishment for you to try to design a poetic appeal to the king in your present state, Labres. Besides, deep night is the time to make poetry, and I will wake you, I promise."

The poet shifted uneasily on his bench, but any argument he was about to make dissolved into a yawn, which proved quite contagious. To stave off collapse, Derval rose.

"I must go find Johnnie," she announced.

The brehan, lavender-eyed, smiled sweetly but shook her head. "My dear, Holdfried will see to that. I sent him out as soon as he had eaten, and he will bring your friend to us."

Derval felt her brow corrugate, and wished she were more alert. "But . . . Holdfried has never met John. He doesn't even know . . . or at least I haven't told him what the fellow looks like." She turned from MacCullen to Ailesh, questioning them wordlessly.

"I surely did not describe him," said Ailesh.

The little brehan rose, folding the napkin on the table. "On the contrary, my treasure, but you did. You all did.

"You, Ni Goban, called him Eoin the Fair. You, Iníon Cuhain, said that his accent was worse than that of a Dublin Dane, and you, my friend and son of my friends, jested that the man looked even smaller riding the shoulders of the bell cow than he did usually. Therefore I sent Holdfried out to find a small blond stranger with terrible Irish. Though Dublin is a rather large city—for this island—still there are not so many who fit that description. And Holdfried knows every corner of the town."

Both Ailesh and MacCullen made noises of appreciation for the brehan's cunning. Derval's "Elementary, my dear Watson," spoken in English, was taken as more of the same. But Derval said in Irish, "I could have shortened his task considerably. I could have told the man to look for Johnnie around beer or boats."

John shifted his ale to his left hand, moved into the square of light thrown by the doorway, and drew on the hearthstone a sketch of a clinker-built rowboat. "Better," he said in English. Why not in English, when this Snorri didn't understand a word of his laborious Irish anyway? "Less caulking." The other followed the line of John's stick with a blunt finger, in critical appreciation. He stuffed a smoked sausage into John's unused left hand.

The publican came behind, to ascertain what damage his customers were doing to his hearth. Seeing John's jauntily ranked sketches, he paused, smiling. "You do good, fellow," he said slowly in his bad Irish: so slowly even John's unpracticed ears caught the words. "Maybe we could finally do something about the walls in this place, if you do not charge too much."

The ale, the food, the warmth of day and the warmth of appreciation all sparked a small golden sun glowing in John's middle section. He felt it a special victory that his idiosyncratic style (damned as "consciously naïve," and "self-limiting" at the reviewed shows at Cooper Union) should have found such a niche of welcome. He was about to explain to the publican just how inexpensive he came, when the light of the door darkened.

A moment's irritation turned into panic as John remembered the warring Saracens. He, Snorri, and the publican turned: a united front against the invasion.

But it was no lean figure in a burnoose or pegged trousers that stepped through the low doorway of the alehouse, but that of a man larger even than Snorri, dressed in Dublin style: knee-length long-sleeved tunic, belted at the waist, trousers, and leather shoes. He stood in the room's shadow and surveyed the company for a few seconds, and then stepped directly over to the three at the hearth.

"Holdfried!" The publican greeted him. "It has been a while since you gifted us with your company. How is the brehan, Holdfried?"

Holdfried answered all with a nod, and then furrowed his pale forehead in concentration. "John Thornburn," he said quite clearly. "I am sent for you," he added in Irish.

John's jaw dropped and his dirty, vague, and sunburnt face looked even more unfinished than usual. "S—sent for me? You mean by . . ."

"Holdfried is the brehan Clorfíonn's man" explained the publican.

"And the brehan Clorfíonn is . . ."

"The speaker of the law, of course."

"I thought so," replied John, his ears ringing. Everything in the alehouse seemed to withdraw to a great distance. "What does he want me for, do you know?" He glanced up at the square face that was so obviously that of a policeman that it made his overfull stomach churn.

"She, not he," corrected the publican affably.

"Clorfíonn will tell you," Holdfried said. He put out an enormous, work-hardened palm, as though he intended to walk John hand in hand through the streets of Dublin to the station. That hand looked as formidable to John as handcuffs.

And that was exactly how John did go—his own hand lost in the meaty depths of Holdfried's, like a boy parading beside his father on a Sunday afternoon. But he had gotten no farther than the sunlight at the alehouse door when he also felt his neck weighted by a brawny arm. It was ruddy-skinned Snorri once more, and he whispered into John's ear a message of unflagging friendship and support, regardless of the penalties of civil law or king's insolence—none of which John understood at all.

Between the bulk of Holdfried and that of the Icelander, John stumbled frequently.

Derval woke again with great reluctance, hearing a voice echoing loudly through the house. There was another voice, much less forceful, but familiar. She clawed the linen sheet back from her head and peered around.

That hump was Ailesh; she could tell by the frizzy hair. The larger one by the wall was Labres MacCullen. Neither budged an inch. But where the old brehan had lain was only a crumpled blanket and bolster. Derval lugged herself through the clinging bedclothes to look at the door.

There were the tennies and loose-hanging trouserlegs of John Thornburn (spindleshanks that he was). But the rest of John was eclipsed by the mass of a great red-bearded man whose hand was on the hilt of large, serviceable belt knife. He was speaking Norse, and it was his voice that had disturbed Derval.

She knew old Norse to read sagas—especially with a crib sheet beside the text—but its spoken form was mostly a loss to her. She caught the words "crime," "protection," "oath bond," and (odd in the context) "little brother." She saw that the man's arm was around John's neck, and that John's hand was clasped tightly by the brehan's servant, and she hoped against hope that John hadn't done anything unforgivable to the stranger's little brother.

But Clorfíonn was standing by the doorway, her white silk leinne, embroidered with scarlet birds at the throat and hem, fading into the whitewashed and brightly painted wall. Her quiet words were lost to Derval, but her gesture of welcome could not be mistaken. John shot into the mattress-covered room as though shoved from behind (which he had been) and gaped around him with no intelligence in his face at all.

Derval sighed. "Do you have to shame me in everything you do, Johnnie?"

"Eh?" John Thornburn turned around, leaving complex-patterned tennis-shoe prints on the white linen. He focused on Derval.

"Take off your shoes. This is a bed," she said. Obediently he sat down and did so.

One by one John made out the shapes of his companions

lying cuddled on the downy mattresses, under blankets. His eyes stung with woodsmoke and sentiment, feeling a warmth even at meeting MacCullen's ironic eye. It occurred to him that he had perhaps caused these people some worry. He felt a pang of regret, for in his weariness and relief he found he liked them all very much. Been through a lot together. He grinned at little Ailesh, whose bright eyes peeped out from her covers like those of a bird in a bush. "I'm not under arrest then, eh, Derval?" he asked, and his question turned into a yawn. Without another glance at Clorfíonn, his hostess, he sank down onto the corner of one heather mattress.

"Under arrest? What the hell for?" Derval rose up, regardless of nakedness. The round blue eyes of the man at the door widened, looking at her.

"What would you be under arrest for, you mucking sap? Where have you been, and by the by what did you do to that boy-o's little brother?"

But John was asleep: solidly, unshakably asleep.

Derval sighed again and stood up. She considered kicking the limp shape beside her, but remembered Ailesh's words and the presence of the brehan before her. It was a dirty shame—neither of them had ever had to baby-sit John Thornburn, that they should criticize her handling of the brute.

Her irritation woke her fully, and she looked up to find herself the object of the ruddy Norseman's great attention. "What are you staring at, I ask?" She spoke to the man in Irish.

The brehan stepped between them. "It is only, my treasure, that the strangers are not accustomed to the sight of the unclothed body. It is a sort of . . . gaès with them."

"Oh." Derval blinked down at herself. "I . . . uh . . . forgot." She grabbed her borrowed shift and threw it over her head, amazed at herself.

MacCullen was now awake, and from his pillow he stared at the intruder without welcome.

"This good man," continued Clorfíonn calmly, "has sworn himself the friend and protector of your John." She said the foreign name clearly and with a good French *j*.

Derval fastened her belt and gave Snorri back a stare as good as he'd given. He returned a grin and a wink.

"And why, Bhean Uasail Clorfíonn," asked Derval frigidly,

"has he done that for a perfect stranger?" The brehan spoke to Snorri again, and her tact so far placated him and reassured him as to John's present safety that the man's knife was once more hidden under the folds of his tunic, and his face split in expansive jollity. He began a long explanation which was half charade. Derval watched with interest as he chopped, swung his arms, and jumped up and down in the doorway.

At last the brehan translated for Derval. "It seems that your John, whom this gentleman calls Jan Thorboern, saved his life from an attack by two Saracens."

"Saved..." Derval's voice failed her for the body of the sentence, returning only in time to squeak "two Saracens?" at the end.

Snorri nodded his large head forcefully in agreement and pointed at the limp, childlike figure sleeping on the corner of the mattress. John had shoved his thumb-knuckle into his mouth. "With nothing but a bowl of curds," he added in Norse.

"Our Eoin is a man of unexpected talent. I have said so before." The drawling, amused voice was that of MacCullen, who was by now sitting upright by the wall, clothed in his long-sleeved linnia.

With an appraising glance at the stranger, he stood, and spoke in Norse as excellent as that of the brehan. "I am Labres MacCullen, Chief Poet of Leinster, trained at the Munster Academy, and we share this most valuable ally, Eoin Cattle Leaper." He pointed at John's recumbent figure.

There was something in MacCullen's ironic courtesy that took Snorri aback. He stepped again into the doorway, conscious that he had not been invited into the house. "I am Snorri Finnbogison, shipwright. I name myself Snorri the Unfortunate, also, for only this year I was on my way to Greenland with all I owned when worms ate through the hull of my ship and she began to take more water than we could bale. She broke up and sank in heavy seas. My life itself and what I get through the skill of my hands is all I possess to me now, and but for this man Jan Thorboern I would have lost all that today."

MacCullen listened to Snorri in the blank-faced way he had when putting things into memory. He narrowed his eyes as he replied. "Finnbogison? That name is familiar to me. Would it be the Finnbogi who was son of Grim that is your father? And would that be Grim Geitskor who walked the breadth of Iceland and brought the All-Thing into being?" Snorri shrugged and nodded. "Then yours is a high lineage, my friend." And MacCullen smiled genially at Snorri's puffy face.

The Icelander shrugged as though embarrassed. "I had a pretty good grandfather. We got on."

MacCullen's eyebrows rose. "Pretty good? It makes no sense, man, to denigrate the greatness of one's kin, where that exists. There are people enough to pretend to birth that is not theirs, for—"

Snorri took in a great lungful of air and blew it out his nose, all the while staring at the brehan's packed cow-dung floor. "It makes no sense to claim another man's worth as your own, though that man be your father. I am proud of my kin. But if I am anyone, I am Snorri the shipwright. That is our way, in Iceland."

"I am corrected," said MacCullen, still smiling, but in a condescending manner.

"You're nothing of the sort. You spoke well. I'm just explaining... And by the way, that's a fine-looking woman you've got there: the dark one."

MacCullen looked startled for a moment. His eyes turned away from Snorri toward Derval. He was fairly sure she understood nothing. He did not reply to the compliment, however, but pursued the first subject. "I should have remembered that the Icelanders are all free men: free from king, from clan, from history—free from all constraint save that of the blood feud."

The bulbous blue eyes wrinkled at the corners and Snorri shifted his considerable weight from foot to foot. "I am party to no feuds, poet. Never my life long, and least of all would I feud with the companion or kin of this man who has saved my life." He rested his hand on John's sloping shoulder. "Not if I am given the choice."

MacCullen's genial (though superior) smile froze into a smirk. "It would take," he said slowly, "more than one roaming Icelander to hold a feud with Labres MacCullen, Chief Poet of Leinster."

Derval, who had understood hardly one word in three of the preceding, turned away. For lack of anything else to do, she tucked a blanket around John Thornburn. The rather heated conversation died immediately, as both men watched her action. Snorri glanced appraisingly at MacCullen, who did not meet his eyes. To the surprise of everyone awake, the big Icelander giggled and made a bow in John's direction. He stepped out of the doorway and sat himself, solid as a door pillar, on the limestone stoop, where he seemed to meditate upon the lean, wandering piglets on the street outside.

MacCullen found the brehan standing close behind him. Her straw hat, with its oddly assorted feathers protruding from the brim, was on her head, and her leather glove was being drawn on. "Another time," she said languidly and just for his hearing, "you will see the humor in two men squabbling over a woman bound to neither of them. And another time, Labres, you might allow me to be the host in my own house."

She went out of the house immediately and engaged in courteous conversation with the man on her doorstep. Grinning broadly, he bowed to the brehan, and followed her into the garden again, holding her basket. She weeded garlic and the medicinal plants until the evening sun set behind the houses across the street and then she came in and brought Snorri Finnbogison with her.

Chapter Eleven

•

> Suddenly as Gunnar and Kolskegg rode up to the Rang River, a stream of blood appeared on the halberd. Kolskegg asked what it could mean. Gunnar replied that when that sort of thing happened in other lands it was called the death rain: a sign of imminent battle.
>
> —*Njaal's Saga*
>
> Translated by Magnus Magnusson

The heavy smoke from the never-failing fire in Olaf Cuarán's law hall rolled out the doors and clung to the earth like a nest of snakes, beaten flat by the gray and regular rain. The walls of the hall (or of the halls, as Sigtryggsson's palace was made up of four long buildings that touched at the corners and created thereby a square central courtyard) rose black and slick as the hull of a ship turned over. Indeed the whole affair looked like a square of knorrs turned keel up on dry land, for the roof was clinker-built of boards and ran smoothly to the ground, windowless save for small shuttered louvers high on the sides and untouched by ornament or color of any kind, except a grimacing animal head at the end of each gable. These added a nightmare quality to the hogbacks.

"Jesus!" John whispered to Derval. "This is where a king lives? It looks like a dungeon." John hadn't wanted to come.

"You're right," Derval replied. "H-block. but in these days every palace is a fortress." She raised her voice slightly and glanced at MacCullen as she added, "Even when the king merely bought his kingdom."

The poet's eyes flashed with alarm. "Scholar Iníon Cuhain, we're not going to be helped by talk like that. Remember that a king is a king—especially in his own hall. If you are unsure what manners are current in this court, I suggest you wait in an outer chamber."

Derval's chin hardened. "I wouldn't miss this for the world's fame, Poet." Then, seeing real worry in his face, she smiled at him. "I'll be as silent as the grave."

"How auspiciously phrased," murmured the brehan Clorfíonn, and she led the small company under the black eaves of the law hall, throwing back the hood of her outer brat of boiled wool as she did so. A spatter of drops darkened the wooden doorsill.

MacCullen and Derval followed, and behind them came Ailesh, shepherded by John.

Since last night's supper the girl had said very little, and now her white face shone like the pale, odorous water-repellent cloaks worn by all the company. Her red hair (she had allowed Hulda to henna it this morning upon rising) turned her pallor into something ghostly. Her silk gown was white and unadorned.

MacCullen's golden hair had been cut and limed and his eyebrows blackened with walnut-hull juice. Over his leinne he wore a gown belonging to the brehan, which became on him a knee-length tunic with three-quarter sleeves. It was made of white silk and decorated with scarlet bands of embroidery Derval recognized as Chinese work. All the brehan's personal jewel ry had been leant to him for this appearance: a gold neck-ring and bracelets and a silver-gilt kite brooch.

(Derval had been nonplussed to see the Ollave decked out in the old brehan's clothes. She had even ventured to ask him if he weren't dressed rather like a woman, a question he had answered with a steely glare, along with the words "I always dress like a woman in public, Scholar. It is the custom of an Ollave." This had shut her up completely. John had merely remarked that the olive had a cruel mess of gear on him.)

Clorfíonn looked like herself, in a leinne of exquisite sky-blue material and a well-woven gray inner brat fastened with a simple penannular brooch with red stones. She was spotlessly neat, but without any bravery or show about her person which might make it seem she was taking notice of Cuarán's law hall.

Derval wore Hulda's best gown, for nothing of the brehan's would fit her. It was Norse style, and the two saucer-sized brass buttons which attached the straps of the pinafore stood out on her torso. She felt rather foolish in the dress until she came into the torchlight of the hall, where she discovered that this sort of gown was the rule among the females of the court.

In the general stir of the morning John had been forgotten, and so was dressed and groomed as John: jeans, T-shirt rather large and stretched out in front, all of which was covered by a brat hiked up to allow his hands in his pockets. He had combed his hair but had forgotten to wipe the mud from his tennies.

There was another person who accompanied them and was of their party and yet not of it. That was Snorri the Icelander. In some respects, he had little idea of the errand, but sure that something important was afoot, he tagged along at the rear, cautiously. He was not certain of the extent of John's involvement in all this and was determined not to get himself into more difficulties than necessary.

Snorri's trust was not in kings.

The fire ran a third of the length of the hall, dividing it as though the molten earth had riven the place in two. And because it was a fire of oak mixed with pine and aged, damp turf, it produced a great deal of smoke. This gathered at the ceiling in strings, awaiting egress through the cracks of the louvers. The ceiling was the light-consuming color of lamp-black, coated by forty years of this hearth's work. Torches hung from wall stanchions, half surrounded by guards of iron to keep the leaping flame away from the wooden walls. Consequently, as the company, led by MacCullen, proceeded down the hall toward a spot of greater color and light at one end, each concealed flame flashed out of the dark and then was gone. The bottom of the hall was fairly empty, save for a few Norse attendants, dressed in what seemed to be Russian-style frogged jackets.

"Gustav Doré," said John to Derval.

"What?" She scowled privately at him.

"Doré. His illustrations for Dante," explained the Canadian. "It all just reminded me." He hiked his shoulders to his ears and let them fall.

In a moment all Derval's anxieties had transferred themselves into irritation at John. This was such a pleasant transformation she was almost grateful to him. But at the same time she felt obliged to remind him once more to keep his mouth shut, lest some inanity of his ruin their cause.

"Didn't want to come at all," he replied, speaking through clenched teeth. At a tremulous sigh from Ailesh, both Derval and John shut up.

It seemed the hall was divided by more than just the long hearth. This end of the upturned "keel," was lit by lamps of oil and a single tall wax candle, however around the dais was a three-sided screen of heavy tapestrylike rugs to reduce drafts. Up in the curtain space two high seats had been set. The one on the left was built upon four oars of ivory, richly carved and pierced through. The bench and the chairback, too, were ivory—narwhal ivory—and the cushions were gold and red brocade from the Levant. In the blackness of the hall it glowed like a moon. On this chair sat a man whose colors mirrored his surroundings perfectly, for his round face, heavy-set and heaviest through the cheeks, was carved with ivory-white wrinkles, and his hair and beard, despite his obvious age, were golden. But there was that about the set of his head and his eyes, as they stared and shifted here and there among the people assembled below him, that was more like the empty dark hall with the hidden light of torches, than like candles, ivory or gold.

At the other side of the long hearth the high seat was not so high, and it was of black wood which faded so into the darkness that its carvings or lack of same were impossible to make out. And the hair of the woman who sat upon the seat was as black as the soot on the ceiling. But her face had a glow beyond that of ivory and her eyes were sky blue. Her dress, woven of fine wool the color of flame, fell down the sides of the chair and lay in a gorgeous puddle at her feet.

Around Gormflaith gathered a retinue mostly of women, and some of these in Gaelic dress. Around Olaf Sigtryggsson the audience was much larger and almost exclusively Norse. As chance or MacCullen had planned it, the party had walked along the fire on the queen's side and now found itself before Gormflaith.

But the queen was not looking at them, nor was any of her retainers. She sat propped against the right arm of her chair, looking at a fair watchful young boy who sat on the stairs of the dais playing with a small dagger. This boy, in turn, had his attention fixed by something that was happening at the feet of his father, the king.

MacCullen did likewise, and though the hearth was raised with flat stones he could see a flash of white, as though someone were dancing about in his shift, and he heard a raised voice pleading in such bad Norse it could scarcely be understood. And he heard the king laugh.

"We are not the first here today to implore the king's justice," he whispered—he thought—into Derval's ear. But it was not the tall woman but John who stood beside him, craning his neck to see over both stone hearth and the ring of courtiers opposite.

"What is that? What is that?" cried John Thornburn. "I hear something, I—"

MacCullen had to resist an urge to pick the small man up as one would a boy and set him on his shoulders. "It is another case, Eoin, brought by the wharf merchants. And it will go heavy for the defendants, if carried. They are accused of dueling within the confines of the *margad*, and as the brehan can tell you, both will lose all their goods to the king.

"The most interesting part is that these travelers came very far, indeed, to come to such scrapes in Dublin, for by their dress and face, these are Saracens."

"I thought so," cried John. "My Saracens!"

And then MacCullen did pick John up and set him on his shoulders.

"He cheated me!" The Turk spat. "Of the price of five healthy slaves. I did not contract for seven-year indentures, but that's what he gave me. This coal-faced Moor is a disgrace to the merchants of all the earth."

"I do not doubt it," answered the king, grinning down in great amusement. He shared his mirth with the three gray men in black who sat on the bench to his left. Then he shifted in his seat and flicked his hand at a daunted ship's captain, who had been brought under guard to translate for the Moor. "What does the black say in his turn?"

The captain's colloquy with the Moor was short. "He says he did nothing: neither cheated the man nor drew sword on him. The captives were fairly described and priced, and if the Turk did not know the Irish laws of indenture—"

"Indenture is not at issue here," said the whitest of the three gray men.

"I beg leave to doubt any merchant's word, when he claims to be free of the taint of cheating," the king interjected, "but as old Ovaegen says, it's not at issue." And here Olafr Konig paused to allow the titter of laughter to spread itself and die in the hall. "What is at issue is dueling, which is forbidden in the marketplace."

A murmur of agreement from the bench.

The Moor spoke into the ship captain's ear, spreading his pale palms wide for emphasis. The captain nodded. "He asks, O King, whether it is not lawful to draw weapon when a man is chasing one with sword raised above his head, having stated his intention to kill."

The king opened his eyes very wide. They were the color of water in a pail of tin. "Is that the case? Did this poor unfortunate fellow get chased around the city of Dublin by an angry Turk? Both of them with gowns fluttering like butterflies, I suppose." The heavy lower part of his face raised itself almost to the cheekbones with his enjoyment. "I am only sorry no one thought to call me to watch!"

The court roared.

"Are they calling it a duel? It wasn't, you know," whispered John to MacCullen, once he'd been put onto his feet again. "The lighter-skinned fellow just up and went for him."

MacCullen, who had suffered an infection of jollity at the picture the king had evoked, looked down at John with a face gone suddenly both sour and intent. "You saw this?"

"Eh? Yes, of course. That's what I'm saying. The lighter fellow took out a mucking big scimitar and went for the black. But his aim was so bad the blow would have gotten Snorri—only I didn't know he was Snorri then—but I raised up the bowl. Then the black rolled around on the floor before he made it out the door, with that crazy chasing him. You see, eh?"

"I see," replied MacCullen. "As the king does not. And I curse the evil fortune that endows me with this sight! But truth is truth. Come—before he delivers an ignorant judgment."

The poet took John by the hand and leaped upon the hearthstones, dragging him behind. Together they jumped the burning embers and came down in the middle of the rioting law court.

"Humorous or not, King of Dublin," MacCullen called loudly to both Sigtryggsson and his court, "this is a history which can be verified."

"What was that about?" Derval whispered to Clorfíonn. "Why did they jump the fire like that? Is it a ritual?"

The old brehan nodded. "It is Labres MacCullen's special ritual, young Iníon Cuhain. Above men's pride or his own claim to justice he must always defend the undefended truth."

It was very exciting for John, miming the sword fight for the court. He had a very good memory for certain things, oddly enough, and movement was one of them. He danced around with sword raised, after the manner of the Turk, and rolled to safety as though encumbered by a long burnoose. He was Snorri, flinching from the blow, and he was himself, raising the wooden bowl on high, and then at last he was the Moor, bursting out the door of the alehouse, with the Turk (also himself) in hot pursuit. The enthusiastic encouragement of the Norse courtiers flushed him as though with wine, but when he was done and his choreographic testimony given, he looked up into the face of Olaf Sigtryggsson and suddenly felt he'd made a great mistake. John took a step backward and ran into Labres MacCullen, who stood like a rock, awaiting the king's pleasure with quiet eyes.

"The Ollave of Leinster," said Olaf, lowering his faded blond eyebrows. "I have missed you of an evening, MacCullen. I admit there is no skald of Norse extraction here with your ready wit and gift of language. Did you bring this buffoon into my session today in hopes he would entertain me?"

MacCullen's battle with his temper was brief and invisible. "It seems the law case did that well enough, Noble Sir. I only brought you a witness with the power to untangle it."

Olaf Sigtryggsson peered down at John with his eyes unfocused. His face had slackened to pear-shape. "And to steal from my purse a great forfeit, perhaps. How do I know to trust his word?"

MacCullen made a wave of the hand which was the courtly version of a shrug. "Jan is no courtier, King of Dublin, having neither good Norse nor good Irish. But he is an honest man, and a craftsman of skill. But if he is not to your taste, Noble

Sir, I believe there is an Icelandic shipwright outside who could corroborate his words. And you could certainly have the keeper of the alehouse brought to you."

"I am not outside but here, Olafr Konig," Snorri spoke up loudly. "The Saxon craftsman speaks the truth, and he is no buffoon." Snorri's arms were folded across his chest. He looked directly up at the old monarch, respectful but without any visible fear.

Sigtryggsson rested back in his chair and for a moment the sag of his back revealed his age. "You misunderstand, Ollave. He is to my taste, for I have been horribly bored all morning, waiting for a son-in-law who does not come, and have no mind to sit before a serious law session at all."

MacCullen extended his sympathies with a nod of the head. "Even a king cannot order the wind and tide, Noble Sir. But I came to this hall neither to relieve boredom nor to save the property of a Moor. I came with a very serious case. I come to sue for a murder price, and no small one. I came for redress."

The old king pursed his mouth. "By bloody Odin, MacCullen! What bad timing. I tell you I am not ready for such business today. Thirteen prime cattle are roasted and nearly ruined and the retinue of my household is in confusion. It is Olaf Tryggvason I expect: Prince of Norway, and the new husband of my daughter Gyda. If your kind have been in a brawl, you will have to wait for your time!"

Sigtryggsson lifted his head only an inch, but that was enough signal to start the court's obedient titter. The king laced his fingers in front of him. "Enough of this. Unless my counselors refute it, I accept the Saxon's testimony."

The three gray men blinked at their king. The eldest nodded ponderously.

"Good then. Release the blackamoor. I find the Turk alone guilty of assault while on the ordained earth of Dublin's marketplace. His goods and all property within the limits of Dublin are forfeit. So be it." Sigtryggsson clapped his hands together. The slack muscles of his forearms jiggled in response, like the long udders of a sow.

Although she was too far from the throne to make out conversation, Derval heard the clap and the subsequent howl of the Turk as he was led through a convenient door behind the thrones. She saw the black man follow, gesturing at his enemy in a manner both obscene and triumphant, and somehow she doubted strict justice had been done here. She did not claim to care about this particular Middle-Eastern crisis, but the amount of laughter it had raised boded ill for her own cause. She let Clorfíonn Iníon Thuathal lead her and Ailesh to the foot of the high seats, before the hearthstones, where they all bowed to the queen before proceeding decorously to Olaf Sigtryggsson's court.

Derval glanced covertly up at Gormflaith in her chair and then looked away, and there was something oddly familiar about the queen's face that left her feeling unsettled. Ailesh, following her, stood stock-still, staring first at the face of the queen and then at Derval herself. This wasn't the fair Woman who had petted her eight years before. This woman was beautiful, and she looked very much like . . .

The brehan took her arm and gently pulled her on. "Quite right," she whispered in the girl's ear. "They could be sisters. But don't be obvious in your stares. Perhaps the Dark Woman of Sovereignty would not be flattered by the comparison with a woman in the dress of a servant."

"So, Labres MacCullen," began the king, when the noise of the previous case had subsided. "Do you insist?"

MacCullen stood a moment in silence. "Circumstances make it impossible to wait. For your honor as well as mine."

"My honor?" The king sat bolt upright. "Be careful, Poet of Leinster."

MacCullen stood silent.

"Well, then." Sigtryggsson scraped against the grain of his beard with one clean fingernail. "Let us have your case, though it would have made better entertainment a week from now." Sigtryggsson leaned forward, resting his elbows on his thighs, and he regarded MacCullen from between his spread knees.

MacCullen had gone white, but there was no weakness in his voice as he said, "Noble Sir, you must not mistake the function of a poet with that of a jester."

He turned his face from left to right, and those whose eyes he met fell quiet. He let three seconds of silence build.

"Blood and burning. Like the treacher hounds,
Breedless dogs, disgraced, mouthing madness,
Who tear the heifer calf, the herdsman's hope.
Consuming nothing. Consumed themselves by fury,
So the human brute has had great glut.
Hear this horror—my tale of terrible loss.
I, Labres—poet—tell you of murder.
Fast following, here drawing close . . ."

Was this MacCullen—the smooth-spoken, the collected? What had roughened his voice like that, and lowered his speaking by an octave? Why, he was another man, declaiming in Norse. What was he saying, Derval asked herself. He surely can't show the horror of the dead abbey in this saga meter. It was made to glorify blood.

But the poet's transformation had had its effect, and the hammer strokes of the meter had taken the attention of the Norse listeners by force. Even the old king's head moved in jerking time. The minutes passed and the surges of rhythm drove Derval herself from one foot to the other, desiring action.

". . . Soft vale, home of artifice,
Gift-giver, gold scattering on Leinster
Sweet sister among the settlements of Eire.
Hill of Ash Trees, you lie in pitiful ruin!

And woe to me! Woe for the sword in my side,
Less bitter than the sacrilege,
Less bitter far than the death of Caeilte my clan brother!
White my heart for grief of him, young Caeilte, whose name was sweetness.
Honey-sweet his bright strings and the music of them,
Never more in this hall among my friends resounding.
Never to his mother, the only son returning . . ."

Derval felt the free slide of the rhythm, and the slide of feeling accompanying it, though the words were lost to her. She made out the name of the harper amid the Norse words.

Good, she told MacCullen silently, as she peered around. He had them. He had them. Fat Cuarán himself was intent.

"Nor is this story ended. Worse will come.
Carrion crows are hungry night and morning.
Feast, however ruinous and rich
Does not slake them. Dublin, look to the south!
I come, storm-tossed, with words of heavy warning."

There was a metallic silence in the hall, through which the spit and hiss of the fire could be heard over the gray drone of the rain. The courtiers and supplicants, Gaelic and Norse, stood dumbly, their eyes on either the king or the queen. Gormflaith herself sat gripping the arms of her chair, her face turned down along the empty hall. Sigtrygg, who had crept closer and closer to MacCullen as he spoke, now ran his fingers up and down the length of his dagger blade and blinked warily at his father. Olaf Sigtryggsson had not moved since MacCullen began his poem. Five seconds stretched into ten.

The king spoke. "Very moving, MacCullen. But it would have gone down more sweetly with music behind it. What have you done with your infant harper?"

This question struck MacCullen just as the fire and the force engendered by his work had begun to go cold and his training took over from passion: just at the moment his eyes had focused to watch and his ears to listen for his audience's reaction. It inserted itself like steel into the poet's moment of weakness.

And it killed the reaction that MacCullen's story had been building among the court, for the king's words cut short the beginning of a hiss and rumble of pity, inaudible except at its being suddenly cut off. Derval heard the murmur and its extinguishment, and not knowing what Sigtryggsson had said, she knew he had purposefully stepped on MacCullen's punch line. Her anger was red and immediate, but so was her perception that the king of Dublin was very good at what he did. She heard Clorfíonn beside her, whispering too softly to be understood. Derval felt suddenly too discouraged to curse. She looked up at random and her eyes met those of the queen.

At Gormflaith's feet were fewer women in Norse dress, now, and more men of the Gaels. Her rose-damask face held no expression whatsoever, but her hand was tight on the sleeve of her son, who was turning the sharp blade over and over in his small hands, his fair head turned away from her. Derval, on impulse, glanced behind herself at the long, dark hall, dotted with guards.

"Shall I tell you again, in lesser words, Noble Sir, that Caeilte is dead?" MacCullen asked Sigtryggsson.

The king leaned farther forward. His beard and hair gleamed so golden against the aged skin that Derval guessed he had been using onion skin to dye it. "Oh yes. That's what it was about, wasn't it? It is so rarely I hear you orate on contemporary subjects, MacCullen. And I did warn you I wasn't prepared for such a tale today.

"Well. A tragedy," he murmured. "And your kinsman as well as your harper, was he not?"

MacCullen nodded briefly.

"And you come here to me for his murder price? I never set young Caeilte under my protection, that I can remember, poet, but no matter of that. I have heard his harping in my hall often enough, and I will pay for him."

"I do not come here for gold, King of Dublin, as though a stone from your kitchen had crushed Caeilte by accident. I come with news of war and broad murder, and the blood price is that of the Abbey of Ard na Bhfuinseoge and all whom it contained!"

Sigtryggsson stared at MacCullen and then firmly shook his head. It was a private message, for afterward he let his eyes roam vacantly over the heads of the assembly. "Ard na Bhfuinseoge?" Another five seconds.

"Never heard of the place."

He glanced over to his bench of old men. "Have I heard of the place?"

The middle gray man scratched his knees through his gown. "A . . . settlement of the Christians twenty miles south and inland."

The king's cheeks rose visibly as he said, "Thank you. So there is such a place. I have learned enough of Gaelic to know it means 'hill of the ash trees.' That's more than I could have told you five years ago, MacCullen. But as I am not a Christian, I don't know what that is to me. I've sacked my share of your shrines, but the Christian kings have outdone me in that almost two to one!"

Against the pallor of the poet's face rose two blotches of

red. He stared straight ahead of him at the long tusks of narwhal that made up the king's chair. "Then learn this, also, King of Dublin. Since twenty years ago, this abbey has paid you for your protection in both cattle and in artifice."

"Is there record of that?"

The men at the benches by the wall murmured unintelligibly.

"There is," replied the brehan Clorfíonn, stepping out from behind Derval's shadow. "And if the writing of a justice is found more worthy of attention than the words of a poet, I will go into my records or your own and find it."

Sigtryggsson straightened abruptly and snorted. His lips drew back from his old-man's teeth. "By Frigga sucking! It's the Ui Neal woman again, at court after all these years, and still waiting to stir my bones with her flesh fork." He pointed his finger at her.

"I tell you, old woman, you have failed in your life's work, for here I am and here I stay, King of Dublin and York! You will not live long enough to triumph at my death!"

Clorfíonn's eyes were of green ice. "I never triumph on the occasion of death, Child out of Ivar's sons. It is too regular a visitor. And whether I live beyond you or you beyond me will make no difference to the code of law it is my profession to serve." Her quiet voice filled the hall.

"Can any of you, man of law or Norse lawyer, refute that Olaf Sigtryggsson signed a pledge of protection with the Abbey of the Hill of the Ash, which was paid for in cattle and artifice yearly?" Her weathered face smiled as she added to Sigtryggsson, "And more specifically, that that pledge had its instigation with the Buyer of the Throne of Dublin, not with the abbot."

The king recoiled from the title she had bestowed upon him as though from a slap. "So—do the penurious think to insult the wealthy by calling them so? Well, old crone, if I have signed a contract with this unpronounceable place I will certainly fulfill its terms. Bring me an inhabitant of the place, that I may put gold into his hand. But bring him to me at my convenience."

"It is not yet time to talk of gold, nor yet of convenience, King of Dublin, while the enemy is feasting within your realm, and his ship's pillars are set up where your own fief stood last week?"

Olaf in his throne hung over MacCullen like a cat in a tree

over a bird. "The enemy, you say? Which enemy? What is his name? Are you clever enough, Poet of the Munster Academy, to name my enemy for me?"

"I believe his name to be Holvar Hjor," replied MacCullen stolidly. "That, at least, was what a friend of mine heard said. And with him came a many score of reavers. Against him I claim a flesh wound and a bone wound for myself, and a flesh, bone, and marrow wound for my sister's son, Caeilte, who got his death by being so wounded."

The king used his elbows to raise himself in his chair. "Holvar Hjor—the Sword? I know the name. Norwegian. Just a moment ago this woman of the Ui Neals called me Child of Ivar. He was a man of Norway, surely, but I have no control over every Viking Norwegian."

MacCullen lifted his chin. "I call you King of Dublin. It was a protectorate of Dublin this marauder destroyed. Need anything more be said?"

The king waved aside the last part of MacCullen's response. "Do you call me King of Dublin, MacCullen? Do any of you Irish call me that, when my face of power is not before you?" He spoke this last in a contemptuous Irish, which was surprisingly good in syntax and in accent.

"My father did!" It was Ailesh who spoke. She elbowed her way forward from between Derval and John, and she walked to the foot of the narwhal chair. "I'm the person you called for, Noble Sir. I am the survivor of Ard na Bhfuinseoge. And this high seat you're sitting upon is the work of Goban MacDuilta, my father, which he built for the King of Dublin in the year before I was born. Often he told me about it: how it had taken him eight years to collect the sea horns, and how the crystal in the mouths of the dragon finials had been bought in Alba by his agents.

"It was a Gael who made you your throne, King Olaf, and it was to him you promised protection.

"Goban is dead now, and I was saved from his fate only by the intercession of Holy Bridget, and because I was able to kill the man who ravaged me. All my community is dead, where you were known as the King of Dublin without question. We gave you cattle! What else could we have called you but king, though never having seen either your city or your face, Awley Cuarán?"

Ailesh Iníon Goban looked about at the housecarls who

surrounded her, and at last she knelt before the throne of the king, her hands caressing her father's work. "I was," she said, her voice breaking in anger, "a maiden. I had never known man. Now I know only to hate, and the blood he rent from my body . . . the blood he rent from my body—"

Ailesh didn't recognize the sounds she heard around her, but they were enough to stop her weeping and drive her to her feet again. She stepped in a clumsy circle over the wooden floor of the dais, mouth open and staring.

For the housecarls who stood before the king's throne were laughing at her. Olaf himself wore a grin, which tightened at the look of reproach which Ailesh cast at him.

"It's your own fault, girl. If you're in such a hurry to publish your shame, what can you expect?"

MacCullen put his arm over Ailesh's shoulder and pressed her head against him. John, never quite understanding, stood close and glared at the fat old Swede on the high chair. All the Gaels in the court stood frozen, their gaze fixed on Gormflaith, who only watched her son turn his little dagger over and over and over.

Olaf snorted. He glanced almost angrily at his young wife and ran his hand over his thin hair. "What do you want out of me, child? Your father was paid for his carving. Shall I get you another Norse husband? You used up the first one fast enough. But I tell you—I tell you all—that you'll get no more recompense from me than that."

Snorri was by this time so angry that he elbowed his way to the front. The insult to the little woman, the child of another craftsman, had stung him hard. Still, he opened with flattery, just to be on the safe side. "Noble Gold-Ring Giver, do you remember me?"

"Of course." Olafr laughed a little, raising his hand in greeting. "I just paid you for a ship. Aren't you satisfied, Finnbogison?

"Only a dragon would be unsatisfied with the payment you heaped on my hands, Olafr Konig. But I am here to give my support to these people. This I ask. Tell me if it is not true that in these lands you rule a craftsmaster who has made goods for a king is not given a wergeld—a murder price—of one-third of that of the king himself?"

Clorfíonn Iníon Thuathal smiled slyly. Snorri did know something of the old law. Olaf's features worked as he wrestled with his confusion. He beckoned the advisors to him. They whispered for a moment, and then nodded in assent. "It appears to be true," Olaf said warily.

Snorri stepped closer to the king and lifted his hand in pleading. "Forgive the proud words of these people. Grief has stirred up their hearts. Surely you can overlook that. If you are generous to this girl and this poet, lasting fame will be yours."

Snorri's face was eager, as if expectant of a change in the king. He was disappointed.

"I've had enough of this. I can't be responsible for every cattle raid. Your case falls. So say I, who am the King of Dublin." And Olaf brought his hand down on his chair arm with a smack.

"King no more," said MacCullen, not taking his arms from Ailesh.

"Now you have said it!" Olaf hurled the challenge with satisfaction at the poet's face. "I have seen your face today only because you hoped to see Domnall here. Do you think me a fool? You come here with your poetry for no other reason! You have looked for a long time for an excuse to heap curses on me. You engineered this to bring ridicule on my name and for no other purpose."

"I have said it because I have witnessed it this day," replied MacCullen. "I have seen Olaf, Child of Ivar's Line, reject his own throne under the beams of his hall. Your kingdom, I believe, rested upon Ard na Bhfuinseoge, this place of which you have never heard.

"By my own state and honor I, Labres, son of Cullen son of Duach, now proclaim Olaf son of Sigtrygg of word faithless and of honor forfeit, polluted by twisted judgment. I will sit upon his doorstep fasting until he fulfills his pledge . . . or departs Dublin to do penance."

"Will you?" The king stood beside his narwhal throne. "Will you do that, indeed, MacCullen? That saves me the trouble of putting a spear through you. You will go very hungry through my feasting today."

"That is upon you."

An idea occurred to the old king. "King Domnall Cloen, my prisoner, will eat with me. I will see to it he hears nothing of your madness until he has feasted."

"That is upon you also," replied the poet, though his hands

balled to fists, and he led his company down the length of the torch-lit hall.

John went last, as he had come. When halfway to the far door, he turned his head to look back toward the light. There, a spot of light surrounded by shadow, Queen Gormflaith sat staring after him, sitting quite alone, and holding in her hands her boy's little dagger.

The Gaels of Dublin had set up a light pavilion. From somewhere had come benches and a table for writing. The pounded dirt of the doorway had been carpeted by clean reeds. MacCullen's bivouac before the law hall was comfortable in every respect save one.

John could smell each individual roasted cow in the far kitchen, and the onions in butter (not normally his favorite food), and honeyed oat cakes, and the fried fish were driving him mad. He sat curled on the straw with his back against the curved wall of the building. Occasionally he coughed on smoke.

"Don't be . . . this way, Ailesh," said John Thornburn. He slapped her arm with spurious roughness. "That old man is a . . . a . . .

"How do you say 'fart' in Irish, Derval?"

Derval raised her head from her hand. "Leave her alone, Johnnie," she said in Irish. "You're not helping."

"He is certainly doing no harm," MacCullen corrected her quietly, and answered John's distrustful glance with a smile of quiet friendship and understanding. John thought of all the nasty things he had wanted to say to the poet in the last few days and he blushed as though he had said them. John stared at his own feet.

Ailesh's tears had fallen off and on all day, with the rain. Like the rain, they were cold and almost soundless. She bit her lip to hold them back. "Where is this shame the king talked about, my sister Derval? What is it I have done that I ought to feel ashamed?"

MacCullen let his blue eyes focus on the girl. They were lit with a very strange light. "There is no shame here except in the man who calls himself King of Dublin. He raped you with words and fouled his mouth for all time."

The poet sat on a low bench without back support. There

was something oriental in his erectness and self-possession. It was as if he were gathering power into himself. "What we do now is beyond shame and not of our own choosing, Daughter of Goban. But know that no king can stand against all opinion. And be comforted that my calling is sacred.

"Even this one, false king and Gaill that he is, will not touch me, and while you are at my side, I believe you will be safe."

Then the brightness died from his face. "But I worry about others . . . the brehan. They are old enemies, Clorfíonn and Cuarán, and when Cuarán came back to the throne of Dublin, she left for many years' far travel. Now in the king's—in Olaf's—hate and old anger, he might commit the sacrilege of murder upon her."

"But not the sacrilege of killing you, Labres MacCullen?" Derval poked him in the leg in proprietary fashion.

He looked uncertainly back at her, as though he could not decide whether to take her words as concern or scorn. But she continued, "John's big Icelander friend is with the brehan. What could we do that he can't? But I also don't trust the old . . . fart, as John calls him, and my fear is that he may leave the flower and wealth of Ireland's history in blood."

Now MacCullen turned from her and examined the reeds by his feet. "This sort of flattery is a new art with you, Derval Cuhain."

"No flattery," she replied. "I value knowledge. You are more full of this land's past than any great book."

He colored. "I have not shown you that, woman. The one time I ventured to speak in my calling—"

"I knew that one fact, Ollave," said Derval, tracing the weave of her brat with her fingers on her lap. "You knew a hundred others around it. And then—you listened to me. That is the mark of the real scholar."

He gave a small sigh. "So what would you have me do?"

She lifted her hem. "Not you, but me. I'm carrying a knife in my boot."

He smiled at her. "My champion! I will have no more fear." Then his face grew serious again. "Woman, if I lock you up and feed you nothing but the cream of choice cows for a month—"

"Do what to me?"

"Eh?" John tuned in to the conversation.

MacCullen laughed. "And then if I could dress you in the gowns you deserve, and put gold around your head and your throat, then the fabled beauty of Olaf's queen would be nothing to yours."

Derval sat back and gaped at the poet. "Oh. So you can't even try to flatter me without it ending in insult. Well, hear this: among my people the saying is, 'You can't be too rich or too thin.'"

MacCullen's blackened eyebrows bristled. "But that is nonsense, on both counts. A man dead of starvation is too thin, while as for wealth, the story of Bres, the king of the Dannans, who was deposed for covetousness much like that of this false king, ought to teach us—"

But Derval was sputtering with laughter. "Curlytop, someone ought to teach you not to argue with a proverb."

His answering smile was tentative. "Curlytop?"

So this was the substance of MacCullen's friendship, thought John Thornburn. And of Derval's faithfulness. He glanced up at the tall poet, who met his eyes with a sudden confusion, and John's anger was replaced by depression as dark as the rain. When had Derval promised him anything, that he should now feel betrayed? It was merely that back home she had found it easier to hide the fact she kept many strings to her bow. John rose, almost pulling over the heavy linen awning. "I'll go watch the brehan," he said, and disappeared into the drizzle.

Derval did not watch him go, but neither did she speak any more to MacCullen. Faithful or faithless, Derval stared out at the rain-slimy logs of the street, afraid to meet the censure of Ailesh's eyes. MacCullen only sighed and shifted.

Silence amplified the drum on the awning.

The rain ceased an hour before twilight and almost immediately after, with a horn squeal and a shout from the wharf, Olaf Tryggvason was welcomed to the docks of Dublin.

Neither MacCullen nor Derval saw anything of him, for he entered at the far corner of the fortress. But behind the oaken door, the sounds of laughter multiplied, and soon the rattle of platters and knives was added.

The casual sprinkling of Gaelic loiterers on the street

changed its makeup, but remained constant in number. Derval found her fingers and toes growing chilly. It was close to dark.

What had she gotten herself into? This affair, begun as an attempt to dispose humanely of an awkward visitor—and Derval had to sneak a glance at Ailesh as she sat in all her red hair and hurt, to make sure this was the same madwoman who had barricaded herself in John's bedroom—had grown and blossomed into a confusion of Irish politics. What did this fast represent to the brehan? To the nameless loungers along the street, or Ailesh herself? Derval felt nothing but hungry.

And what would it lead to? Derval searched her brain for some memory fitting the time and place. But the tenth century had never been her period, and all she could remember at the moment was the Battle of Clontarf. What would that be—forty years away? No help. Brian of the Tributes was alive now, surely. Should be king of Munster.

"Hey," she began, nudging MacCullen. "You were trained in the Munster Academy, weren't you?"

The poet admitted as much.

"Then why weren't you there—among the Gaels, instead of roaming near Dublin?"

MacCullen half took offense. "Because of Domnall. Besides, it happens my own people live just north of here, woman. And from the first, I was good in my Norse. Why should I not—"

"No reason," replied Derval, shrugging. "I only wondered if you knew the king of Munster."

With a touch of vanity he replied, "I know every true king on the island, Scholar Iníon Cuhain."

"What do you think of him—Brian, I mean."

He took a breath and held it for a moment. "He is, like all kings, proud. And a lover of violence, jealous for the supremacy of his own tribe."

"What if he became Ard-Ri?" Derval pressed.

"God turn it aside!" was MacCullen's quick answer. "He is of the DalCais. His foot would be heavy on the necks of Leinstermen. Other than that he has no real blemish."

She sat slumped on her low stool and thought about Brian, the man who would die near this place in forty years' time, having unified Ireland with much killing and burning.

Unified it for a moment.

With a heavy grinding the iron hinges of the door behind

her began to turn. Derval pivoted on her seat to squint at the light of torches. There were three serving men, dressed in the strange Russian-style costume, and they carried plates.

Derval smelled beef and pork and honey through the onions. She saw, centered on a platter that might as well have been gold as brass, the shape of a bird, steaming, covered in bright feathers. Gladness bubbled up within her, both for the light in her wet darkness and for the wonderful food. But immediately it was replaced by fury, that someone would tempt them this way. And she wondered if she would be able to sit with Labres MacCullen and die slowly, for a matter of principle.

The poet had risen, not in reaction to the servers but to someone behind them. Derval rose also, to look into that face that unsettled her: that woman with a complexion of black and damask-rose, clothed still in the flame-colored dress she had worn in her husband's hall.

"Dark Lady of Sovereignty. Queen of this place." MacCullen spoke with deep respect, and Derval remembered about Gormflaith.

The queen bowed her head and sent the servers away. "Please eat," she whispered to the three fasters. "You will do no good, here, this way.

"I myself," and she took Ailesh's cold hand in hers, "will pay you a price out of money that is mine. Fat cows without number will be yours. I will find you a good husband."

Ailesh stole an awed glance from the queen to MacCullen. "I . . . I thank you, Bhean Ri. But I don't want to take gifts, but rather what is mine."

"You want vengeance so much then?" Her hurried eyes sought each face. "A heap of skulls for your dowry? You'll get no marriage with that."

MacCullen answered. "If to want killed the wolves that are harrying Dublin's villages is vengeance, then yes, that is what we want. And then, she has been made a laughingstock. That in itself is a heavy wrong to be compensated."

I want to go home, said Derval to herself, as emotion and hunger made her reality slip away once more. I don't want to talk about vengeance or wolves. I want to eat a sandwich. I want a Guinness.

"Whatever you call it, you will not get it from Olaf," said

the queen. "You will only get a slow death in the streets, while he feasts and makes mock of you."

"He feasts?"

Her black hair shook loose in her face. "Of course, Poet. His customs are not ours—yours. We are welcoming his daughter's husband."

"You, Queen? Do you join the feast? Do you, Queen, woman of bright honor, daughter of a great king?" His question was very gentle.

She shook her head. "No. No. I haven't. I . . . don't want a poet's curse on Sitric's young head."

Sitric—Sigtrygg. The last bell went off in Derval's swimming head. She stepped forward.

The queen stood with her hands humbly over her gown, over the jeweled box brooches made of gold which adorned her breasts, as she said, "I want only that he grow to be the force that welds Olaf's people and mine into one—"

"Is that what you want?" Derval found herself saying. "Well, you are doomed to disappointment. He will betray you, Lady. His loyalty will be foreign, and his sword on the necks of the Irish people."

Gormflaith shone white in the shadows, and then her face reddened in anger. "You know nothing of it! Sitric is a good, kind lad, and only eight years old. It's very easy to make up a future and call yourself a seer, but—"

"Not easy at all," answered Derval, swaying as the dark world began to go pale around her, and her ears filled with ringing. "It's been very difficult, and likely to end in death, for Johnnie and me.

"Queen, your troubles ought to be no more than footnotes in a history to me. I have my own troubles. And fears. Be glad you don't know *my* fears: then you'd have something to lose sleep over. I don't need to tiptoe around the ego of some fat squarehead with a kingdom the size of a very small bus route."

Gormflaith stared uncomprehending at the unfamiliar words. Derval found herself sitting on the edge of a bench, breathing hard. "Do you know what I am, Queen of Dublin? I am she who has no mother on this earth, nor any father. Nor are the bones or ashes of my parents to be found by any skill. I come without family, clan, or relation into this world. I have known the facts of your life and death, as well as those of your husband and son, since I was a child.

"You." Derval pointed at the queen quite rudely, and sat straddle-legged on the bench, panting with effort. Her hand, despite the cold, glistened with sweat under the torchlight. "You are most afraid of being like the other Gormflaith, who had three kings for husbands and died in a nunnery. Your fate will be very much like hers. You will outlive this husband of yours and marry again. The Ard-Ri will be your next husband, and then the king of Munster, and no happier than this shall those unions be. You will be taken by force from one and repudiated by the other. As for your son, Sitric, he will marshal Gentiles from Alba, Wales, and the Orkneys, from York and Mann, to stand against the men of Ireland. There will be a great battle when Norse shall oppose Gael, and Christian oppose pagan. At the end of that all Ireland will be united under one clan. For the moment."

Gormflaith's breath caught. "United under what lineage?"

Derval laughed and flung herself to her feet. "Pity to you, who will see the bloody mail shirts stacked up in this place."

"What lineage?" Gormflaith insisted. "What lineage, shadow woman, my double? What lineage?"

"What lineage do you think, woman of Erin?" and then it seemed as though the dim, swimmy world went out for her. She fainted in a heap at the queen's feet.

Gormflaith's red robes were almost black against the keel wall of the fortress. She shuddered convulsively twice, and it seemed as though she might join the prophet in unconsciousness on the carpet of reeds. But she remained upright, and asked, "MacCullen. Iníon Goban. Who is this woman?"

The poet swallowed. He made a clumsy gesture to lift Derval in his arms. "Lady, at . . . at this moment, I cannot say I know who it is that she is."

"Unless," said Ailesh, "she is your twin walker, come from the sidhe world, Noble Lady. You and she are very like."

Gormflaith shuddered a third time.

Ailesh added, "The Bhean Uasal Derval is the friend and protector Holy Bridget sent to save me in the hour of ruin. She is a terrible warrior, and went into the camp of the reavers and came out unseen, with knowledge and treasures. She saved the Ollave and rescued young Caeilte's harp. I did not know she was a seer, though."

Gormflaith made the sign of the cross. "Christ grant that she be a false seer and her words empty!"

The blare of a horn rang through the doorway. "I must go back," the queen whispered, and clapped for her attendants, who had stood waiting on the slick wooden street, their hands—those not holding torches—stuck in swordbelts for warmth.

The sputtering torches illuminated Derval's worn features, as she lay stretched out along a bench under the awning. MacCullen raised his head from her long enough to call for the last servant through the door to take the filled plates back with him.

Derval woke from her swoon to find herself lying on wood, with her head supported by something warm and firm. It was the poet's hands beneath her neck and head, and his face was close.

"Who are you, woman?" he whispered.

"Derval Mora Caitlin Daughter of Cuhain," she answered, and then sighed heavily. "Doctor of History at Trinity. Thirty years old. Spinster. Now resident in Dublin."

His long fingers massaged her neck. "And have you lied or told the truth here, Doctor of History Cuhain?"

She worked her brow in headachey fashion. "The truth?" A chuckle escaped up her nose. "I don't claim your ancient virtues, MacCullen. I lie when it suits my purpose." Then her pale, dark-smudged eyes focused. "But I didn't lie to Gormflaith, if that's your question. Whether I ought to have told what I know—that's another question, but I felt so odd..."

"And how do you know these things—about Olaf's son and the king of Munster?"

Derval closed her eyes against the red light, reflected off the linen awning. His hands were warm against her ears. "I am from the far future, poet," she said, with a feeling of having leaped off a bridge. "John Thornburn and I have come a thousand years into the past with Ailesh. You people are my history."

She felt the hard bench against her head as his hands were withdrawn. MacCullen stared at the featureless, rain-soaked wall.

Chapter Twelve

•

Bloody decks to ya!
—Newfie blessing to sealers and fishermen

"That is very well done," stated Snorri Finnbogison. "VERY well done." He took the flat shard of limestone and lay it upon his knees under lamplight, regarding his own exophthalmic visage in miniature.

"It's a . . . a cartoon, you understand." John spoke in Irish, for the brehan to translate, throwing in the English word "cartoon" in desperation. "I don't mean to say you really look like that."

Clorfíonn gave him a startled glance. "But he does look like that, John Thor's Bear. Exactly like that." Then she translated for Snorri.

"Indeed," agreed the Icelander. "It is my very image." Snorri leaned forward over the low table. His very heavy and intricately ornamented sword banged against the bench.

John wiggled in an ecstasy of embarrassment, but when Hulda, in a small voice that contrasted with her strapping physique, requested her own likeness drawn, he added another sketch to the white stone. He had never learned how to flatter a model, but he did his best with an outline of waving hair (not filled in with pencil, to show it was blond) and larger-than-life eyes. Hulda was very happy. Holdfried, her twin brother, appeared on the stone beside her, their fraternal resemblance exaggerated as much as was in John's power. Soon the stone was covered with cartoons.

The four of them, John, Snorri, Holdfried, and Hulda, sa bunched around the slight figure of Clorfíonn Iníon Thuathal very closely. At her left was Hulda, in her canary-yellow dress, and at her right was John Thornburn. Clorfíonn leaned toward the left to avoid snagging her silk on the rough stone. John also leaned left to avoid bumping his drawing arm against Holdfried's sword, which was flat, dull, and hammered out of a single length of iron. The brehan's servant had no such nicety as a sheath; the weapon ran through a ring of brass attached to his belt. Two oil lamps burned quietly before John's work. No draft disturbed the flames, for all the doors and windows of the brehan's house were shuttered and bolted. It was a very late hour of the night, yet no one had suggested going to bed.

Clorfíonn stood, saying she would find something else for John to draw on.

"Let me," said the maidservant. Hulda pressed the brehan down into her seat again. Smiling ruefully, the old woman whispered in her ear and Hulda scuttled off into the shadows of the house.

These shadows loomed uneasily as the others waited for her. Silence in the room brought the silence of the street outside into focus. John heard the grunt of a pig outside the garden gate, perhaps trying to find a way in to eat the onions. MacCullen's blue-eyed mare, or else the hinny, dropped a hoof behind the house. It was very close also. John felt himself sweating beneath his woolen brat.

Hulda came back with a leather bag, painted all over in a key pattern of crimson and gold. Opening this, the brehan took out a book which she handed to John.

"There are many blank pages scattered through it," she said to him. "I will provide a pen and some good imported ink."

He took the book on his lap. It was small, almost paperback-sized, and its leather cover was dark and soft with cow's-foot oil and the oil of hands. He opened it to a page of painted vellum and gasped.

"This is a missal."

The brehan's face rounded into a Buddha-smile. "And so you must draw nothing irreverent in it. But you are certainly as good as the others who have decorated it, and pages were meant to be filled."

It had been put together with a minimum of gold ink. The pictures in the margins—birds, the eggs of birds, cats leaping after birds—were casual and unrelated to the text. Yet the script was beautiful and the illuminations fine. The doodles completely enchanted John. He handed the book back to Clorfíonn and his hand shook.

"I'm sorry, Your Honor, but I don't dare."

Her smile widened at his peculiar form of address. "One picture, perhaps? Of me? I would be grateful."

And John lowered his head and played with the ink stick and quill until they were to his liking. He drew Clorfíonn Iníon Thuathal's face, and then, under it, a small sketch of a bird in the style of the man who had done the marginal drawings, making the bird also look very much like the brehan. When he gave it back to her he felt all eyes in the room staring at his little work, and he himself wondered if there were something ominous or at least portentous about the sketch. The shadows loomed more heavily.

John stood himself up, clumsily, slapping the circulation back into his legs. "I think I know how to get more drawing surface." Stepping over the bench with the limestone in his hand (he carried it more easily than one would think, looking at him), he sought out Ailesh's hammer. This she had left behind on her trip to the law hall, as a forbidden weapon. It had been cleaned of its rusty stains. John picked it up and weighed it in his hand.

"Time you returned to your legitimate functions," he whispered to the hammer. He glanced from Snorri's side to Holdfried's, and then gestured to the brehan's servant to come to him.

The stone was placed endwise on the floor. Reluctantly, Holdfried rested the blade of his sword along the top of the stone. John placed his brat-tail over the sword, raised the hammer and brought it down. A deep, almost warlike grunt escaped him as he did so, and the limestone broke with a sharp crack. It fell into two flat pieces—each with a virginal white side exposed.

John laughed. Holdfried laughed. And then time froze, as all within the room turned to follow the horrendous blow against the door, and saw the blade of an ax blooming among the slivers of oak.

All the people in the house sat without stirring, almost seeming without interest in the event, and the only movement was Hulda's, as she tugged at her belt of rope.

The first assassin stepped forward, and it still seemed no

man in the brehan's party had the power to act. But as the flaring ax blade rose above her head, Snorri's hand twisted at his side, and the ax fell, chipping the floor. John found himself staring at the gold-plated hilt of Snorri's sword, which protruded from the assassin's crotch like a jewel-encrusted cock. The blade had vanished upward through the man's body.

The second assassin was only a moment behind the first, however, and as he struck sideways at Clorfíonn, a third ax-wielder threw himself into the room. The brehan ducked quite limberly, and then Hulda was on the man's back, and her belt of hard hemp was around his throat.

Snorri could not free his blade from the body of the man he had impaled, for his victim was kicking as his life ran out. As he pulled, bent over, and braced against the assassin's thigh, the third man swung down at him.

Holdfried's black sword intersected the ax and broke. The ax was deflected so that it bit deeply into the fallen man's breast. That one cried out and died, while Holdfried slashed his broken sword across the attacker's face and throat, which opened red in the lamplight. Three times the Saxon smashed the snapped end of the sword into the juncture of the attacker's neck and shoulder before he was ready to believe the man dead.

He held up his shortened sword and laughed. "It has never been so sharp before!"

The remaining assassin stood flailing his ax around him, while his other hand clawed wildly at his throat. Hulda, big as she was, hung behind him, tossed like a dog at the neck of a bull. John sprang over the bench, but could find no way through the rain of blows to help.

The man bellowed, sounding also like a bull, and tossed the Saxon woman above his head. The ax struck backward and hit Hulda flat on the forehead. She fell.

But in that moment John leaped up and forward and Ailesh's hammer smacked the black head. There was a sound like a wooden bowl breaking.

John stood for a moment, balanced wide on his legs. When he saw there were no more enemies standing, he put his head down and ran until he hit the wall of the house. There he threw up. When he saw what horror he still held in his hand, he dropped it.

Hulda sat on the floor, her legs tangled with those of the dead. She held her head in both hands. Her eyes were crossed. Holdfried came to her and pulled her to her feet. Snorri at last freed his sword from the body of his enemy.

The brehan sat quietly weeping on her bench, in the wavering light of the oil lamps, and the neighbors, full of sleep and carrying rude weapons, started to arrive.

"How could they be Gaels? How could they be Gaels and do this?" asked Hulda once more, as bitterly as though her own people had betrayed her.

"They were dressed as Gaels," said Holdfried, stating the obvious, in Norse.

"I could wear the skin of an ass," replied Snorri, fingering the edge of his sword gingerly. "Would that make me one? Or any more of one?" he added, with a faint smile. "They didn't say anything, that I recall."

"There is no difference between the Gael and the Gaill," said Clorfíonn, who had been wrapped in blankets, "when they lie still in death."

"Oh, I don't know." The Icelander's face reflected a flicker of interest. "I think I can usually tell an Irishman." He took a lamp in his hand and stepped out into the garden, where the bodies of the assassins had been dragged. His light floated in the dark like a will-o'-the-wisp.

"I think," he announced on return, "that the one with the split face might be Irish. Hard to tell, now. The others . . . I'd say no."

"It doesn't matter," said Clorfíonn. "I don't even want to know." She looked about her, at her house filled with bustling nocturnal activity, as the woman who lived next door mopped the vomit out of the corner, while three others worked at the congealing blood in the middle of the room.

Hulda sat beside her mistress, a wet poultice on her forehead. The tall blonde was developing two black eyes. She smiled triumphantly at Clorfíonn.

The brehan squeezed Hulda's rope-burned hand. "I am surrounded by loving family," she said into Hulda's ear.

The lamps flickered as someone came through the open doorway. It was Labres MacCullen, who stared about the shambles-smelling room and threw himself at Clorfíonn's feet.

"Foster mother! Clorfíonn, forgive me. This violence is my

fault and my doing! If I had listened to your voice of wisdom . . ."

Clorfíonn chuckled. "Instead I listened to your voice of honor, Labres. Well, so be it. If there were not someone to match wisdom with honor occasionally—like you, my dear boy—all our wisdom would become mere cunning."

She petted MacCullen on his hair, which was damp with the night mists. She saw Derval O'Keane follow him into the room, her eyes still large from the sight of carnage outside. Ailesh came last of all, and she sat down at Clorfíonn's feet, wrapping a blanket over her head.

Derval found John by a wooden bucket, scrubbing at bloodstains on the pages of the missal. His face was pasty and his mouth trembling. "This is the work of months, Derval. I can't let it be ruined."

In Derval's cold and hunger, John seemed to be standing at the end of a tunnel. "A human being is the work of nine months," she said, perhaps inconsequentially.

"I would ask you one favor, Labres my child," Clorfíonn whispered, half asleep with closeness and the reaction of fear. He raised his fine head. "Anything, Clorfíonn."

"Leave Dublin with me."

After a moment, he nodded.

He needed light to cut the runes, so Thorfinn held the lamp close. Snorri grunted softly as the hammer struck the chisel, driving it into the ash stake.

"You're very reckless to do this," his companion whispered.

"Reckless, hah! He is crazy." An indignant female voice answered from the bed curtains.

"Give up, Ermingerd, it's no use to persuade, let alone shame him into prudence." A face appeared where the drapes parted in the bed alcove. "Don't pretend to agree with me. You just want me to be silent. You are bringing unnecessary danger into the house of a family that befriended you!"

"That's enough, wife," Thorfinn scolded.

A big woman, heavy with child, lowered herself rather painfully onto the bench just outside the bed. Her hair was uncovered, but she was so upset she forgot her kerchief.

While she held her belly with both hands, her eyes drilled into Snorri's back. "There will be killings after you do this! And what house have you lived in? What house?" Her lips trembled and she began to sob aloud. Her husband burst out in rage.

"No one could possibly take action against us as long as you keep your mouth closed, woman!"

The hammer fell several more times. Thorfinn said nothing more for a while. He was as terrified as his wife, but he was held under control by the duties of friendship and by a fear of disgrace greater than his fear of the king. "Since she lost the last child she has been distraught. Forgive her."

"No pardon is necessary," Snorri said, sighing. "She is right. I was stupid and ungrateful to come here tonight." Snorri said it loudly enough for Ermingerd to hear it. She began to sob louder. Snorri continued, "If you are questioned concerning this, I urge you to publicly repudiate me. But I cannot turn back now. I have killed a king's man and it's likely Olaf wants me dead anyway. A lawless king is the worst of evils.

"There. It's finished."

Snorri held up his work, examining it for error. The stake was twelve feet long and sharpened at both ends. Part of it, of course, would go into the ground. On top would rest the horse's head he'd bought from the butcher. But along six feet of it was written: SHAME TO OLAF, SON OF SIGTRYGG, INSULT TO HIS JUDGMENTS. SNORRI FINNBOGISON CARVED THESE RUNES

Ermingerd, overcome with curiosity, rose from her place and waddled around to the hearth to look at it. She was an intelligent woman and a good housekeeper, when not sick. But that was all too often now. Pregnant for the sixth time, she had buried or miscarried four of Thorfinn's children, but she once had been beautiful, and Thorfinn had not forgotten that. He was very worried about her. For all the bulk of her body, her face was thin and yellow.

"Where are you going to set it up?" she asked.

Snorri looked up into her face. "At the Thingmount."

"That's the best place, if you are going to do such a thing," she agreed quietly. "He . . . he was once a good king." She hesitated to say more. "He—my father fought beside him in York. We received wedding gold from him." She turned away and headed slowly toward the bed. "Don't come back to Dublin after this."

"I know, Thorfinn's wife. I'm sorry to bring this grief to you," Snorri said gently. "I will go out through the byre. No one will see me that way."

It was the end of the barrel, and Holvar was aware of the dregs floating heavily near the bottom. "Ah well," apologized the alehouse keeper, "who would have anticipated that we should go through two great tuns in one week? But between the festivity at the law hall and all the uproar among the natives—the Gaels . . ."

Holvar's ears stretched upward half an inch toward the top of his head, bringing wrinkles to where the hair was thin. His nervous feet scraped the bag at his feet. He expressed his interest in a mumble which the man scarcely needed to keep talking.

"With the poet's complaint to the king, you know—or you ought to know, as I'm told it was a work of some power. And the attack of the Saracens, under this very roof!"

Now Holvar's mumble was more frankly confused. He took his meather of ale and peered into it with vague dissatisfaction, hoping the strainer had not let slip too much of the slime from the cask bottom.

"And now all the Irish are talking about a Viking raid on Dublin. Supposedly by Norwegians, just as the prince of Norway is enjoying the hospitality of the king. What a flock of silly sheep these Gaels can be."

The alehouse keeper's words were spoken in an undertone, strictly for the ears of this Norse visitor. He did not notice the two shocks which hit the Norseman's frame, the first at the mention of raiders and the second—and stronger—when the name of the prince of Norway was spoken. Long training and longer years kept Holvar Hjor from displaying his surprise more obviously.

"The prince of Norway is not called that by all," Holvar grunted.

"He is by all in Dublin," the publican contradicted him equably.

Holvar looked into the gloom of the windowless house, where figures in simple dress crouched on the floor or on low benches, under the smoke layer. One young fellow in the shirt of a peasant was cavorting by the hearth, illustrating by gesture some sort of sword battle. He appeared positively sorcerous in the half-light of the fire. After an explanation in such bad Norse that Holvar could not understand, he rolled on the floor, smacking the stones around him as he did so, and laughing.

Tryggvason in Dublin.

The alehouse keeper was saying, "It is their religion that makes them so. They fill the earth with saints and spirits, and depend on them for everything, letting their wills die from lack of use. Never met a Christian who wasn't plain superstitious." He cast a close look at this square-built, hard-faced traveler and took a chance. "Now, a man who worships Thor in reasonable manner—"

Holvar snorted. "Thick-tongued god of slaves. They confuse him with their bleeding Christ, with all their crosses that look like Thor's hammers." He stooped, picked something up out of the bag, and tossed it lightly between his hands.

The publican blinked. "Don't take that to heart. The Irish rarely know who their own fathers are, let alone the gods. Thor is still Thor."

"And will never be All-Father," murmured Holvar to himself. "Why do they believe there will be an invasion of Dublin?" he added in a louder voice.

The innkeeper sighed, looked out the door, and struck a posture. "That . . . was the burden of the poet's complaint. He had been in the Abbey of Ard na Bhfuinseoge—the place where all that fine carving comes from—and Vikings attacked it, leaving no stone upon a stone. And further, he said it was no simple raid, but an invasion, and that the reavers comb the coast for blood even now."

Holvar could not speak for a moment. He stared from the carved crystal to the cup beside him on the bench, where dark masses of matter swirled in a circle. A man survived also? A poet? A rich man? Who had friends? Holvar suddenly saw Skully's arrogant, adolescent face in his mind's eye. Anger washed hot and was gone. "But a Gaelic poet does not carry weapons. He survived this terrible attack?" The alehouse keeper nodded.

"Then it was obviously not Norwegian raiders," stated Holvar, with a smile of satisfaction.

The publican blinked again at his customer. He was no Norseman himself, but a Dubliner, and uncomfortable at the direction the conversation took in this stranger's mouth. His eye was caught by the sparkle in Holvar's hands.

"Probably it was just a war with Irish neighbors," the Norseman continued, "and this fellow does not want to admit he ran away." Holvar was very pleased with himself, producing this story. He was not normally a man of ready wit, and here was a tale that rang true even to himself. It was proof of the one-eye's inspiration.

The alehouse keeper slouched back a step, as though dissociating himself from the tenor of the conversation. "It would be hard to convince anyone in the city, Norse or native, that the Ollave MacCullen lied. He's well known...sort of a local champion. Besides, my friend, he was not alone in his experience."

Holvar was now beyond startlement. He sat still, making no more encouraging grunts. They were not necessary. His cup weighed heavy in the hand that held it, and he listened to his heart beating. He also counted the men in the house.

"There was also the daughter of Goban, the very carver who made the king's throne of narwhal horn, and two strangers who are Gaill—excuse me—foreigners to the land. It is not two days since the little Saxon of their company sat in my house—where you are sitting, friend—and drew pictures of a strange skill on the stones of the hearth. There. Lean forward and they are visible yet."

Holvar leaned obediently forward and looked at the drawings his mind did not see. "These all escaped the sacrifice—the slaughter of this abbey?"

The other man shrugged. "They are of MacCullen's party. They went to the king together."

Holvar stretched his neck from side to side casually. "And what did the king say to this story?"

The publican was silent. Perhaps he shouldn't have let this conversation start. The town was full of Tryggvason's men, and who knew what was safe to say? He honed his answer. "With the great visit, it was an inconvenient time to approach the king, I believe."

"Sigtryggsson wasn't impressed." Holvar felt a smile sliding over his face. The luck of Odin's favorite. "He is not out for vengeance."

The alehouse keeper stirred the dregs in the tun with his wooden ladle, knowing he shouldn't do that, knowing he was making things worse. "No," he said to the Norseman. "And because of that the poet cursed him, and began a fast on his doorstep: a fast which the king desecra— Which the king did not enjoin. Then there was an attack (no one knows by whom) on the poet's foster mother, Clorfíonn." He congratulated himself on the subtlety of his tongue, in not admitting what the whole world knew: that it was the king's friends who had gone to kill the brehan. "Now they have all departed together, the poet having proclaimed Olaf Cuarán no king." He glanced from the tun to see the Norseman's hand playing with a dead twig of charred wood on the hearth. His hands might have been those of the talented Saxon. The publican caught the man's sullen eye and saw that he was laughing.

"You don't believe in the power of a poet's curse?" the alehouse keeper asked.

Holvar appeared to consider the question. "Depends upon whose poet is cursing." He rose from the bench.

"Where could I sell this in Dublin?" He let the alehouse keeper finger the ball of crystal.

It was intricately cut. Snakes or dragons chased one another over the surface of the stone, and there was a bird with its wings outstretched. The alehouse keeper sighed in critical appreciation. He wished Jan the artist was still about, so he could show the crystal to him.

"I don't know," he said, staring into the unclouded depths of the stone, where the small light of his doorway fled and multiplied. "It is work one does not see every day, even in Dublin. Fit for a noble's house. You could show it to Olaf himself."

He put it down and sighed more deeply. The mention of Olaf Cuarán and the sight of the stone together made a connection in the alehouse keeper's mind. "What does this remind me of? There was someone who worked in crystal. Imported crystal, much like this. And ivory, I think. Someone well-known. Now where . . ."

He raised his head from musing to find the Norseman gone.

Behind Tryggvason sat his wife, Gyda, a woman as pale and conventionally pretty as her mother, Olaf Sigtryggsson's first wife, had been. The king and the prince sat across from each other at the high table while the nuncheon grew cool and the juice of the meats gelled.

Next to his father, young Sigtrygg kicked his heels and let his little crystal ball slide from hand to hand. His attention was all on the grownups. He hadn't seen the younger of the two Olafs in a long time and he had missed him very much. The prince had brought little Sigtrygg a present, of course: a belt of silver gilt plates and a small purse to go on it. It went well with his dagger and sheath. His silky blond hair, uncut and long as a girl's, fell forward over his eyes like a veil as he looked down at the new treasures around his waist. He grinned with pleasure and then frowned. He wanted so badly to go hunting with young Olaf today. It was raining, however, and of course there was the feast that made it impossible. He didn't get to go hunting often, in fact, for his father was so tired that he didn't go out much nowadays. Guthrim, his cousin, took him out sometimes, but mostly he had to content himself with the pleasures of the women: chess, music, and trips to the market. He felt slighted.

Olaf kept Sigtrygg close to the house, lest harm come to the precious child, who it was hoped would not get himself killed like Ragnall, nor have more loyalty to his Irish relatives than to his father's kin, as Gluniairn Iron-Knee seemed to have.

The boy looked up at his father. The old man was talking earnestly with his son-in-law. Now he's truly my brother, Sigtrygg thought gleefully. Suddenly the boy stood up on the bench and, pulling his knife, balanced it delicately between the thumb and forefinger. He was good with his knife, and as eager to show off his prowess to Olaf as he was eager to kill his first man.

"Gyda, look at this," he cried out in his high-pitched child's voice as he threw his dagger straight across the room, where it snuffed the light from the tall wax candle at the dais. Conversation was for the moment arrested by laughter and cries of encouragement. "See that," Olaf Sigtryggsson said. "He'll be apt for battle. No hope for the assassin who pursues my son."

He had to keep that in mind with all the Irish kings he himself had murdered: all the Ui Neals and Ui Fáeláins.

"Come here, Sigtrygg, my rose of many thorns." Olaf beckoned to the boy, who had run to retrieve his weapon, his best-beloved toy, from the shadows on the floor. Sigtrygg was now the center of attention and, for now, entirely happy. He climbed into his accustomed place, his father's lap, and received a kiss from the old man. Then he curled up like a lap dog with his fair head against the king's breast.

The light was quickly rekindled by an attendant. Fruit and hazelnuts were placed on the table. Ale was strained and poured into drinking vessels.

"This first horn should be dedicated by you to the female deities of increase," the king suggested to his son-in-law. Sigtrygg heard the breath rumble in his father's lungs as he said this. Olaf Tryggvason stood, took up the horn, but then just before he was going to utter the blessing, he lowered it.

"Father—I'll make a bargain with you. I will spill ale to the old gods if you will spill ale to Christ and to the saints."

Olaf Sandal shifted in the chair. Sigtrygg knew it was time to get up out of his father's way. He slid out of the chair as his father stood up.

"Don't bother me with this again, especially today." He said it with such an air of exasperation that even the women laughed. "Have you been baptized; is that what you're trying to tell me?"

"I've been primsigned." The younger Olaf smiled and nodded.

The king of Dublin coughed and wheezed. "Well, what of it? I've been dipped in incense and it didn't make a bit of difference to me. All right—whatever makes you happy. I'll drink to your poor sniveling little Christ if it makes you happy. I've done it for the Bishop of York, so I guess I can do it with you."

The prince of Norway smiled and lifted the horn. "This ale to you, Mothers of the Earth. Bring me increase. Health to all who drink here together." Olaf Tryggvason let a few drops fall to the floor of beaten earth between them, then drank deeply.

"Mothers of the Earth, bring vigor to the loins of my son and daughter," chanted the old king. "Timely and quick births of strong children." He spilled and drank.

They worked through all the deities. An hour passed. Each had to stop the libations once to piss.

"It's time to make vows," Olaf Cuarán suggested as they sat down again. The women, hearing this, retired. Gormflaith, who had not joined in the drinking, came to take Sigtrygg off to bed, but Olaf insisted that he stay. This led to some shouting on Olaf's part, fueled by ale, and she left angry, while her husband laughed. "She needs a good bedding," the old king told his son-in-law lewdly. "I can still do it, but not often enough to make her keep her temper." He wiped off his beard with a napkin. "I swear"—he raised his voice—"that if you make my daughter queen of Norway, I will cover your bedquilt with gold and silver to the depth of three fingers."

Gasps ringed the assembly hall. Sigtrygg grinned. There was no one like his father. His magnificence shamed all others. "My father, the King—the Gold-Scatterer!" cried the boy, who, drunk with ale and pride, lifted his own small horn and toasted him. Praise rang through the hall. It was a moment of glory.

But Olaf Cuarán was not finished. He was building to a crescendo of drama. This would be his last great feast; he was sure of that, and it would not be forgotten by anyone in the hall. He had beggared himself to make it so. Signaling to his steward, he caused the crotta and timpan players, and the *clàirseirs*, to burst into music, and a procession appeared. Eight beautiful girls and an equal number of young men, all dressed in the great novelty of identical clothes, carried the edges of a coverlet of embroidered rainbow-colored Byzantine silk. It was lined and edged in furs of the best quality. Olaf Tryggvason groaned aloud with pleasure. "Here is the bedquilt that I will cover with wealth," old Olaf announced. "These choice slaves are also yours and Gyda's. I selected them personally for their intelligence, strength, and accomplishments."

"Father, I am overwhelmed." Tryggvason crossed the space between them and embraced the old man.

"But of course you must have a ship to carry all this in. So I built a longship for you. It is not yet put into the water. Would you like to see it?"

Night had fallen, but torches made light enough for their progress, and the alcohol made the night warm and inviting. Sigtrygg walked hand in hand with his father, going to the wharf and coming back. The prince of Norway was more than pleased, for the ship was a masterpiece. The carving on the keel ends was lovely and expert work. Nothing was lacking, and in addition to the luxury, Tryggvason could see that it was as practical, as strong, and as perfect for warfare and traveling as it was beautiful. It was huge, longer than any longship that he had seen.

He got the point too. Here was the warship with which he was expected to win the crown. Cunning even in his affection and generosity: Tryggvason had always known Olafr of Dublin to be that way.

Tryggvason had been all but raised here in Dublin, after his uncle had rescued him from slavery in the Baltic. He was very fond of this old man who had fostered him, but he saw the backside of every smile of Olaf's, the expectation behind every gift. The Norwegian prince knew it was his turn to make vows.

"If it is in my power, I swear," he told the old man, as he stroked the gilded twining animals on the new ship, "Gyda will be queen of Norway! And moreover, Sigtrygg, your son, will have my support in fortune and trouble even as I have had yours." He said it loudly.

Olaf Cuarán hugged him and slapped his arm. His rotted teeth glinted in the torchlight as he smiled. "I also vow to sacrifice oxen, horses, swine, sheep, and fowl. I will sacrifice twelve captives, too, if the gods strike down Haakon. May his death come soon, who keeps you from your high seat."

Tryggvason grew silent after this, as if it did not please him. It was a short journey back to the hall. More ale and more time passed. Nearly all the guests had left, except members of the royal family and their intimate retainers. Sigtrygg lay asleep on top of sheepskins by the fire. "How is Astrid, your mother?"

"She has had another child," Tryggvason answered.

"That's good. Is she well?"

"Very well. Lodin isn't the man I would have chosen for her, but under the circumstances I am satisfied. Not every man can buy a queen at a slavemarket, but at least he has treated her with honor."

The old king nodded. "I saw a shadow come across your face, my son, down at the ship. What is troubling you?"

The prince rubbed his forehead, and then vigorously rubbed his scalp, leaving his golden hair fluffed up around his ears.

"Nothing, except that I think it is unlucky to vow prisoners now. Haakon has taken to that: he and those Jolmsvikings he loves so much. I hope that the allegiance of God cannot be bought but is given to the just. Haakon's arrogance is beyond all bounds now; some of his berserkers have raided close to York. One of your favorite earls and mine is killed."

"Who?" Olaf Cuarán sat bolt upright in his ivory throne.

"Oswald Cadmusson."

"Dog's blood! It can't be."

Tryggvason nodded and rubbed his hands together. "He and eighteen armed housecarls. They cut the blood eagle into the backs of all the survivors. A badly wounded servant pretended to be dead and so was spared. He said the party was led by Haakon's retainer from the Jolmsburg: Holvar Hjor Roptson. It almost makes me laugh, too, because word reached me from the Orkneys that Haakon is angry with Holvar Hjor, too, for some reason—I don't know what." The prince lifted his silver-chased horn to drink.

Out of nowhere Olaf Cuarán said, "I will make you a present of this human pig's head. Would you like that?"

The prince swallowed his ale and stared with surmise at his father-in-law. He smiled.

The old king got up, rubbing his aching spine and rubbing his backside by the fire. Then he bent for a moment to smooth the silken hair of his sleeping son. Doing so, he lifted the crystal jewel, with its incised birds and serpents, from the boy's relaxed fist and balanced it in his palm. The hall was reflected dark in its glass surface, except for the swimming specks of the lamp's light.

Chapter Thirteen

•

> Eochaid reached the Brugh Mac Og. A tall man came to them and would have turned them out of the country, but they avoided him. In that night he killed all their horses, and in the morning came back and said, "Unless you get out of this country, I will bring death to the whole lot of you."
>
> *The Death of Eochaid,* from
> The Book of the Dun Cow

"I'm sorry you could not at least see Domnall Cloen," the girl said to MacCullen.

"I'm not," he replied. "What could this story do but add to his load of bitterness?" He shielded his face from an overhanging pine bough.

Ailesh stumbled over the rock in a path and caught herself on an elm sapling. Everyone had to stop in place, from her to the hinny laden with books and the heavy iron caldron, while she pulled her hair free of the twigs.

"Ouch! This is no cow path at all, but a deer path, eh? It goes straight up." She turned a sunburnt face toward John, smiling.

Derval cleared her throat. "There is no need for you to be imitating John's bad Irish, heart of my heart."

"But 'eh' is a very useful word. It can mean anything, I think." Ailesh's voice was teasing, and as John Thornburn glanced at her he remembered how young the girl was. He remembered, also, that she *was* a girl.

"Can not," he replied gruffly. "It means . . . it means . . ."

"Anything that you want it to mean."

"Not true. Sometimes it means 'Don't you agree with me,' or 'Wouldn't you like to,' but mostly it means 'Give me an answer so I know you're listening.'"

"But being shorter than all these, it is better," stated Ailesh. "Eh?"

Then Derval laughed despite her blisters, and also Ou Neal, seated on the white mare. But Labres MacCullen twitched from his blond head to his feet in irritation. "Is that the attitude you take to the language and culture that has nourished you, Daughter of Goban? Then we could all save a great deal of trouble if we gave up speaking altogether and grunted like pigs. The Saxons love to be silent, and then grunt at one another after long times empty of speech."

Days spent in the Ollave's close company had eroded Ailesh's deference. She giggled. Clorfíonn Iníon Thuathal only smiled, her old eyes green under the leaves. "Who are you to lecture like the oldest monk in the abbey, Labres? If you have turned thirty years old, I don't remember it."

He lifted his handsome head. "Then you don't remember yesterday, foster mother, for I turned thirty on the morning we left Dublin."

Clorfíonn caught her breath. "So it is! I grieve that I forgot, Labres. And here on this deer path (as Ailesh so correctly calls it) there is nothing I can do to mark the event."

"Happy birthday," said Derval ceremoniously, in English. John echoed her. MacCullen bowed from the waist. "I will bake bread on the coals tonight," promised Ailesh, "and we will pretend it is a feast."

"Then it will be," said the poet. He spared a glance from the path. "Iníon Goban, Cuhain, Thorboern, it is to you three that I owe my thirty-first year. But for your courage I would be under Christ's judgment now. Or sleeping in some new mother's womb, forgetful of all I was and all I cared for."

"Is that what you think?" asked Derval casually. "About death? Either judgment or reincarnation?" She was once more struck by the amount of paganism this Culdee Christianity had managed to absorb without indigestion.

But MacCullen shied visibly away from her, and his eyes widened. "If you know otherwise, far traveler," he whispered, "I am not ready to hear it. And if you know the manner of my death, I beg you never to tell me." He strode forward hurriedly, up an incline that caused both hooves and booted feet to skid.

"I don't," said Derval, panting. "I wouldn't." She kept her eyes to the stony, overgrown earth, feeling obscurely guilty.

Late in the afternoon there was a brief scare, as it was discovered that the hinny Hulda was leading had lost her burden of manuscripts. In the urgency of turning back for them, Clorfíonn came off her horse and landed on her back on the rough and stony trail.

For a moment she lay flat, staring at the sky dazedly. Holdfried cried out and would have plucked the tiny woman from the ground, but that his sister shoved him away. "Are you all right, Benefactress?" the tall Saxon woman whispered, kneeling by Clorfíonn's head.

Clorfíonn blinked attentively at Hulda. "Shouldn't wonder if I was," she said, and she drummed her fingers on the hard ground. Slowly she curled onto her side and put her feet under her. Hulda and Holdfried brushed the leaves gently from her back and shook out her brat. "I guess my dancing days are not yet over, children." She chose to walk behind the horse from that time on.

Luckily the leather bags were found only a hundred yards behind, where they had snagged on a blackthorn bush. But as they congratulated one another for the discovery, the sound of heavy hoof falls silenced the whole party.

"There is nowhere to hide," whispered Ailesh. "Nothing but slick bare hill."

The brehan groaned. "Forgive me, my dear ones. If this is a hireling of Olaf's, it is me he is seeking. And but for me, you would not be fleeing in the wilderness this way."

MacCullen exploded. "But for you! Clorfíonn, but for my insistence on the matter, you would not have involved yourself in our war with the false—"

"Let me by," cried the brehan, striving to force her way past MacCullen, to be first in the path of the unknown. But he held her by her léinne.

Ailesh took out her hammer. "Brace yourselves," said John, in an English only Derval understood. Hulda and Holdfried flanked their mistress, obscuring her completely.

Around a corner of gorse bushes came a tall black horse, sweating and scrabbling with the climb. Its neck was nearly as thick as an Irish pony's body, and it wore a harness of brass and black leather. Sitting upon it was a man also in black, his woolen surcoat thrown back to reveal a mail shirt lined with a quilted cotton. A helm fit over the man's head, hiding the face completely. It was fashioned like an eagle, wings uplifted.

He yanked the bit till the horse's chin nearly touched its neck. The beast strutted on the slippery path, its eyes white-rimmed, dropping sweat from its sides to make black spots on the rock. A huge, gaudy-hilted sword spanked the horse's side as it pranced. The rider lifted his gloved hands upward.

Ailesh, likewise, lifted her hammer. John started, stared at the sword, and bulled his way to the front. "Snorri!" he cried. "Goddammit. It's Snorri the Icelander, decked out like the black prince!"

As the helm came up, Snorri's broad features were revealed. He was sweating as much as his horse. "You left me!" was his first statement, and he made it an accusation. "I go out to the wharf to buy a little something, and I come back to find you flee without me!"

MacCullen stepped up beside John. He regarded the Icelander's outfit with obvious approval. "We did not think you to be in any danger, my friend. Or none that would not depart when we did."

He motioned for John to hold his horse's head. John did so with trepidation, for the animal was thicker through than Derval's Tinker, and it glared at him wickedly. Snorri Finnbogison swung his leg over the table-sized croup and hit the ground. His knees buckled for a moment and he leaned against the horse's side, "What," he began, "do you think I went to the market for, I ask you? Or do you think I bought all this to sit in the alehouse and be admired?

"Of course the danger is yours, Irish poet. But while it is yours it is Thorbeorn's. And while it is Thorbeorn's, it is mine. So the circle is closed."

"With Eoin at the center, once more," muttered MacCullen, thoughtfully. He raised his eyes to Derval. "I have said before, scholar, that our cattle leaper is no ordinary man."

Derval snickered and glanced at the Canadian with amused fondness. John, not having understood the beginning of the exchange, looked from one to the other and then back at Snorri.

Black from head to foot, and redolent with the smell of well-cured leather. The helm turned Snorri's fleshy head into a fantasy. "You look," said John, searching his vocabulary for any word in Irish, Norse, or English to fit. "Just . . . bitchin'!"

Snorri grinned at the approval. "You could all have horses," he said with a shade of resentment. "And war gear. I was going to buy it for all who wanted it. We would have left Dublin like a royal parade!"

MacCullen met his glance soberly. "Then we would have been too much in your debt, Finnbogison."

Snorri growled and led his horse forward, favoring a right leg which long riding had sent to sleep. "What is the money for, then? I have no family, but for two older sisters who are glad to see my butt off the hearthstones. My ship and stock are at the bottom of the sea."

He laughed mordantly and dropped his spiny helmet into John's care. "My money comes from the king of Dublin. I built him a longship this spring: the best he's got. If we can use my gold to beat this sow's son who would send three warriors after an old woman, then better the joke on him!" The garnet eyes of the stylized hawk that adorned the crest of the helmet glinted in perfect oneness with Snorri's own.

They camped in a rocky dimple at the crest of the hill they had spent all afternoon climbing. Ailesh's pot bread was a great success and all toasted MacCullen's thirtieth birthday with enthusiasm.

"We are out of Cuarán's country by now," murmured the poet to Clorfíonn. "Another day's travel and we will be with your kin." She glanced up from her bowl of cheese, to see Labres MacCullen sitting rapt by the orange campfire, his waving hair tossed back by the heat, his eyes dry and mouth slightly open.

A poet makes a strange sort of man, she thought. A great poet must be a madman. She was happy to see that Labres grew madder every day.

"But we must not relax," she said. "For if he will not protect what is within his boundaries, then who can be sure he will respect what is without?" Without waiting for a reply she asked, "What then, Labres? After I am deposited with my kin in Brega? Will you stay with us? All these—your new foster brothers and sisters—are welcome wherever I am in the true lands."

He rested his chin on his fist and his fist on his knee. "I am grateful, Clorfíonn. But I have a heavy duty before me, and that will take me south again."

"To tell Cennait about Caeilte?"

"That's it. And the longer I wait, the harder it becomes.

"And then, for at least Ailesh and me, there is a question of a murder price unfulfilled."

Clorfíonn nodded, unsurprised. "And of the others . . . the foreign friends? What is their interest in the matter, Labres, and what are their plans?"

His eyes, when he raised them, blazed like the fire. "It is gaes for me to talk of that." He rose from the fireside and shook out his blankets.

John found himself quite heartened to have Snorri along, even though, never having asked for a translation, he had no idea why the Icelander was there. He suspected it had something to do with him, though, and it was a new thing with John for someone to go out of his way for the sake of John's company.

As long as the light lasted John played, monkeylike, with the black battle harness.

Delbeth eased himself off his dun pony, trying not to disturb the harp. He stared around him at the Dublin wharves in a confusion so great he began to drool. To ask—to merely ask—after the people he sought was beyond him. The tall buildings and taller ships loomed over him in their angularity and he felt crushed. A man in Norse costume brushed by him, causing the harp to sing an out-of-tune protest. Though he knew this was no reaver, his hand tightened on his spear haft.

All the men were dressed like that, except for the very dark one with a cloth wrapped around his head like a huge bandage, who sat with his back against a pier and cursed outlandishly.

Delbeth led the pony along the waterside, between close housefronts and stalls of beads and axheads. Merchants wished him to the devil as the gangling boy and the wide pony with baggage brushed by.

Though the day was cool, sweat dripped along Delbeth's nose. He had never been in a city before, let alone the largest city in Ireland, and he had never been without clan protection.

Indeed, who ever was without clan protection? It was like being a severed finger (if a severed finger had the power to grope on its own). Thinking of that last interview with the taiseach, Delbeth did not curse but rather got tears in his eyes. To be so deluded by guests. Yet it seemed to him that a year's banishment was an unjust punishment for the crime of letting prisoners go, when he hadn't been told they were prisoners.

And when he stroked the clàirseach in its leather wrappings, Delbeth remembered the honest eyes of the poet MacCullen and those finer yet of the dark woman with him, and his resentment faded for the moment, and he tried to believe there had been some other explanation to the story they had told him that night in the cattle enclosure: the story the taiseach had called a lie. All in all, the young man couldn't have said whether he was chasing after MacCullen for vengeance or sympathy.

There was a fat man, dressed in Gaelic linnia, sitting on a stump beside one of the featureless housefronts. He grinned at Delbeth with a mottled mouth. "Harper, is it? Come to replace the one the Munster poet lost in the raid, boy?"

Delbeth stared stupidly, while he made connections between this man's supposition and his own information.

"Well, I'm sorry to say you're too late," the fat man continued. He paused to scrape dried turnip from his yellow shirt. "They've all gone already. Left in the night. Heard they had no choice."

Delbeth leaned wearily against his pony, who leaned in turn against Delbeth. The complexity of Dublin chattering around his head almost drove him to his knees. "Gone?"

"Because they were dedicated to Odin," stated Holvar. The sullen face of Skully, with bloodshot eyes and black scab on his nose, did not turn away.

"So tell Odin they got away."

Holvar had to restrain an impulse to set his sword between the duelist's chin and shoulders. To see that insolent head go bouncing over the ground now... "Ours is not a god of failure," he answered the boy evenly.

"What will he do about it?"

"Grant us short lives, shameful death, and the afterlife of a slave." Holvar spoke with conviction. "Though it is no true warrior that has to be driven into Odin's embrace by fear. If you had a good heart, it would throb to serve him!"

Glancing around at his dirty and very tired subordinates, Holvar Hjor wondered if he had gone too far. "My heart is throbbing for a Dublin alehouse," came a murmur, unlocatable. Holvar had not intended to speak about the prince of Norway's presence in the city, lest fear or foreboding of failure unman his warriors. But now he said, "Then you'll die hanging over the Dublin gates, fellow, for the man who had declared us outlaw in England is in the city, and he is son-in-law to the Dublin king. And if that is not enough peril for you, know that the sacrifice that escaped us is traveling now to recruit an army of Irish to drive us into the sea!"

Now he'd got their attention. Holvar raised himself off the ground and pointed eastward, over the sloping downs to the sea. "Just today I heard that news, in Dublin City."

"Did you get any money in Dublin, Battle Chief?" was all Skully's reply. "Will we at least be able to eat while we track this perilous Irish wench over the length and breadth of the island?"

Holvar growled. "That was a mistake. The toys I took were signed by the maker. That squat man we found by the stone was known in Dublin, it seems. A man of importance."

Skully scratched a pimple on his youthful face, and the pull on his skin made the scab on his nose smart. "Too bad, then, that we didn't hold him for ransom."

Holvar lost patience. "We couldn't! Not after dedica— Oh, dog's shit. We leave in the morning."

The Vikings groaned like so many galley slaves.

What a farce: keeping watch on a night of no moon. Derval sat wrapped in blankets on the lip of the dell on the hilltop and tried to make sense of what she saw. Luckily the limestoney earth tended to reflect what light the stars gave out, so she at least could tell heaven from earth and the road from the underbrush. But how useful would that be, if an army came pelting up that shimmering path? But, she reasoned, she was as invisible as they were, now that the fire had burned low.

At least the dark and quiet sharpened her ears. She could hear a night bird cry with a voice like a saw on wood. She heard the wind in the hazel, which sounded different from the same wind blowing through oak leaves. She heard every stir and creak of John Thornburn as he rose from his spot by the dying fire and sought her out by feel.

"Here," she whispered. "Ten feet from you. On a boulder."

She removed a seeking hand from the vicinity of her mouth. "Right here. Sit down so I can listen again."

"Listen to what?" asked John, rather too loudly. He bit off his own words.

"I'm on watch." Again the hazel wind, the oak wind, and the bird like a buzz saw.

John gazed down at the trail. "I thought," he said much more quietly. Hesitant. "I can't sleep. I thought we could take a little . . . walk."

"A walk. Why would . . . oh. No, Johnnie. I'm on watch." Still he sat beside her. The wind lifted his flaxen hair and it shone like limestone under the stars. His oversized arms lay over his thighs, with his relatively small hands dangling.

Derval sighed. "What are we going to do, Johnnie? Not these people, I mean—they've got their business—but you and I? How are we going to get back to the cross?"

"I haven't thought about it," he answered.

Just like you, Derval thought, but aloud she asked, "Don't you want to go home?"

He smiled. His teeth glimmered in the darkness. "Sure. All these onions . . . I'm farting myself to death."

"By now they must think we're dead," whispered Derval, looking up at the stars.

John gave a sad little laugh. "No. They'll think I killed *you* and ran away."

"Johnnie, you are so fucking paranoid. They can't convict you of murder without a body, and I don't think—"

"I think I heard something," John interrupted very quietly.

Derval's sentence ended in a tight exhalation. The blackness she had almost forgotten closed in heavily. In an instant she had gooseflesh on her arms and a pit of black terror within her. "Don't scare me like that, Johnnie. It's bad enough sitting here—"

He put his finger to her lips, or near her lips. "I heard something."

"Oh, dear God!" Derval sat and listened. The saw bird, the hazel wind, John's breathing and her own.

A crackle of leaves.

She could hear his muscles tighten. He could hear her rise from her seat. "A deer, maybe," he whispered. "Or a raccoon."

"No raccoons," she said weakly. "Fox."

"Hush."

She heard it again, and also a rustle from a different quarter. Her breath caught.

Derval felt the pressure of invisible eyes all around the hill. She slid back toward the fire. Her bladder threatened to fail her for the first time in twenty-six years.

There was no dealing with this terror. She had not felt anything like it in the Vikings' camp. Surely the noise of her breath whistling through her lungs would draw them—whoever they were—to the camp. Surely the tiny warmth of the dying fire would call.

She looked at the faint outline of blankets. Only eight bodies. Only four men. Only two swords. Perhaps it would be better not to wake them at all. Better to die asleep than screaming and pissing oneself in terror. But as Derval thought this, her hand was shaking MacCullen by the shoulder, and her other palm was over his mouth.

"I see a man, I think," said John at the watch stone. He sounded calm as stone himself.

MacCullen, in turn, crept over to Snorri, who lay on his stomach with his fingers locked on his sword hilt. He called his name, and when Snorri's hand tightened on the sword, MacCullen put his own hand over it. "Peace, Icelander. The enemy would not bother to wake you up."

The poet sought out Derval, to thank her for her warning, only to see what might have been the woman's shadow huddled over at the edge of the camp. And his eyes hadn't played him false; she was relieving herself on the ground.

By Mary's face, what a cool woman. But perhaps she had information. Perhaps some saint or spirit had told her she would not die tonight. MacCullen sighed, well aware no one had said as much to him.

Around the fire they stood, in a circle with shoulders touching. Clorfíonn had Snorri at one side of her and Holdfried at the other. John stood between Derval and Ailesh, holding in his hand a carving knife of the brehan's that felt very awkward to him. MacCullen, he noticed, held nothing: not even leather to shield him. He stood tall—taller even than Snorri or bulky Holdfried, with one hand on the shoulder of each of the women. Looking at him John's eyes stung. He could forgive the man any arrogance. Any crime—even that of cutting him out with Derval O'Keane. That weaponless confidence of MacCullen's made it possible for John himself to face death without horror. Starlight circled the hill like the ring of flame around a candle.

A voice on the hillside. John's stomach tightened. His hand was slippery on the knife's wooden handle, but what he felt was more anger than fear. I don't want to die like a rabbit, he thought. I don't want to be made to look like a fool and then die.

Spitted like a pig. Spitted like a pig, ran the words in Derval's head. She couldn't have brought me here to be spitted like a pig. But the saint or goddess sent her no comfort at all. She glanced to the right, at John, to find in his face the emotionless concentration he had always saved for his art. For five seconds she stared at his sharp, severe face. So, she said to herself, this time I have followed him all the way. Now I understand John Thornburn. She could not have said what it was she understood, but it put out her fear like a candle. She gave him a smile meant to say it all, but he did not turn his head to see.

Now there was no mistaking the men on the hill. One could hear them talking to one another. And as minutes passed and the rustlings became neither louder nor softer, and the voices grew no closer, the circle on the hilltop began to sway with fatigue.

"Why don't they come for us?" Holdfried asked, his voice cracking.

"Because they don't want to, obviously, though I can't imagine why," Snorri replied, laughing. "We can't make them, you know." He drew a slow circle in the air with his sword blade.

MacCullen turned in place, peering into the night. "Perhaps they will not attack until dawn."

Derval gave a half-smothered scream. "By dawn I will be dead on my feet!"

"That is one reason why they would do it," the poet answered her.

"I hear something," said John, tilting his head.

The circle tightened.

Soon all their straining ears could make out a rumble on the earth. John stared out at the ribbon path where it broke from the forest growth and came to the crest of the hill.

"Maybe this is what they've been waiting for," he said. "The horses."

They broke out of the shrubbery at a trot and clambered up the hill: over a dozen horses, most of them white, with riders in mail, bareheaded, their iron helms lashed behind to the saddletree. In front of them rode one wearing a tarred coton and the garb of a Gaelic warrior. The shield at his horse's flank bore the insignia of Olaf of Dublin: an eagle with a hooked beak and outspread wings.

Ailesh stepped through the ashes of the fire, kicking them to a glow. She watched the approach of the horse troop and she defied it, hissing like a cat. She swung her hammer in the air. "Swine! Paid dogs of the Gaill! Some of you will never go home to your master again."

John put his back against hers, feeling the heat of the fire through his tennies. The riders had not made him forget the men coming through the bushes. At least this girl for whom he had gone to such trouble would not be stabbed from behind. At least that.

The shod horses scrabbled and slipped on the rock just below. A cry rang up from the captain of the company, and he waved his shield into the air.

"Thor hulf!" Snorri answered it, and he placed himself in front of his friends, huge, naked, and with his gentleman's sword raised before him.

The captain quieted his horse. "Peace to you, stranger. We seek the Ollave MacCullen, of Leinster."

Before Derval could restrain him, MacCullen stepped out. "You have found him."

With a sigh and a weary rubbing of the eyes, the captain said, "Then know I am Finnchu MacImidel and these are my sworn men. We are sent from the king of Dublin for your aid."

Twenty-six people and twenty-one horses made the dimple at the hilltop a very crowded place. It was very lucky that the troop had brought their own beer and jerky, also, for there was nothing in that dry place with which to make hospitality.

"Again, please? Forgive the slowness of an old woman, but tell me what exactly Olaf said to you?"

Finnchu knit his brow and answered as politely as he

could, for he was a Dublin Gael and had been raised with a great respect for Clorfíonn the law giver. "The king said that you hunted reavers, and by error had left the city before he could direct us to you."

Clorfíonn nodded, and in the light of the rebuilt fire her eyes went the color of mist.

"Well, I'll be damned! Why *not* trust them?" whispered John to Derval. "If they wanted to kill us, it'd be done already, eh?"

"There's that." Derval turned to the nearest of the horsemen, a young man with hair faintly reddish, wearing a leather tunic so worn and old as to resemble linen. "Tell me, honored warrior, why do your foot soldiers not come to refresh themselves in the firelight with us?"

The young man puzzled visibly over her words. At last he replied, in Norse-Gaelic, "We have no foot soldiers, Bhean Uasail. We are eighteen men and eighteen horses. As you see."

Derval sat silent for a moment and then gave a small squeak, staring out into the night.

At dawn they made an awkward procession over the dry highlands, as riders who had slept little worked to rate irritated horses to the speed of MacCullen's walking company, who had not slept at all.

"Agreed that there had been a cold camp down the hill from you," said Finnchu MacImidel to MacCullen. "There is no way to prove it was last night's, or that it was inhabited by your enemies. You are a big enough party to perhaps make other travelers wary for their own sakes, and reluctant to show themselves openly."

"Why are you so slow to believe, Captain? It was not my ears alone that heard men encircling us. Do you not believe in the very reavers the king sent you to destroy?"

MacImidel was a fair man, with a nose turned red by the sun. He played thoughtfully with his flowing mustache. "The tale was of raiders to the south, as I remember." Whether he believed it a true tale, he did not explain. "I find it difficult, Ollave, to believe in rescue coming so aptly. It smacks of the miraculous, and if I were party to the miraculous, I imagine some sense of mine would tell me."

MacCullen stumbled over nothing, and stared at the Captain of Horse. His face colored, but he did not open his mouth.

Ailesh Iníon Goban, however, spoke up boldly. "Yet the miraculous has us in its grasp very often, Honored Captain, as I have reason to know. If you do not see it, you must work to open your eyes."

MacImidel glanced grinning at the rosy girl. His young horse, iron gray and restive, swung its head up and down as though to agree with her. "I will remember that fault in my next confession," the horseman said to her.

Ailesh stole a glance at MacCullen, uncertain whether to count him a friend or foe in this issue. But the poet now walked at a slower pace and his head was bowed.

"But whether your neighbors were friend or foe, they did not attack. Nor will any sane body bother us, many and strong and armed as we are, in broad light between here and the Abbey of Domnach Sechnaill, where there will be time to take stock."

Derval had at last taken off her riding boots, and her bleeding feet picked a way carefully along the path, avoiding the green nettle and crawling briar. John winced as he looked down. "Ye Gods and little fishes. They're . . . suppurating!"

"I never noticed."

John clucked with his tongue and kicked casually at a thistle. "Try Nikes. I wear them for everything and never a blister."

Not ten hours ago Derval had felt herself in possession of the mystic truth about John Thornburn. This morning that truth was locked by pain somewhere in a black closet of her mind. The face she turned upon John caused him to shrivel. "Thanks for the advice. And where's the nearest outlet? I wore boots because I had been riding, remember? And didn't expect any nature hike. Sweet Jesus, I wish I *was* riding. What I really wish I had here was Tinker."

John danced lightly around a deposit left by MacImidel's mount. "There's scads of horses here, Derval. If you want to ride—"

She sniffed. "Haven't ridden a pony since I was eight. It's Tinker I want. He's big and he's well taught. These little sausages know nothing more than to stop at a yank and to go at a kick. If you're lucky."

"Myself, I'd like to have my hat," John announced, to have something to say.

As always, Derval's tempers took years of maturity away from John. As he walked beside her now, kicking pebbles and smashing weeds with his toe, he might have been a well-spoken twelve-year-old. "I dunno that I agree with you. About the ponies. I like them. The way they sorta roll along, without the jitter-jitter of a trot. And they have such kind eyes."

Her blue eyes, pale with pain, held contempt. "Don't get ideas. You're not ready to branch out yet, Johnnie. Not till you've really mastered cow riding."

He laughed at himself, hoping to put her in a better mood thereby. His laughter failed in the middle. Derval sneaked a glance at his face and the dark closet opened. Her own ill temper disappeared as though it hadn't been. "They almost got us last night, Johnnie. Didn't they?"

He shrugged up his brat and put his hands in his pockets. "Yeah. But who is 'they'?"

Ailesh was also barefoot. She bore it much more easily than did Derval. Her embroidered cloth belt tapped her knee with every step. With surprise she noticed that the place where the cloth of the belt had been pulled and twisted by the knot for over a year now lay in a few inches down the slack of it. How much weight she had lost, without noticing! She shook her léinne around her hips. Yes, she was thinner. But she did not feel sick. In fact, it seemed her young system had had all the misery it could take and was determined on recovery. She felt light, and her steps bounced over the grainy earth.

Why should I be happy when I don't know where I'm going and my kin are all dead or far away, she asked herself. She looked around her at the high hillside and the wide plain below. The tails of the horses in front swished like the backsides of self-important ladies. The young soldiers in their leather were pictures from a book; Ailesh, abbey-bred, was not used to seeing so many warriors.

Right behind her was Labres MacCullen, his hair waving fountains in the sun. He might as well be a true brother to her, in his kindness. Surely she took a sister's liberties with him. After him came Iníon Cuhain and Eoin, his hair dangling in his eyes, his thin legs wrapped, as always, in coarse blue trousers. By his slouch she could tell that Derval had been pecking at him again.

This morning she could not be bothered by that. There was a bond between them, it was clear, no matter if the bhean uasal chose to appear a shrew. Looking over her shoulder at her friends, Ailesh Iníon Goban sighed with affection.

Hooves very close to her. Ailesh turned her head the rest of the way round, spinning her body behind it. The young redheaded soldier grinned down at her. He was missing only one tooth. "You must be tired, maiden. Come up on the horse with me for a mile or two."

His Norse accent caused a shudder of revulsion in Ailesh, but she berated herself for it. "I doubt your captain would like the sight of that," she replied, and her nervous hands played with her belt.

"Hah! Why should he care? Are we in a forest, where enemies might pop out of the trees? Come, maiden. We redheads must stick together, for no one else will do a thing for us!"

The day would be warm. The wind blew from the west. "Why shouldn't I?" asked Ailesh of no one in particular, and she hopped up on the pillion behind him. She decided that perhaps she hadn't lost her looks.

The small grasses and brush of the hill faded, and the hooves of the horses sparked off white stone. They marched through a very simple landscape, with wind whipping the fringe of their brats against their faces. It was all downhill, from here. Ahead was the great bowl of Ireland, fertile and full of creatures: the wide plain of Brega.

But after meadow had followed meadow through the morning, they came to a hollow in the land, and a county so filled with green it might have been piled with grass cuttings. And near the shore of the lake rose a low wall of stone. Within the ring were buildings of stone, ranging from small to smaller. The smallest were domed hives. The least small was a corbeled rectangle of Romanesque architecture which could be nothing but a church.

"There it is," MacCullen called ahead. "The Abbey of Domnach Sechnaill. There we can rest and ask ourselves what comes next."

Chapter Fourteen

•

> More, daughter of Donn og McKeally, queen of Ireland, died in this year. Moglekyeran O'Magney was cruelly tortured and martyred to death by the Danes of Dublin. He was a cowarb of St. Coloumbekill.
>
> *Annals of Clonmacnoise* (A.D. 980)

As they came close to the monastery, trees cut off the voice of the wind, leaving a thick silence in the air. John smelled water. Rock turned to gravel and then to black dirt beneath their feet. Ahead was a stand of red sally among lush grass, as inviting to sore travelers' feet as carpets.

Clorfíonn, whom chance had put at the head of the line, let out a heartfelt "Thanks to God. The face of disaster from us!" and climbed stiffly off her horse. Holding her shoes in her hand she stepped barefoot over marshy ground. John and Ailesh scampered after her, with Derval limping behind as best she could. The body of the company went slower, engaged in talk.

At the edge of the willow grove the brehan paused, one foot lifted half off the ground. Then she bowed from the waist, her hands folded in front of her.

John pelted up in time to send a red fawn bolting for cover. He skidded on the west earth and stood blinking at a small two-point stag with wide eyes and a naked, hairy man standing beside it, his hand on the animal's antler. His shoulders, his face, his arms, and the root of his penis were deeply tanned. As John met his eyes, the man sank wordlessly down on his knees. In mud.

John stepped back as quickly as he had approached. He

turned to find Ailesh behind him. "A crazy," he whispered. "I think." He glanced back to find nothing in trampled grass except the prints of two knees. The brehan had gone on ahead.

Ailesh glanced back at John with curiosity. "A naked man, all over hair. With two deer. They disappeared."

"A holy man," replied Ailesh.

"Again? Isn't anybody here ever holy in a comfortable way?" As John looked down at them, the kneeprints were filling with water.

Ailesh giggled. "I am sinful in a comfortable way, Eoin. Will that do?"

John smiled one-sidedly at the girl from the height of his many years. "You don't know what you're saying, Ailesh."

Her gaze was more puzzled than ever.

Just beyond the willows, water spread like a smooth sheet over half an acre. Close to the rear bank there was a thing like a pier with arms sticking out. John could not imagine the function of it, for the single hide curragh the pond boasted was upturned in the shade of the trees. Coming closer he found it to be carved very realistically in the shape of a man, with arms and hands outstretched. As he passed it, it sniffled.

"Another holy man, Ailesh?"

She prodded him from behind. "Don't disturb his prayer."

The ground rose again and became firmer. Fruit trees, carefully pruned and tended, lined the path. They could hear the rhythmic thuds of a hoe biting the earth. John entered the trees to locate it.

The kitchen garden was on the south side of the orchard. The gardener stood among his pea stakes, leaning on his hoe. His hair was black and long in back, tied into a pigtail, but shaved from the forehead to a line running between the ears.

"Looks like a bloody samurai, doesn't he, Johnnie?" came Derval's voice in his ear. The man looked up at the sound.

"Good day to you, slave of Christ."

"The blessing of Mary's son upon you, honored visitors. Welcome to the house of Holy Sechnaill."

The monk had a most engaging smile, and John felt himself relax into it.

"Before you offer us welcome, know that we are twenty-six

in number, with almost as many beasts, and we come pursued by trouble."

The monk's smile faded, but not into alarm. "Then all the more need for welcome, my sister. I will take you to the abbot."

He stepped carefully among his hills of greens and turnips, and John could see his lips moving. He suspected counting the crop, rather than prayer, was the purpose of that movement, and felt the chagrin of any unexpected guest.

The enclosure was low, only four feet or so in height. Its wooden gate ran on a post which rotated into a deep hole in a stone footing. As they passed singly through, Finnchu MacImidel put his hand out in a warding gesture. The last man through, the orange-haired Norse youth, had ready a foxglove pod which he tossed over the gate pole. Ailesh, already inside the enclosure, saw him wink at her. She blushed, for the gate was known as the union of male and female. Then she giggled, remembering how the captain of horse had feared it. There was a great diversity in men.

"If at all possible, Brother Eochaid," repeated the poet, "I would like to see the abbot himself."

The monk who had met John in the garden sighed. "I'm sorry, but it really isn't possible. He is at his meditations."

MacCullen tried to be reasonable. He sat himself down on the refectory bench. "I value his meditations, and it is my great hope that my own soul may feel the cleansing of them. But this is a matter of some urgency."

Eochaid said, "Most especially I may not therefore disturb him, for he meditates with the aid of mushrooms today."

MacCullen's eyes widened momentarily. He nodded his understanding.

"Would you like to speak to the abbot's wife?"

MacCullen broke out in a grin.

"I'm sorry, Ollave, but I am a very simple fellow and out of practice in dealing with visitors. The director of the scriptorium, then?"

MacCullen nodded heavily. "Take me to him."

Father Blathmac was tonsured in the Roman style. He came to the door and squinted watery eyes at the sunlight. He listened to Eochaid's explanation.

"I see, Brother. Well. Perhaps it would be better if one in the position of our dear Father Conoran left such strenuous disciplines to the wild men in their cells. But that can't be helped. Bear and forbear. Bear and forbear." Blathmac turned and led the way into the scriptorium.

John came to listen, though it was against his habit. But he could not resist the appeal of the place, inherent in the very smell of ink and leather.

Monks, either in the old tonsure or that of Rome, sat at a long table, with small bottles of ink at their right hands and fresh feathers in a pile above each working page. A few of the workers had neither tonsure nor the hooded linnia of the monks. One was a very heavy woman of middle years, dressed in canary yellow. In order to supply light for these scribes, some of the thatch roof louvers had been raised, and rested propped on stout timbers. But despite that, John would have been hard pressed to make a fair copy in such gloom. He sat carefully away from the table, watching the woman press a dust-thin film of gold leaf over the letter *n*. When she had done it to his satisfaction, he rose and began to look over the open missals at another table.

"It would, of course, take a large or foolhardy band of Gaill to attempt an assault on the monastery," MacCullen said to reassure Father Blathmac, who seemed to need reassuring. "But it would be wise for all who live here to know that reavers are in the neighborhood."

"Sweet savior!" whispered the priest. "And all the wealth in this room alone—"

Suddenly a gasp, followed by a cry, filled the room. As one, all the copyists raised their quills up into the air, studying their work anxiously for the suggestion of a blot. MacCullen swiveled on his bench. "It's Eoin again. Never the expected."

He found John Thornburn on his knees, his hands over his mouth, his face a few inches from the surface of a book.

"This is it! This is the Book of Kells!"

Father Blathmac walked over, scowling. "That might have ruined much labor, Brother Eoin."

John heard none of it. He hovered above the Gospel of Matthew, hands fluttering like butterflies, not daring to touch. "Oh God, oh God, oh God," he cried in English. "It's the real thing, and even old already. A century old, maybe, and look at it . . ."

MacCullen took the priest's arm. "You must understand

about Eoin. He is a great artist in his own right, and . . . far from home."

Father Blathmac looked at John with a shade more toleration. "He surely has the proper taste. Would that any one of my monks could do such work! But that book is heavily flawed. Beneath its gold and colors it is so full of copyist's errors it can scarcely be read. And to my amazement it contains tables and indexes which refer to nothing at all. Such is the state of learning in these northern monasteries . . . We have the book only for repairs, anyway. It will return to—" Father Blathmac broke off at the sight of John's unabated exaltation.

Joh focused on the men standing above him. Awkwardly he got to his feet. "Please," he said to Father Blathmac, "please turn it to the Chi Rho page."

Blathmac's scanty eyebrows rose. "So you know the book, Brother Eoin? Then, assuming your hands are clean, turn the page yourself."

"Myself?" John's voice cracked. Then, with infinite care, he put his hand on the book.

Like a flea on a bald head, thought Holvar Hjor bitterly. Like a fly buzzing in milk, did they stand out on this bare table of rock. Who knew what eyes were watching in the distance? Two Irish had seen them so far, since they crept away from Dublin. One had run too fast to be cut down. That was disturbing, and could not lead to good.

Wind threw his thinning hair into confusion. He brushed it from his eyes and noticed that Ospack, the old helmsman, had matched his pace to Holvar's.

Ospack smeared the tears of sun and weather from his squinting eyes. "This has been an ill-starred voyage, Captain," he said. "All has been bad with us since those killings in England."

He spoke in tones of depression rather than resentment. Holvar could think of nothing to say. Ospack was no Skully Ulfson to be beat into behavior by swordwork or threats. Ospack had carved the altar stakes at Jolm with his own hands. He had obedient grown sons. He had yearly gone on Viking raids with Holvar over England, Ireland, and the Baltic since both were young men.

"Not ill-starred, old friend, but full of obstacles. We will leave this island with great wealth *and* the favor of Odin. He leads us on, in the persons of these dedicated ones who have escaped the sacrifice."

Ospack blinked. "Well, you have always understood far more about such matters than I, Godi. But how he can show himself in the persons of these Irish who are running away from his fulfillment so speedily—"

"That is his raven cunning. Ofttimes we do the work of the god best when we believe we are evading him!" Holvar felt a moment of satisfaction in this answer. "And our journey into the land of the enemy will reward us for its peril by enough wealth to build our city on the shores of the Baltic."

Ospack scuffed the limestone with the sole of his high-thonged sandal. "Hah! Our city by the Baltic. How I will ever get Freydis there I don't know. I don't even know where she is living, since winter."

Holvar paused, looking suspiciously at a black dot on the horizon. After a moment it flew away and he laughed. "Then get yourself a new young wife, Ospack, and sire another dozen children."

Ospack regarded his captain sidelong. "Easy enough for a widower to say."

Another man matched his strides to theirs. It was Orm, the Swede who had joined them since their Northumbrian disaster. He was very close to Skully Crow.

"Captain, have we any particular reason to believe our wild sheep went this way?" Orm's words were more respectful than the tone in which they were uttered.

Holvar stared cooly at him before answering. "I think we do. I was told they were going over the hills. Inland. Besides—who climbs to the top of a ridge only to parade along it? One goes over. And then, of course"—and here he pointed at a pile of wind-hardened horse manure—"we are following somebody."

Orm listened, shifting uneasily in his leather harness. Skully, more bold, replied, "The hills are full of these little wild horses. As they are full of caves, where a couple of frightened Irish sheep can conceal themselves for days."

Holvar nodded. "But at this point we are talking about more than a score of Irish, most of them mounted, and so not so likely to be as frightened as you think. Do not dismiss the anger of the Gaels, lad, just because you have taken one village without a fight."

Skully grinned. With the scab on his nose, the effect of it was frightful. "I fear no one but their girls. But as to the mounted men—then, Captain, why did we miss our chance to slaughter the camp last night, when we had them, and before the Dublin horseboys arrived?"

Holvar, by habit, clenched the hilt of his sword. "Never! To attack these at night would be unredeemable shame!"

"Shame?" echoed Ospack in disbelief. He had never known Holvar to be so scrupulous. Perhaps it would be ritually better—a greater weapon-feat—to have killed them in the light of day, but to his whole memory, Ospack could not recall that he had heeded such courtesies. Perhaps it would have been far more impressive for Holvar to have killed them in a fair fight, but now it seemed like an error again, in a series of error after error. Luck, that indefinable essence that showed life was going with you, or was strong in you, was gone. Loss of luck meant your days were running out. Great priests often lost their kin and then their lives, Ospack remembered. Maybe Holvar's dead were drawing him. Ospack shuddered at the thought. The dead wife and since last year two dead sons.

He looked up at the sky. A pair of crows, big ones, passed from the left to the right. He sighed quickly with relief. That was a good sign. Maybe not death for me, Ospack thought to himself. Maybe just for Holvar. he was a priest of Odin and he seemed now to be following the pattern: the usual astronomical rise to leadership, victory after victory, fame, the trust and gold of kings, followed by the jealousy of kings, and then what? A gradual turning toward a violent death. Odin's love was always the same. They would not drink together this Yule, he thought regretfully, for he was very fond of his godi.

There was a smudge on the edge of vision. Holvar peered and squinted at it doubtfully, and then climbed a bare bulb of rock which projected over the table. Ospack clambered up beside him, cursing his knee joints.

There was the green plain in the distance, its patterns of forests, lakes, and fields, as shapely at the cleft in a woman's bosom. There were farms laid out, and orchards, and water. There were the tiny round buildings, the rectangular church, and a slender round tower. And as Holvar perceived them all, a sense of meaning descended on him, heavy as a giant hand. He could scarcely breathe. The clouds in the sky seemed to roll over his head. But for the support of the helmsman, Holvar would have fallen.

"There." He pointed to the distance and spoke for the ears of all his men. "There it is. There our quarry is waiting for us, and there the favor of the rune winner will be shown to all who fight with untainted hand. Gold for a second Jolmsburg; its fame will never die out. So . . ." And here Holvar's voice dropped to a whisper. "So he has revealed to me."

John hunched against the north wall of the church, guarding the book from sunlight and blowing dust. Ailesh perched on her heels beside him. She was very impressed with the book, and still more impressed with all he knew about it.

"See this little man with the green coat? He was drawn by a different hand than the others on the page. If you look in the back, there are three names: Ferches, Rafn, and Hengisson. Father Ferches was an Irishman born who worked at the Abbey of Iona in your grandfather's time. I think the other two were his assistants. I'm guessing it was Ferches himself who did the drawings for the Chi Rho. His style is far more confident than that of the others."

"And yet the book is almost a century in age, Eoin. It leads me to ask how old you are."

He glanced up vaguely. "Twenty-nine. Oh. Of course I wasn't around to know all this. Father Blathmac told me about Ferches, and the rest I studied in books. Other books."

"There is much I don't know," answered Ailesh simply. As this is a sentiment never difficult for a listener to hear, John raised his head and grinned at her.

Brother Eochaid strode by, his hoe over his shoulder. He smiled sweetly and waved as he passed them. John's mood made him expansive. "That fellow is what I like to see in a holy man. Not cold water or crawling naked in the weeds. A comfortable sort of holiness."

Ailesh's eyes narrowed. She bit the sour end of a stalk of grass. "But holiness is by its nature not very comfortable. Especially not for the one who is holy."

"Don' see that." John thumbed slowly through the sheets of heavy parchment.

"I do. Your own holiness, now... when you are at work upon your drawings, is not at all comfortable to watch. Your face goes... idiotic."

John glanced up in astonishment from the Gospel of Matthew. "Eh? Idiotic, maybe. Holy, never. I don't even know what I believe."

Instead of replying directly, Ailesh giggled and said, "My father was a very holy man. Or idiotic, if you prefer."

Derval looked up from the bronze harp strings she was cleaning with a linen mitt filled with powdered chalk. MacCullen also glanced across the refectory to see a man enter. He was heavy, very tan of face, and either tonsured in the old manner or bald at front. His steps hesitated. His manner was diffident. He began with an apology.

"Forgive, my friends, that in your hour of need I was not available. Had I known there would be visitors..."

Both MacCullen and Derval rose hurriedly, to greet the abbot.

"...As it was I discovered... in my meditations... that there was need of decision, though I know not whether it was a message from the Son of our Lady or merely that I heard strange voices. I came out into the sunlight, and my brother Eochaid informed me of your grievous trouble." After a moment he added, "I am Father Conoran."

MacCullen introduced Derval as the scholar Cuhain, and himself. "Though our trouble is serious, Abbot, it is not so immediate that you must wrest yourself from deep medicines and fasting. I myself know what it is to fast."

Derval stared at MacCullen. It occurred to her that between one thing and another, she hadn't seen him in the act of eating since the meeting with Olaf. Not even his own birthday "cake." Surely he hadn't continued his fast, with the long walking and the impossibility of his deprivation affecting the king of Dublin at all?

"I am in no danger," said the abbot, lowering himself onto the bench. "This abbey is under the protection of the high king. His namesake founded it. Besides, Mealseachlinn is stepson to Olaf. Between Dublin and Teamair we have no enemies here. I hope there is no danger in any respect, now that you are here. You believe the Gaill to have followed you all the way from Ard na Bhfuinseoge?"

MacCullen nodded. "Though it sounds very odd, Father, and I myself have no notion how they discovered our escape, nor what would drive them to such ceaseless pursuit . . ."

"Except piety, perhaps," answered the abbot shrewdly, with an odd little smile on his face. "Piety will drive men to mad deeds, and the northern heathen have a very wild sort of piety."

MacCullen, not denying this, drummed the tabletop. "We will be gone tomorrow, Father, and expose your monastery to no more danger."

Derval plucked an experimental octave around the sister strings. The abbot's head turned and his eyes softened in expression for all the thirty seconds that the bell-like note rang in the stone chamber. At last he said, "What is to say we will not be raided by this group of pious heathens after you are gone? Or that they might have found us without your aid? We are not poor in works to grace the sacrament, and our scriptorium is as good as the best in Eire.

"Stay, my friends. My great-grandfather, the first abbot of this place, had a belt of skulls that he wore, trophy of the enemies he had killed in his youth. I still keep it in my cell, under the breviary table, since Father Blathmac will not permit it to be stored with the other relics of the monastery. As I am rather fat and take up the girth more than my ancestor, I might be able to fit a few more heads on it. I shall ask Eochaid what he thinks."

With a complacent smile, contrasting oddly with the look of dreamy sensitivity the Amanitas had given his eyes, the abbot went out the door.

MacCullen leaned over the table to Derval and grinned broadly.

Derval had no intentions of falling into the role of minding John's belongings just because she took responsibility for the animal that had borne them. She presented him with the packet of his belongings and suggested he wash his socks.

The packet consisted (besides those socks of battleship gray which the softness of the old Nikes made unnecessary) of his clasp knife, house keys, and an odd pound in change. All these had been in his pocket when he had made the great step backward in time. With them was the shirt that had been drenched in MacCullen's blood.

He glanced at this unappealing item for a moment and dropped it back in the bag in which Derval had kept it. Strange to remember how very sick Labres had been. (John called him Labres simply because he called John by his first name, and a Canadian is impatient with dignities.) Obviously there had been change in the species in this last thousand years, and not for the better, either, for John knew that the wound the poet had suffered would have put him low for a long time, if not six feet under.

The bell of noon was ringing from the church. It awoke a host of echoes from the rocky walls of the valley and beyond: echoes so delayed they developed off-tones and rhythms among each other and were hard to recognize as having originated in the simple dingdong from the monastery. He had been told that the noon bell was rung a half hour early, because some of the herb gatherers of the community wandered a long way into the upper rocks. John looked over the drowsy landscape of the enclosure, where red cows competed with pilgrim penitents for grassy places in which to pray. Among the gray and white gravestones with their crosses and their "*ora pro . . .*" inscriptions. One old gentleman who had green thistles stuck at odd places into his léinne knelt by the wall of the church with his arms outspread. John was thinking once more of the superior sort of holiness of the gardener—he did not agree in any sense with Ailesh's comments on his own condition—when the sun sparked off a church window set with glass.

John scuttled toward the church. Only an hour ago Father Blathmac had shooed him out of the scriptorium, saying his elation was disturbing the concentration of the scribes. But he had (mark of great favor from the Roman-trained priest) been allowed to carry the great book out with him. Only in the compound, Father Blathmac had warned him. John had not needed a warning. He carried the Book of Kells wrapped in his brat, very close to his beating heart.

His luck was in, for there was no mass being offered within the church, and the sun of midday lit it as effectively as John's illuminated worktable at home. John tiptoed warily past certain religious who stood with arms in the position of crucifixion at odd places in the building's nave. Why they felt they had to do this, rather than a simple folding of the hands and bowing of the head, was more than he could say. But it might have been a factor in the production of some of the blacksmith-sized shoulders he'd seen among the monks.

He missed the presence of regular pews, with high seats and backs, as he settled down onto a bench, his bones crackling. The white-painted churches of his childhood (with the list of drowned and missing fishermen carved in stone in the vestibule) had their attractions. Yet when was the last time he had visited a church, except to take rubbings?

He knew better than to put the book in direct sun, temptation though it was to see the pigments glow. Calfskin, like any leather, degenerates and cracks to nothing under such treatment. So he placed himself in a position where the sunlight, filtered through small round panes of glass, merely tickled his thigh.

An active sort of contentment spread through John Thornburn as he leafed from page to page. The soft light put a glow to the coat of Saint Mark's lion, and the eyes of the saint himself seemed radiant. He flipped from face to face, feeling the work of the forgotten artist in the tendons of his own forearm. After a while he came upon the page illustrating the Virgin, and stopped at it.

Why was there no other female figure in all this wealth? And why did this one lack the rotund complexity of all the other saints portrayed? John doubted it was by Ferches.

John felt something like pique at the monks who would design such a beautiful thing and leave out something as important as females. It was not a political response on his part, brought on by contact with Derval's feminism, but rather an aesthetic one. John himself preferred to draw women and thought there was more in a female worth drawing. Especially for any artist who preferred a curve to the straight line. He imagined himself engaged in minatory dialogue with the good Father of Iona.

The sun had been crawling toward him as he sat in reverie, and now, like a daring puppy, it came up and licked his eyelids. John shut his eyes against the brilliance and then gasped, for behind his eyelids came the image of Bridget as he had seen her, in rags and glory.

Though he had not exactly been asleep, John woke up. He heard the self-directed babble of the child in the corner, and the groans of one poor pleader whose position was at the feet of the altar cross. He looked at the altar, at a painted wooden Christ with large blue eyes and arms as stiff as the crosspiece of a telephone pole, and he looked into those blue eyes. He felt his breath go harsh and felt, also, oddly, the stirrings of his penis within his jeans.

"What?" he said aloud, staring through the Christ. "What is this all about, please?" He stood up.

"Why did you bring me here?" It was a question John had never asked before. Never thought to ask. The book slid in his hand, and as he caught it, he saw the sunlight shining through the parchment as if through amber wax, and he could make out the backward Latin on the other side.

On impulse John put the book back in his brat and yanked at the string of his bag. He drew out his rusty-brown shirt and unrolled it. In the front pocket was the many-folded sheet of tissue he had left there, and despite the dried blood it came open as cleanly as waxed paper. He stared once more at the obliterated pencil work. He went to the glass window with it.

Without thinking of the horror of what he did, he put the four corners of the sheet into his mouth, one by one, and got them wet. Then he pressed them against the flatter area of the glass and they stuck. The sun's light, through the stained paper, was the color of dead leaves.

But the lines were there—every little clear-etched spiral. John growled to himself in satisfaction. He rummaged for his knife. The end of the corkscrew attachment he fitted against the groove made by repeated tracings. He began to whistle.

Worshipers looked up. Dobarchu, wife of Brother Aidhne, the cook, glanced over, frowning. The White Lady knew there were different rites in the church and different churches among the faithful, and what with the odd prayers of the Welsh and Hebrideans, not to mention the acerbic Romans themselves . . . But to make such noise at one's devotions, in the church itself. Dobarchu had no fear of taking responsibility on her shoulders, and so after waiting a decent time, she lifted her skirts and proceeded toward the source of the disturbance.

It was with her own eyes she saw the shining cross of blood upon the window, eclipsing the sunlight in its brilliance. And there was no mistake that the little poorly dressed stranger jumped for joy to see it, and cried out for sheer happiness as he cast himself into it and was gone.

Dobarchu spread herself flat out on the carved stone floor and praised God in a voice more loud than the stranger's whistling.

Chapter Fifteen

•

> "It would be a mad world completely, the people would be putting their bicycles upside-down on the road and pedalling them to make enough mechanical movement to frighten the birds out of the whole parish." He passed a hand in consternation across his brow. "It would be a very unnatural pancake."
>
> Flann O'Brien,
> *The Third Policeman*

After the rosy beauty of the gate dissipated, John found himself in total darkness. For a moment he thought he had come to some terrifying half-world, and that he would never escape. But there was a ground, and he could move along it. As he bumped into the drafting table and fell face forward onto the floor, he realized that he had made it back into his house. He wondered why night and day, for the first time in his temporal zigzagging, were off sequence.

John stumbled to the light switch and turned it on. The inside of the room was as it had always been, albeit even more dusty. But the sixteen-paned French windows in front of the drawing board had been covered crudely with plywood. All the windows had been so treated, and that was what had put the room in darkness. John shut the switch off again and waited for his eyes to adjust. Pinpoints of light shone through the cracks.

So the house had been boarded up—by the police, certainly, since Mrs. Hanlon would have no interest in disfiguring her property in this manner. He tried the door handle. The latch moved, but the door, nailed shut to the frame, wouldn't budge.

Confused for the moment, he walked over to the refrigerator and opened it. He wrinkled up his nose and slammed it shut again.

"*Pists,*" he whispered. (He had always cursed easily in Irish.)

A click sounded in the living room, and John went to investigate. It was the stereo turntable, which he now remembered he had left without turning off. He walked over and was quite surprised to find that apparently nothing had been damaged. He lifted the arm back into its cradle, and shut it off.

Why would the police have left this going, when they had taken the trouble to board up the house? It didn't make sense, but John dismissed it from his mind. He had more important things to think about, so he sat on the couch and thought about them.

He had certainly solved the problem for Derval and himself. All he had to do was to usher her through the church window and into his bathroom. And it was no bad time to do it, now that Ailesh was safely in the monastery of Domnach Sechnaill.

But this vision, roseate as the gate of Bridget, faded as he considered it, and as he considered the import of the boarded windows and nailed doors. Arriving in his own home century was going to be a bit of a problem. Explanations. John had no gift for explanations.

Derval did, of course. But Derval, if John was any judge, was not going to be too eager to leave the tenth century, now that things had at last quieted down and she could rummage about to heart's content. Showing off to the locals. And come to that, neither was John Thornburn himself too eager to leave. After all, when all this Ailesh business was done, they did plan to bury the gate for good. There'd be no going back.

When all this Ailesh business was done . . . John gave a large sigh and dangled his hands between his knees. He had a desire to do something for the girl, if he was going to say good-bye for good. While he was at it, he'd do something for Derval too. Help her display herself to best advantage in front of the olive.

Hurriedly he changed his clothes, washed himself, and shaved. Then he noticed something he'd been missing for days. In the corner of the hallway lay his fisherman's cap; the battered, lumpy blue hat that was almost part of his head. As he got himself together he popped it on and felt immediately better. Then he headed back into the bathroom.

The bathroom window might be easier to get open. It would certainly have required fewer boards to cover it. Standing on the toilet he gripped the heavy shower-curtain rod. (He knew it could hold him, because he'd played with it before.) Swinging himself out, he kicked the window. The glass shattered and the flimsy plywood waved from one nail and then dropped noiselessly into the weeds below.

Daylight streamed into the bathroom. John checked his pockets for his wallet, passport, and bankbook, then gently lowered the leather satchel with its precious contents to the ground. He jumped.

Suddenly he felt the presence of the twentieth century. Inside the boarded-up house he had been protected from the noise, but as he walked to the bus, a deafening bombardment of sounds assaulted him. Somehow, the week that he had spent in that other place had made him vulnerable.

What a shame. He had thought this was a quiet street. It looked pleasant enough: the old trees, the wide, uneven paving, fancy iron- and brickwork fences in front of old semi-detached houses, small front gardens graced with beds of roses and annuals. Greystones wasn't O'Connell Street, after all; he had felt as at ease here as anywhere in Ireland. But now he was followed by an electric broom, an aircraft, two radios, a television tuned to the BBC, a domestic argument, a group of small children fighting, and of course, dozens of automobiles. They whizzed past with an alarming din at frightening speed. He covered one ear, but that brought no relief. He stuck his finger into the ear.

At first it was individual sounds that bothered him. Then he heard the underlying roar of Dublin itself, stretching across the miles. It was a noise made up of hundreds of sounds. It was a hum that set his teeth on edge. It unnerved him so much that he hardly realized that the bus was passing him on the way to the stop. He ran to get there, only to find a waiting line long enough to delay the driver for all the time that he needed. He mounted the steps and climbed up to the second tier.

Up here he was nearly alone. He felt his shoulders sag slowly down from his ears. A tightness in his throat dissolved. He watched the green grass and gray pavement go by.

As the bus wound its way toward the city the ticket attendant finally got around to coming upstairs. He walked down the aisle and asked John for his destination. For just a moment John panicked. The sound of the English shocked him so much that he struggled to remember what to say. Finally "Dame Street, Trinity Gate" came out. The conductor asked for thirty p.

John counted out the coins, and watched the fellow clip them into his change belt. "Thanks," said the conductor.

"Right you are," John answered casually, having rehearsed the answer all during this transaction. Then he was alone again.

It was impossible that he could be thinking in Irish, after only seven days' exposure. He had had four years of French in school and never succeeded in making that leap. And everyone in . . . in that other place told him how bad his Irish was. But still, he found his native tongue sounding very odd.

His mind was working differently; he could say that without fear he was being blinded by conceit. He had never before felt safer on the roof of a bus than in the middle. It had never before seemed reasonable to invest his money in needles.

There was a stop. A large crowd got on: workers from a small factory or office. They filled half the seats on the upper tier. So much for his privacy. Their speech provided another stimulus and shock. Of course, he still knew English, knew intellectually what the words meant, but he had to follow the sentences carefully and put them into Irish in his head for comprehension to take place.

John's palms were sweaty. He wiped his hands off on the clean corduroy pants. How would he live this way again, he wondered. How long would it take before he could ignore the noise? What if he never readjusted? Holding tightly to the leather book satchel for reassurance, he took his eyes from the rows of brick houses and the whizzing cars. He took his nose away from the automobile exhaust that made his gorge rise, and brought the intricately tooled leather up to his face.

There was a comforting scent, mixed of peat smoke, tallow, oak bark, and cows. He followed the soothing patterns with his eyes. Variety and order were both there.

Nothing else around him seemed as real as that book sack.

It was getting late in the day by the time he got off in front of the Bank of Ireland. The bell on College Green was ringing four o'clock. People were already knocking off from their jobs. It was the beginning of rush hour. Long queues were forming at the commuter stops for the buses out to the neighborhoods. The names on the signs told John of the names of the ancient monastic houses: Tallagh, Drumcondra, Santry, Glasnevin. They had ringed the village of the Ford of the Hurdles, once. In my time, John thought, I have heard their bells ring. And the bell at Trinity. How many others could say that? He felt like Methuselah, he thought. But no—he had outdone Methuselah. That old man lived for nine hundred sixty-nine years, and John's memory stood over a thousand.

He wondered if this sort of thing happened to other people, and if so, why no one seemed to know about it.

In between the whizzing streams of traffic stood the statue of the man who had written "A nation, once again." John looked at it, for a moment, trying to decide whether to go straight to the bank, or to head over to the Trinity Library. It was Friday—a long bank day, so there might be time . . .

The noise was still deafening, but he was gradually getting used to it again. For a moment he hesitated, and then started walking toward the college.

The library had won. Or rather, John's curiosity had. It seemed great crack to compare the two books (or the one book in its two ages), and he was hoping that Kieran Hakett was on duty today. With Kieran and a bit of luck, he might actually be able to touch the manuscript.

Kieran and John were old friends, or rather, old for his stay in Ireland. They were drinking buddies and had both worked in a graphics shop together when John had first come over—he as paste-up man, while Kieran was printer's devil—and the position hadn't worked out for either one of them. John quit, and Kieran was sacked for referring to his employer in highly original language while the man was in earshot.

One thing John worried about was the possibility that someone who had read about a "mysterious disappearance" might run into him here, so he took a circuitous route through the halls, avoiding the green entirely.

The library was closing up for the day, but he asked the fellow at the door to see Kieran, and he slipped in just as the attendant locked the front door.

"Well, hello, my man, you old bastard, ya!" Kieran saluted him in the neatly pronounced but slightly nasal accent of Kimmage. "How the fuck are ya?"

"Good enough, eh?" John slapped his shoulder and shook his hand warmly. "Good enough."

"And what brings you here to this den of shameless bibliomania? Would you like a cup of tea? I'm just getting ready to knock off." Kieran loosened his tie and sat down on his desk.

He was a good-looking fellow, rather nicely built, a long head and face, with curly light-brown hair, blue eyes, and a clipped, slightly reddish beard. He was an insane hurling fan and belonged to a good amateur team.

Derval hated him with a pure hate.

John admitted he could endure some tea.

"Good man." Hakett disappeared into the staff room and came back with tea and two heavy china mugs. "Would you fancy a biscuit? Oatmeal or jelly centers?"

John replied that he didn't care much.

"Then you'll get the oatmeal, 'cause I've a terrible hunger for jelly centers. Some Ald One—some dithering old cunt, God love her—left her parcel in here and as we've no way of uniting the lost little bikkies with their mammy, all we can do is inhale them, right?"

John grinned. "I've no moral objections."

Kieran ate noisily and neatly. "You never did say what brought you here."

Instead of replying, John laid the satchel down on the desk. His companion saw the tooling and made appreciative noises.

John pulled out the Book of Kells.

Kieran gasped audibly at the sight of the gilded silver cover, dazzling with filigree plaques and irregular cabochon jewels. "Jesus, Mary, and Joseph! Where the fuck did you get that? Whose bloody throat did you have to cut to get your shithooks on it?"

John smiled and opened to the carpet page.

"Jesus! Jesus Christ!"

John had never seen his friend so abashed, and that in itself was a pleasure, for Kieran was one of those young men who affect a fashionable indifference to everything. Now he was simply twitching with admiration. "Jesus, shit, oh dear," he said. "Are you going to tell me you did this?"

"I did not," John replied truthfully. "I'm taking care of it for a friend of mine. I wanted to see the two of them together, just for the crack."

"It must be worth a fucking fortune."

John made no denial, but said instead, "It was commissioned for a priory. To be used for the mass."

"Good enough. Good enough." Kieran nodded his head. "Let's not be near it with the tea, nor the grease off the food."

He whisked everything back to the staff lounge. John could hear him washing his hands furiously. He could also hear him getting the keys. John's heart began to beat fast. What would happen if an object met that part of itself existing in another time? Would the book blow up? Would the world blow up?

Maybe just John himself would blow up.

But the matter was literally out of his hands now. For Kieran was back. He had put on his conservator's white cotton deacidified gloves. Tenderly he lifted the jeweled wonder on the desk. Together they walked to the pH-controlled and humidity-regulated case where one of the chief treasures of the world lay. Kieran handed what he thought was the copy to John and opened up the glass.

"Don't touch her, for fuck's sake," he warned. "I'll just slip her 'child' in with her and we'll have a look-see."

It was done. John held his breath. The old Book of Kells was at the Chi Rho page. Kieran turned to the same one in the new copy and pushed them close. The edges touched. John's heart nearly stopped.

Nothing happened. There was a long sweet silence.

The vellum had darkened with age, and the colors faded just a little. There were little stains and frayed edges. But otherwise they were exactly the same.

John stood amazed. Even stripped of its book shrine, mutilated and cuffed about by time, it had exactly the same power to move. It was a magical thing: a talisman. Of what, John wondered? It had the life of Jesus written four times over in it. Was it a symbol of the bond between deity and humanity—a true product of spirit and body? But it wasn't Jesus who had been responsible for John's being able to fondle the great book in its completeness. It was Bridget, and she was . . .

John tossed that question aside. He looked over at Kieran, who had stepped back so as not to let the tears fall on the precious books. "Jesus, they're lovely, aren't they?" Kieran said softly. "Fucking gorgeous."

John turned away in embarrassment from all this emotion.

"What got me just now," Kieran continued more composedly, "was that the one who did the copy didn't just duplicate it—it's a reconstruction of what she must have looked like when she was first finished. Look at how they matched the vellum." He pointed to a shadow made by a grouping of creamy white blood vessels on both pages. "They used the exact same part of the animal on this. It's not just a surface replica. It's a fucking masterpiece."

Kieran removed the "new" one and gave it back to John, locked up the case, and readjusted the instruments. "Who did this?" he asked.

"A team of craftsmen," John answered. "A priest did the metalwork."

"Where?"

"In Scotland."

Kieran took off the gloves and wiped his eyes with his handkerchief.

"It's a great comfort to me to know that something like this has been done. You never know what could happen. It's stupid to have anything like this in a major city in times like these."

"Oh yes, the sulphur dioxide."

"That and the chance of the fucking bomb."

John opened his mouth and then closed it again. Kieran went for the tea, and John slipped the book back into the satchel.

"These accessories: the shrine and the bag. They're not copies?" Kieran asked.

"They are not."

Kieran smiled slyly. "Trying to sound like an Irishman, John? Or have you been reading James Stephens?"

John made no sense of this remark, but hadn't the energy to question Kieran. He sipped his tea: a great comfort after the ordeal of introducing the book to itself. That bout of fear had come upon him unexpectedly and he had suffered it in total silence, without raising any suspicion on the part of his companion. You really ought to think about things beforehand, he told himself. You really ought to.

Kieran caressed the dark surface of the satchel. "They did an incredible job on these accessories. It really brings it off. The style is perfect."

John nodded in agreement and tossed off the tea. He had already spent too much time indulging himself. He had things to do. And anyway, he didn't feel like talking to Kieran just now. Not after looking through the two books. The *Book*. John loved its spectrum-bright, unfaded colors far better than he had realized. He felt a sudden foolish passion to make all things in life—acts and words and colors—pure.

"I've got to be off now. Must get to the bank, eh?"

"Well, I must say, you know how to make a smashing impression of yourself. You've made my day. No! My effing week!" Kieran brightened up. "I'll meet you after. We'll have a few jars."

John refused with a good imitation of regret. He shouldered the satchel and walked briskly around to Dame Street. Despite its being a long bank day he got there just before the bank closed and withdrew every penny he had. Fifty-three pounds, sixpence. He began to walk briskly toward O'Connell Bridge.

The rush hour was now full on and the sidewalks packed. Close to the bridge a horse-drawn wagon, a flat-bedded rubbish hauler, turned in to join the cars. A whole family was on it: traveling people. The father stood up in the front, the reins in his hands. Behind him on a pile of filthy clothes and bedding sat a bunch of dirty-faced but obviously healthy children, all of them with hair that was fiery red.

The bridge was lined on either side with fruit sellers. Buskers, a fiddler and an accordionist, made wild music, a hat out in front of them. John threw money into it.

The Liffey seemed too narrow to John now. Successive generations had forced it into tighter and tighter banks, which had then been frozen into stone. It was fairly deep and very dirty. The river Pottle—the water that John and company had crossed outside the gates of Dublin—was gone, and the black pool with it, all covered over with streets. They were now nothing more than drainage patterns, unknown to anyone except the civil engineers. John sighed as he swiftly crossed over the short span, passed poor old Daniel O'Connell, gobbed with pigeon shit.

In the middle of O'Connell Street stood Clery's department store. John disappeared into it and emerged half an hour later with forty pounds of his money spent. He had sewing needles, a shoebox full, as well as dozens of spools of brightly colored silk buttonhole twist. It was a stroke of genius, he told himself, remembering how Ailesh had braved considerable danger to retrieve her single brass sewing needle. A steel needle of the quality sold in the twentieth century would be worth the equivalent of thirty pounds in the tenth. Silk, he knew, was also expensive and sought after. Best of all, these goods were compact and he could carry a king's ransom in a small shopping bag. Of course the clerks had all thought he was insane, but what skin was that off his back? Ailesh would have cows.

Feeling successful and lavish he headed for his favorite chip shop. Evening was getting on. The street lamps were just being turned on as he made a right onto the Drumcondra Road. He was now in the old Georgian neighborhood, where the houses were made of brick, with slate roofs. Fanlights ornamented the brightly painted front doors of the small shops, pubs, off-track betting establishments, and homes. He passed a turf accountant. He passed MacGill's Public House, a red-lacquered, gold-lettered sign over it. Behind the counter of a little grocery store, the whole family were watching the RTE evening news, everyone with a dinner plate balanced on his lap. John caught this glimpse in the open door as he went by. He could smell O'Donnell's all the way down the block, and he was so hungry that he quickened his pace to meet it.

It was an old place, which had been in operation since the twenties. Bare, unpainted concrete floor, low ceilings, wooden tables and bentwood chairs . . . Dark wood moldings set off creamy colored plaster walls. A sentimental German oleograph of the Sacred Heart adorned one wall, with a red electric vigil light in front of it. There was also a poster of the Declaration of the Irish Republic, and a calendar. Over against the rear was the chipper. The first time John had come in here, it had been love at first sight. The frying machine filled the whole back wall. It had bright green and pale yellow enamel art deco panels in a fan shape, with fancy chrome counters, warmers, and deep-fat fryers. Elaborate glass and chrome racks held the dripping hot fish and chips.

There was no variety at O'Donnell's. One either got potatoes or fish or both together. Hot tea and cold beer were sold, and milk for the children, but that was it. Still, the portions were generous and very fresh. And as the cook-owner knew his business, it was delicious as only simple good food can be.

O'Donnell was a proud man. He kept the chipper spotlessly clean. The customers who came in here were from the neighborhood, working people, and John always felt at home among them.

As it was suppertime, there was a line of people getting large orders of take-out for their families. A few individuals were treating themselves. Over in the corner a young couple on a date were feeding each other and laughing. John got to the end of the queue and tried to decide whether he wanted tea or beer just now. He had already resolved on the number one portion: four large pieces of cod on a mountain of fried potatoes. And he wanted a beer, too, but he was afraid that the alcohol would make him sleepy. No, he thought to himself. I'd better have the tea. I have to ride a horse tonight.

He felt something jab his leg. Feeling down his trousers he discovered that the needles were getting him. Some of them had worked their way out of the paper envelopes. He turned the bag around the other way and saw a big fellow standing behind him who grinned and nodded.

"Handsome rucksack, that."

"Thanks."

"Reminds me of something I saw a while ago."

"Oh, really. Fancy that, eh?" John replied in a rather flat, discouraging tone. He didn't want to go through a big conversation just now. He wanted to eat and be on his way. This was especially true since he no longer enjoyed speaking English very much. The stranger kept on, undiscouraged.

"I work for Board na Mona, you know."

John answered, "Really."

"My cutter turned up a piece of stone a while back, covered with little knots and swirly things just like that pack you've got."

John didn't reply. There was a humming in his ears beyond

that of the uproar of Dublin. He remembered the peat-darkened shards of Bridget's cross, and that memory made him endlessly weary. "Grabbed in the ass by fate," his father used to say about coincidences like this. If there were coincidences like this. If there were coincidences . . .

The stranger kept talking. "I'd be in your debt to know where you got it. It's a pure pleasure: a good piece of work like that."

The line moved up. John found himself at the counter. He ordered quickly. The fellow kept talking. "Did you get it from prisoner's aid?"

John turned around to look at him. "I did not. I mean, a friend of mine did it. I've just got it for a few hours and I'm returning it to her."

The stranger smiled. "The name's Burke—Peter Burke, but my friends call me the Smasher."

John didn't think it was a name of good omen. Then he got the point of the nickname; it was a compliment. Peter Burke is wonderful (*is maisin*). Smashing, as the English language had adopted the expression. He was huge, sturdily built, strong-faced, but with a personal warmth.

"Your supper and tea. That's ninety pence."

John took his plate and mug and turned away from the chipper to face the man behind him. "I'm J—uh—Eoin Thornburn. I'm in a big hurry, but if you want a good look at the satchel, you're welcome."

Burke thanked him with a grin.

John sat down and began dousing the plate with malt vinegar. He was well into the second piece of cod when the Smasher came over with his own meal. "You don't mind if I sit here? Thanks. You know, it's not often I've been in Dublin. My teeth have been killing me lately, and I went to see my cousin Tim Cooney. He's got a clinic on Eccles Street. And by the way, if you need a good cheap dentist, he's the very man! At me all day and I can eat tonight!"

John smiled and nodded. He realized just now that if he had trouble with his teeth in the tenth century he was going to be up a creek. But then, he wouldn't stay long enough to worry about that.

But what would his life have been like, if he hadn't been able to get back? Short and brutish, like history had told him? Or bright as the movie *Camelot*? Neither one, of course, but a lot like every life. Toothache, disease, death, and crying babies. But we die once anyway, wherever. But that was not to say things would be the same.

He smiled, letting his thoughts wander. He could be an historical figure. Eoin Cattle Leaper, they'd called him. John the . . . the headachy was closer to the truth. But if he couldn't be a hero, he could be at least an ancestor. What if this man sitting here was one of his and Derval's descendants—imagining that they had gotten stuck where there were no little pills or condoms.

The odds were rather for than against this fellow being a descendant of that mythical child of his and Derval's. Everyone in the tenth century who had a reasonable number of living children could be and probably was an ancestor of millions of people. John had put the satchel up on the table. The Smasher was gently examining it with his finger following the knotwork pattern. His hands were enormous, with blunt, thick fingers. But the way the nails were shaped and the turn of the thumb was not like his, nor Derval's, but more like Ailesh's, and those of her father. His snub nose was like Ailesh's too.

A hard place formed again in John's throat. The Smasher, who was usually a silent person, had been talkative only because he was so nervous about accosting a stranger. Now, deep in art appreciation, he was himself again. Both men sat silently, John eating and Burke examining. "You'd better eat your supper," John said, as he finished the dregs of his tea and popped the last pieces of potato into his mouth. (God, how he'd missed potatoes. How he hated onions.)

"The line isn't perfect on this one, but it's still a fine-looking article," Burke confided.

"Eh?"

"The line. It's not like it was on the pieces of stone I found. On them the swirls were all connected. It was . . . amazing."

John replied, "Yes. Amazing." He nodded. How many others would have noticed that, he wondered, even as he tried to keep his face bland.

"Your friend doesn't make 'em to sell, by any chance?" Burke asked a little desperately.

"No, I'm afraid not."

"Well, too bloody bad."

John stood up to go, picked up the satchel and his parcel. He looked down at the Smasher just in time to catch his eye. "Why don't you make yourself one? You've had a good look at it. For twenty pounds you could get the leather and the tools. I bet," he added meaningfully, "that you've got it in you to do it."

"What, me? Go on!" The Smasher shook his head, embarrassed. "No, I've never . . . Well, God bless. And thanks."

Burke offered his hand. John shook it strongly and said in old Irish, "The blessing of Mary's Son, the Maiden Bride, and all the saints to you."

"Jesus, I'm sorry. I have no Irish at all anymore," the Smasher answered and sat down to eat his food.

John caught a bus for Houston Station, took a commuter train to Greystones and a cab out to Mrs. McCaffrey's farm. By the time he got there it was late: about nine-thirty. There was no moon to guide him down from the road to the stables and house. He could see in the distance that the stable lights were turned off, for which he was profoundly grateful. Still he had to go past the bungalow. Halfway down the road he heard the dog coming, barking a little. John cursed it, but there was no way to escape now, so he stood his ground as the big Doberman came rushing up. "Tancred! Be quiet!" John called out in a stage whisper. The beast stopped barking, but what happened next was almost worse. He knocked John flat onto the road, whining and slobbering over his face. John extricated himself from the dog's tender affections with difficulty and stood up, dusting himself off.

"Good lad. Yes, you're a good old lad, you old son of a bitch. Yes, and you are one too." He was wondering whether Mrs. McCaffrey had heard him. If she had, he had better go talk to her before she called the police, with disastrous results for everyone.

Tancred was no longer barking, so he was able to tiptoe to the lighted window of the bungalow. Through transparent, lacy white curtains he could see a tall slim woman with silver hair. She was reading by the light of a table lamp. Another dog was asleep at her feet. It seemed she had no suspicion that anything was going on. Very carefully, John stole past the house toward the stables, with Tancred in close attendance.

As he entered the building, he was greeted with welcoming nickers, and these sleepy sounds reminded him of how long it had been since he'd had a good night's rest. Going first to the windowless tackroom, he switched on the light. He took Derval's saddle and bridle. With the saddle in his arms he stalked around until he discovered Tinker. The big gray horse was turned out in one of the large paddocks surrounding the stable itself. At the stable door he made out the heavy shape of Mrs. McCaffrey's own western stock saddle, hanging from a stand. This was more John's idea of a saddle. Feeling extremely wicked, he took it, replacing it with Derval's close-contact jumping saddle. He rather suspected Derval's was worth more, anyway, despite its smaller size.

Tinker was dozing. John patted him and whispered, "You old hefalump: how 'bout going out a bit, eh?" Standing next to the big animal, whose withers were above John's head, he was not at all sure he could control it. In Newfoundland, he had handled harness animals, but his efforts as an equestrian were limited.

Derval's pride and joy was a crossbred Irish farm horse/Thoroughbred. Derval became infuriated when the English sporting press referred to Tinker as part "Irish draft horse," because she denied that there was draft-horse blood in any native Irish equine, and considered it just one more ethnic slur by the English. Tinker looked much more like his gray mother than his stakes-winning father, and had her dark eye and easy attitude. He stood over seventeen hands high at the withers.

As John fumbled with the cinch, this usually patient animal began to wiggle. John's progress grew even slower, and his whispers shifted from endearments to curses. Somehow he got the pad and saddle on. Then the bridle. The horse opened his mouth reluctantly to take the snaffle bit and John felt a twinge of sympathy. He had worn braces as a child. Finally he led Tinker out of the paddock.

He lifted his left leg and sprang off his right, aiming his left foot for the stirrup hanging far above his knee. With the first touch of his weight, the big rectangular saddle slipped neatly down under Tinker's belly. The horse widened his eyes in alarm. Using his shoulder, John shoved the saddle back into place. He tightened the cinch further, wondering why it was now so loose, when it had been very snug when first put on.

He was very proud of his cloverleaf cinch knot. Though it came from macrame, not horse training, he knew it was correct.

This time he led Tinker toward an upturned section of log which had been set beside the stable door. The horse stood beside it calmly and John flung himself into the saddle. Tinker let out a grunt.

Perhaps he ought to tie himself on, John thought, as the great animal began to move. Perhaps he could find a rope in the stable, and . . . But no. John remembered the saddle hanging under Tinker's belly and imagined himself dangling down between the nervous hooves. Better to fall cleanly off.

Now that John had mounted up, the dog Tancred was just delighted. Apparently moonlight rides were something he was occasionally allowed to enjoy. He began to prance around John and Tinker, and then finally to run around in circles, joyfully barking. John urged the horse around the side of the stable away from the McCaffrey bungalow. There was a beam of light in the distance, and Mrs. McCaffrey's voice. "Tancred. Get in here and stop raising hell, you big, dumb dog!"

Tancred whined and drooped at both ends. A romp over the Wicklow Mountains was much more attractive than sleep. "Tancred! Heel!" The dog dropped his tail and obeyed. "No rabbits for you tonight," she scolded. "And no bailing you out of jail, either." The light from the open door disappeared. John sat immobile for some time, while the horse shifted from foot to foot, impatiently. As he waited in the dark, he decided not to ride up the road. She would surely hear it, if he did. No—he would ride the horse across the pastures, where the soft grass would cover the sound.

The horse was very fresh, and not content to walk. But his ground-eating trot bounced John like the proverbial sack of potatoes, which pleased neither horse nor rider, and at last the horse compromised in a long, swinging walk that covered a great deal of ground.

When he had crossed the main road, it took John a little while to find the boreen over the mountains that Derval had used only last week to get to his house. He had only been with her a few times, but once he located it, it was relatively clean going. Tinker knew the way very well.

He was having certain problems with Tinker. The horse was used to Derval's understated dressage signals. John's commands were so crude, even when correct, that the horse wasn't sure what was expected of him. John had never mastered posting, either, and even if he had, the western saddle would not have cooperated, so whenever Tinker broke from his walk John would call a hearty whoa and bring him to a complete halt before starting over. The bags on John's back bounced with every step, of course, and the cloth shopping bag with the needles in it dug into his back. After twenty minutes of suffering he rode up to his house.

It was close to ten-thirty. Except for an occasional car, the streets were deserted. He felt a real sense of urgency now. If he was noticed by his landlady, or still worse by the local garda, it was all up. He had to get into the house without attracting attention, and that of course meant that somehow he had to pry the piece of heavy plywood off the door without making a sound. It was impossible to sneak the horse back through the bathroom window.

He tied Tinker up to the fender of the Morris Minor, where the shadows from the trees made him a little less conspicuous. How, he wondered, do you make a horse inconspicuous? Then he sneaked around to the back and, unlocking the messy little garage, he located by feel the crowbar hanging up on a nail.

It took him some time of very careful prying to loosen the plywood. He stood it gently to one side, unlocked the door, and, untying Tinker, led him easily into the house. Once inside, he tethered him to a leg of the kitchen table. The horse was unable to raise his head much above his back in the seven-foot ceiling.

John dropped his bundles onto the sofa, went back out and, as gently as he could, closed the door, placed the plywood back against it so that the cops wouldn't see anything amiss on their walk. Then he crawled back through the bathroom window, and after blundering around in the dark, he opened the refrigerator door. It would give him just enough light to do what he had to do.

John shouldered the shopping bag and the book satchel, wadded up his Irish clothes inside a beloved Hudson's Bay blanket, and tied it all to the saddle horn with a piece of clothesline.

He turned on the stereo on the very lowest setting at which it was still audible. He put the needle at the accustomed spot of the record, hoping that its week's abuse would not have destroyed it entirely. To his astonishment, the sound of a concertina filled the air.

The disc had been changed. It was now a selection of Canadian songs collected by Alan Lomax. The song he was listening to was one called "The Shores of Newfoundland." That struck him as very odd. Could it have been the gardai who put this on for amusement while boarding up his house? He felt a moment of householder's outrage. Then for an instant he knew fear. What had they done with the music that would take him back through time?

To his relief, he found the album neatly stowed with all his others in the rack below the stereo. Trembling he changed the record back. He turned on the fluorescent tube on his light table which illuminated his much-worked first tracing of Bridget's cross. Picking up a burnishing stylus, he began to follow the pattern to the accompaniment of the piper. Behind him it began to happen. A red glow like a gorgeous sunset began to compete with the sickly blue-green of the light table. Finally John put down his stylus and turned around to see the pulsating, living spirals that filled the gate.

Tinker snorted, looking wild-eyed at that which had formed in front of the bathroom door. John took the reins and attempted to lead him in, but the horse refused to move. Tinker neighed and then pissed onto the musty carpet. John cursed, then he laughed. He could see two policemen with a forensic specialist down on their knees. "This seems to be horse piss, Lieutenant." In the end, John picked up a dish towel, and then wrapping it around Tinker's eyes, as though leading him through a fire, he took the cheek strap of the bridle, and the huge bulk of the horse and the small man disappeared into the impossibly tiny room. In a moment the house was totally empty. The only sound was the broken water tap, dripping away, and the needle of the stereo, circling around at the edge of the paper label.

He felt the dirt under his feet as he blinked into the darkness. The bulk of the horse pushed him into grass. "No," said John quite loudly. "No. It's a church! I came out of the church, and I have to return to a church!"

But it wasn't a church, as his eyes told him moments later.

It was a path parted in the high June grasses, where a week before bodies had lain bleeding. There before him under starlight were the scars in the soil where a great, broken stone had been dragged.

Ard na Bhfuinseoge. Vikings. John pivoted, twisting the horse's neck almost back to the saddle, but the attempt was futile; the red gate had closed almost immediately behind them.

Chapter Sixteen

•

> "Are you better than Christ? He came to redeem woman no less than man. No less did he suffer for the sake of woman. No less do they enter the kingdom of heaven. Why should women not come onto your island?" Shame reddened the cheeks of Senan. "Enter here for the glory of God, then."
>
> Saint Canair's reproof of Saint Senan,
> from the Book of Lismore

The news came to Derval O'Keane in the little round refectory as she sat in conference with MacCullen, Clorfíonn Iníon Thuathal, MacImidel, Father Blathmac, and the Abbot Conoran. The director of the scriptorium had just slapped his hand smartly on the tabletop, saying, "The way of Christ is not the way of bloodshed," when Dobarchu clawed through the cattle guard across the door. Abbot Conoran had only time to reply, "But if blood is to be shed, would not the Lady's Son prefer it to be that of heathens than of his own faithful?" When he and all around him were silenced by the wildness of the cook's wife's expression.

"Miracle! Miracle!" She fell onto her plump knees before the bare wooden table. "I have seen a saint taken bodily into heaven before my eyes and in our own sanctuary!"

All stared. Conoran narrowed his eyes in perplexed doubt. "What and where, good woman?"

"The little fair stranger, Abbot. In front of the window of glass in the church. It was our savior's cross that came for him, shining like the sun of morning, and he faded into the light of heaven and was gone. Gone—and there is nothing left but his relics behind him, drenched in the blood of Iosa."

Labres MacCullen smiled his fond, superior smile. "I suspect our Eoin Cattle Leaper is again showing his quality—" But in the middle of this sentence he glanced over at Derval, and his thoughts were startled from his mind. For she stood beside her chair with her mouth agape and her skin was mottled gray.

"The gate!" she shrieked in English, and as she thrust herself out from the table she came near to fainting, and her knees hit the clay floor roughly. But Derval crawled forward unfeeling, rose again, shoved brutally past Dobarchu, and went out the doorway of the refectory.

The company could do nothing but follow.

MacCullen found her by the tall west window, shaking and shivering, dry-eyed. Before her was the sheet of paper, still creased and darkened, stuck to the lead and the glass. He stood behind her and put his hands on her shoulders. "What has he done, woman?"

As though his touch and his words were keys to unlock her from her paralysis, Derval slumped in his arms. Tears came out of nowhere.

"He's gone home. Without me."

MacCullen winced to see her pain, and shuddered at his own imaginings. He put his arms around Derval and locked his fingers together. With her face turned to the wall, Derval wept.

"What is this story?" asked the abbot. "I will not hide from you the truth that I am easily confused today!"

Derval said nothing. She put her hands up toward her face, but the poet's hold restrained her and she let them drop.

"Our Eoin has a power," MacCullen answered for her. "I know not all about it and wish to know less, but he has come to the aid of the Gaels from . . . from a far place, and brought with him this warrior and noblewoman."

"He went and left me behind!" cried Derval with childish shrillness. She choked with the violence of her tears. MacCullen hugged more tightly.

"Then he is no man, Daughter of Chadhain. And whether he goes or stays, he surely was never the man for you!"

Derval turned with difficulty and faced him, struck dumb by his vehemence. Her eyes were soaked and her nose slimy. The poet kissed her on the lips.

The abbot and MacImidal regarded this scene with no

trace of comprehension. The brehan Clorfíonn only smiled and wandered, green-eyed, to the window.

"I don't think," said Derval in a small voice, "that he meant to abandon me, you know. He doesn't mean to do anything. He's just a fool sometimes . . . a lot of times."

"Well I know!" replied MacCullen, letting her slip free. "And were he not such a natural, I would have fought with him long since over the poor care he's taken of you, woman."

Derval wiped her face with both hands. Her dark brows drew together. "Why should Johnnie take care of me at all?"

MacCullen picked up one of her hands and put it to his lips. One by one he touched her fingertips with his tongue. "In a year, noble lady, I could teach you not to ask such a question."

She let her hand slip onto his broad shoulder. There was still a shade of puzzlement, or else malice, in her voice as she said, "But I'm too thin. And talk like a servingwoman. I dug a hole in your side like I was digging onions and I . . . Ooof!"

"Perfect memory is to be reserved for poetry," MacCullen stated. His embrace came close to breaking Derval's ribs. Her own response startled her, and it had to do with fear.

Clorfíonn saw fit to interrupt at this point. "It is a heavy power of Eoin's, to be certain, if it was his power that took him away. For Dobarchu did not exaggerate about the blood."

MacCullen freed his mouth from Derval's black hair. "Blood there is, foster mother, but not that of our savior. It is only the blood of my battle wound that stained Eoin's work."

"Is it, Labres?" asked Ui Neal very softly. "Look at it and tell me that again."

Her tone pulled him over to the window, with Derval O'Keane, hand in hand. He caught his breath.

The tracing paper was there, firmly pressed to the window. Each knot and spiral of it stood out as thin and clear as knife cuts. But it was red, not brown. Red with blood as fresh as cherry juice, and though the sun beat on it, it remained clear.

There was a beating on the door of the sweathouse. Ailesh, huddled in her misery, ignored it. Brother Eochaid went to the door with a lamp, scratching his pubic hair casually. On his way he tripped over the sullen bulk of Snorri Finnbogison. Eochaid engaged in low conversation through the door and then shut it again. "It was only Father Blathmac. He thought I shouldn't be in here with you alone."

Ailesh raised her head dully. "Why?"

Eochaid considered the question. "I suppose it to be because he is Roman trained. Rome seems to teach monks to be great worriers." He squatted down beside the girl again. "I told him the Icelander was with us, however, and with that he made content."

Ailesh lost interest in the matter. She groaned, not for the first time. Eochaid shook her gently. "Fortitude, my sister. Would you like the fine redheaded horseman to see you with your face all twisted like this?"

"Piss on the redheaded horseman!" Ailesh's sobs were smothered by her knees.

"Even if he had to go," she hiccoughed, "how could he have gone without saying good-bye to me? Did he think I would try to keep him—to restrain him from going home? I would not!"

Eochaid patted her on the head and gazed off into the blackness of the sweathouse. He sighed. "Perhaps he meant to come right back from his far home. Perhaps he still does."

Ailesh's head came up instantly. "Of course! That must be it! It explains everything—" Then her confidence slackened. "But Derval doesn't think so. She wouldn't have been so distressed if she thought he would return for her at any moment."

Brother Eochaid grimaced his annoyance to the hot stones on the floor. He produced another consolation. "Are we so sure that the bhean uasaluis in Eoin's complete confidence? Could it be he had secrets even—"

"That's it!" Ailesh raised her head and smote her knees with both palms. "I say she is not! How could she be when her every word is a scourge on his back? If I were Eoin, it would be a long day in winter before I told her anything of my plans!"

Now she turned on the inoffensive monk. "And another thing, Brother Eochaid. Eoin did not leave for fear of the Gaill! It is only this week that he saved the life of Snorri here with nothing but a bowl of curds to match against a Saracen's sword, and the next night he slew an assassin with an ax, practically before my eyes."

Snorri Finnbogison, hearing his name coupled with the

word "Saracen," grunted in agreement. He added a long statement of his faith in Jan Thorboern's wisdom and integrity, which, though in Norse, was completely intelligible to Ailesh.

"I believe you," answered the monk stoutly. "He must be a hero of classical proportion. Such a man would never leave his friends in trouble. Nor would he take away with him a book of immense value that does not even belong to us. (I tell you quite frankly that Father Blathmac is more upset about that than about any possibility of Norsemen at our door!) It must be he has thought of some plan for our aid."

Ailesh, with the emotional flexibility of both love and youth, thrust out her hand and found Eochaid's ear. "You have comforted me, Brother! I am perfectly at ease now. And—eh? What was it he said about you? Oh. Eoin said he liked you best of all the monks, Brother Eochaid, because you had such a comfortable sort of holiness."

Eochaid flinched away with a grunt. "Holiness? Comfort was better said indeed. Far from being a holy man, child, I have been so obstinate in my will as to refuse the orders of priest and abbot, preferring instead my own peace of mind."

"Then you have much in common with Eoin! I understand you both!"

Eochaid grinned. "No doubt you do. But who on this earth is fine enough, my sister-child, to understand you?"

In the early darkness, under no moon at all, MacCullen went walking with Derval O'Keane. From the apple orchard they could look downward to a lake full of broken stars, surrounded by black lowlands.

He sat down on the turf and pulled her beside him. But then he turned his face from hers and said nothing for five minutes. A wariness, a preparation for rejection, seeped into her. Finally he said, "I have a thing to say to you, woman, that should have been said long since."

Something went hard and ancient inside Derval. She took her hand out of his. "I know. A wife and five children."

He blinked at her in astonishment. "Not at all, Derval, pulse of my heart. Do you think I could have a wife and not have mentioned her in all these days? There are men so secretive, I know, but by my office, woman, they are not myself!" His quick grin went out again.

"No. What I must tell you is a thing of shame which will perhaps ruin your trust in me, and now that I have . . . Now I would regret that with great grief."

Derval's spine crawled, as all the shames she could think of paraded before her. "Then don't tell me, Labres. Just lie here with me and be quiet."

He did lie down, but his chuckle was rueful. "Lying down is about all I can do with you, lady with hair of night. For I have not broken fast since I met Olaf Cuarán in the law hall of Dublin, and what with the journeying and the worry I might as well be an infant in wrapping for all the use I can be to a woman."

Derval shook him in fury that was only half pretense. "Still fasting? I suspected it! You bloody, bloody fool! Why?"

"Because I set a fast," he replied, wrapping her up in his brat. "It grates on me to fail in it, merely because there is a perjuring Gaill on the throne of Dublin."

"Well, I know a man can live a long time without eating, if he starts out fat, but you—having a wound in you I could poke my fist into . . ."

MacCullen sank onto his back again and regarded the stars behind the apple leaves bleakly. "That *is* my shame, Derval O'Keane. For you see I have no wound on me at all. And perhaps that is why I feel I must fast, that I do not escape all suffering—"

"You what?" Derval propped herself up on her elbow. She could hear a single cricket in the grass nearby. "You don't have a wound? By Jesus you had a wound, as you and I both know!"

He sighed heavily. "By Jesus and by his Mother I did. But not since the saint, whom I denied, showed herself to us in the woods. I was healed with young Ailesh."

Derval puzzled. "You were? Then why did you work so hard to convince us it was a sham—a false visitation?"

MacCullen looked over at her. His eyes glistened faintly. He dug his fingers into the brat which covered them both as he said, "Because I didn't know her when she came before me."

She could feel the tension in his arms. A thread of wool snapped. "I am an ordained poet," he said, "and my duty and my labor—and my glory, if glory I can find—is to be open to the inspiration of the unseen world. I tell you in truth, Derval, that I have had more labor than inspiration in my life: though I studied as no other boy at Munster in my time, I never felt the touch of the Spirit in my poetry. And why should I, I ask myself? None in my family before me have been poets. Poetry is a divine calling, and a man may wonder if perhaps he has misheard the call. Perhaps he was not called at all and has no business—"

Derval put her hand to his cheek but said nothing. He stopped for a moment to kiss that hand.

"And what good was I at Ard na Bhfuinseoge, with all my learning and the respect they gave me? There is no greater power than true poetry. But they are dead, and I live by accident and by the compassion of one who didn't know my name. Oh, Scholar, believe I was not quick to admit that the vision of the saint of Kildare in her beauty had been granted to two who seemed to me Dubliners of the serving caste, if not runaway Saxon slaves!

"And when the daughter of Goban, who also was not permitted to see, found she had been healed of all her injury, I, too, put my hand to my side and found whole flesh. Scholar Chadhain, my heart was hardened like that of the king of Ulster who raced the woman Macha against his horses when she was heavy with child."

Derval leaned over him. She laughed in her nose. "That explains a lot," she said. "I thought you were superhuman."

"I have thought I was. Now I would be very content to believe myself only a decent man. But I have allowed my dear foster mother to praise me to my face for my honesty! That was both crime and its own punishment."

"Forget it." Derval smiled. "It was never your fault that you failed to recognize the old goddess—er, saint. She has her purpose, and remember what she said to you? That one day you would curse and rave with the best of them. By her authority, I forgive you for denying her, Labres MacCullen." She kissed him lightly on the face.

He took her face between his hands. "You have the authority of Bridget, Daughter of Cuhain? God be with us! How did that come about?"

She grinned and kissed him, openmouthed. "I'm a woman, curlytop. And I'm overjoyed to find you sound, however long you concealed the fact. Now I don't have to worry that you're going to fall dead at my feet at any moment."

His teeth shone. "If I fall at your feet, lady, it will not be because I am dead." Growling, he drew her down on top of him. Nothing was said for a few minutes, though much was accomplished, until he murmured in her ear, "Three days is not such a time to go without food, it seems."

Derval snuggled into the bedding in the little beehive cell she shared with Ailesh and two of the female penitents in residence at the abbey. This dividing of her from her companions was Father Blathmac's Roman idea, and might have caused some sharp words between Conoran and his director of the scriptorium, had not the two women decided it was better to go and keep the peace. The light of a single, stinking tallow rush light showed her the features of the worn, middle-aged woman across from her. As Ailesh was not in bed yet, Derval shared her overwhelming happiness with the stranger, in a smile so sweet it would have astonished many who knew her well.

Her heart was full of radiance, and she had not felt this way since the day she got her first horse. Each time her thoughts drifted back to MacCullen (and they were never far away) she found another grace or quality to cherish. His fine face, his perfectly proportioned body, the generosity and expertise of his lovemaking . . . He was intelligent, endlessly loyal, and he threw himself into his work with a dedication which she knew how to value. Even the aspects of his character which had put them into conflict, and would undoubtedly do so again, could be reevaluated. After all, who wanted a horse anyone could ride? Derval, despite her temper, could be a strong and tactful rider.

Rider. Her mind, by its own pathways, drifted back to his expertise in lovemaking. "Poor Johnnie," she murmured to herself with compassionate dismissal. She glanced covertly at her companion in the cell and determined to sneak out when she was sure Father Blathmac would have retired to his joyless Roman-trained meditations. But no sooner had she closed her eyes than there was a noise in the doorway, and Ailesh stood framed by night.

"Derval! Wake up; it is the Gaill! The reavers have found us, and their fires surround the abbey wall!"

Behind the low stone wall small lights flickered, moving between one building and the next. There was no one in the place sleeping tonight, Holvar reflected. And that was fitting, for a man needed time to prepare for death. In the end he would kill them all, of course, for this he did was not sport.

He wondered how many there were, in there, and how many of them were women. Without queasiness of any kind his mind slid to a contemplation of his oldest daughter, who slept on a bed of down and rushes, warmed by the bodies of her seven children. He yawned. It would be a long time before he saw Thjodhild again, if ever, for she had not suffered under the decree of banishment like her father.

It was just as well Halldis was dead. Had died before knowing her sons—Holvar's sons—pyre-burned on the English shores. Before seeing her homeland disappear behind the ship's wake forever. Halldis would have called the raid a bad bargain; she had never any passion in her for Odin. What woman did?

Holvar saw movement, white in the distance. A man approached from the direction of the abbey church. He was tall and well built. He glimmered in the darkness. Holvar found himself looking up into the face of a man he had killed the week before.

MacCullen also recognized Holvar, but as he was a subtle man, he let no clue of that recognition pass. He only stared down at the red, wind-roughened arm which had held the sword, and he said, "My name is Labres MacCullen, and I am a poet of the Munster Academy, and Ollave of the kingdom of Leinster. Why did you come here, Godi?"

The voice was as much a shock as the Gael's reappearance, for he spoke in perfect Norse, with a more cultivated accent than did Holvar himself. "I have pursued you through the woods of the island, as you well know, man. Know also that you are the dedicated victim of Odin and will not escape him again."

MacCullen took this with seeming calm. "Of Odin, you say? Well, I was dedicated at the age of seven to Jesus, son of

Mary, and to the saint of Ireland who serves them, so I feel that may have precedence."

"Take care your words, lest you go to the god's presence defiled, Irishman."

MacCullen stared coolly at the Norseman. By leaning over the wall he was able to make a certain use of his height. "I? Defiled? You are incomprehensible, reaver. But tell me—am I your only object in this place? For if that is so, it seems to me a great waste of substance for your men to throw themselves upon both a fortress full of monks—"

"Monks!" Holvar tossed out the word in contempt.

MacCullen smiled grimly. "Irish monks. There is a difference. And a troop of Dublin cavalry as well—"

"Plowboys on ponies, man. Do not try to cow me with such threats. Know that in Northumbria just this year my men took a fortress of a hundred, and when the sun was high there was not one of them left, and we lost but eight men. And I doubt there is a man here to fight the equal of Cadmusson."

"I know about Cadmusson, Holvar Hjor," replied the poet. "The captain from Dublin told me. I know further that neither your rightful king nor the king you have chosen to follow smiles upon you. I suggest, ere you add destruction to folly, that this morning see a battle of different sort: between your chosen champion and me alone."

Holvar took a step backward. He forced his eyes from the tall poet's face and looked at the stars. He thought of a battle against a man that could not die and he suppressed a shudder. He said, "An Irish poet challenges me? But I have always been told such a man is a bull without a pintle, for all the good he is in war."

This pulled MacCullen upright. Holvar put his hand to his sword hilt, half-believing the Ollave would attack him with bare hands. But after a moment's silence, MacCullen said, "My weapons are not common ones, Gaill, but you may find there is a point in them."

Holvar laughed, almost against his will. "Perhaps so. But I am a skald of my people, Irishman, and the voice of the Wolf's-Father. I know that great songs come after great deeds and not in place of them. Odin has promised this place to us and sent us to it through hardship. Tomorrow he will deliver it—and you—to us. Your lives will be a sweet offering to my god, and your riches will build us our city to replace the home fortune has denied us."

MacCullen opened his mouth to curse the Norseman for a devil, but instead he heard himself saying a very different curse. "Holvar Sword, I tell you that after tomorrow morning you will not go down from this mountain to trouble Ireland any more. Both my land and the country that has vomited you out will be quit of you forever. So shall it be."

Holvar hissed between his teeth and braced his hand against the cold stone of the wall. "You! You're a dead man already!"

But MacCullen was walking away.

Delbeth did not know where he was going, but the pony seemed to. It was well-known that a dun horse could see through a wall of stone, so Delbeth merely clung to Sedna's mane and hoped he would not lose his head to any low-hanging branches. But as the night drew on, and the cold with it, the track evened under Sedna's hooves and there was a feeling of space around him. He looked up to find himself in an ocean of stars, and he caught his breath. Even the stars—the Lady's lamps—shone on him in unfriendly manner. Nothing was right for a man without dirbfine.

Delbeth was glad when the pony sniffed, whickered, and broke into a running pace, for he was just about as weary as he had ever been, and this exposed hilltop was no place for a campfire. He descended into the low country now undisguisedly relinquishing control of the journey to Sedna. The clàirseach tied to the saddle scraped against sally wands with a sweet protest.

The ground was mucky, and then dry again. The pony called out, and was answered by a horse in the distance ahead. There were lights. Delbeth found himself in a clearing, with a cattle wall before him. Behind it he could see a row of beehive cells. An abbey.

But not all the lights were before him. In the bare, closely grazed space around him were fires. And men about them. How odd. With clumsy hands Delbeth pulled Sedna to a halt.

Someone approached the boy. Politely Delbeth slipped off his horse. His feet, travel-swollen, stung where they touched the ground. He stared at a short, broad man dressed in a leather skirt and tunic. The man spoke to him, and Delbeth did not understand a word.

Surely the fellow was no monk from the abbey, thought Delbeth. He had no tonsure, and the leather and padded cotton tunic bore no resemblance to a religious habit. And why would a monk be carrying a sword that nearly brushed the ground? After that one long greeting (if greeting it had been) the man had said nothing at all, but only stared at Delbeth thoughtfully. Another came to stand beside him: a thinnish fellow with very bright eyes and something wrong with his nose. Delbeth felt his hair pulling itself upright. His shudders woke the harp. He led the pony quickly to the gate in the wall.

"In the name of the gods my kin swear by, who comes here?"

The voice behind the wickerwork spoke Irish. Delbeth replied, "It's only me. Delbeth of. . . of. . . I have brought the poet's harp to him."

Brother Eochaid opened the door. He had a small lantern. He peered beyond Delbeth and then at him. "Come in and God protect you," he said. "God protect us all."

MacCullen came to Delbeth from the refectory, where council was being taken. He met the boy by a poor lamplight and found himself wishing he could read the expression on Delbeth's face. "I have returned the harp," Delbeth said.

"You must have come a hero's road to do so tonight," replied MacCullen, a bit uncertainly.

"No one bothered me, if that's what you mean." He handed over the clàirseach in its sheepskin case. MacCullen did not look at Delbeth as he took it. "Those men out there. Are they Gaill? Reavers?"

Now the poet raised his eyes. "You passed through them and did not know it?"

Delbeth sighed and rubbed his long nose with two fingers. "When I came to Dublin I found everyone looked like the Gaill. These men look no different. And they didn't hinder me."

MacCullen's confusion turned to pity. "Their intent is to kill us all at dawn."

Delbeth heard this through a sort of cold gray fog, like old woodsmoke. "To kill us? So. Well, it hardly matters. . . to a man without kindred."

"Without kindred?" Suddenly the reason behind Delbeth's presence became clear to the poet. His face darkened in a leonine scowl. "You are without clan? Because of this? Of us?"

The boy's hidden anger found vent for a moment and he glared at MacCullen without words. Then he dropped his eyes as he said, "You lied to me, Ollave. Perhaps it doesn't matter much to you—I'm only a cowboy. But you left me with nowhere to go."

"No word of it was a lie!" And then MacCullen flinched away from Delbeth and the little oil lamp he held threw wild shadows between the two. "O saints of God, I am entirely undone!" he cried. "I, who spent a life in boast of my word!"

MacCullen dropped to his knees. The lamp fell and spilled, making a platter of flame which the earth drank and put out. He wrapped his arms about Delbeth's bony legs and touched his head to the boy's knees. "Honest man! In honor far beyond me! My dirbfine be yours, and my cattle also, and my brotherhood and my blood! Delbeth, once of Ui Garrchon, take me for your lesser brother, that you may be a model to me in truth, honor, and humility."

Delbeth frowned and blushed horribly, thinking the poet was making fun of him. But the force of the big man's grip on his legs and the hot tears against his legs made this impossible to believe. He sank down, losing his balance, and squatted before MacCullen. "Ollave. Ollave! It is not worth this! Believe me; my anger is over. I was not very angry at all, for I knew you must have had your reasons. And the taiseach never liked me a great deal, I think. I'm the son of one of his father's other wives, anyway."

MacCullen took Delbeth's knobbed, unfinished hand in his own. Delbeth winced at the strength of that grip. "Still you are my brother, Delbeth MacCullen."

"The honor is too great," replied Delbeth, wonderingly.

MacCullen snorted and sat back then. Suddenly he felt how tired he was, and how cold. "It may be a short-lived honor for both of us, Delbeth. Tomorrow the sun is like to shine on a lake of our bright blood."

The gawky boy cast his eyes left and right, but the dark was thick and he could think of nothing to say. At last he propped up his knees and rested his elbows on them. "The harp is undamaged," he said encouragingly.

* * *

Wearily MacCullen returned to the meeting. Blathmac was talking, as he had been when the poet was called out. Derval Iníon Chadhain was no longer at the table. MacCullen narrowed his eyes in sheer disappointment, for no other face besides hers could bring him comfort at that moment.

"Does no man here long to stand among Christ's martyrs, should it come to that?" the priest was saying.

"Whether I long for that blessing or no, Blathmac," replied a burly monk, "I don't want it visited upon my daughter, who is but three years old!" There was a growl of support for this. Blathmac tightened his lips and muttered.

"I didn't ask you to bring a woman and children here."

"Your mind is not very open and charitable to the rest of your brothers. Did not Saint Brendan carry the sword?" asked a brawny, dark-haired monk. He stood up to look about him at the frightened eyes of his companions. "My ancestors were among the first to embrace the snow-white Hero, but we didn't shrink from a fight either. This is the day I will give myself bravely to Mary's son, but it will be because I stand before his house steadfastly, defending the sacred things here. Will the words spoken by our Lord, written in scarlet in the Gospel books, be used to line the shoes of these Danish dogs? Not while I can lift a hoe or a reaping hook." He sat down, folded his arms, and waited for an answer.

For a long time there was silence. Then a monk MacCullen had not noticed before, one with the old tonsure, began speaking. "No one knows of these Danes better than I do myself. Isn't it myself who swam from Dalkey Island to escape from slavery not two years ago? It is true that the sacred things must not be defiled, especially the blessed sacrament." MacCullen caught the glistening of the man's eyes. "The body of Christ must be totally consumed before morning. All the books should be hidden. Inside the graves of some of our holy dead would be a good place, where the marks of digging would be covered by the stones. Then maybe, if we live, we can retrieve them. Or others who come after us here will find them. But as for my choice, I'm willing to offer myself up to our enemies with a word of forgiveness and blessing. I'm willing moreover to go out to them with all the gold and silver vessels that they covet and offer my life to them in exchange for those of the women and children here. I invite all true heirs of Christ to do the same with me. Perhaps our example—"

He was cut off in midword by Father Blathmac. "You would just give them the sacred treasure? This is sinful beyond belief! Just what I would expect from someone with the apostate's mark on his forehead!"

The man who had offered to give his life looked at Blathmac with an air of patient sadness. "My dear brother, our treasure here cannot be taken from us by anyone. He has promised us that. No glory of this world is worth a human life. Better that we should give them everything here than that they should sin by stealing it. Better that we should offer up our bodies to martyrdom than that we should do murder. You may not kill; His law is clear. I, too, come from a lineage of fighting men, but when I left Corkaduibne to be married to the Word of God, I knew I must put aside violence for all time."

MacCullen looked at the face of this man, getting comfort thereby. His features were beautiful: large, heavy-lashed eyes, a straight and perfect nose, and the shape of his head was oval as pieces of ancient stonework that he had seen. What was the cause of this Kerryman being so far from his home? MacCullen decided it must be to escape from the violence of his own tribe's quarrels.

MacCullen walked to the side of Abbot Conoran and cleared his throat. In the presence of the whole company he made his request. He described in detail what he wanted and why he wanted it. There was a moment's silence.

"By Benedict!" said Blathmac. "A bloody bull's hide! That completes it."

"It is an old and sanctified ritual: the wattles of knowledge," replied MacCullen, "and I—"

"Old I will grant you, poet. As old as the standing stones in the cowfields. But no more sanctified than any work of ignorant, pagan hand. Next you will ask for dog's flesh to eat, so that a spirit may speak through you. It is all of a piece with this place," stated the small priest, bringing his hand down on the tabletop. "There is no monastery in Ireland, I think, where so much ritual of heretical or simply pagan inception has been permitted to grow and flourish—"

Conoran was stung into reply. "What was pure Christianity in my grandfather's time cannot be heretical in mine, Father

Blathmac. My grandfather was abbot here and so am I, may I remind you, though not by my choice. Mine is the authority to say whether we fi—"

"Yours is the authority?" Fury drove Father Blathmac to his feet. "Then tell me, Prior Conoran, who is your bishop, who granted you this authority? Or does the Holy Father speak to you directly in your drug-induced dreams?"

Father Conoran, whose white, sweaty face and red-rimmed eyes marked how harshly either the drug or the discussion was treating him, opened his mouth in protest, but could not break in.

"Or do you here set yourself up as an Irish Papacy? I would believe that, as easily as anything else. A fine Church you would make of it, with ax-wielding monks indistinguishable from barbarians."

"The question is not, Blathmac, what I or any of us in the old tradition are doing here. The question is, out of all the monasteries of Ireland, why did you choose to come plague us?" Now Conoran stood as well as Blathmac, on opposite sides of the table.

"Peace!" called Brother Eochaid, who sat in a badly lit corner. All turned to him and there was silence.

Conoran sobbed. "Eochaid! Let me go. I never wanted to be abbot either."

Eochaid bent his half-shaved head. "Forgive me, Conoran. I have been selfish, I know." He rose from the bench and walked slowly to the head of the table, where Conoran had already risen from the tall-backed armchair. He sat down, slump-shouldered. Conoran took Eochaid's position at the bench, and on his round pale face settled a look of sweet relief.

MacCullen took the opportunity to speak. "You may call the wattles of knowledge heretical or pagan, Fathers, but I had it from my teacher Erard Mac Coyssie, of Munster, and I know it to be neither of these. Whether to use physical weapons or not is not a choice I have to make. My *gaesa* forbid it. And tomorrow, at dawn . . . very soon, now . . . I will face a test beyond anything I have known. Perhaps it will be the last for me, as perhaps tomorrow will be the last morning for us all. I have"—and here MacCullen stumbled on his words—"I have in the past been found unworthy. I—" Here he paused and gathered breath.

"Indeed I would be very happy to be the vessel through

which a spirit spoke—a spirit of God—for I know I myself have not the power to create a poem to save us from the madness of the Gaill. If there is any way to be tried—" And here he broke off, not knowing quite what he wanted to say.

"I will pray for you, Labres MacCullen," said Brother Eochaid, looking closely and compassionately at the poet. "My prayers may not have the power of the wattles of knowledge, but that is for Iosha MacMarie to decide. And, we have no time to kill and skin the bull and bury you in the hide before dawn."

MacCullen bowed. He felt oddly relieved at the brother's words and left the room without any feeling he had been denied a thing.

Now Eochaid turned back to the gathering at the table. "Captain MacImidel," he said, gesturing to the fair man who slouched at his left. "What chances have your men against this assault if none within the monastery rise and help you?"

MacImidel stretched and smothered a yawn. "Most of my men," he said, "have never seen battle before."

A hiss of dismay passed down the table. MacImidel thoughtfully cracked each of his knuckles in turn before adding, "But then the question might also be asked, how much of an advantage would it be if you did fight? At least my men have been taught which end of a sword does the cutting."

A voice called out, "We're not infants, Captain."

"Nor Romanists," added another.

"That is quite obvious," came a third voice, of a young gingerhead in round tonsure. Blathmac shot his supporter a chiding glance. He stood again, soberly this time.

"I beg you all to forgive my temper—my besetting sin. I have been thinking since I last spoke, as I ought to have before speaking. As director of the scriptorium, I cherish the relics and art within our keeping as much as any man alive. But there is no book worth murdering for."

"How about dying for, Father Blathmac?" Conoran asked. Blathmac shook his head.

"There is not. And for that reason I suggest giving them up—or rather giving up their jeweled covers to the Gaill." Having said this, he bowed his head in silence.

MacImidel smiled. "Paying them off? Hah! There speaks a man with his head in a barrel."

Brother Eochaid replied more respectfully. "But they haven't come to take our books, Father. They have sworn to kill us all. Sworn to their god."

Blathmac stared at Eochaid. "Sworn to kill us all? Why on earth—"

"It seems to be a vow they've taken." He turned to Conoran, met his brother's eyes, and then smiled. "We will fight, Conoran and I," he said to the horseman. "And whoever will come with us. God's love upon all of us within these walls, wherever conscience lead them."

He went to his brother's side and put his arm around him. "Good cheer, Conor. Remember what a great brawler you were as a boy!" Conoran grinned back.

MacCullen found Derval by the sound of the harp. She sat on a log bench at the west side of the church, and there was no light around her but starlight. She turned as he sat down and rested her head on his shoulder. "I couldn't bear it any more. Too much like a department meeting."

He didn't bother to ask what a department meeting was. "It's a sweet music," he whispered, touching the clàirseach gently.

Derval was playing one-handed. She touched her free hand to his lips. "'Maible Ni Chaillaigh.' By O'Carolan, they say. It doesn't sound strange to you?"

"Only beautiful."

"Then maybe it's older than they say."

He was quiet for a few minutes, listening to the slow, many-parted melody. Then he kissed Derval on the lips.

"Lady and scholar, but for the intercession of the Powers we will die tomorrow. But whether or no, my heart is yours for all my life."

"I love you, Labres," Derval said, and then she put her hands to the strings again.

MacCullen left her there as he found her, He went to a cell to find even greater darkness and deprivation of sense than night could bring. Within it he lay down and wrapped himself in blankets, to plead with the green woman and to give birth to his poem.

* * *

Tinker shook the dish towel from his face. The big horse looked right and left and then sighed.

"Well you might say!" said John to him. "Well you might say!"

Leaning against the leather of the saddle fender, John tried to think. Could he get back to the bathroom? Perhaps. If the Vikings (as they had had reason to suspect) had followed the party north, then he would be free to find the pieces of the cross again. And then what? Drag them back to the base? Ye Gods—it had taken six men to drag them away. And then what—stick them together again with spittle?

And even if it all worked, what would be the good of finding himself in his hallway in Greystones? He'd be back in the twentieth century with no way into the tenth except the path he'd just now come. John whined in his throat and the horse stared at him. "No good, Tinker. It's my mistake, but I'm afraid it's you who will have to do the hauling to make up for it."

Cautiously he led Tinker along the sloping path until they came to the Hill of the Ash Trees. It seemed a shame not to look at the place once more. There was no smell of rot in the air, but in the silhouette of the hill against the stars there was nothing to see, neither house nor tree, but only sad lumps of clay and ash, and broken branches pleading between sky and earth.

One sight of it changed John's mind. He turned the horse once more to find the path occupied by a doe deer and her spotted fawn. She was very small: much littler than the whitetail John was used to, and she approached the gray horse stiff-legged, and snorted audibly.

Tinker gave back a companionable sniff. In his heavy face his eyes blinked as benignly as a whale's. The deer and fawn brushed by John, touching the back of his hand. The baby stared into his eyes and its ridiculous ears flicked. Then they were gone, up the hill and bouncing over the ruins of the cattle enclosure.

John found he had been holding his breath. Shoving his cap more solidly on his head, he grabbed a handful of mane and attempted to emulate the deer, bounding onto Tinker's back. He barely made it, coming down with a thump that stung his bottom. Tinker grunted and John apologized, stroking his neck. He turned the horse down the path away from Ard na Bhfuinseoge.

This was much better than blundering through the wood, as they had done last week. Feeling confident that this small track would eventually meet Slige Chualann, John decided to chance the perils of the road rather than suffer through the brush once more. And as the passage of wagon traffic had barbered the trees overhanging this little road, there was little chance of being knocked from the horse by branches. He was emboldened to give Tinker's sides a little kick.

Suddenly he was hanging on to the horn with one hand and the horse's mane with the other. The rubber-coated jockey's reins were tangled through his fingers, but the reins themselves flopped loose against Tinker's neck. Hooves hit the earth like forge hammers and the horse's breath made a heavy, bellows accompaniment. How fast the world went by.

John's small equestrian background had consisted of riding well-trained and overworked horses, with the nose of his horse against the rump of the one ridden in front of him. Always these trail or trekking horses had worn curb bits, and John had been told not to hurt his mount. Being of rather tender sensibilities, he had followed this warning carefully. He had never ridden a horse "on the bit" in his life.

Tinker had never worked any other way, and now that he felt his head thrown away completely, he obediently flung himself forward, over mile after mile of lovely, mossy, quiet woodland path. He had been at complete rest for a week, and wanted nothing more than to run all night.

After the first mile or so, John found himself more exhilarated than frightened, for Tinker was very steady gaited, and never shied or twisted in his stride. Starlight speckled the hoof-pounded path; it unrolled gently before them like a ribbon through the blackness.

The sides of the blackness opened out for a moment on either side and then closed. John blinked confusedly and recognized that they had just passed the intersection of the path with a wider road. The Slige Chualann the Great, going north into Dublin. "Whoa!" John shouted, and he attempted to gather in the futile, flopping reins. "Whoa!" He leaned back and pulled on the single side he had found.

Tinker spun like a cow pony, but John's shouted command

and (more importantly) his exaggerated weight shift had slowed him down enough that John only lurched in the saddle. The horse shook his head in disapproval, and the hardware on the bridle jingled.

John apologized again and, sitting perfectly still in the saddle, asked Tinker to go back to the intersection and turn right. Tinker was twelve years old and had seen many things in his competitive life. He had no idea what this little rider was saying, but he was aware something was wanted, so he made his own decision, trotted back to the intersection, and turned right.

John looked at the high-arching dome of branches above Slige Chualann—a road wide enough to run a good cattle drive without injury to man or beast—and wondered if this could be the same road he had thought of last week as a forest trail. He shortened the reins of the snaffle carefully in his left hand, apologized in advance, lest he was doing something wrong, and gave Tinker an experimental squeeze with his legs.

Tinker tucked to the feel of the reins and set out at a nice trot along the north road. His irritation with his rider turned into an amused tolerance, for John sat quietly and did nothing to interfere with the horse's enjoyment of this night ride.

No autos, no paved surfaces on which one might skid onto one's bleeding knees, no crowds, no loudspeakers, and no fences one must plan in advance. Tinker passed an hour without altering stride.

John's back hurt. He found a posting rhythm which helped that, but then his knee hurt. He twisted in the saddle, and immediately heard Derval's scathing denunciation of people who went off balance and bruised a horse's back muscles. He cursed Derval aloud, but stopped twisting. Up hill, down hill, and then up a lot more hill. He decided he simply had to stop, and he said as much to Tinker, who was now not sorry for the rest.

They were at the top of a hill. He looked down a long slope and there was grass, and a broad river, and a few yellow sparks in the shadows beside the water. He stared at these wearily, wondering, until he recognized them as fires.

Dublin. Ye Gods and little fishes, could it be? From Ard na Bhfuinseoge to Dublin in maybe an hour and a half? It had taken at least two miserable days before. John petted Tinker with awed respect. No wonder Derval had picked him above everything else . . .

Tinker took the soft slaps as a signal to move forward again. He picked his way down the long hill carefully, his rider rigid with nerves and leaning on the horn. In the wet grass west of the palisade of Dublin City Tinker threw up his head and whinnied. From behind the wooden walls came the answers of the Irish ponies, weak and treble next to the power of Tinker's lungs. He was now where the Slieg Dala, the Road of Assembly, met the Lands of Dublinn. He crossed a small bridge and rode quickly on past.

John looked at the black pool and the black wall of the city and felt a species of fear, remembering Olaf Cuarán and the assassin's ax in Clorfíonn Ui Neal's door. He ignored his body's pain (he was sure he'd pulled a muscle in his groin) and turned the horse's head north.

The low ground was slushy and the road soft, even in June. Starlight beat down into the cleared valley, illuminating the bare tree stumps ahead and east, where one day the row houses of Glasnevin would be.

He approached a tiny wooden shed, lit from within. He stopped the horse once more, fearing the unknown presence. But before the door of the building rose a stone cross, larger than Bridget's cross but very like it, and that symbol encouraged him. Still mounted, he looked into the open doorway.

It was empty, except for a low table with a cowbell of brass and an oil lamp upon it. The walls were intricately painted and the floor covered with heather. Garlands of wilted flowers lay all around.

It was obviously a shrine. St. Molua's, he remembered, stood by the Ford of the Hurdles. John's glance returned to that heavy bell. It was very yellow: perhaps not brass at all. Surely not gold? But it was very yellow. He was more curious every moment. He lifted one leg from the saddle.

Or he tried to. The leg didn't seem to get the message. He considered pushing himself sideways off the horse, but he was quite certain that once he was on the ground, there would be no way on earth he could climb up again. So unwillingly he left the shrine behind him.

In front was the Liffey, breaking starlight into swirls which bespoke shallowness. Two posts stood by the road, showing the place to enter the water. But would Tinker cross water? John had sat futilely on horses that wouldn't. He placed the gelding at the edge of the river and gave a good nudge, thinking strong thoughts all the while.

Tinker would have been outraged had he known of his rider's doubts, for he had never refused a water obstacle in his competitive life. He entered the Liffey with a grand leap and splashed over and among the wicker baskets full of stones which had been set to provide footing. John clung to the horn, his eyes shut against the splashing. Three hundred yards later the horse rose out on the north bank.

To John's relief, he found Sliege Mid Luchra right where he remembered it, northwest of Dublin and going up into the hills. Tinker, no longer fresh but still strong, climbed up and out of the Liffey Valley.

John fought off sleep, not so much because he feared he might fall, but because he did not want to miss the unmarked turnoff west over the mountains. He came to it within the hour and then did not have to worry about sleep again, for the trail Ailesh had called "no cow path but a deer path" slapped him in the face mercilessly. John was forced to lean forward in the saddle, bent over the high roper's horn, while Tinker flailed over stone and bulled his way between the trees.

He passed the place where he had kept watch—when? Only last night? Ye Gods. He erupted onto the flat and treeless table of the low hills, where both he and Tinker felt themselves abashed by the stars. After a mild canter over this tableland he rode down to the wide plain of Brega, and to St. Sechnail's monastery. Tinker drank from the pool among the willows where John had seen the wild hermit. No one was praying in the cold water tonight.

John heard chanting. He was glad there was someone still up. Wouldn't Derval be surprised to see Tinker? A smile stretched itself across his weary, dust-caked, and branch-switched face.

They were in the middle of the packed field outside the enclosure when John saw the Vikings and the Vikings saw him.

Derval sat with the sound box of the harp on her lap and rested her chin on the bow. "Damn Johnnie," she mumbled aloud. She gazed blankly out at the night, listening to the prayers of the assembled people of the abbey, and the occasional shout from the camp of the Gaill. She began thinking how much darkness there was here. It seemed twenty-three hours of every day since she had come—since she had been brought into the past—had been spent in the dark: darkness of night, of woods, of buildings . . . It needed strong faith for a person to put one foot before the other. An absurd faith it was, too, since one fell more often than not.

Still, she had seen Bridget. The saint, the goddess. (Being a scholar of old history, Derval felt more comfortable thinking of her as goddess.) Did that seeing mean Derval would escape death in the morning? She wanted very much to believe that it did, for though she was not afraid (how could she be afraid with the memory and smell of the poet's love surrounding her?) she wanted most passionately now to live.

Certainly one miracle made another miracle more easily believable. Feeling the force of the old woman by the road was enough to convince her that life was not the collision of blind matter that nightmare often hinted. What more proper than for Bridget to reach out her hand and save the one she had put her mark upon?

Or perhaps not to save her at all, but to call her to . . . whatever. It was well-known that people who were about to die saw things. Even in the world of plastic and pavement (and of light. Easy light) from which Derval had come, people who were dying had visions of a certain kind. Psychologists studied them, called them near-death-experiences, and invented dozens of pragmatic explanations involving neural decay.

Psychologists had never seen Bridget.

It was as likely that the aisling vision meant Derval's doom rather than her salvation. Likely she was already close to the edge between life and that cold country. Likely it was by her death that time was to protect itself against interference, leaving of her no trace in a burnt field of battle, where even the stones of the wall would be taken by the crofters of five hundred years from now and put into other walls.

There was the book. It was known that the book survived. But John had taken the book and disappeared. Derval shuddered at this reminder. They had fallen through time together, but the doom of it was hers alone. Damn him. Damn him. And her shudder grew into a fear that took the ability to move away from her.

Then Derval was no more the scholar but the daughter of Pat and Mary O'Keane, and the difference between the goddess and the Catholic saint bothered her no more than it did the people at the abbey around her. She folded her hands over her face and implored Saint Bridget to intercede with Christ that she might not die. But her anger at John Thornburn placed itself between her and her prayers and Derval remembered the early teaching of Sister Therisita at school, who had told her that she could not ask good of God while intending evil of her neighbor. It was Johnnie who had done the evil, she thought resentfully. But for him she would be . . . what? Safe? Perhaps? Not alone? Well, she was not alone. She had Labres MacCullen, and could want no better companion in the world. Derval threw away her resentment of John, not in exchange for divine assistance, but because it seemed suddenly silly.

She raised her head. The air was getting damp, and there was a dent in her chin from the carved bowpillar of the harp. She heard two monks walk by in front of her. Evidently the mass was over. "God to you," said one to the other and they smiled as they walked away in different directions.

Damn religious group of people, she sighed to herself. Excessively religious. Even for the Irish. Perhaps because there was so much dark to trip in. But it was all a shade ridiculous, on the eve of massacre. Derval herself smiled grimly as she prayed, "Bridget, please don't make me religious tomorrow."

There was a sound of hoofbeats outside the wall. The Vikings didn't have horses with them. What was this—reinforcements? For the Dublin forces, or for the Gaill? Derval stood up.

It was one horse. Long-strided. Much different in action from the Celtic ponies, or from the bull-necked horses of the Dublin Danes. Derval knit her brows and put the harp down on the bench behind her.

There was a pale glimmer far beyond the wall, moving fast. Derval saw light flash from a sword under starlight as the animal charged through the Norse camp. Her eyes strained to focus. She recognized the beast. Then Derval spoke a name: not the name of a horse.

She saw him clinging to the mane with his belly leaning against the gray's heavy neck. In wonder she made out the blocky shadow of McCaffrey's western saddle. Surely the high pommel and horn of the thing was poking a hole into the rider's stomach. Surely he wasn't going to try to jump the wall like that, with flopping reins and in the darkness. Surely neither horse nor man had so much ridiculous faith as to . . .

Derval saw Tinker size up the jump, adjust his stride, gather . . . He was up and over, and oh Christ he was coming down right on top of one of those stone beehive cells where he was about to be broken and his rider with him.

But the eyes of the horse and his reflexes were better than she had feared. Tinker snapped up his hind legs and arched his back as though he were a leaping hound. He came down on the dome of rock with all four feet and sprang up and off, touching earth twenty feet away, and he danced his way between the little round buildings, reins dragging.

His rider touched earth in a different place, flat on his back. His cap covered his face.

Derval ran to John, holding Tinker's reins in her hand. The small blond man was already blinking and gasping for breath. She lifted his head.

With difficulty he made out her features above him. "Idiot gate!" he said. "Didn't know enough to bring me back here. Took me to Ard na Bhfuinseoge, instead.

"I brought your horse, like you wanted," John explained, and then winced as he picked himself up from the dirt. "And my hat."

"I know I am judged unworthy," whispered MacCullen in his private darkness. "Perhaps I was never called to poetry at all. But Lady, I am the only one these people have. I beg your aid." Then he opened his mind.

But instead of making poetry, Labres MacCullen fell into a sleep—a sleep which troubled him so he tossed on his mattress of heather until he was wound in his blankets as tightly as any prisoner. And in that sleep he had a dream.

There was a tree before him, and in its branches a sweet bird singing. And then it turned to ash, both tree and bird. He turned and there was a great house, and in a moment it, too, was gray ash. And a woman stood before him, with the face of Derval, and she, too, was consumed. All this was under a light of horrible brilliance. He struggled away from this, until he knew that he was dreaming, and then—still dreaming—he changed the dream.

The dirty old woman sat at the end of his bed, bent and splayed as she had sat by the campfire on the road to Dublin. "Tell me why you're short of the mark, boy. Or why do you think I measure you so?"

She waited for his answer like one waits for the end of a joke which promises to be a good one. MacCullen grew warm with resentment, but the bedclothes held him still. "I couldn't see you. You didn't let me. Though I was dedicated to your service at the age of seven, Lady, still you have never let me see you. Those others—"

"Those others have their own problems, Labres. Leave them out of this. Some men need dedication—others need visions. And as far as seeing things, well, you can't see a person standing behind your back, can you? Not even if she's very close. Close enough to touch."

There was a prod against MacCullen's back: not too gentle. He twisted, but there was nothing beneath him but the fragrant, dusty heather. And she was laughing at him, as he had known she would. Distantly he heard a voice speaking: his own.

"Are you behind me then, Eire? And have always been? I doubt it, or else I would have far different welcome in the world. They call me clever, you know. Not inspired but clever. How is 'clever' going to help these good souls defend themselves against the wickedness of destruction? How can it even help them to die well, if it is a hard, fierce death you demand of us this morning?"

Old Bride listened to him calmly. "But you are a clever lad, Labres, and have been so from birth. Don't abuse the gift you're given, even if it is not what you asked for. So clever you are, that if I showed you the pretty face you have been mooning to see, why, in a moment your mind would be so busy deciding whether my eyes were more like blue sky or seawater that you might as well be staring at a painted picture of me."

"Then I am beyond help!"

Bride grinned, and her smile made her no less plain. "Not so, lad. Yours is a road of stones—no mistake—but then so is mine."

MacCullen closed his mouth in wonder to hear this, and forgot entirely that he had been dreaming. His rough swaddling fell away from him, and he was naked at the old woman's feet.

"Come, Labres, spouse and son. Share in my work with me once more. Let us make a glorious poem!" The poet wrapped his arms around Bridget's angular old knees and she put her hand upon his head.

He woke from his dream on the cold stone floor of the cell, feeling he had slept a night through. He threw on his léinne and over it his brat, glad to see by the position of the plow in the sky that there was still some time before daybreak. In his mouth rested the poem Bride had given him. He feared even to whisper it aloud.

In the church he found all the people he sought: Eochaid, MacImidel, Ailesh, Finnbogison, and of course Derval Iníon Chadhain. Also he met one he had not thought to see again. In the dancing light of yellow oil lamps, John Thornburn was arguing with Father Blathmac. Snorri Finnbogison stood so close to the small foreigner as to hide him from view, and with a broad grin on his face the Icelander punched John regularly on the upper arm. Emotion made John's Irish almost incomprehensible, and every good-natured blow from Snorri rattled it further, but MacCullen heard the name of Bridget spoken and with his dream fresh in his thought he stepped forward, as one closely involved.

"It has nothing to do with devils," John repeated himself, slapping his hand on his knee. "It was Bridget who brought Derval and me here, and Bridget can take us all safely away."

"A saint is not God Omnipotent! The only power of the holy dead is to intercede for us with the Father, from whence all power for good originates."

Father Conoran, so recently the abbot of the monastery, sat on a little stool and blinked his dilated eyes. "All power originates in the Father? I don't know, Blathmac. I think perhaps you are saying too much there. Surely the saint who visited Eoin here did not say anything about power originating—"

"She didn't say anything at all!" shouted John, with so much venom in his voice that Snorri took a step away from him. "Not a damn, fucking thing! She just opened the damn, fucking gate that we can all just—"

"Why don't we try it?" suggested Eochaid. All seemed surprised to hear the new abbot speak. He now stepped over to the bloody paper affixed to the window, which night had colored glossy black. "We can more easily judge the sanctity of this method of escape once we have seen it work." Father Blathmac opened his mouth to protest, but the abbot continued. "Blathmac can pray for the safety of our souls as we make the venture." John sighed, puffing out his cheeks with relief. He nodded at Eochaid.

"Take the lamps out to the other side of the window, so I can see through the paper," he said. The little lights wafted ghostily out the door.

John was conscious that someone had stepped close to him. He felt a light, dry kiss against his face and heard Ailesh's voice in his ear. "Please don't be angry with me, Eoin," she said. He turned, startled.

"Don't be angry with me, but I cannot come back with you into your house. I belong here, where the murder price of my father is to be decided."

John hissed between his teeth. "You little idiot. Didn't you see enough blood? What do you expect to do against those mean mothers out—" He cut off short, realizing he had been speaking English.

Derval came up on his other side. "Don't lose your temper, Johnnie. I didn't think you could convince Ailesh to run away."

"Eh? I don't have to convince her. I'll just throw her through!"

"She'll brain you," came the woman's reply. "Or I will." John felt, rather than saw, MacCullen behind him, standing very close to Derval. He turned to confront the tall poet.

"Don't say a word, Labres. I know already. I'm quick that way. Congratulations." He stalked over to a bench, shoving Conoran aside and barking his own shins in the process. When MacCullen sat beside him he edged away.

"Eoin, we thought you had left us."

John snorted. "Very flattering, I'm sure. And as for Doctor O'Keane, I wish you a great deal of luck. And a thick skin. You'll need both. I suppose you won't use the gate either."

MacCullen's reply was thoughtful. "Not . . . not while anyone remains undefended in the abbey, I will not. I could not, by my vows."

"Then help me convince them all."

The twin lights wavered outside the window, lending a ruby glow to the assemblage within. John stood, still shaking with anger, weariness, and frustration. "Be quiet," he said rudely, and walked to the tracing, holding his pencil before him.

He cleared his throat and tried to clear his mind. He began.

It wasn't right, and he knew it wasn't right, but stubbornly he persisted, until Derval spoke out. "Johnnie. That's not the right air. You're humming 'The Coast of Newfoundland.'"

John Thorbeorn groaned. In his weariness he swayed toward the paper, which was redolent of a familiar, not very pleasant smell. "Oh shit! Damn that idiot cop! And I think the tracing's finally going too. It stinks."

He backed up a step. "Whistle the right tune for me, Derval."

"I can't," she admitted. "But I can do it pibrochaid, in voice alone. Start . . . now!"

After ten seconds John stopped tracing. "That's 'The Coast of Newfoundland' again."

Derval choked on her singing. "Is it? Christ, you're right. They're so alike, the one has driven the other from my head. Ailesh, you try."

The girl was willing, for she had no desire to push others into her private battle. A small three-holed *cuislean* was fetched for her, and John began again. This time he was almost through with the tracing before he recognized that the tune had slipped from the pipe air to the chantey, and he continued anyway. At the end of it, his hand was dripping with the inexplicable blood that soaked the paper.

There was a creaking and a distant shushing noise, broken by the bleak, thin cry of a bird. A splotch of color appeared before John Thornburn, only to fade again immediately. John sniffed. "There it is again. The smell. I think the gate is rotten."

Derval put her hand out, but the brief apparition was over. "Not . . . rotten, I don't think. But we certainly got it wrong this time."

"Perhaps you are not meant to get it right," growled Blathmac, but then Father Conoran brushed by him, eyes alight. "I *saw* something, Eochaid. I did. In front of the bleeding cross. I saw a bird, all in white, and it spoke to me."

Eochaid lifted his black eyebrows. "What did it say?" But Conoran merely shook his head and sat down again.

John stumbled outside. The fresh air hit him, and for a moment he could almost put a name on the stink that came out of the misopened gate. "Damn the idiot garda who played with my stereo. Now I can't remember the real tune."

"What idiot garda?" Derval, with Ailesh by the hand, caught up with him. She laughed when he explained. "Ah well, Johnnie. Tunes are like that. Don't worry. There's still tomorrow."

He gave her a sick, hurt look in reply.

Chapter Seventeen

•

> "And what was it that sustained your life so," Patrick asked. Caeilte answered, "Truth was in our hearts, strength in our bodies and what we promised, that we did."
>
> *The Colloquy of the Ancients,*
> from the Book of Lismore

At the cold hour, just before the eastern stars went muddy, the abbey entered in upon its day's worship, just as though everyone had slept. John sat bundled in a brat on one of the low benches that surrounded the church, watching MacCullen be washed all over with bitter-cold water. It seemed odd; surely the worst thing one could do when preparing to give a speech was to court laryngitis. But the poet scrubbed himself—even his hair—with a gusto John found repellent.

So that's what can turn Dr. O'Keane's head around, he thought to himself. (He found it easier now to refer to her as Dr. O'Keane.) Well, she was welcome to it.

There was something about this morning's bustle that was very like a funeral, he considered. He didn't mean the obvious, that it was their own large funeral to commence with the sun's rising, but rather that it was like that of John's grandfather. Bleakness, lack of sleep, and a great deal to do for everyone. Everyone except John. He turned his hat around and around under his hands, feeling the band his grandfather had knotted for him so long ago.

Despite all the traditional hatred between the Church and the College of Poets, MacCullen was being given all the blessings and deference possible under the circumstances. Mass was said by the priest from Kerry, and though he had only seen a Catholic service once before, John could tell that a lot had changed in the last thousand years. A lighted menorah was held up as the Epistle was read on the left-hand side of the altar. Then the Bible was carried across to the right hand, where the Gospel was read, and the menorah was extinguished immediately thereafter. John was struck by the Jewishness of the Mass. He no longer wondered why they called the unbaptized the Gentiles.

The knowledge that he would die today did not bother him at all, for he did not think about it. Not thinking about things was John's specialty. But he did feel very bad about forgetting the magic tune that might have got everyone to safety. Hell, they might have just filed into his hallway and then gone out again to Ard na Bhfuinseoge—nothing even to upset Derval (Dr. O'Keane). Or the garda. He also resented somewhat that she, who was supposed to be so damn musical, let his mistake twist her own memory. What a bitch of a turn.

Having filled a vessel with mead from the kitchen, Snorri Finnbogison prowled about until he found a secluded place where no priests would interrupt him. He had had his Mass and Communion like the good Christian he was, but now—Christ was good, but so was Thor. Snorri lifted the wooden bowl up to the stars. Muttering, he spilled out some of the drink. He sipped it, then lifted it, and finally spilled the whole lot of it out onto the grass. "Never have you failed me, Thor, true friend of brave men. Accept this ale. If I survive this battle, I will give a feast in your honor. I will sacrifice a bull, a stallion, and a goat. Hail Thor the Mighty!" He raised both his hands. Then quietly he turned back to the church, feeling he had done all that he could do.

Derval rubbed Tinker's legs with energy, talking to him as she did so. "I know you're tired, baby horse. I know you did good, with that sack of potatoes bouncing on your back and sending you over a wall where there was no place to come down. You showed good heart, Tinker. Good bottom.

"But now you've got to do more, even more for Ma. This morning we're going to play Spanish Riding School, and I know we haven't done that in a long time, but you just search your endless equine memory for the cues and we'll be just fine. There's nothing like you in this whole world, darling. Nothing at all like you." She rubbed a speck of mash from the huge gray's nose and adjusted the blanket—her blanket—more securely on his steaming back. Tinker rested his chin on the windowledge of the calving shed where he had been stalled, and gave out a long, sweet-smelling sigh.

Ailesh watched John as he sat, lost in his meditations. She had brought him to this—she, Ailesh Goban's Daughter. Bridget had given her grace such as no Irishwoman knew, outside of story, saving her life and bestowing upon her protectors from far away. Not mortal men. But no—in that Ailesh could only delude herself, for she had looked into Derval's face and seen one prepared for death. But not ordinary men.

Did not the old gods sometimes die? Bridget had said she'd lost a son. She had lost a foster son, too, if the histories were right, for the Son of Mary died. Eoin could—would—die.

If I had not shocked him so, saying I would not go to safety with him, then he might not have forgotten the magic. Immediately as this thought arrived, Ailesh chided herself for conceit. Eoin did not think so much of her. Derval was his heart's love, and she had left him this night for another. For MacCullen, who in all his show and arrogance could no more compare with gentle Eoin than a frog compete against birdsong.

Tears stung her eyes and chilled her face. She put her hand over the cold iron head of the hammer in her belt, thinking if her heart did not let her be, she would be useless in the fight.

Turning away from the sight of bundled Eoin, she ran smack into Snorri Finnbogison's chest. The big man was already clothed in his black mail shirt, with his grand sword at his back. He grinned at her. As she apologized a voice—Eoin's voice—spoke from close behind her.

"Snorri says a hammer is a good weapon to use from a horse, because if you miss you can keep on going. I—er—he thinks you should ride behind him. Only you have to be careful where you swing the thing, eh?"

Ailesh looked from one man to the other, and the wetness on her face became tears of cold and wind.

"Of course you could also ride behind Derval—she'd be glad to have you. But with what she's planning to do with Tinker, you'd probably get seasick, even if you didn't fall off."

"But you, Eoin. Since you have a hammer also, what horse will you ride into battle?"

A look of great pain crossed Eoin's face, and Ailesh was suddenly shy. "I. . . I have ridden enough for one day," he answered her. "I don't think my legs will go that far apart again."

Ailesh found herself grinning like the Norseman, who seemed to understand at least part of what Eoin said. "It is true what the scholar says, then. The cow is your true mount."

Even John smiled to that, though it was an awkward smile. "No. A boat. You should see me ride a boat, Ailesh. Haven't fallen out of a boat since I was a boy."

The three were laughing when Holvar Hjor winded his horn.

Dressed in a priest's vestment of red with an undergown of embroidered white linen, Labres MacCullen stepped into the chariot. Two ponies were hitched before it, one with black mane and tail and one with staring blue eyes. Delbeth, his driver, took up the lines and sent the ponies through the open gate.

At the edge of the trampled earth around the enclosure the Norsemen stood ranked, their swords and spears upon the ground before them. MacCullen glanced from face to face, and though the light was still dim, many of those faces he remembered from Ard na Bhfuinseoge. He took a breath, feeling the openwork of the léinne oddly rough against his shoulders.

Out from the line stepped a short man, dressed in boiled leather and black iron rings like any of his fellows. It was Holvar Hjor, and he carried a banner blazoned with a black crow. He strode forward but did not approach the chariot closely, lest he have to look up at the poet. He spoke.

> "Ere steel-spangled combat
> The sun-rivaling bloodstars ply
> To word-war.

I challenge you, poet-brother,
To wit-sharp dueling."

MacCullen savored the elegance of the couplets, then smiled slowly. He shook his head a little, like a spirited horse, then he looked into Holvar's eyes—into the blue fire burning in there.

Extemporaneous composition was of course the most difficult of all: the poetry of heroes. All the more so when made at the point of a sword. Death hung heavily over both of them, despite the flimsy ritual truce.

But MacCullen had no time to be afraid. In heart and eye, the two had already begun the battle.

"Yes, utterances of learned beauty
The twisting wiles of wordcraft speak
No hesitation
For he who stumbles now
The web goes wry."

MacCullen's answer matched the challenge so perfectly in meter that it would have seemed to anyone unaware of the circumstances that they were reciting verses of a poem well-known to both of them. There were grunts of appreciation from the spectators. Holvar grinned with fierce pleasure. MacCullen was a true man, he decided. A worthy opponent. Like a pair of rutting stallions they energized each other.

Holvar raised his right arm in an elegant gesture.

"Rushing headlong into rhyme
I call the rune master. Ropt,
The masked one
Upon the living world-tree struggling
Against your coward Christ."

MacCullen answered him immediately (though a little clumsily, he thought).

"Matchless is the Son of Mary
I will defend him ever. Iosa
The loving one

Against the cunning of the world
Returning good for evil."

Holvar closed his eyes. He seemed to shake himself, or maybe he trembled—MacCullen couldn't tell. The godi drew his sword, raised his arms over his head, and, with one eye wide open and the other shut tight, began to chant:

"The carrion crows
That westward fly
Scan well the earth
With watchful eye
By now the news
Of battle here
Has reached exalted
Odin's ear.

Soon shall the first of warriors come
The guardian of earth and sun

Across the void
The eight-hoofed steed
Bears close the lord
To mark our deed
To hear the praise
I heap on him
Giver of victory
Dearer than kin . . ."

Holvar's voice caught. Stumbled.

"Dearer than kin.

While in the forest wolves awake
Their cries of joyous worship make.

Upon the branches
Of tall pines
The hawk his prey
At noon divines.
The noble bird
Shall take his kill

It is the great
All-father's will.

From death and fear come life and meat
Unto the strong the hunt is sweet.

Within the bed
The virgin cries
As virile man
First with her lies
Yet from her blood
A child will spring
From father's seed
And mother's pain.

To Froeya's lover now I pray
To potent Odin, conqueror of Froey.

Magic spell
And poet's skill
The healer's art
Are his to fill.
So vain are they
Who for their part
Try to outrun
His fatal dart.

One day the honor come to me
Of spear and noose and holy tree."

He cut open his forearm. Blood dripped from the blade as he raised his arms over his head.

"Brother of iron
Bitter tongue of steel
Release the blood
From sword-arm spill.
And this red ale
Unto him bear
God of the slain
Accept all here."

Holvar shouted the last two lines, in which he offered everyone present to Odin. Then, with eyes bugged out in parody of madness, with bared teeth he hissed:

"Tonight the cold-eyed maidens choose
The bravest dead, who win or lose."

Holvar ceased, swaying. The trance faded into exhaustion, and horrified, he became aware that he had offered himself—himself—as sacrifice to Odin.

MacCullen watched his enemy's gyrations with a distant pity, a distant contempt. He is trying to force his god to him, MacCullen thought. But I don't believe he came, the crow-god. I don't believe he came.

And then the Ollave took one step forward. He felt the warmth of a Presence by his side.

"Odin one-eye, old in oath-breaking,
Fearful equally in foe-wrath or friendship.
Kindling killing alike among stranger and kinsman
Cold comfort ken I, in all your rune cunning.

Vileness, I name you, and short-sighted victory your vassal.
Troll-biter of bleeding breasts upon the boughs of slaughter.
Sweet unto you, the slave's sad lamentation.
And dearer still, the maddened swordsman's laughter.

But force is not freedom, nor a gibbet, justice.
No courage can cleanse the cruel slayer of bloodstain.
Your valor is vain, then, Odin black-tongue,
When matched against that of Thor, whom thralls pray to.

Loving not war, nor unseemly land-strife
Not livid light that leaps off wielded weapon.
But those fair words of truthful telling
Deeds faith of friendship all fullfilling

And unto you I will spill out my ale-gift
Best in battle, great in gentleness and goodness
Thor, lightning lifter, my choice champion
Larger in worth than all the world's weak wickedness!

And all I would ask, ere the ending
Is to stand in the shield wall beside you till stricken.
Nor would he, the Christ Lord, begrudge it to me.
Nor would she, the Lady who bore them. So be it."

There was silence, and the Vikings stared at MacCullen with the same rapt attention as did the Gaels behind the abbey wall. Then came a shriek, and the Norseman standing closest to the poet lifted his spear and flung it at MacCullen.

The poet did not move, but his driver did. Delbeth flung himself between the flying weapon and MacCullen, and with his hands attempted to ward the thing off. His hands did not stop the spear, but his breast did. Delbeth MacChatháin fell back against the poet as he crumpled from the cart. The horses spooked and the little chariot rattled into the Viking lines.

Holvar Hjor stared wonderingly from the scene before him to Skully the duelist, who stood panting from his long cast. With his face still filled with wonder, Holvar strode over to Skully. His hand moved, and Skully's head bounced twice on the pounded earth. The rest of him took a strangely long time falling.

MacCullen bent to Delbeth's body, which lay arched over the spearhead protruding from the boy's back. Delbeth was far beyond hearing what MacCullen whispered to him as he pushed the shaft of the weapon through the gory wound. Then, using only his two hands, MacCullen broke the spear in two and pulled the pieces free. He stood and regarded the Norsemen, his face frozen. He threw the broken spear at Holvar's feet and walked away, back through the wicker gate.

Holvar wiped his sword. He heard a rattling and looked up to find Ospack leading the little chariot into the trees behind their camp. "First spoil," Ospack said to his chief, as he had so often before. But there was no triumph in his words and Ospack's face looked gray and old.

In sudden dismay Holvar looked down the line of men. He met the eyes of a dozen men, and in no pair of them did he find the growing madness of possession. They are as abandoned as I am, he thought. Shamed and abandoned at the beginning of battle.

It was the power of the Irishman—the poet. Who said he had weapons that might cut, though he had never lifted a blade. The first man Holvar had ever struck without the presence of Odin lifting his arm, and the first who had not died. Holvar had been fool enough to let that power touch his men and now . . .

"Today," Holvar announced, "Odin has promised us our heart's desire." He turned his face toward the enemy.

Tinker sniffed at the bloody thing MacCullen carried, but did not shy. Derval was sitting on his back stark naked, for the long léinne and brat had been intolerably constricting on horseback. Her flesh was flushed with cold and her nipples stood out. She looked uncomfortable in the enormous stock saddle John had brought with the horse. MacImidel sat beside her, and the difference between Tinker and the Dubliner's pony made him appear the size of a child. Snorri Finnbogison sat on his heavy black horse with difficulty, for the animal was fresh. Ailesh clung behind him, looking through the crowd for one face.

The poet delivered Delbeth's body to other hands and looked over the milling horsemen to Derval, high above all. John came to join them, his hat in his hand and his hammer in his belt. He looked down at the horses' legs.

"It is only a sortie," MacImidel was explaining to the abbot. "There is no value in having horse soldiers unless the horses keep moving. We will swing through their line and then return. Have the gate ready."

Derval called over, "We need something to break through their lines. Something big, to make a hole we can fight in."

MacImidel replied in irritation, "Fight? So speaks a woman who will not carry a weapon in her hand?"

"I am riding my weapon."

Abbot Eochaid patted Tinker's heavy shoulder. "Well, I can believe that! There is nothing bigger than this in the monastery, except the great cross and my great black bull."

Derval narrowed her eyes, gazing down at Eochaid's unkempt tonsure. "Your great black bull?"

He met her eyes, and then, without a word, ran off to the cattle sheds.

Three monks returned with him, dragging a very large chunk of night, horned like an aurochs, between them. The bull plunged and swung his head left and right. Finally he was placed with his nose at the gate.

It is now, thought Derval, and her insides lurched.

"Open the gate and release him." It was MacImidel who spoke, and a half-dozen tonsured monks moved to obey. But in the three seconds it took to open the gate and slip the ropes free, someone had leaped into the middle of them, grabbed the beast by the rough hair between his horns, and heaved up onto the animal's neck.

"Johnnie!" Derval cried.

"Eoin! My Eoin Ban! If I had known you would ride, I would have come behind you!" shouted Ailesh, and she raised her hammer in salute. "Eoin, my hero and my man, now and for my life!"

John stared at her, mouth agape, bobbing as the bull threw itself against its constraints. At last a grin stretched his indeterminate features and his white face flushed. At that moment the huge black bull was released.

John Thornburn erupted out of the abbey swinging his hammer by its long leather thong and screaming in a falsetto that was half terror and half the pain of abused thigh muscles. Holvar saw him and believed for a moment that Thor, the rude hammer god, had come in response to the Irish poet's call. But as the maddened animal bore down upon them, bucking and bellowing, and Holvar saw the horsemen charge out of the gate behind it, his fighting reflex took over. Even if it was Thor himself they fought today, they were the men of Odin, and victory was theirs.

Halfway to the waiting Norsemen, the bull turned about, and with an enormous toss of his shoulders and head, threw John spinning into the air. Derval on Tinker's back passed beneath him as he arced through the air, and then he was lying very flat on the ground, on the very spot of blood where Delbeth had met death. The entire horse troop passed over him, untouching.

The gray horse and the black horse hit the Norse lines together, but where Snorri came on with sword unsheathed, not feeling the spear that glanced off his thighpiece of boiled leather, Derval rode straight on and cued Tinker into a capriole.

It was a very bad capriole, for Tinker was terribly unprepared. He rose only three feet off the ground and his four legs kicked out unevenly. What was worse (to the horse's limited perceptions) was that three of those legs hit things as they struck out. He came down stumbling and embarrassed, determined to do better at next signal.

Next signal came immediately and the horse gathered himself and sprang.

"By the teeth of Fenris," cried Ospack in Holvar's ear. "It is no mortal beast!"

"Then make it mortal!" Holvar threw himself at the great gray, only to be blocked by the flanks of a black horse that thrust itself in. A shadow of a man on the black shouted, "Death to Holvar, shame of the Norse!" and a sword sliced down at his head.

Half-contemptuously, Holvar blocked it and, on the return stroke, made ready to sever the black horse's tendons. But there was a woman's shriek and his sword rang in his hand. Holvar found himself staring at a broken blade and a hammer, which had dug a hole in the sod at his feet. The end of the broken blade had cut Holvar's scalp in its flight. The woman—the flinger of the hammer—cried out in Irish, which Holvar did not understand.

But then the black horse itself screamed and bounded forward with a knife haft sticking out of its ham. Holvar found himself with Ospack, who grinned with his bad teeth, handed Holvar another sword (Skully's sword) and said, "You owe me a knife, Battle Chief."

MacImidel came into a snarl of horses and weapons and his men followed him. "Swing wide!" he called to them. "Stay clear and wide!" Then he had no attention to spare.

The first Dubliner to touch the Norse line went down, as his pony's forelegs were hacked away. The rider, falling with a leg under his mount, was dead and unrecognizable in moments. Behind him came another horseman, whose pony leaped the dead bodies in terror, to come down upon a spear. In less than a minute there was neither Norse line nor charge of horsemen, but a tangle of ruin and blood.

"This is better!" called Ospack to his chief. "This is the play I crave!" Holvar returned a grin of teeth, but both knew it to be a lie. There was blood in Holvar's mouth and his scalp stung like acid. Odin was not with them this morning. He would not forgive.

Derval made the great loop along the edge of the clearing. Her concentration on Tinker was so intense she did not see the enemy below her, nor feel the wind of the swords that struck at her face. But she felt perfectly every connection those big hooves made with flesh, and she held him to the course so abhorrent to the gentle horse. When the Jolmsviking's sword pricked his belly she felt it as surely as Tinker did, and in fury she turned the excited animal and forced it to trample its attacker into the dirt. Then she booted Tinker toward the monastery.

Christ! Derval looked back to see the Dublin troop hacked and fallen behind her. Only five horses were up. MacImidel had not exaggerated their inexperience. They had allowed the enemy to re-form the shield wall she herself had opened. There was Snorri, however, riding toward her on a beast that limped badly. And there was MacImidel himself, still upright. He saw her and turned his pony's head. Ax raised, he headed toward her.

But in his path was a squat Viking, no taller than Johnnie. Derval saw that it was the man who had led the Vikings in song on the night she had raided their camp. His sword feinted toward the pony's neck. As the beast shied off, the stroke re-aimed itself at MacImidel, who reversed his ax and parried. Letting the force of the contact swing the ax around, MacImidel struck at the attacker's shoulder. And missed. He kicked his pony forward before the Viking chief could retaliate.

"Here!" called Derval.

But as soon as the horse captain had ridden far enough to view the battle as a whole, with his men down on either side and hardly a live horse to be found, he grimaced, let out a hiss, and galloped back. Snorri glanced at Derval, who shrugged and followed.

There were three men standing and one with a broken leg, whom Derval hauled onto the back of her saddle. These ran, protected by the remaining horses, toward the abbey gate.

The gate was opened for them, but there was something in the way. Tinker swung wide around John Thornburn, refusing, even today, to trample someone he knew. Derval looked down and saw John. Cursing his stupidity, she reached to grab him and got only his cap. He had the knotted band in his hands; it came off. Then she was through the abbey gate, with Snorri's black horse behind her, and behind them the broken and wounded Dublin troops.

"Johnnie! Are you with us?" She heard no answer.

* * *

John Thornburn had seen too much without understanding. He stood in the middle of a ring of battle, quite untouched, except by the blow of the earth against his head. Twice in a day's time. Hardly fair. It left him very dizzy. John's back was soaked with blood and he had no idea if it was his or not. It didn't seem to matter. He watched Ailesh's new red-haired friend go down, his head rolling across the ground like a soccer ball. He wondered if Ailesh would mind very much.

He also wondered if he were dead already and that was why he felt so invisible and unconnected to all that was happening. If he were dead, though, why did it hurt so much? Well, perhaps it would stop soon, and he'd be able to rise away from here, into the sky. Or something.

He played with his hatband absently. It seemed to relieve his head. This band of his grandfather's was also the first piece of macrame John had ever studied. When Derval shot by and grabbed the cap out of his hands, he refused to let the band go.

The horsemen were past and now the Vikings were running toward him. Soon it would all be over. John found himself singing "The Coast of Newfoundland."

Too bad it was the wrong song; he knew it so much better than the other. "No more will I go roaming on the coast of Newfoundland/With the seaspray making faces burn and the rope burning my hand/ Oh lie, did die di fingle and oh lie did die di cann." Because he had learned it from his grandfather, John had originally believed the refrain to be in Micmac.

Here came the Vikings.

This was the man whom Holvar had believed to be some kind of deity. He stood in the path, holding a knotted cord in his hands, and Holvar wiped the blood from his eyes to stare at him. And as he looked, the battle chieftain's eyes grew wider.

It was his own younger son he saw, who died with his brother in Northumbria. It was not this, but rather Holvar's own face, in the mirror of recollection. It was more the weathered, patient face of his wife, who was buried alone in Norway. Holvar, who had been at sea when she was buried, could never return to visit the grave.

It was none of these, but a familiar-looking young man who regarded him without fear, anger, or even very much interest, and sang a Saxonish song not very well. Holvar raised his sword and then put it down again, thinking I won't kill him. I'll leave it to some other to kill him.

But then the song was over and it seemed his men were all gone ahead. Holvar heard a voice—a familiar voice—calling, "Hurry, Holvar. You are late." It was a very familiar voice, as the young man's face was very familiar, and though the voice chided him (and he knew he was very late), it promised forgiveness. Holvar sprinted forward.

When the song ended perfectly in time with the knotwork, John knew that this time it had been right. And the cold, strong smell that filled the air, as it had filled the stuffy church, had a name.

Fish?

Cod.

He turned to see the green glowing gate behind him, with two dozen Norsemen standing with their feet in the water of the surf at L'Anse aux Meadows, looking very surprised. John was very surprised, too, for the Norsemen were standing where the net gallows should be but wasn't.

It's a dream, he thought. All this. Not just the medieval thing but the whole Irish ball-of-wax. I'm home. I have only to wake up. He started toward the beach, believing that he would see the top of the school bell tower right around the corner of the green gate.

Too much Book of Kells, he told himself. I've studied too much. Jeesus, imagine me trying to tell that to any of my teachers at school—that I've studied too much. Me, John Thornburn, the great slacker.

As he approached the blue water that lapped so naturally and inexplicably out of the trampled sod, his delight at waking became mingled with regrets. This place—looking so much like Newfoundland, so much like his home. And he thought about the language that had been in his ears here, so much sweeter than English. He recalled the scriptorium, where a row of pens was always engaged in the best possible work upon paper. He thought about the face of Bridget. Was that a dream? Had he the capacity to make up—that?

He thought of Ailesh and his dizziness receded. The bad dream quality which made everything absurd and meaningless around him was broken, and he remembered clearly what Ailesh had called him: "My hero and my man, now and for my life!"

"You're just a teenager, my maid," he whispered with some bitterness. "Full of ramlatch notions. I'm no one's hero and not much of—"

At the edge of the water John stopped and hung his head. He shuddered once. "Ailesh?" he called out.

Then the water went out, and the smell of fish dissolved in the air of Ireland. Sun touched the wall of the cattle enclosure before him, but John's heart was a cold ball inside him.

The only gate was the gate of the abbey, and it was empty. Ailesh herself came out of it and flung herself toward him. "No one's hero, and not much of a man," he said to her with some intensity, and then he allowed her to lead him in.

There were the monks, some with axes and some with swords. There was the poet and Snorri. All were kneeling, even Derval. John Thornburn thought he'd better kneel too. He heard singing: much better singing than his. He leaned forward and rested his head on Ailesh's shoulder and passed out that way.

Chapter Eighteen

•

> That's all gone by now, and the high heart and the fun are all passing from the world. Then we take the homeward way together, easy and friendly after our long revelling, like the children of one mother, none doing hurt or harm to his fellow.
>
> Tomas O'Crohan, *The Islandman*

John woke in darkness with a terrible head. He hadn't felt the aftereffects of a migraine this badly since he was a child. But of course, he hadn't any drugs here. He felt a moment's depression as he realized that his hope that the Beautiful Face had cured him of headaches along with everybody else was false. Then he remembered. This was no migraine; he'd fallen off a horse. No, a bull.

Both.

He tried to sit up, feeling his spine stretch very painfully along his back and neck as though it had come loose from its socket. Groaning, he sank back down. But the noise brought about events. There was a rustle of cloth and daylight played over wicker walls above his mattress. A beautiful face appeared before him. Her eyes were goldish-greeny-brown and her cheeks blushed like a rose. After a moment's strenuous focus he recognized it was not Bridget but Ailesh. She smiled at him with a sweet happiness, and it occurred to him that much could be done with the lines of that face.

John discovered that if he kept his face from moving, the pain was greatly reduced. Ailesh lifted his head carefully and held a metham to his mouth. The brew tasted like peppermint and garbage.

"We—we won the battle?" he asked, amazed and gratified at how pitiful his voice sounded. "We must have, or else . . ."

Her eyes went perfectly round. "How can you ask, Eoin? How can you, of all people, ask that question?"

His only reply was to close his eyes, so Ailesh added, "Don't you remember?"

"I fell off a muckin' huge bull. I remember that."

"You sent the reavers away."

He actually turned his head. "I . . . sent them away? I just went up to them and said, 'Here, you. I think it'd be better all around if you just went—' "

Ailesh giggled. "How sad you alone should forget your own miracle. You sang a great prayer and Bridget or the Son of Mary opened a hole and took them. I think it must have been the saint, for she shows such an interest in you."

John really did sit up. "Ye Gods and little fishes! I've sent the Vikings to my house!"

"No, no." Ailesh lowered him down. "I know well the gate of the red cross. This was a round, green shining, and they charged through it as though they did not see."

John laughed: laughed and winced. "Maybe I've sent them to Halifax."

"Wherever that may be."

"It's the bad place. Or—" John had a jumbled memory. Then it went away. "I don't want to think about it," he said. He curled his hands under his chin and fell asleep.

He had been having a good dream and awoke with one hand on his tumescent cock. As though the dream hadn't ended, there was Ailesh hovering over him. It seemed she had noticed the quality of his dream. He sighed, clearing cobwebs, and then his face set in disapproval.

"I'll bet you're fifteen years old, Ailesh."

Her eyes widened. "Every day of it! But surely I am not past the age of bearing, and whatever beauty I had a few years ago I still possess."

His smile turned into a wince. "You're smashing, Ailesh. But I'm twice your age; I can't take advantage—"

She put a soft hand over his mouth. "It's therefore for you to take care of me and teach me the wisdom of age." John found himself kissing the fingers that covered his lips. "I love you, my heart's heart. I will be to you whatever you choose me to be; if I am too young and silly for you, I will be your young and silly sister, and if I am . . . not a great enough woman for you"—Ailesh paused here, for John had put his hand over her own and was kissing it repeatedly—"then I will be your companion and student in work. But what I most desire . . ." She touched his trousers.

John looked quite surprised. Then he dropped her hand and struggled up. "I just thought. I forgot the needles." He made repeated wry faces as he stood on his feet and peered around the floor of the chamber. "My bag. My bag, eh? Did anyone find—" There in the corner, where a monk had reverently placed it, was the leather satchel which John had carried for a thousand years and then a thousand years back. He felt through it and drew out a spine-broken cardboard box.

"Here, Ailesh. I brought this for your—whattacallit—marriage portion." His voice softened as he added, "Your bridal cows."

Ailesh took the box and walked to the door, for light. There within were the papers of needles, all shining, perfect, as numerous as the trees in a wood. And beside them dozens of spools of bright silk caught the afternoon sun.

"By the Powers, Eoin! This is astonishing wealth! I did not believe so many needles existed in the world!" Then her excitement went out.

"But there is no need, Eoin, my treasure. I offered myself to you. For your bed. I had not the effrontery to declare myself your bride! It is not for me to make a price in such circumstances."

"Eh, Ailesh?" John's eyes narrowed. "What's this? You mean a little fun, but no—uh—commitment?" He threw in the English word, speaking with increasing bitterness. "I brought the needles from my home for you, because you were in trouble, and not with the thought of forcing you into something you don't want . . ."

Staring without comprehension, Ailesh put the box down. "Eoin Ban, you have saved my life, and the lives of all in this monastery. What is this talk of forcing—"

"I don't want your bloody gratitude, my maid, nor for another damn woman to sleep with me out of charity. The needles are for you, but as for the rest of this—"

Ailesh grabbed him about the neck. "Ow," said John.

"Out of charity? Eoin, blessed Eoin, bright as sunlight, my dear craftmaster, I could slay her for that!"

"Slay who?" John's headache added to his confusion.

"Derval Iníon Chadhain, if it was she who took your worth from you in this manner. Eoin, I say you can have me without cows—or needles. The honor of touching you is enough for me."

"The honor of—" John's incipient giggle died. The girl was on her knees before him. Slowly and with some pain he sank down beside her. "I'm sorry, love. I misunderstood you. I . . . I've never . . ."

John Thornburn took a breath. "Ailesh, Daughter of Goban (whom I wish I had known), you have the beauty of young Bridget, and the kindness of Iosha's own mother. I have wanted you since I fed you sausage in my kitchen, that time which seems so long ago. I was thinking all the while you were too young to feel for me in return."

"There was Derval," said Ailesh in a small voice.

"There was, and good luck to her, Ailesh, but—"

"But she is here no longer," the girl finished for him.

John kissed her on the lips. "I want to keep you, Ailesh. Take the bloody needles!"

All day long he heard singing, outside or echoing from under stone. He had a vague idea it was Easter. The garbagey drink was very potent. Derval was there once when he woke up. She pushed the hair from his eyes and said nothing. Snorri came in with a roast rabbit and tried to make him eat it. When John refused with great stubbornness, Snorri squatted down beside him and ate it himself. Ailesh chased him out.

Labres MacCullen came quietly in and sat by the wall for a long time. He was there at twilight, when John awoke for a few minutes, feeling better.

The next day he was on his feet, walking stiffly as a man in a body cast. He remembered nothing after the bull. (He did not try very hard.) He walked slowly into the church, with a vague idea he would like to do something nice for God. The place was garlanded with flowers, and the numerous people sitting, standing, or sprawled on the stone floor all knelt down when he walked in.

He started to back out again, only to bump into Derval.

Her eyes were filled with a confidence close to triumph. "I remember the tune, Johnnie."

He blinked at her and then flexed his fingers experimentally. "As long as I keep my mouth shut and don't blow it for you."

"Not worried about that at all, love."

Ignoring the reverence surrounding him, John walked over to the tracing blood-stuck against the wall. It was half-concealed by gifts of flowers and early fruit. Did the red of its dye seem a trifle browned? He put his finger to the paper.

"It's drying, Derval."

She nodded. "We can't wait. I'll get Labres." She turned and paused again. "You know he's coming with us, Johnnie?"

John wrinkled his forehead. "Eh? Well, what about paradox."

"Paradox can suck its own . . . I mean, it will take care of itself. He's needed, Johnnie. He . . . he shared my bad dream." When John continued to stare she explained, "We have our own reavers, in our world. Bridget said she would put the old into the new as well. How could we refuse that?"

"Such self-sacrifice." John smiled a bit wryly, but added, "Much luck to both of you."

"Should you be up, Eoin?" It was Ailesh's voice. The girl stood in the light of the church door. She carried a basket of bloody bandages, for she had come from tending those few of MacImidel's men who had come from the encounter alive.

Instead of answering, he asked, "Do you want to go back to my house, Ailesh? Labres is going, I'm told."

She dropped the basket on the floor. "Back . . . back there? To the glass house? Away?" She put both hands to her face. "If you go, of course I will follow."

"You don't sound very happy about it."

Ailesh gave John a lopsided smile.

"You don't want to." It was a statement. John nodded. "I thought so."

He turned to Derval, grinning. "Two came; two will go back. I do wish you a lot of luck, Derval." He sought reflexively in his shirt pocket for the pencils he'd left a thousand years away.

"You're not going?" Derval's mouth hung open.

"No." Her expression made him grin even more broadly.

"Oh, don't worry. I can't imagine it's all hardship and bloody battles here. I expect it to be very quiet, and you know I like things quiet."

"But—but if I go back without you, it'll look like I . . ."

John laughed outright, until the church echoed. "Scary thought, isn't it? But they can't convict you of murder without a body, you know. And besides—you can say we had a fight and I took a bus. It's something I would do."

The church darkened, and John turned to see Derval's elephantine horse bend his head very low to step in, led by MacCullen. Had the doorway been an inch lower, the passage would have been impossible. Tinker sniffed the floral offerings and extended his head, greedily. Labres MacCullen, with a wondering, solemn expression on his face, glanced over at Derval and handed John a stylus.

"What about your king, Labres?" asked John, remembering about Domnall Cloen. He looked up at the big man.

Sorrow pinched MacCullen's face. "Ocho, Eoin! My grief! But what can I do for Domnall any more, or he for me? Poor Leinster is torn by the dogs of many tribes, and her heart has ceased its beat in her. It may be that I am the last poet she will have as living nation!

"Yet the Powers have created me poet and my poetry is not yet written. Derval Iníon Cuhain has shown me what I must do."

"Derval? I believe it!" Then John's grin faded into something sweeter and more sad. "Take care of each other," he said to them both. He went to the window, where light through the tracing blushed his face to rose. Derval came up beside him and touched her lips to his.

"I'm sorry I'm not a nicer person, Johnnie. I'll miss you. May Bridget and the Son of Mary bless you and keep you all your days." She spoke in the English none but the two of them understood.

"And all the same to you," he answered, in his bad Irish.

Glossary

•

Awley: The way Olafr sounds to Gaelic speakers. The name of the king of Dublin.

Bhean: Woman, as in bhean shidhe-woman of the other world, or in bhean uasail-nobel woman. An honorific term.

Blood Egale: Horrible Norse sacrificial custom in which the victim's back was cut open on either side of the spine and the lungs pulled out like wings.

Bo: Cow, as in Bo aire-cow-man, term for respectable man.

Bord na mona: The government peat bog agency in modern Ireland.

Brat: Cloak or blanket worn as outer garment in medieval Gaelic counties.

Brehon: Lawyer or arbitrator in old Ireland.

Cailleach: Old woman, hag, mighty, old woman.

Caoruheacht: Cattle skill, knowledge of the herds.

Clàirseach: Triangular frame harp with metallic wire strings, used all over Europe in the Middle Ages, believed to have been important in Ireland by 800 A.D.

Coibce: Marriage portion of women.

Cotun: Cloth armor, stiffened with pitch or other substance, often padded or many layered. Worn all through early medieval period.

Craic: Fun, a good time with friends.

Cruit: Rectangular flat-box lyre, like Saxon rote or crotta.

Cuisleen: Early Irish whistles or reed pipes. Examples from excavation in Dublin resemble English tabor pipe.

Dean deifer: Make haste!

Dia Linn!: God be with us.

Dirb fine: Kin group based on common great-grandfather.

Duan uasail: Noble person. Term of respect.

Effing: Modern Dublin slang, euphemism for stronger four-letter word.

Fine: Kin group of any size.

Ful-ya, Ful-ya: Onomonopoetic cattle-soothing vocables from west coast of Ireland, especially the Connemara district.

Gaese: Personal taboo.

Gaill: Stranger, term of derogation meaning "foreigner."

Gardai: The police in modern Ireland.

Inion: Or Ni, daughter of. An honorific title.

Inuit: The true people. The name the Eskimos call themselves.

Léinne: Shirt of linen or silk (though that was less common, silk being an imported luxury). This shirt was generally dyed a bright color, and was ankle length when not kilted up for work. It seems to have been sleeveless at an earlier period, but in the tenth century A.D. it usually had wide, long sleeves. Much later on, in the Renaissance, the sleeves became enormous bags.

Mac: Son of: Honorific title, normally preceeding the father's name.

Mether: Three- or four-sided, carved, wooden drinking vessel, often with several handles.

Mumhan: The kingdom of Munster, one of four major political and ritual divisions of Ireland's territory.

Ollave, Ollam: Professor, doctor of poetry and literature, unless otherwise specified in the story.

Pitis!: Gaelic explicative, meaning vulva, but not an obscenity. There are no obscene words, in the English sense, in Gaelic.

Sheelta: The language of the Tinkers, the traveling people of Ireland.

Shiun: Sister.

Slua: Host. A massing of people or beings of any kind.

Tain Bo Cualighne: The Cattle Raid of Cooley, oldest known epic poem in Irish literature. Probably contains elements from Bronze Age.

Taraigeacht: War party or, more specifically, cattle-raiding and reraiding party. Very little loss of life is believed to occurred during the course of these actions.

Timpan: Bowed lyre with any number of sympathetic strings, which were struck with the player's thumbnail while bowing.

Taoiseach: War chieftan.

Rafted: (Newfi) In bad shape, angry.

Ramlatch: Total absurdity, bullshit (Newfi).

Righ: King, royal.

Ui: The people of. Indicates very large kin group.

Uillinn pipes: Literally, elbow pipes, the national bagpipe of Ireland. Developed in eighteenth century, probably from the Northumbrian Half Long pipes, of Northeast England. There are close to 200 different bagpipes in Europe alone, with many others in the Arab countries. They are believed to have originated in classical times, in the Mediterranian area.

Coming in September 1985 from Bantam Spectra Books:

THE DREAM YEARS

by Lisa Goldstein

> "THE DREAM YEARS is fresh and stimulating . . . Ms. Goldstein brings to literature the sparkle of renewal that is needed in every enduring novel." —Han Suyin, author of THE ENCHANTRESS

Few novels have the power not only to contribute something fresh and new to the art of fiction, but to change the way we perceive the world as well. Lisa Goldstein's THE DREAM YEARS, the haunting second novel by the American Book Award-winning author of THE RED MAGICIAN, is just such a work.

Beginning in 1920s Paris, THE DREAM YEARS tells of a young Surrealist writer transported forward through time by a beautiful, mysterious woman to the 1968 Paris riots, where they must prepare the way for a visionary war of dreams in the 21st century. At once a tour-de-force of fantasy and a stunning recreation of history, THE DREAM YEARS is a groundbreaking work that challenges the boundaries of modern fiction.

THE DREAM YEARS will be available in hardcover beginning September 1, 1985.